Paul Kelver by Jerome K. Jerome

Jerome K Jerome's early life of poverty exacerbated by the death of his parents in his early teens helped to cruelly mould the young Jerome. After early stints on the railways, as an actor, a journalist, a school teacher, a writer and a solicitors clerk he had some minor success with a collection of comic memoirs "On The Stage – And Off" about his earlier stint as an actor. Shortly thereafter he married and his honeymoon on the Thames became the inspiration for Three Men In A Boat. This of course was a wild success both critically and commercially and also his creative highpoint. Although he was now able to write full time he was never able to attain all the heights of that classic humorous novel. However he was prolific at the shorter form and it is from that rich seam that these stories have been mined. Here we publish another of his classics 'Paul Kelver'.

Index Of Contents

PROLOGUE.

IN WHICH THE AUTHOR SEEKS TO CAST THE RESPONSIBILITY OF THIS STORY UPON ANOTHER.

At the corner of a long, straight, brick-built street in the far East End of London, one of those lifeless streets, made of two drab walls upon which the level lines, formed by the precisely even window-sills and doorsteps, stretch in weary perspective from end to end, suggesting petrified diagrams proving dead problems, stands a house that ever draws me to it; so that often, when least conscious of my footsteps, I awake to find myself hurrying through noisy, crowded thoroughfares, where flaring naphtha lamps illumine fierce, patient, leaden-coloured faces; through dim-lit, empty streets, where monstrous shadows come and go upon the close-drawn blinds; through narrow, noisome streets, where the gutters swarm with children, and each ever-open doorway vomits riot; past reeking corners, and across waste places, till at last I reach the dreary goal of my memory-driven desire, and, coming to a halt beside the broken railings, find rest.

The house, larger than its fellows, built when the street was still a country lane, edging the marshes, strikes a strange note of individuality amid the surrounding harmony of hideousness. It is encompassed on two sides by what was once a garden, though now but a barren patch of stones and dust where clothes, it is odd any one should have thought of washing, hang in perpetuity; while about the door continue the remnants of a porch, which the stucco falling has left exposed in all its naked insincerity.

Occasionally I drift hitherward in the day time, when slatternly women gossip round the area gates, and the silence is broken by the hoarse, wailing cry of "Coals, any coals, three and sixpence a sack, co-o-o-als!" chanted in a tone that absence of response has stamped with chronic melancholy; but then the street knows me not, and my old friend of the corner, ashamed of its shabbiness in the unpitying sunlight, turns its face away, and will not see me as I pass.

Not until the Night, merciful alone of all things to the ugly, draws her veil across its sordid features will it, as some fond old nurse, sought out in after years, open wide its arms to welcome me. Then the teeming life it now shelters, hushed for a time within its walls, the flickering flare from the "King of Prussia" opposite extinguished, will it talk with me of the past, asking me many questions, reminding me of many things I had forgotten. Then into the silent street come the well-remembered footsteps; in and out the creaking gate pass, not seeing me, the well-remembered faces; and we talk concerning them; as two cronies, turning the torn leaves of some old album where the faded portraits in forgotten fashions, speak together in low tones of those now dead or scattered, with now a smile and now a sigh, and many an "Ah me!" or "Dear, dear!"

This bent, worn man, coming towards us with quick impatient steps, which yet cease every fifty yards or so, while he pauses, leaning heavily upon his high Malacca cane: "It is a handsome face, is it not?" I ask, as I gaze upon it, shadow framed.

"Aye, handsome enough," answers the old House; "and handsomer still it must have been before you and I knew it, before mean care had furrowed it with fretful lines."

"I never could make out," continues the old House, musingly, "whom you took after; for they were a handsome pair, your father and your mother, though Lord! what a couple of children!"

"Children!" I say in surprise, for my father must have been past five and thirty before the House could have known him, and my mother's face is very close to mine, in the darkness, so that I see the many grey hairs mingling with the bonny brown.

"Children," repeats the old House, irritably, so it seems to me, not liking, perhaps, its opinions questioned, a failing common to old folk; "the most helpless pair of children I ever set eyes upon. Who but a child, I should like to know, would have conceived the notion of repairing his fortune by becoming a solicitor at thirty-eight, or, having conceived such a notion, would have selected the outskirts of Poplar as a likely centre in which to put up his door-plate?"

"It was considered to be a rising neighbourhood," I reply, a little resentful. No son cares to hear the family wisdom criticised, even though at the bottom of his heart he may be in agreement with the critic. "All sorts and conditions of men, whose affairs were in connection with the sea would, it was thought, come to reside hereabout, so as to be near to the new docks; and had they, it is not unreasonable to suppose they would have quarrelled and disputed with one another, much to the advantage of a cute solicitor, convenient to their hand."

"Stuff and nonsense," retorts the old House, shortly; "why, the mere smell of the place would have been sufficient to keep a sensible man away. And", the grim brick face before me twists itself into a goblin smile, "he, of all men in the world, as 'the cute solicitor,' giving advice to shady clients, eager to get out of trouble by the shortest way, can you fancy it! he who for two years starved himself, living on five shillings a week, that was before you came to London, when he was here alone. Even your mother knew nothing of it till years afterwards, so that no man should be a penny the poorer for having trusted his good name. Do you think the crew of chandlers and brokers, dock hustlers and freight wreckers would have found him a useful man of business, even had they come to settle here?"

I have no answer; nor does the old House wait for any, but talks on.

"And your mother! would any but a child have taken that soft-tongued wanton to her bosom, and not have seen through acting so transparent? Would any but the veriest child that never ought to have been let out into the world by itself have thought to dree her weird in such folly? Children! poor babies they were, both of them."

"Tell me," I say, for at such times all my stock of common sense is not sufficient to convince me that the old House is but clay. From its walls so full of voices, from its floors so thick with footsteps, surely it has learned to live; as a violin, long played on, comes to learn at last a music of its own. "Tell me, I was but a child to whom life speaks in a strange tongue, was there any truth in the story?"

"Truth!" snaps out the old House; "just truth enough to plant a lie upon; and Lord knows not much ground is needed for that weed. I saw what I saw, and I know what I know. Your mother had a good man, and your father a true wife, but it was the old story: a man's way is not a woman's way, and a woman's way is not a man's way, so there lives ever doubt between them."

"But they came together in the end," I say, remembering.

"Aye, in the end," answers the House. "That is when you begin to understand, you men and women, when you come to the end."

The grave face of a not too recently washed angel peeps shyly at me through the railings, then, as I turn my head, darts back and disappears.

"What has become of her?" I ask.

"She? Oh, she is well enough," replies the House. "She lives close here. You must have passed the shop. You might have seen her had you looked in. She weighs fourteen stone, about; and has nine children living. She would be pleased to see you."

"Thank you," I say, with a laugh that is not wholly a laugh; "I do not think I will call." But I still hear the pit-pat of her tiny feet, dying down the long street.

The faces thicken round me. A large looming, rubicund visage smiles kindly on me, bringing back into my heart the old, odd mingling of instinctive liking held in check by conscientious disapproval. I turn from it, and see a massive, clean-shaven face, with the ugliest mouth and the loveliest eyes I ever have known in a man.

"Was he as bad, do you think, as they said?" I ask of my ancient friend.

"Shouldn't wonder," the old House answers. "I never knew a worse, nor a better."

The wind whisks it aside, leaving to view a little old woman, hobbling nimbly by aid of a stick. Three corkscrew curls each side of her head bob with each step she takes, and as she draws near to me, making the most alarming grimaces, I hear her whisper, as though confiding to herself some fascinating secret, "I'd like to skin 'em. I'd like to skin 'em all. I'd like to skin 'em all alive!"

It sounds a fiendish sentiment, yet I only laugh, and the little old lady, with a final facial contortion surpassing all dreams, limps beyond my ken.

Then, as though choosing contrasts, follows a fair, laughing face. I saw it in the life only a few hours ago, at least, not it, but the poor daub that Evil has painted over it, hating the sweetness underlying. And as I stand gazing at it, wishing it were of the dead who change not, there drifts back from the shadows that other face, the one of the wicked mouth and the tender eyes, so that I stand again helpless between the two I loved so well, he from whom I learned my first steps in manhood, she from whom I caught my first glimpse of the beauty and the mystery of woman. And again the cry rises from my heart, "Whose fault was it, yours or hers?" And again I hear his mocking laugh as he answers, "Whose fault? God made us." And thinking of her and of the love I bore her, which was as the love of a young pilgrim to a saint, it comes into my blood to hate him.

But when I look into his eyes and see the pain that lives there, my pity grows stronger than my misery, and I can only echo his words, "God made us."

Merry faces and sad, fair faces and foul, they ride upon the wind; but the centre round which they circle remains always the one: a little lad with golden curls more suitable to a girl than to a boy, with shy, awkward ways and a silent tongue, and a grave, old-fashioned face.

And, turning from him to my old brick friend, I ask: "Would he know me, could he see me, do you think?"

"How should he," answers the old House, "you are so different to what he would expect. Would you recognise your own ghost, think you?"

"It is sad to think he would not recognise me," I say.

"It might be sadder if he did," grumbles the old House.

We both remained silent for awhile; but I know of what the old House is thinking. Soon it speaks as I expected.

"You, writer of stories, why don't you write a book about him? There is something that you know."

It is the favourite theme of the old House. I never visit it but it suggests to me this idea.

"But he has done nothing?" I say.

"He has lived," answers the old House. "Is not that enough?"

"Aye, but only in London in these prosaic modern times," I persist. "How of such can one make a story that shall interest the people?"

The old House waxes impatient of me.

"'The people!'" it retorts, "what are you all but children in a dim-lit room, waiting until one by one you are called out to sleep. And one mounts upon a stool and tells a tale to the others who have gathered round. Who shall say what will please them, what will not."

Returning home with musing footsteps through the softly breathing streets, I ponder the words of the old House. Is it but as some foolish mother thinking all the world interested in her child, or may there lie wisdom in its counsel? Then to my guidance or misguidance comes the thought of a certain small section of the Public who often of an evening commands of me a story; and who, when I have told her of the dreadful giants and of the gallant youths who slay them, of the wood-cutter's sons who rescue maidens from Ogre-guarded castles; of the Princesses the most beautiful in all the world, of the Princes with magic swords, still unsatisfied, creeps closer yet, saying: "Now tell me a real story," adding for my comprehending: "You know: about a little girl who lived in a big house with her father and mother, and who was sometimes naughty, you know."

So perhaps among the many there may be some who for a moment will turn aside from tales of haughty Heroes, ruffling it in Court and Camp, to listen to the story of a very ordinary lad who lived with very ordinary folk in a modern London street, and who grew up to be a very ordinary sort of man, loving a little and grieving a little, helping a few and harming a few, struggling and failing and hoping; and if any such there be, let them come round me.

But let not those who come to me grow indignant as they listen, saying: "This rascal tells us but a humdrum story, where nothing is as it should be;" for I warn all beforehand that I tell but of things that I have seen. My villains, I fear, are but poor sinners, not altogether bad; and my good men but sorry saints. My princes do not always slay their dragons; alas, sometimes, the dragon eats the prince. The wicked fairies often prove more powerful than the good. The magic thread leads sometimes wrong, and even the hero is not always brave and true.

So let those come round me only who will be content to hear but their own story, told by another, saying as they listen, "So dreamt I. Ah, yes, that is true, I remember."

CHAPTER I

PAUL, ARRIVED IN A STRANGE LAND, LEARNS MANY THINGS, AND GOES TO MEET THE MAN IN GREY.

Fate intended me for a singularly fortunate man. Properly, I ought to have been born in June, which being, as is well known, the luckiest month in all the year for such events, should, by thoughtful parents, be more generally selected. How it was I came to be born in May, which is, on the other hand, of all the twelve the most unlucky, as I have proved, I leave to those more conversant with the subject to explain. An early nurse, the first human being of whom I have any distinct recollection, unhesitatingly attributed the unfortunate fact to my natural impatience; which quality she at the same time predicted would lead me into even greater trouble, a prophecy impressed by future events with the stamp of prescience. It was from this same bony lady that I likewise learned the manner of my coming. It seems that I arrived, quite unexpectedly, two hours after news had reached the house of the ruin of my father's mines through inundation; misfortunes, as it was expounded to me, never coming singly in this world to anyone. That all things might be of a piece, my poor mother, attempting to reach the bell, fell against and broke the cheval-glass, thus further saddening herself with the conviction, for no amount of reasoning ever succeeded in purging her Welsh blood of its natural superstition, that whatever might be the result of future battles with my evil star, the first seven years of tiny existence had been, by her act, doomed to disaster.

"And I must confess," added the knobbly Mrs. Fursey, with a sigh, "it does look as though there must be some truth in the saying, after all."

"Then ain't I a lucky little boy?" I asked. For hitherto it had been Mrs. Fursey's method to impress upon me my exceptional good fortune. That I could and did, involuntarily, retire to bed at six, while less happily placed children were deprived of their natural rest until eight or nine o'clock, had always been held up to me as an astounding piece of luck. Some little boys had not a bed at all; for the which, in my more riotous moments, I envied them. Again, that at the first sign of a cold it became my unavoidable privilege to lunch off linseed gruel and sup off brimstone and treacle, a compound named with deliberate intent to deceive the innocent, the treacle, so far as taste is concerned, being wickedly subordinated to the brimstone, was another example of Fortune's favouritism: other little boys were so astoundingly unlucky as to be left alone when they felt ill. If further proof were needed to convince that I had been signalled out by Providence as its especial protege, there remained always the circumstance that I possessed Mrs. Fursey for my nurse. The suggestion that I was not altogether the luckiest of children was a new departure.

The good dame evidently perceived her error, and made haste to correct it.

"Oh, you! You are lucky enough," she replied; "I was thinking of your poor mother."

"Isn't mamma lucky?"

"Well, she hasn't been too lucky since you came."

"Wasn't it lucky, her having me?"

"I can't say it was, at that particular time."

"Didn't she want me?"

Mrs. Fursey was one of those well-meaning persons who are of opinion that the only reasonable attitude of childhood should be that of perpetual apology for its existence.

"Well, I daresay she could have done without you," was the answer.

I can see the picture plainly still. I am sitting on a low chair before the nursery fire, one knee supported in my locked hands, meanwhile Mrs. Fursey's needle grated with monotonous regularity against her thimble. At that moment knocked at my small soul for the first time the problem of life.

Suddenly, without moving, I said:

"Then why did she take me in?"

The rasping click of the needle on the thimble ceased abruptly.

"Took you in! What's the child talking about? Who's took you in?"

"Why, mamma. If she didn't want me, why did she take me in?"

But even while, with heart full of dignified resentment, I propounded this, as I proudly felt, logically unanswerable question, I was glad that she had. The vision of my being refused at the bedroom window presented itself to my imagination. I saw the stork, perplexed and annoyed, looking as I had sometimes seen Tom Pinfold look when the fish he had been holding out by the tail had been sniffed at by Anna, and the kitchen door shut in his face. Would the stork also have gone away thoughtfully scratching his head with one of those long, compass-like legs of his, and muttering to himself. And here, incidentally, I fell a-wondering how the stork had carried me. In the garden I had often watched a blackbird carrying a worm, and the worm, though no doubt really safe enough, had always appeared to me nervous and uncomfortable. Had I wriggled and squirmed in like fashion? And where would the stork have taken me to then? Possibly to Mrs. Fursey's: their cottage was the nearest. But I felt sure Mrs. Fursey would not have taken me in; and next to them, at the first house in the village, lived Mr. Chumdley, the cobbler, who was lame, and who sat all day hammering boots with very dirty hands, in a little cave half under the ground, his whole appearance suggesting a poor-spirited ogre. I should have hated being his little boy. Possibly nobody would have taken me in. I grew pensive, thinking of myself as the rejected of all the village. What would the stork have done with me, left on his hands, so to speak. The reflection prompted a fresh question.

"Nurse, where did I come from?"

"Why, I've told you often. The stork brought you."

"Yes, I know. But where did the stork get me from?" Mrs. Fursey paused for quite a long while before replying. Possibly she was reflecting whether such answer might not make me unduly conceited. Eventually she must have decided to run that risk; other opportunities could be relied upon for neutralising the effect.

"Oh, from Heaven."

"But I thought Heaven was a place where you went to," I answered; "not where you comed from." I know I said "comed," for I remember that at this period my irregular verbs were a bewildering anxiety to my poor mother. "Comed" and "goned," which I had worked out for myself, were particular favourites of mine.

Mrs. Fursey passed over my grammar in dignified silence. She had been pointedly requested not to trouble herself with that part of my education, my mother holding that diverging opinions upon the same subject only confused a child.

"You came from Heaven," repeated Mrs. Fursey, "and you'll go to Heaven, if you're good."

"Do all little boys and girls come from Heaven?"

"So they say." Mrs. Fursey's tone implied that she was stating what might possibly be but a popular fallacy, for which she individually took no responsibility.

"And did you come from Heaven, Mrs. Fursey?" Mrs. Fursey's reply to this was decidedly more emphatic.

"Of course I did. Where do you think I came from?"

At once, I am ashamed to say, Heaven lost its exalted position in my eyes. Even before this, it had puzzled me that everybody I knew should be going there, for so I was always assured; now, connected as it appeared to be with the origin of Mrs. Fursey, much of its charm disappeared.

But this was not all. Mrs. Fursey's information had suggested to me a fresh grief. I stopped not to console myself with the reflection that my fate had been but the fate of all little boys and girls. With a child's egoism I seized only upon my own particular case.

"Didn't they want me in Heaven then, either?" I asked. "Weren't they fond of me up there?"

The misery in my voice must have penetrated even Mrs. Fursey's bosom, for she answered more sympathetically than usual.

"Oh, they liked you well enough, I daresay. I like you, but I like to get rid of you sometimes." There could be no doubt as to this last. Even at the time, I often doubted whether that six o'clock bedtime was not occasionally half-past five.

The answer comforted me not. It remained clear that I was not wanted either in Heaven nor upon the earth. God did not want me. He was glad to get rid of me. My mother did not want me. She could have done without me. Nobody wanted me. Why was I here?

And then, as the sudden opening and shutting of the door of a dark room, came into my childish brain the feeling that Something, somewhere, must have need of me, or I could not be, Something I felt I belonged to and that belonged to me, Something that was as much a part of me as I of It. The feeling came back to me more than once during my childhood, though I could never put it into words. Years later the son of the Portuguese Jew explained to me my thought. But all that I myself could have told was that in that moment I knew for the first time that I lived, that I was I.

The next instant all was dark again, and I once more a puzzled little boy, sitting by a nursery fire, asking of a village dame questions concerning life.

Suddenly a new thought came to me, or rather the recollection of an old.

"Nurse, why haven't we got a husband?"

Mrs. Fursey left off her sewing, and stared at me.

"What maggot has the child got into its head now?" was her observation; "who hasn't got a husband?"

"Why, mamma."

"Don't talk nonsense, Master Paul; you know your mamma has got a husband."

"No, she ain't."

"And don't contradict. Your mamma's husband is your papa, who lives in London."

"What's the good of him!"

Mrs. Fursey's reply appeared to me to be unnecessarily vehement.

"You wicked child, you; where's your commandments? Your father is in London working hard to earn money to keep you in idleness, and you sit there and say 'What's the good of him!' I'd be ashamed to be such an ungrateful little brat."

I had not meant to be ungrateful. My words were but the repetition of a conversation I had overheard the day before between my mother and my aunt.

Had said my aunt: "There she goes, moping again. Drat me if ever I saw such a thing to mope as a woman."

My aunt was entitled to preach on the subject. She herself grumbled all day about all things, but she did it cheerfully.

My mother was standing with her hands clasped behind her, a favourite attitude of hers, gazing through the high French window into the garden beyond. It must have been spring time, for I remember the white and yellow crocuses decking the grass.

"I want a husband," had answered my mother, in a tone so ludicrously childish that at sound of it I had looked up from the fairy story I was reading, half expectant to find her changed into a little girl; "I hate not having a husband."

"Help us and save us," my aunt had retorted; "how many more does a girl want? She's got one."

"What's the good of him all that way off," had pouted my mother; "I want him here where I can get at him."

I had often heard of this father of mine, who lived far away in London, and to whom we owed all the blessings of life; but my childish endeavours to square information with reflection had resulted in my assigning to him an entirely spiritual existence. I agreed with my mother that such an one, however to be revered, was no substitute for the flesh and blood father possessed by luckier folk, the big, strong, masculine thing that would carry a fellow pig-a-back round the garden, or take a chap to sail in boats.

"You don't understand me, nurse," I explained; "what I mean is a husband you can get at."

"Well, and you'll 'get at him,' poor gentleman, one of these days," answered Mrs. Fursey. "When he's ready for you he'll send for you, and then you'll go to him in London."

I felt that still Mrs. Fursey didn't understand. But I foresaw that further explanation would only shock her, so contented myself with a simple, matter-of-fact question.

"How do you get to London; do you have to die first?"

"I do think," said Mrs. Fursey, in the voice of resigned despair rather than of surprise, "that, without exception, you are the silliest little boy I ever came across. I've no patience with you."

"I am very sorry, nurse," I answered; "I thought"

"Then," interrupted Mrs. Fursey, in the voice of many generations, "you shouldn't think. London," continued the good dame, her experience no doubt suggesting that the shortest road to peace would be through my understanding of this matter, "is a big town, and you go there in a train. Some time, soon now, your father will write to your mother that everything is ready. Then you and your mother and your aunt will leave this place and go to London, and I shall be rid of you."

"And shan't we come back here ever anymore?"

"Never again."

"And I'll never play in the garden again, never go down to the pebble-ridge to tea, or to Jacob's tower?"

"Never again." I think Mrs. Fursey took a pleasure in the phrase. It sounded, as she said it, like something out of the prayer-book.

"And I'll never see Anna, or Tom Pinfold, or old Yeo, or Pincher, or you, ever anymore?" In this moment of the crumbling from under me of all my footholds I would have clung even to that dry tuft, Mrs. Fursey herself.

"Never any more. You'll go away and begin an entirely new life. And I do hope, Master Paul," added Mrs. Fursey, piously, "it may be a better one. That you will make up your mind to"

But Mrs. Fursey's well-meant exhortations, whatever they may have been, fell upon deaf ears. Here was I face to face with yet another problem. This life into which I had fallen: it was understandable! One went away, leaving the pleasant places that one knew, never to return to them. One left one's labour and one's play to enter upon a new existence in a strange land. One parted from the friends one had always known, one saw them never again. Life was indeed a strange thing; and, would a body comprehend it, then must a body sit staring into the fire, thinking very hard, unheedful of all idle chatter.

That night, when my mother came to kiss me good-night, I turned my face to the wall and pretended to be asleep, for children as well as grown-ups have their foolish moods; but when I felt the soft curls brush my cheek, my pride gave way, and clasping my arms about her neck, and drawing her face still closer down to mine; I voiced the question that all the evening had been knocking at my heart:

"I suppose you couldn't send me back now, could you? You see, you've had me so long."

"Send you back?"

"Yes. I'd be too big for the stork to carry now, wouldn't I?"

My mother knelt down beside the bed so that her face and mine were on a level, and looking into her eyes, the fear that had been haunting me fell from me.

"Who has been talking foolishly to a foolish little boy?" asked my mother, keeping my arms still clasped about her neck.

"Oh, nurse and I were discussing things, you know," I answered, "and she said you could have done without me. Somehow, I did not mind repeating the words now; clearly it could have been but Mrs. Fursey's fun.

My mother drew me closer to her.

"And what made her think that?"

"Well, you see," I replied, "I came at a very awkward time, didn't I; when you had a lot of other troubles."

My mother laughed, but the next moment looked grave again.

"I did not know you thought about such things," she said; "we must be more together, you and I, Paul, and you shall tell me all you think, because nurse does not quite understand you. It is true what she said about the trouble; it came just at that time. But I could not have done without you. I was very unhappy, and you were sent to comfort me and help me to bear it." I liked this explanation better.

"Then it was lucky, your having me?" I said. Again my mother laughed, and again there followed that graver look upon her childish face.

"Will you remember what I am going to say?" She spoke so earnestly that I, wriggling into a sitting posture, became earnest also.

"I'll try," I answered; "but I ain't got a very good memory, have I?"

"Not very," smiled my mother; "but if you think about it a good deal it will not leave you. When you are a good boy, and later on, when you are a good man, then I am the luckiest little mother in all the world. And every time you fail, that means bad luck for me. You will remember that after I'm gone, when you are a big man, won't you, Paul?"

So, both of us quite serious, I promised; and though I smile now when I remember, seeing before me those two earnest, childish faces, yet I think, however little success it may be I have to boast of, it would perhaps have been still less had I entirely forgotten.

From that day my mother waxes in my memory; Mrs. Fursey, of the many promontories, waning. There were sunny mornings in the neglected garden, where the leaves played round us while we worked and read; twilight evenings in the window seat where, half hidden by the dark red curtains, we would talk in whispers, why I know not, of good men and noble women, ogres, fairies, saints and demons; they were pleasant days.

Possibly our curriculum lacked method; maybe it was too varied and extensive for my age, in consequence of which chronology became confused within my brain, and fact and fiction more confounded than has usually been considered permissible, even in history. I saw Aphrodite, ready armed and risen from the sea, move with stately grace to meet King Canute, who, throned upon the sand, bade her come no further lest she should wet his feet. In forest glade I saw King Rufus fall from a poisoned arrow shot by Robin Hood; but thanks to sweet Queen Eleanor, who sucked the poison from his wound, I knew he lived. Oliver Cromwell, having killed King Charles, married his widow, and was in turn stabbed by Hamlet. Ulysses, in the Argo, it was fixed upon my mind, had discovered America. Romulus and Remus had slain the wolf and rescued Little Red Riding Hood. Good King Arthur, for letting the cakes burn, had been murdered by his uncle in the Tower of London. Prometheus, bound to the Rock, had been saved by good St. George. Paris had given the apple to William Tell. What matter! the information was there. It needed rearranging, that was all.

Sometimes, of an afternoon, we would climb the steep winding pathway through the woods, past awful precipices, spirit-haunted, by grassy swards where fairies danced o' nights, by briar and bracken sheltered Caves where fearsome creatures lurked, till high above the creeping sea we would reach the open plateau where rose old Jacob's ruined tower. "Jacob's Folly" it was more often called about the country side, and by some "The Devil's Tower;" for legend had it that there old Jacob and his master, the Devil, had often met in windy weather to wave false wrecking lights to troubled ships. Who "old Jacob" was, I never, that I can remember, learned, nor how nor why he built the Tower. Certain only it is his memory was unpopular, and the fisher folk would swear that still on stormy nights strange lights would gleam and flash from the ivy-curtained windows of his Folly.

But in day time no spot was more inviting, the short moss-grass before its shattered door, the lichen on its crumbling stones. From its topmost platform one saw the distant mountains, faint like spectres, and the silent ships that came and vanished; and about one's feet the pleasant farm lands and the grave, sweet river.

Smaller and poorer the world has grown since then. Now, behind those hills lie naught but smoky towns and dingy villages; but then they screened a land of wonder where princesses dwelt in castles, where the cities were of gold. Now the ocean is but six days' journey wide, ending at the New York Custom House. Then, had one set one's sail upon it, one would have travelled far and far, beyond the golden moonlight, beyond the gate of clouds; to the magic land of the blood red shore, t'other side o' the sun. I never dreamt in those days a world could be so small.

Upon the topmost platform a wooden seat ran round within the parapet, and sitting there hand in hand, sheltered from the wind which ever blew about the tower, my mother would people for me all the earth and air with the forms of myth and legend, perhaps unwisely, yet I do not know. I took no harm from it, good rather, I think. They were beautiful fancies, most of them; or so my mother turned them, making for love and pity, as do all the tales that live, whether poems or old wives fables. But at that time of course they had no meaning for me other than the literal; so that my mother, looking into my eyes, would often hasten to add: "But that, you know, is only an old superstition, and of course there are no such things nowadays." Yet, forgetful sometimes of the time, and overtaken homeward by the shadows, we would hasten swiftly through the darkening path, holding each other tightly by the hand.

Spring had waxed to summer, summer waned to autumn. Then my aunt and I one morning, waiting at the breakfast table, saw through the open window my mother skipping, dancing, pirouetting up the garden path.

She held a letter open in her hand, which as she drew near she waved about her head, singing:

"Saturday, Sunday, Monday, Tuesday, then comes Wednesday morning."

She caught me to her and began dancing with me round the room.

Observed my aunt, who continued steadily to eat bread and butter:

"Just like 'em all. Goes mad with joy. What for? Because she's going to leave a decent house, to live in a poky hole in the East End of London, and keep one servant."

To my aunt the second person ever remained a grammatical superfluity. Invariably she spoke not to but of a person, throwing out her conversation in the form of commentary. This had the advantage of permitting the party intended to ignore it as mere impersonal philosophy. Seeing it was generally uncomplimentary, most people preferred so to regard it; but my mother had never succeeded in schooling herself to indifference.

"It's not a poky hole," she replied; "it's an old-fashioned house, near the river."

"Plaistow marshes!" ejaculated my aunt, "calls it the river!"

"So it is the river," returned my mother; "the river is the other side of the marshes."

"Let's hope it will always stop there," said my aunt.

"And it's got a garden," continued my mother, ignoring my aunt's last remark; "which is quite an unusual feature in a London house. And it isn't the East End of London; it is a rising suburb. And you won't make me miserable because I am too happy."

"Drat the woman!" said my aunt, "why can't she sit down and give us our tea before it's all cold?"

"You are a disagreeable thing!" said my mother.

"Not half milk," said my aunt. My aunt was never in the least disturbed by other people's opinion of her, which was perhaps well for her.

For three days my mother packed and sang; and a dozen times a day unpacked and laughed, looking for things wanted that were always found at the very bottom of the very last box looked into, so that Anna, waiting for a certain undergarment of my aunt's which shall be nameless, suggested a saving of time:

"If I were you, ma'am," said Anna, "I'd look into the last box you're going to look into first."

But it was found eventually in the first box-the box, that is, my mother had intended to search first, but which, acting on Anna's suggestion, she had reserved till the last. This caused my mother to be quite short with Anna, who she said had wasted her time. But by Tuesday afternoon all stood ready: we were to start early Wednesday morning.

That evening, missing my mother in the house, I sought her in the garden and found her, as I had expected, on her favourite seat under the great lime tree; but to my surprise there were tears in her eyes.

"But I thought you were glad we were going," I said.

"So I am," answered my mother, drying her eyes only to make room for fresh tears.

"Then why are you crying?"

"Because I'm sorry to leave here."

Grown-up folks with their contradictory ways were a continual puzzle to me in those days; I am not sure I quite understand them even now, myself included.

We were up and off next day before the dawn. The sun rose as the wagon reached the top of the hill; and there we paused and took our farewell look at Old Jacob's Tower. My mother cried a little behind her veil; but my aunt only said, "I never did care for earwigs in my tea;" and as for myself I was too excited and expectant to feel much sentiment about anything.

On the journey I sat next to an exceptionally large and heavy man, who in his sleep, and he slept often, imagined me to be a piece of stuffing out of place. Then, grunting and wriggling, he would endeavour to rub me out, until the continued irritation of my head between the window and his back would cause him to awake, when he would look down upon me reprovingly but not unkindly, observing to the carriage generally: "It's a funny thing, ain't it, nobody's ever made a boy yet that could keep still for ten seconds." After which he would pat me heartily on the head, to show he was not vexed with me, and fall to sleep again upon me. He was a good-tempered man.

My mother sat occupied chiefly with her own thoughts, and my aunt had found a congenial companion in a lady who had had her cap basket sat upon; so I was left mainly to my own resources. When I could get my head free of the big man's back, I gazed out of the window, and watched the flying fragments as we shed the world. Now a village would fall from us, now the yellow corn-land would cling to us for awhile, or a wood catch at our rushing feet, and sometimes a strong town would stop us, and hold us, panting for a space. Or, my eyes weary, I would sit and listen to the hoarse singing of the wheels beneath my feet. It was a monotonous chaunt, ever the same two lines:

"Here we suffer grief and pain,   Here we meet to part again,"

followed by a low, rumbling laugh. Sometimes fortissimo, sometimes pianissimo; now vivace, now largo; but ever those same two lines, and ever followed by the same low, rumbling laugh; still to this day the iron wheels sing to me that same song.

Later on I also must have slept, for I dreamt that as the result of my having engaged in single combat with a dragon, the dragon, ignoring all the rules of Fairyland, had swallowed me. It was hot and stuffy in the dragon's stomach. He had, so it appeared to me, disgracefully overeaten himself; there were hundreds of us there, entirely undigested, including Mother Hubbard and a gentleman named Johnson, against whom, at that period, I entertained a strong prejudice by reason of our divergent views upon the subject of spelling. Even in this hour of our mutual discomfort Johnson would not leave me alone, but persisted in asking me how I spelt Jonah. Nobody was looking, so I kicked him. He sprang up and came after me. I tried to run away, but became wedged between Hop-o'-my-Thumb and Julius Caesar. I suppose our tearing about must have hurt the dragon, for at that moment he gave vent to a most fearful scream, and I awoke to find the fat man rubbing his left shin, while we struggled slowly, with steps growing ever feebler, against a sea of brick that every moment closed in closer round us.

We scrambled out of the carriage into a great echoing cave that might have been the dragon's home, where, to my alarm, my mother was immediately swooped down upon by a strange man in grey.

"Why's he do that?" I asked of my aunt.

"Because he's a fool," answered my aunt; "they all are."

He put my mother down and came towards us. He was a tall, thin man, with eyes one felt one would never be afraid of; and instinctively even then I associated him in my mind with windmills and a lank white horse.

"Why, how he's grown," said the grey man, raising me in his arms until my mother beside me appeared to me in a new light as quite a little person; "and solid too."

My mother whispered something. I think from her face, for I knew the signs, it was praise of me.

"And he's going to be our new fortune," she added aloud, as the grey man lowered me.

"Then," said my aunt, who had this while been sitting rigid upon a flat black box, "don't drop him down a coal-mine. That's all I say."

I wondered at the time why the grey man's pale face should flush so crimson, and why my mother should whisper angrily:

"Flow can you be so wicked, Fanny? How dare you say such a thing?"

"I only said 'don't drop him down a coal-mine,'" returned my aunt, apparently much surprised; "you don't want to drop him down a coal-mine, do you?"

We passed through glittering, joyous streets, piled high each side with all the good things of the earth; toys and baubles, jewels and gold, things good to eat and good to drink, things good to wear and good to see; through pleasant ways where fountains splashed and flowers bloomed. The people wore bright clothes, had happy faces. They rode in beautiful carriages, they strolled about, greeting one another with smiles. The children ran and laughed. London, thought I to myself, is the city of the fairies.

It passed, and we sank into a grim city of hoarse, roaring streets, wherein the endless throngs swirled and surged as I had seen the yellow waters curve and fret, contending, where the river pauses, rock-bound. Here were no bright costumes, no bright faces, none stayed to greet another; all was stern, and swift, and voiceless. London, then, said I to myself, is the city of the giants. They must live in these towering castles side by side, and these hurrying thousands are their driven slaves.

But this passed also, and we sank lower yet until we reached a third city, where a pale mist filled each sombre street. None of the beautiful things of the world were to be seen here, but only the things coarse and ugly. And wearily to and fro its sunless passages trudged with heavy steps a weary people, coarse-clad, and with dull, listless faces. And London, I knew, was the city of the gnomes who labour sadly all their lives, imprisoned underground; and a terror seized me lest I, too, should remain chained here, deep down below the fairy city that was already but a dream.

We stopped at last in a long, unfinished street. I remember our pushing our way through a group of dirty urchins, all of whom, my aunt remarked in passing, ought to be skinned. It was my aunt's one prescription for all to whom she took objection; but really in the present instance I think it would have been of service; nothing else whatever could have restored them to cleanliness. Then the door closed behind us with an echoing clang, and the small, cold rooms came forward stiffly to greet us.

The man in grey went to the one window and drew back the curtain; it was growing dusk now. My aunt sat on a straight, hard chair and stared fixedly at the three-armed gaselier. My mother stood in the centre of the room with one small ungloved hand upon the table, and I noticed, for I was very near, that the poor little one-legged thing was trembling.

"Of course it's not what you've been accustomed to, Maggie," said the man in grey; "but it's only for a little while."

He spoke in a new, angry voice; but I could not see his face, his back being to the light.

My mother drew his arms around us both.

"It is the best home in all the world," she said; and thus we stayed for awhile.

"Nonsense," said my aunt, suddenly; and this aroused us; "it's a poky hole, as I told her it would be. Let her thank the Lord she's got a man clever enough to get her out of it. I know him; he never could rest where he was put. Now he's at the bottom; he'll go up."

It sounded to me a very disagreeable speech; but the grey man laughed, I had not heard him laugh till then, and my mother ran to my aunt and kissed her; and somehow the room seemed to become lighter.

For some reason I slept downstairs that night, on the floor, behind a screen improvised out of a clothes horse and a blanket; and later in the evening the clatter of knives and forks and the sound of subdued voices awoke me. My aunt had apparently gone to bed; my mother and the man in grey were talking together over their supper.

"We must buy land," said the voice of the grey man; "London is coming this way. The Somebodies" (I forget the name my father mentioned) "made all their money by buying up land round New York for a mere song. Then, as the city spread, they became worth millions."

"But where will you get the money from, Luke?" asked the voice of my mother.

The voice of the grey man answered airily:

"Oh, that's merely a matter of business. You grant a mortgage. The property goes up in value. You borrow more. Then you buy more, and so on."

"I see," said my mother.

"Being on the spot gives one such an advantage," said the grey man. "I shall know just when to buy. It's a great thing, being on the spot."

"Of course, it must be," said my mother.

I suppose I must have dozed, for the next words I heard the grey man say were:

"Of course you have the park opposite, but then the house is small."

"But shall we need a very large one?" asked my mother.

"One never knows," said the grey man. "If I should go into Parliament"

At this point a hissing sound arose from the neighbourhood of the fire.

"It looks," said my mother, "as if it were done."

"If you will hold the dish," said the grey man, "I think I can pour it in without spilling."

Again I must have dozed.

"It depends," said the grey man, "upon what he is going to be. For the classics, of course, Oxford."

"He's going to be very clever," said my mother. She spoke as one who knows.

"We'll hope so," said the grey man.

"I shouldn't be surprised," said my mother, "if he turned out a poet."

The grey man said something in a low tone that I did not hear.

"I'm not so sure," answered my mother, "it's in the blood. I've often thought that you, Luke, ought to have been a poet."

"I never had the time," said the grey man. "There were one or two little things"

"They were very beautiful," interrupted my mother. The clatter of the knives and forks continued undisturbed for a few moments. Then continued the grey man:

"There would be no harm, provided I made enough. It's the law of nature. One generation earns, the next spends. We must see. In any case, I think I should prefer Oxford for him."

"It will be so hard parting from him," said my mother.

"There will be the vacations," said the grey man, "when we shall travel."

CHAPTER II.

IN WHICH PAUL MAKES ACQUAINTANCE OF THE MAN WITH THE UGLY MOUTH.

The case of my father and mother was not normal. You understand they had been separated for some years, and though they were not young in age, indeed, before my childish eyes they loomed quite ancient folk, and in fact my father must have been nearly forty and my mother quit of thirty, yet, as you will come to think yourself, no doubt, during the course of my story, they were in all the essentials of life little more than boy and girl. This I came to see later on, but at that time, had I been consulted by enquiring maid or bachelor, I might unwittingly have given wrong impressions concerning marriage in the general. I should have described a husband as a man who could never rest quite content unless his wife were by his side; who twenty times a day would call from his office door: "Maggie, are you doing anything important? I want to talk to you about a matter of business." ... "Maggie, are you alone? Oh, all right, I'll come down." Of a wife I should have said she was a woman whose eyes were ever love-lit when resting on her man; who was glad where he was and troubled where he was not. But in every case this might not have been correct.

Also, I should have had something to say concerning the alarms and excursions attending residence with any married couple. I should have recommended the holding up of feet under the table lest, mistaken for other feet, they should be trodden on and pressed. Also, I should have advised against entry into any room unpreceded by what in Stageland is termed "noise without." It is somewhat disconcerting to the nervous incomer to be met, the door still in his hand, by a sound as of people springing suddenly into the air, followed by a weird scuttling of feet, and then to discover the occupants sitting stiffly in opposite corners, deeply engaged in book or needlework. But, as I have said, with regard to some households, such precautions might be needless.

Personally, I fear, I exercised little or no controlling influence upon my parents in this respect, my intrusions coming soon to be greeted with: "Oh, it's only Spud," in a tone of relief, accompanied generally by the sofa cushion; but of my aunt they stood more in awe. Not that she ever said anything, and, indeed, to do her justice, in her efforts to spare their feelings she erred, if at all, on the side of excess. Never did she move a footstep about the house except to the music of a sustained and penetrating cough. As my father once remarked, ungratefully, I must confess, the volume of bark produced by my aunt in a single day would have done credit to the dying efforts of a hospital load of consumptives; to a robust and perfectly healthy lady the cost in nervous force must have been prodigious. Also, that no fear should live with them that her eyes had seen aught not intended for them, she would invariably enter backwards any room in which they might be, closing the door loudly and with difficulty before turning round: and through dark passages she would walk singing. No woman alive could have done more; yet, such is human nature! neither my father nor my mother was grateful to her, so far as I could judge.

Indeed, strange as it may appear, the more sympathetic towards them she showed herself, the more irritated against her did they become.

"I believe, Fanny, you hate seeing Luke and me happy together," said my mother one day, coming up from the kitchen to find my aunt preparing for entry into the drawing-room by dropping teaspoons at five-second intervals outside the door: "Don't make yourself so ridiculous." My mother spoke really quite unkindly.

"Hate it!" replied my aunt. "Why should I? Why shouldn't a pair of turtle doves bill and coo, when their united age is only a little over seventy, the pretty dears?" The mildness of my aunt's answers often surprised me.

As for my father, he grew positively vindictive. I remember the occasion well. It was the first, though not the last time I knew him lose his temper. What brought up the subject I forget, but my father stopped suddenly; we were walking by the canal bank.

"Your aunt", my father may not have intended it, but his tone and manner when speaking of my aunt always conveyed to me the impression that he regarded me as personally responsible for her existence. This used to weigh upon me. "Your aunt is the most cantankerous, the most, " he broke off, and shook his fist towards the setting sun. "I wish to God," said my father, "your aunt had a comfortable little income of her own, with a freehold cottage in the country, by God I do!" But the next moment, ashamed, I suppose, of his brutality: "Not but what sometimes, of course, she can be very nice, you know," he added; "don't tell your mother what I said just now."

Another who followed with sympathetic interest the domestic comedy was Susan, our maid-of-all-work, the first of a long and varied series, extending unto the advent of Amy, to whom the blessing of Heaven. Susan was a stout and elderly female, liable to sudden fits of sleepiness, the result, we were given to understand, of trouble; but her heart, it was her own proud boast, was always in the right place. She could never look at my father and mother sitting anywhere near each other but she must flop down and weep awhile; the sight of connubial bliss always reminding her, so she would explain, of the past glories of her own married state.

Though an earnest enquirer, I was never able myself to grasp the ins and outs of this past married life of Susan's. Whether her answers were purposely framed to elude curiosity, or whether they were the result of a naturally incoherent mind, I cannot say. Their tendency was to convey confusion.

On Monday I have seen Susan shed tears of regret into the Brussels sprouts, that she had been debarred by the pressure of other duties from lately watering "his" grave, which, I gathered, was at Manor Park. While on Tuesday I have listened, blood chilled, to the recital of her intentions should she ever again enjoy the luxury of getting her fingers near the scruff of his neck.

"But, I thought, Susan, he was dead," was my very natural comment upon this outbreak.

"So did I, Master Paul," was Susan's rejoinder; "that was his artfulness."

"Then he isn't buried in Manor Park Cemetery?"

"Not yet; but he'll wish he was, the half-baked monkey, when I get hold of him."

"Then he wasn't a good man?"

"Who?"

"Your husband."

"Who says he ain't a good man?" It was Susan's flying leaps from tense to tense that most bewildered me. "If anybody says he ain't I'll gouge their eye out!"

I hastened to assure Susan that my observation had been intended in the nature of enquiry, not of assertion.

"Brings me a bottle of gin, for my headaches, every time he comes home," continued Susan, showing cause for opinion, "every blessed time."

And at some such point as this I would retire to the clearer atmosphere of German grammar or mixed fractions.

We suffered a good deal from Susan one way and another; for having regard to the admirable position of her heart, we all felt it our duty to overlook mere failings of the flesh, all but my aunt, that is, who never made any pretence of being a sentimentalist.

"She's a lazy hussy," was the opinion expressed of her one morning by my aunt, who was rinsing; "a gulping, snorting, lazy hussy, that's what she is." There was some excuse for my aunt's indignation. It was then eleven o'clock and Susan was still sleeping off an attack of what she called "new-ralgy."

"She has seen a good deal of trouble," said my mother, who was wiping.

"And if she was my cook and housemaid," replied my aunt, "she would see more, the slut!"

"She's not a good servant in many respects," admitted my mother, "but I think she's good-hearted."

"Oh, drat her heart," was my aunt's retort. "The right place for that heart of hers is on the doorstep. And that's where I'd put it, and her and her box alongside it, if I had my way."

The departure of Susan did take place not long afterwards. It occurred one Saturday night. My mother came upstairs looking pale.

"Luke," she said, "do please run for the doctor."

"What's the matter?" asked my father.

"Susan," gasped my mother, "she's lying on the kitchen floor breathing in the strangest fashion and quite unable to speak."

"I'll go for Washburn," said my father; "if I am quick I shall catch him at the dispensary."

Five minutes later my father came back panting, followed by the doctor. This was a big, black-bearded man; added to which he had the knack of looking bigger than even he really was. He came down the kitchen stairs two at a time, shaking the whole house. He brushed my mother aside, and bent over the unconscious Susan, who was on her back with her mouth wide open. Then he rose and looked at my father and mother, who were watching him with troubled faces; and then he opened his mouth, and there came from it a roar of laughter, the like of which sound I had never heard.

The next moment he had seized a pail half full of water and had flung it over the woman. She opened her eyes and sat up.

"Feeling better?" said the doctor, with the pail still in his hand; "have another dose?"

Susan began to gather herself together with the evident intention of expressing her feelings; but before she could find the first word, he had pushed the three of us outside and slammed the door behind us.

From the top of the stairs we could hear Susan's thick, rancorous voice raging fiercer and fiercer, drowned every now and then by the man's savage roar of laughter. And, when for want of breath she would flag for a moment, he would yell out encouragement to her, shouting: "Bravo! Go it, my beauty, give it tongue! Bark, bark! I love to hear you," applauding her, clapping his hands and stamping his feet.

"What a beast of a man," said my mother.

"He is really a most interesting man when you come to know him," explained my father.

Replied my mother, stiffly: "I don't ever mean to know him." But it is only concerning the past that we possess knowledge.

The riot from below ceased at length, and was followed by a new voice, speaking quietly and emphatically, and then we heard the doctor's step again upon the stairs.

My mother held her purse open in her hand, and as the man entered the room she went forward to meet him.

"How much do we owe you, Doctor?" said my mother. She spoke in a voice trembling with severity.

He closed the purse and gently pushed it back towards her.

"A glass of beer and a chop, Mrs. Kelver," he answered, "which I am coming back in an hour to cook for myself. And as you will be without any servant," he continued, while my mother stood staring at him incapable of utterance, "you had better let me cook some for you at the same time. I am an expert at grilling chops."

"But, really, Doctor" my mother began. He laid his huge hand upon her shoulder, and my mother sat down upon the nearest chair.

"My dear lady," he said, "she's a person you never ought to have had inside your house. She's promised me to be gone in half an hour, and I'm coming back to see she keeps her word. Give her a month's wages, and have a clear fire ready for me." And before my mother could reply, he had slammed the front door.

"What a very odd sort of a man," said my mother, recovering herself.

"He's a character," said my father; "you might not think it, but he's worshipped about here."

"I hardly know what to make of him," said my mother; "I suppose I had better go out and get some chops;" which she did.

Susan went, as sober as a judge, on Friday, as the saying is, her great anxiety being to get out of the house before the doctor returned. The doctor himself arrived true to his time, and I lay awake, for no human being ever slept or felt he wanted to sleep while Dr. Washburn was anywhere near, and listened to the gusts of laughter that swept continually through the house. Even my aunt laughed that supper time, and when the doctor himself laughed it seemed to me that the bed shook under me. Not liking to be out of it, I did what spoilt little boys and even spoilt little girls sometimes will do under similar stress of feeling, wrapped the blanket round my legs and pattered down, with my face set to express the sudden desire of a sensitive and possibly short-lived child for parents' love. My mother pretended to be angry, but that I knew was only her company manners. Besides, I really had, if not exactly a pain, an extremely uncomfortable sensation (one common to me about that period) as of having swallowed the dome of St. Paul's. The doctor said it was a frequent complaint with children, the result of too early hours and too much study; and, taking me on his knee, wrote then and there a diet chart for me, which included one tablespoonful of golden syrup four times a day, and one ounce of sherbet to be placed upon the tongue and taken neat ten minutes before each meal.

That evening will always live in my remembrance. My mother was brighter than I had ever seen her. A flush was on her cheek and a sparkle in her eye, and looking across at her as she sat holding a small painted screen to shield her face from the fire, the sense of beauty became suddenly born within me, and answering an impulse I could not have explained, I slipped down, still with my blanket around me, from the doctor's knee, and squatted on the edge of the fender, from where, when I thought no one was noticing me, I could steal furtive glances up into her face.

So also my father seemed to me to have become all at once bigger and more dignified, talking with a vigour and an enjoyment that sat newly on him. Aunt Fan was quite witty and agreeable for her; and even I asked one or two questions, at which, for some reason or another, everybody laughed; which determined me to remember and ask those same questions again on some future occasion.

That was the great charm of the man, that by the magnetic spell of his magnificent vitality he drew from everyone their best. In his company clever people waxed intellectual giants, while the dull sat amazed at their own originality. Conversing with him, Podsnap might have been piquant, Dogberry incisive. But better than all else, I found it listening to his own talk. Of what he spoke I could tell you no more than could the children of Hamelin have told the tune the Pied Piper played. I only know that at the tangled music of his strong voice the walls of the mean room faded away, and that beyond I saw a brave, laughing world that called to me; a world full of joyous fight, where some won and some lost. But that mattered not a jot, because whatever else came of it there was a right royal game for all; a world where merry gentlemen feared neither life nor death, and Fate was but the Master of the Revels.

Such was my first introduction to Dr. Washburn, or to give him the name by which he was known in every slum and alley of that quarter, Dr. Fighting Hal; and in a minor key that evening was an index to the whole man. Often he would wrinkle his nose as a dog before it bites, and then he was more brute than man, brutish in his instincts, in his appetites, brutish in his pleasure, brutish in his fun. Or his deep blue eyes would grow soft as a mother's, and then you might have thought him an angel in a soft felt hat and a coat so loose-fitting as to suggest the possibility of his wings being folded away underneath. Often have I tried to make up my mind whether it has been better for me or worse that I ever came to know him; but as easy would it be for the tree to say whether the rushing winds and the wild rains have shaped it or mis-shaped.

Susan's place remained vacant for some time. My mother would explain to the few friends who occasionally came from afar to see us, that her "housemaid" she had been compelled to suddenly discharge, and that we were waiting for the arrival of a new and better specimen. But the months passed and we still waited, and my father on the rare days when a client would ring the office bell, would, after pausing a decent interval, open the front door himself, and then call downstairs indignantly and loudly, to know why "Jane" or "Mary" could not attend to their work. And my mother, that the bread-boy or the milkman might not put it about the neighbourhood that the Kelvers in the big corner house kept no servant, would hide herself behind a thick veil and fetch all things herself from streets a long way off.

For this family of whom I am writing were, I confess, weak and human. Their poverty they were ashamed of as though it were a crime, and in consequence their life was more full of paltry and useless subterfuge than should be perhaps the life of brave men and women. The larder, I fancy, was very often bare, but the port and sherry with the sweet biscuits stood always on the sideboard; and the fire had often to be low in the grate that my father's tall hat might shine resplendent and my mother's black silk rustle on Sundays.

But I would not have you sneer at them, thinking all pretence must spring from snobbishness and never from mistaken self-respect. Some fine gentleman writers there be, men whose world is bounded on the east by Bond Street, who see in the struggles of poverty to hide its darns only matter for jest. But myself, I cannot laugh at them. I know the long hopes and fears that centre round the hired waiter; the long cost of the cream and the ice jelly ordered the week before from the confectioner's. But to me it is pathetic, not ridiculous. Heroism is not all of one pattern. Dr. Washburn, had the Prince of Wales come to see him, would have put his bread and cheese and jug of beer upon the table, and helped His Royal Highness to half. But my father and mother's tea was very weak that Mr. Jones or Mr. Smith might have a glass of wine should they come to dinner. I remember the one egg for breakfast, my mother arguing that my father should have it because he had his business to attend to; my father insisting that my mother should eat it, she having to go out shopping, a compromise being effected by their dividing it between them, each clamouring for the white as the most nourishing. And I know however little the meal looked upon the table when we started I always rose well satisfied. These are small things to speak of, but then you must bear in mind this is a story moving in narrow ways.

To me this life came as a good time. That I was encouraged to eat treacle in preference to butter seemed to me admirable. Personally, I preferred sausages for dinner; and a supper of fried fish and potatoes, brought in stealthily in a carpet bag, was infinitely more enjoyable than the set meal where nothing was of interest till one came to the dessert. What fun there was about it all! The cleaning of the doorstep by night, when from the ill-lit street a gentleman with a piece of sacking round his legs might very well pass for a somewhat tall charwoman. I would keep watch at the gate to give warning should any one looking like a possible late caller turn the corner of the street, coming back now and then in answer to a low whistle to help my father grope about in the dark for the hearthstone; he was always mislaying the hearthstone. How much better, helping to clean the knives or running errands than wasting all one's morning dwelling upon the shocking irregularity of certain classes of French verbs; or making useless calculations as to how long X, walking four and a quarter miles an hour, would be overtaking Y, whose powers were limited to three and a half, but who had started two and three quarter hours sooner; the whole argument being reduced to sheer pedantry by reason of no information being afforded to the student concerning the respective thirstiness of X and Y.

Even my father and mother were able to take it lightly with plenty of laughter and no groaning that I ever heard. For over all lay the morning light of hope, and what prisoner, escaping from his dungeon, ever stayed to think of his torn hands and knees when beyond the distant opening he could see the sunlight glinting through the brambles?

"I had no idea," said my mother, "there was so much to do in a house. In future I shall arrange for the servants to have regular hours, and a little time to themselves, for rest. Don't you think it right, Luke?"

"Quite right," replied my father; "and I'll tell you another thing we'll do. I shall insist on the landlord's putting a marble doorstep to the next house we take; you pass a sponge over marble and it is always clean."

"Or tesselated," suggested my mother.

"Or tesselated," agreed my father; "but marble is more uncommon."

Only once, can I recall a cloud. That was one Sunday when my mother, speaking across the table in the middle of dinner, said to my father, "We might save the rest of that stew, Luke; there's an omelette coming."

My father laid down the spoon. "An omelette!"

"Yes," said my mother. "I thought I would like to try again."

My father stepped into the back kitchen, we dined in the kitchen, as a rule, it saved much carriage, returning with the wood chopper.

"Whatever are you going to do, Luke, with the chopper?" said my mother.

"Divide the omelette," replied my father.

My mother began to cry.

"Why, Maggie!" said my father.

"I know the other one was leathery," said my mother, "but it was the fault of the oven, you know it was, Luke."

"My dear," said my father, "I only meant it as a joke."

"I don't like that sort of joke," said my mother; "it isn't nice of you, Luke."

I don't think, to be candid, my mother liked much any joke that was against herself. Indeed, when I come to think of it, I have never met a woman who did, nor man, either.

There had soon grown up a comradeship between my father and myself for he was the youngest thing I had met with as yet. Sometimes my mother seemed very young, and later I met boys and girls nearer to my own age in years; but they grew, while my father remained always the same. The hair about his temples was turning grey, and when you looked close you saw many crow's feet and lines, especially about the mouth. But his eyes were the eyes of a boy, his laugh the laugh of a boy, and his heart the heart of a boy. So we were very close to each other.

In a narrow strip of ground we called our garden we would play a cricket of our own, encompassed about by many novel rules, rendered necessary by the locality. For instance, all hitting to leg was forbidden, as tending to endanger neighbouring windows, while hitting to off was likewise not to be encouraged, as causing a temporary adjournment of the game, while batter and bowler went through the house and out into the street to recover the ball from some predatory crowd of urchins to whom it had evidently appeared as a gift direct from Heaven. Sometimes rising very early we would walk across the marshes to bathe in a small creek that led down to the river, but this was muddy work, necessitating much washing of legs on the return home. And on rare days we would, taking the train to Hackney and walking to the bridge, row up the river Lea, perhaps as far as Ponder's End.

But these sports being hedged around with difficulties, more commonly for recreation we would take long walks. There were pleasant nooks even in the neighbourhood of Plaistow marshes in those days. Here and there a graceful elm still clung to the troubled soil. Surrounded on all sides by hideousness, picturesque inns still remained hidden within green walls where, if you were careful not to pry too curiously, you might sit and sip your glass of beer beneath the oak and dream yourself where reeking chimneys and mean streets were not. During such walks my father would talk to me as he would talk to my mother, telling me all his wild, hopeful plans, discussing with me how I was to lodge at Oxford, to what particular branches of study and of sport I was to give my preference, speaking always with such catching confidence that I came to regard my sojourn in this brick and mortar prison as only a question of months.

One day, talking of this future, and laughing as we walked briskly. through the shrill streets, I told him the words my mother had said, long ago, as it seemed to me, for life is as a stone rolling down-hill, and moves but slowly at first; she and I sitting on the moss at the foot of old "Jacob's Folly", that he was our Prince fighting to deliver us from the grim castle called "Hard Times," guarded by the dragon Poverty.

My father laughed and his boyish face flushed with pleasure.

"And she was right, Paul," he whispered, pressing my small hand in his, it was necessary to whisper, for the street where we were was very crowded, but I knew that he wanted to shout. "I will fight him and I will slay him." My father made passes in the air with his walking-stick, and it was evident from the way they drew aside that the people round about fancied he was mad. "I will batter down the iron gates and she shall be free. I will, God help me, I will."

The gallant gentleman! How long and how bravely he fought! But in the end it was the Dragon triumphed, the Knight that lay upon the ground, his great heart still. I have read how, with the sword of Honest Industry, one may always conquer this grim Dragon. But such was in foolish books. In truth, only with the sword of Chicanery and the stout buckler of Unscrupulousness shall you be certain of victory over him. If you care not to use these, pray to your Gods, and take what comes with a stout heart.

CHAPTER III.

HOW GOOD LUCK KNOCKED AT THE DOOR OF THE MAN IN GREY.

"Louisa!" roared my father down the kitchen stairs, "are you all asleep? Here have I had to answer the front door myself." Then my father strode into his office, and the door slammed. My father could be very angry when nobody was by.

Quarter of an hour later his bell rang with a quick, authoritative jangle. My mother, who was peeling potatoes with difficulty in wash-leather gloves, looked at my aunt who was shelling peas. The bell rang again louder still this time.

"Once for Louisa, twice for James, isn't it?" enquired my aunt.

"You go, Paul," said my mother; "say that Louisa" but with the words a sudden flush overspread my mother's face, and before I could lay down my slate she had drawn off her gloves and had passed me. "No, don't stop your lessons, I'll go myself," she said, and ran out.

A few minutes later the kitchen door opened softly, and my mother's hand, appearing through the jar, beckoned to me mysteriously.

"Walk on your toes," whispered my mother, setting the example as she led the way up the stairs; which after the manner of stairs showed their disapproval of deception by creaking louder and more often than under any other circumstances; and in this manner we reached my parents' bedroom, where, in the old-fashioned wardrobe, relic of better days, reposed my best suit of clothes, or, to be strictly grammatical, my better.

Never before had I worn these on a week-day morning, but all conversation not germane to the question of getting into them quickly my mother swept aside; and when I was complete, down even to the new shoes, Bluchers, we called them in those days, took me by the hand, and together we crept down as we had crept up, silent, stealthy and alert. My mother led me to the street door and opened it.

"Shan't I want my cap?" I whispered. But my mother only shook her head and closed the door with a bang; and then the explanation of the pantomime came to me, for with such "business", comic, shall I call it, or tragic? I was becoming familiar; and, my mother's hand upon my shoulder, we entered my father's office.

Whether from the fact that so often of an evening, our drawing-room being reserved always as a show-room in case of chance visitors; Cowper's poems, open face-downwards on the wobbly loo table; the half-finished crochet work, suggestive of elegant leisure, thrown carelessly over the arm of the smaller easy-chair, this office would become our sitting-room, its books and papers, as things of no account, being huddled out of sight; or whether from the readiness with which my father would come out of it at all times to play at something else, at cricket in the back garden on dry days or ninepins in the passage on wet, charging back into it again whenever a knock sounded at the front door, I cannot say. But I know that as a child it never occurred to me to regard my father's profession as a serious affair. To me he was merely playing there, surrounded by big books and bundles of documents, labelled profusely but consisting only of blank papers; by japanned tin boxes, lettered imposingly, but for the most part empty. "Sutton Hampden, Esq.," I remember was practically my mother's work-box. The "Drayton Estates" yielded apparently nothing but apples, a fruit of which my father was fond; while "Mortgages" it was not until later in life I discovered had no connection with poems in manuscript, some in course of correction, others completed.

Now, as the door opened, he rose and came towards us. His hair stood up from his head, for it was a habit of his to rumple it as he talked; and this added to his evident efforts to compose his face into an expression of businesslike gravity, added emphasis, if such were needed, to the suggestion of the over long schoolboy making believe.

"This is the youngster," said my father, taking me from my mother, and passing me on. "Tall for his age, isn't he?"

With a twist of his thick lips, he rolled the evil-smelling cigar he was smoking from the left corner of his mouth to the right; and held out a fat and not too clean hand, which, as it closed round mine, brought to my mind the picture of the walrus in my natural history book; with the other he flapped me kindly on the head.

"Like 'is mother, wonderfully like 'is mother, ain't 'e?" he observed, still holding my hand. "And that," he added with a wink of one of his small eyes towards my father, "is about the 'ighest compliment I can pay 'im, eh?"

His eyes were remarkably small, but marvellously bright and piercing; so much so that when he turned them again upon me I tried to think quickly of something nice about him, feeling sure that he could see right into me.

"And where are you thinkin' of sendin' 'im?" he continued; "Eton or 'Arrow?"

"We haven't quite made up our minds as yet," replied my father; "at present we are educating him at home."

"You take my tip," said the fat man, "and learn all you can. Look at me! If I'd 'ad the opportunity of being a schollard I wouldn't be here offering your father an extravagant price for doin' my work; I'd be able to do it myself."

"You seem to have got on very well without it," laughed my father; and in truth his air of prosperity might have justified greater self-complacency. Rings sparkled on his blunt fingers, and upon the swelling billows of his waistcoat rose and sank a massive gold cable.

"I'd 'ave done better with it," he grunted.

"But you look very clever," I said; and though divining with a child's cuteness that it was desired I should make a favourable impression upon him, I hoped this would please him, the words were yet spontaneous.

He laughed heartily, his whole body shaking like some huge jelly.

"Well, old Noel Hasluck's not exactly a fool," he assented, "but I'd like myself better if I could talk about something else than business, and didn't drop my aitches. And so would my little gell."

"You have a daughter?" asked my mother, with whom a child, as a bond of sympathy with the stranger took the place assigned by most women to disrespectful cooks and incompetent housemaids.

"I won't tell you about 'er. But I'll just bring 'er to see you now and then, ma'am, if you don't mind," answered Mr. Hasluck. "She don't often meet gentle-folks, an' it'll do 'er good."

My mother glanced across at my father, but the man, intercepting her question, replied to it himself.

"You needn't be afraid, ma'am, that she's anything like me," he assured her quite good-temperedly; "nobody ever believes she's my daughter, except me and the old woman. She's a little lady, she is. Freak o' nature, I call it."

"We shall be delighted," explained my mother.

"Well, you will when you see 'er," replied Mr. Hasluck, quite contentedly.

He pushed half-a-crown into my hand, overriding my parents' susceptibilities with the easy good-temper of a man accustomed to have his way in all things.

"No squanderin' it on the 'eathen," was his parting injunction as I left the room; "you spend that on a Christian tradesman."

It was the first money I ever remember having to spend, that half-crown of old Hasluck's; suggestions of the delights to be derived from a new pair of gloves for Sunday, from a Latin grammar, which would then be all my own, and so on, having hitherto displaced all less exalted visions concerning the disposal of chance coins coming into my small hands. But on this occasion I was left free to decide for myself.

The anxiety it gave me! the long tossing hours in bed! the tramping of the bewildering streets! Even advice when asked for was denied me.

"You must learn to think for yourself," said my father, who spoke eloquently on the necessity of early acquiring sound judgment and what he called "commercial aptitude."

"No, dear," said my mother, "Mr. Hasluck wanted you to spend it as you like. If I told you, that would be spending it as I liked. Your father and I want to see what you will do with it."

The good little boys in the books bought presents or gave away to people in distress. For this I hated them with the malignity the lower nature ever feels towards the higher. I consulted my aunt Fan.

"If somebody gave you half-a-crown," I put it to her, "what would you buy with it?"

"Side-combs," said my aunt; she was always losing or breaking her side-combs.

"But I mean if you were me," I explained.

"Drat the child!" said my aunt; "how do I know what he wants if he don't know himself. Idiot!"

The shop windows into which I stared, my nose glued to the pane! The things I asked the price of! The things I made up my mind to buy and then decided that I wouldn't buy! Even my patient mother began to show signs of irritation. It was rapidly assuming the dimensions of a family curse, was old Hasluck's half-crown.

Then one day I made up my mind, and so ended the trouble. In the window of a small plumber's shop in a back street near, stood on view among brass taps, rolls of lead piping and cistern requisites, various squares of coloured glass, the sort of thing chiefly used, I believe, for lavatory doors and staircase windows. Some had stars in the centre, and others, more elaborate, were enriched with designs, severe but inoffensive. I purchased a dozen of these, the plumber, an affable man who appeared glad to see me, throwing in two extra out of sheer generosity.

Why I bought them I did not know at the time, and I do not know now. My mother cried when she saw them. My father could get no further than: "But what are you going to do with them?" to which I was unable to reply. My aunt, alone, attempted comfort.

"If a person fancies coloured glass," said my aunt, "then he's a fool not to buy coloured glass when he gets the chance. We haven't all the same tastes."

In the end, I cut myself badly with them and consented to their being thrown into the dust-bin. But looking back, I have come to regard myself rather as the victim of Fate than of Folly. Many folks have I met since, recipients of Hasluck's half-crowns, many a man who has slapped his pocket and blessed the day he first met that "Napoleon of Finance," as later he came to be known among his friends, but it ever ended so; coloured glass and cut fingers. Is it fairy gold that he and his kind fling round? It would seem to be.

Next time old Hasluck knocked at our front door a maid in cap and apron opened it to him, and this was but the beginning of change. New oilcloth glistened in the passage. Lace curtains, such as in that neighbourhood were the hall-mark of the plutocrat, advertised our rising fortunes to the street, and greatest marvel of all, at least to my awed eyes, my father's Sunday clothes came into weekday wear, new ones taking their place in the great wardrobe that hitherto had been the stronghold of our gentility; to which we had ever turned for comfort when rendered despondent by contemplation of the weakness of our outer walls. "Seeing that everything was all right" is how my mother would explain it. She would lay the lilac silk upon the bed, fondly soothing down its rustling undulations, lingering lovingly over its deep frosted flounces of rich Honiton. Maybe she had entered the room weary looking and depressed, but soon there would proceed from her a gentle humming as from some small winged thing when the sun first touches it and warms it, and sometimes by the time the Indian shawl, which could go through a wedding ring, but never would when it was wanted to, had been refolded and fastened again with the great cameo brooch, and the poke bonnet, like some fractious child, shaken and petted into good condition, she would be singing softly to herself, nodding her head to the words: which were generally to the effect that somebody was too old and somebody else too bold and another too cold, "so he wouldn't do for me;" and stepping lightly as though the burden of the years had fallen from her.

One evening, it was before the advent of this Hasluck, I remember climbing out of bed, for trouble was within me. Creatures, indescribable but heavy, had sat upon my chest, after which I had fallen downstairs, slowly and reasonably for the first few hundred flights, then with haste for the next million miles or so, until I found myself in the street with nothing on but my nightshirt. Personally, I was shocked, but nobody else seemed to mind, and I hailed a two-penny 'bus and climbed in. But when I tried to pay I found I hadn't any pockets, so I jumped out and ran away and the conductor came after me. My feet were like lead, and with every step he gained on me, till with a scream I made one mighty effort and awoke.

Feeling the need of comfort after these unpleasant but by no means unfamiliar experiences, I wrapped some clothes round me and crept downstairs. The "office" was dark, but to my surprise a light shone from under the drawing-room door, and I opened it.

The candles in the silver candlesticks were lighted, and in state, one in each easy-chair, sat my father and mother, both in their best clothes; my father in the buckled shoes and the frilled shirt that I had never seen him wear before, my mother with the Indian shawl about her shoulders, and upon her head the cap of ceremony that reposed three hundred and sixty days out of the year in its round wicker-work nest lined with silk. They started guiltily as I pushed open the door, but I congratulate myself that I had sense enough, or was it instinct, to ask no questions.

The last time I had seen them, three hours ago, they had been engaged, the lights carefully extinguished, cleaning the ground floor windows, my father the outside, my mother within, and it astonished me the change not only in their appearance, but in their manner and bearing, and even in their very voices. My father brought over from the sideboard the sherry and sweet biscuits and poured out and handed a glass to my mother, and he and my mother drank to each other, while I between them ate the biscuits, and the conversation was of Byron's poems and the great glass palace in Hyde Park.

I wonder am I disloyal setting this down? Maybe to others it shows but a foolish man and woman, and that is far from my intention. I dwell upon such trifles because to me the memory of them is very tender. The virtues of our loved ones we admire, yet after all 'tis but what we expected of them: how could they do otherwise? Their failings we would forget; no one of us is perfect. But over their follies we love to linger, smiling.

To me personally, old Hasluck's coming and all that followed thereupon made perhaps more difference than to anyone else. My father now was busy all the day; if not in his office, then away in the grim city of the giants, as I still thought of it; while to my mother came every day more social and domestic duties; so that for a time I was left much to my own resources.

Rambling, "bummelling," as the Germans term it, was my bent. This my mother would have checked, but my father said:

"Don't molly-coddle him. Let him learn to be smart."

"I don't think the smart people are always the nicest," demurred my mother. "I don't call you at all 'smart,' Luke."

My father appeared surprised, but reflected.

"I should call myself smart, in a sense," he explained, after consideration.

"Perhaps you are right, dear," replied my mother; "and of course boys are different from girls."

Sometimes I would wander Victoria Park way, which was then surrounded by many small cottages in leafy gardens; or even reach as far as Clapton, where old red brick Georgian houses still stood behind high palings, and tall elms gave to the wide road on sunny afternoons an old-world air of peace. But such excursions were the exception, for strange though it may read, the narrow, squalid streets had greater hold on me. Not the few main thoroughfares, filled ever with a dull, deep throbbing as of some tireless iron machine; where the endless human files, streaming ever up and down, crossing and recrossing, seemed mere rushing chains of flesh and blood, working upon unseen wheels; but the dim, weary, lifeless streets, the dark, tortuous roots, as I fancied them, of that grim forest of entangled brick. Mystery lurked in their gloom. Fear whispered from behind their silence. Dumb figures flitted swiftly to and fro, never pausing, never glancing right nor left. Far-off footsteps, rising swiftly into sound, as swiftly fading, echoed round their lonely comers. Dreading, yet drawn on, I would creep along their pavements as through some city of the dead, thinking of the eyes I saw not watching from the thousand windows; starting at each muffled sound penetrating the long, dreary walls, behind which that close-packed, writhing life lay hid.

One day there came a cry from behind a curtained window. I stood still for a moment and then ran; but before I could get far enough away I heard it again, a long, piercing cry, growing fiercer before it ceased; so that I ran faster still, not heeding where I went, till I found myself in a raw, unfinished street, ending in black waste land, bordering the river. I stopped, panting, wondering how I should find my way again. To recover myself and think I sat upon the doorstep of an empty house, and there came dancing down the road with a curious, half-running, half-hopping step, something like a water wagtail's, a child, a boy about my own age, who, after eyeing me strangely sat down beside me.

We watched each other for a few minutes; and I noticed that his mouth kept opening and shutting, though he said nothing. Suddenly, edging closer to me, he spoke in a thick whisper. It sounded as though his mouth were full of wool.

"Wot 'appens to yer when yer dead?"

"If you're good you go to Heaven. If you're bad you go to Hell."

"Long way off, both of 'em, ain't they?"

"Yes. Millions of miles."

"They can't come after yer? Can't fetch yer back again?"

"No, never."

The doorstep that we occupied was the last. A yard beyond began the black waste of mud. From the other end of the street, now growing dark, he never took his staring eyes for an instant.

"Ever seen a stiff 'un, a dead 'un?"

"No."

"I 'ave, stuck a pin into 'im. 'E never felt it. Don't feel anything when yer dead, do yer?"

All the while he kept swaying his body to and fro, twisting his arms and legs, and making faces. Comical figures made of ginger-bread, with quaintly curved limbs and grinning features, were to be bought then in bakers' shops: he made me hungry, reminding me of such.

"Of course not. When you are dead you're not there, you know. Our bodies are but senseless clay." I was glad I remembered that line. I tried to think of the next one, which was about food for worms; but it evaded me.

"I like you," he said; and making a fist, he gave me a punch in the chest. It was the token of palship among the youth of that neighbourhood, and gravely I returned it, meaning it, for friendship with children is an affair of the instant, or not at all, and I knew him for my first chum.

He wormed himself up.

"Yer won't tell?" he said.

I had no notion what I was not to tell, but our compact demanded that I should agree.

"Say 'I swear.'"

"I swear."

The heroes of my favourite fiction bound themselves by such like secret oaths. Here evidently was a comrade after my own heart.

"Good-bye, cockey."

But he turned again, and taking from his pocket an old knife, thrust it into my hand. Then with that extraordinary hopping movement of his ran off across the mud.

I stood watching him, wondering where he could be going. He stumbled a little further, where the mud began to get softer and deeper, but struggling up again, went hopping on towards the river.

I shouted to him, but he never looked back. At every few yards he would sink down almost to his knees in the black mud, but wrenching himself free would flounder forward. Then, still some distance from the river, he fell upon his face, and did not rise again. I saw his arms beating feebler and feebler as he sank till at last the oily slime closed over him, and I could detect nothing but a faint heaving underneath the mud. And after a time even that ceased.

It was late before I reached home, and fortunately my father and mother were still out. I did not tell any one what I had seen, having sworn not to; and as time went on the incident haunted me less and less until it became subservient to my will. But of my fancy for those silent, lifeless streets it cured me for the time. From behind their still walls I would hear that long cry; down their narrow vistas see that writhing figure, like some animated ginger-bread, hopping, springing, falling.

Yet in the more crowded streets another trouble awaited me, one more tangible.

Have you ever noticed a pack of sparrows round some crumbs perchance that you have thrown out from your window? Suddenly the rest of the flock will set upon one. There is a tremendous Lilliputian hubbub, a tossing of tiny wings and heads, a babel of shrill chirps. It is comical.

"Spiteful little imps they are," you say to yourself, much amused.

So I have heard good-tempered men and women calling out to one another with a laugh.

"There go those young devils chivvying that poor little beggar again; ought to be ashamed of theirselves."

But, oh! the anguish of the poor little beggar! Can any one who has not been through it imagine it! Reduced to its actualities, what was it? Gibes and jeers that, after all, break no bones. A few pinches, kicks and slaps; at worst a few hard knocks. But the dreading of it beforehand! Terror lived in every street, hid, waiting for me, round each corner. The half-dozen wrangling over their marbles, had they seen me? The boy whistling as he stood staring into the print shop, would I get past him without his noticing me; or would he, swinging round upon his heel, raise the shrill whoop that brought them from every doorway to hunt me?

The shame, when caught at last and cornered: the grinning face that would stop to watch; the careless jokes of passers-by, regarding the whole thing but as a sparrows' squabble: worst of all, perhaps, the rare pity! The after humiliation when, finally released, I would dart away, followed by shouted taunts and laughter; every eye turned to watch me, shrinking by; my whole small carcass shaking with dry sobs of bitterness and rage!

If only I could have turned and faced them! So far as the mere bearing of pain was concerned, I knew myself brave. The physical suffering resulting from any number of stand-up fights would have been trivial compared with the mental agony I endured. That I, the comrade of a hundred heroes, I, who nightly rode with Richard Coeur de Lion, who against Sir Lancelot himself had couched a lance, and that not altogether unsuccessful, I to whom all damsels in distress were wont to look for succour, that I should run from varlets such as these!

My friend, my bosom friend, good Robin Hood! how would he have behaved under similar circumstances? how Ivanhoe, my chosen companion in all quests of knightly enterprise? how, to come to modern times, Jack Harkaway, mere schoolboy though he might be? Would not one and all have welcomed such incident with a joyous shout, and in a trice have scattered to the winds the worthless herd?

But, alas! upon my pale lips the joyous shout sank into an unheard whisper, and the thing that became scattered to the wind was myself, the first opening that occurred.

Sometimes, the blood boiling in my veins, I would turn, thinking to go back and at all risk defying my tormentors, prove to myself I was no coward. But before I had retraced my steps a dozen paces, I would see in imagination the whole scene again before me: the laughing crowd, the halting passers-by, the spiteful, mocking little faces every way I turned; and so instead would creep on home, and climbing stealthily up into my own room, cry my heart out in the dark upon my bed.

Until one blessed day, when a blessed Fairy, in the form of a small kitten, lifted the spell that bound me, and set free my limbs.

I have always had a passionate affection for the dumb world, if it be dumb. My first playmate, I remember, was a water rat. A stream ran at the bottom of our garden; and sometimes, escaping the vigilant eye of Mrs. Fursey, I would steal out with my supper and join him on the banks.

There, hidden behind the osiers, we would play at banquets, he, it is true, doing most of the banqueting, and I the make-believe. But it was a good game; added to which it was the only game I could ever get him to play, though I tried. He was a one-ideaed rat.

Later I came into the possession of a white specimen all my own. He lived chiefly in the outside breast pocket of my jacket, in company with my handkerchief, so that glancing down I could generally see his little pink eyes gleaming up at me, except on very cold days, when it would be only his tail that I could see; and when I felt miserable, somehow he would know it, and, swarming up, push his little cold snout against my ear. He died just so, clinging round my neck; and from many of my fellow-men and women have I parted with less pain. It sounds callous to say so; but, after all, our feelings are not under our own control; and I have never been able to understand the use of pretending to emotions one has not. All this, however, comes later. Let me return now to my fairy kitten.

I heard its cry of pain from afar, and instinctively hastened my steps. Three or four times I heard it again, and at each call I ran faster, till, breathless, I arrived upon the scene, the opening of a narrow court, leading out of a by-street. At first I saw nothing but the backs of a small mob of urchins. Then from the centre of them came another wailing appeal for help, and without waiting for any invitation, I pushed my way into the group.

What I saw was Hecuba to me, gave me the motive and the cue for passion, transformed me from the dull and muddy-mettled little John-a-dreams I had been into a small, blind Fury. Pale Thought, that mental emetic, banished from my system, I became the healthy, unreasoning animal, and acted as such.

From my methods, I frankly admit, science was absent. In simple, primitive fashion that would have charmed a Darwinian disciple to observe, I "went for" the whole crowd. To employ the expressive idiom of the neighbourhood, I was "all over it and inside." Something clung about my feet. By kicking myself free and then standing on it I gained the advantage of quite an extra foot in height; I don't know what it was and didn't care. I fought with my arms and I fought with my legs; where I could get in with my head I did. I fought whatever came to hand in a spirit of simple thankfulness, grateful for what I could reach and indifferent to what was beyond me.

That the "show", if again I may be permitted the local idiom, was not entirely mine I was well aware. That not alone my person but my property also was being damaged in the rear became dimly conveyed to me through the sensation of draught. Already the world to the left of me was mere picturesque perspective, while the growing importance of my nose was threatening the absorption of all my other features. These things did not trouble me. I merely noted them as phenomena and continued to punch steadily.

Until I found that I was punching something soft and yet unyielding. I looked up to see what this foreign matter that thus mysteriously had entered into the mixture might be, and discovered it to be a policeman. Still I did not care. The felon's dock! the prison cell! a fig for such mere bogies. An impudent word, an insulting look, and I would have gone for the Law itself. Pale Thought, it must have been a livid green by this time, still trembled at respectful distance from me.

Fortunately for all of us, he was not impertinent, and though he spoke the language of his order, his tone disarmed offence.

"Now, then. Now, then. What is all this about?"

There was no need for me to answer. A dozen voluble tongues were ready to explain to him; and to explain wholly in my favour. This time the crowd was with me. Let a man school himself to bear dispraise, for thereby alone shall he call his soul his own. But let no man lie, saying he is indifferent to popular opinion. That was my first taste of public applause. The public was not select, and the applause might, by the sticklers for English pure and undefiled, have been deemed ill-worded, but to me it was the sweetest music I had ever heard, or have heard since. I was called a "plucky little devil," a "fair 'ot 'un," not only a "good 'un," but a "good 'un" preceded by the adjective that in the East bestows upon its principal every admirable quality that can possibly apply. Under the circumstances it likewise fitted me literally; but I knew it was intended rather in its complimentary sense.

Kind, if dirty, hands wiped my face. A neighbouring butcher presented me with a choice morsel of steak, not to eat but to wear; and I found it, if I may so express myself without infringing copyright, "grateful and comforting." My enemies had long since scooted, some of them, I had rejoiced to notice, with lame and halting steps. The mutilated kitten had been restored to its owner, a lady of ample bosom, who, carried beyond judgment by emotion, publicly offered to adopt me on the spot. The Law suggested, not for the first time, that everybody should now move on; and slowly, followed by feminine commendation mingled with masculine advice as to improved methods for the future, I was allowed to drift away.

My bones ached, my flesh stung me, yet I walked as upon air. Gradually I became conscious that I was not alone. A light, pattering step was trying to keep pace with me. Graciously I slacked my speed, and the pattering step settled down beside me. Every now and again she would run ahead and then turn round to look up into my face, much as your small dog does when he happens not to be misbehaving himself and desires you to note the fact. Evidently she approved of me. I was not at my best, as far as appearance was concerned, but women are kittle cattle, and I think she preferred me so. Thus we walked for quite a long distance without speaking, I drinking in the tribute of her worship and enjoying it. Then gaining confidence, she shyly put her hand into mine, and finding I did not repel her, promptly assumed possession of me, according to woman's way.

For her age and station she must have been a person of means, for having tried in vain various methods to make me more acceptable to followers and such as having passed would turn their heads, she said:

"I know, gelatines;" and disappearing into a sweetstuff shop, returned with quite a quantity. With these, first sucked till glutinous, we joined my many tatters. I still attracted attention, but felt warmer.

She informed me that her name was Cissy, and that her father's shop was in Three Colt Street. I informed her that my name was Paul, and that my father was a lawyer. I also pointed out to her that a lawyer is much superior in social position to a shopkeeper, which she acknowledged cheerfully. We parted at the corner of the Stainsby Road, and I let her kiss me once. It was understood that in the Stainsby Road we might meet again.

I left Eliza gaping after me, the front door in her hand, and ran straight up into my own room. Robinson Crusoe, King Arthur, The Last of the Barons, Rob Roy! I looked them all in the face and was not ashamed. I also was a gentleman.

My mother was much troubled when she saw me, but my father, hearing the story, approved.

"But he looks so awful," said my mother. "In this world," said my father, "one must occasionally be aggressive, if necessary, brutal."

My father would at times be quite savage in his sentiments.

CHAPTER IV.

PAUL, FALLING IN WITH A GOODLY COMPANY OF PILGRIMS, LEARNS OF THEM THE ROAD THAT HE MUST TRAVEL. AND MEETS THE PRINCESS OF THE GOLDEN LOCKS.

The East India Dock Road is nowadays a busy, crowded thoroughfare. The jingle of the tram-bell and the rattle of the omnibus and cart mingle continuously with the rain of many feet, beating ceaselessly upon its pavements. But at the time of which I write it was an empty, voiceless way, bounded on the one side by the long, echoing wall of the docks and on the other by occasional small houses isolated amid market gardens, drying grounds and rubbish heaps. Only one thing remains, or did remain last time I passed along it, connecting it with its former self, and that is the one-storeyed brick cottage at the commencement of the bridge, and which was formerly the toll-house. I remember this toll-house so well because it was there that my childhood fell from me, and sad and frightened I saw the world beyond.

I cannot explain it better. I had been that afternoon to Plaistow on a visit to the family dentist. It was an out-of-the-way place in which to keep him, but there existed advantages of a counterbalancing nature.

"Have the half-crown in your hand," my mother would direct me, while making herself sure that the purse containing it was safe at the bottom of my knickerbocker pocket; "but of course if he won't take it, why, you must bring it home again."

I am not sure, but I think he was some distant connection of ours; at all events, I know he was a kind friend. I, seated in the velvet chair of state, he would unroll his case of instruments before me, and ask me to choose, recommending with affectionate eulogisms the most murderous looking.

But on my opening my mouth to discuss the fearful topic, lo! a pair would shoot from under his coat-sleeve, and almost before I knew what had happened, the trouble would be over. After that we would have tea together. He was an old bachelor, and his house stood in a great garden, for Plaistow in those days was a picturesque village, and out of the plentiful fruit thereof his housekeeper made the most wonderful of jams and jellies. Oh, they were good, those teas! Generally our conversation was of my mother who, it appeared, was once a little girl: not at all the sort of little girl I should have imagined her; on the contrary, a prankish, wilful little girl, though good company, I should say, if all the tales he told of her were true. And I am inclined to think they were, in spite of the fact that my mother, when I repeated them to her, would laugh, saying she was sure she had no recollection of anything of the kind, adding severely that it was a pity he and I could not find something better to gossip about. Yet her next question would be:

"And what else did he say, if you please?" explaining impatiently when my answer was not of the kind expected: "No, no, I mean about me."

The tea things cleared away, he would bring out his great microscope. To me it was a peep-hole into a fairy world where dwelt strange dragons, mighty monsters, so that I came to regard him as a sort of harmless magician. It was his pet study, and looking back, I cannot help associating his enthusiasm for all things microscopical with the fact that he was an exceptionally little man himself, but one of the biggest hearted that ever breathed.

On leaving I would formally hand him my half-crown, "with mamma's compliments," and he would formally accept it. But on putting my hand into my jacket pocket when outside the gate I would invariably find it there. The first time I took it back to him, but unblushingly he repudiated all knowledge.

"Must be another half-crown," he suggested; "such things do happen. One puts change into a pocket and overlooks it. Slippery things, half-crowns."

Returning home on this particular day of days, I paused upon the bridge, and watched for awhile the lazy barges manoeuvring their way between the piers. It was one of those hushed summer evenings when the air even of grim cities is full of whispering voices; and as, turning away from the river, I passed through the white toll-gate, I had a sense of leaving myself behind me on the bridge. So vivid was the impression, that I looked back, half expecting to see myself still leaning over the iron parapet, looking down into the sunlit water.

It sounds foolish, but I leave it standing, wondering if to others a like experience has ever come. The little chap never came back to me. He passed away from me as a man's body may possibly pass away from him, leaving him only remembrance and regret. For a time I tried to play his games, to dream his dreams, but the substance was wanting. I was only a thin ghost, making believe.

It troubled me for quite a spell of time, even to the point of tears, this feeling that my childhood lay behind me, this sudden realisation that I was travelling swiftly the strange road called growing up. I did not want to grow up; could nothing be done to stop it? Rather would I be always as I had been, playing, dreaming. The dark way frightened me. Must I go forward?

Then gradually, but very slowly, with the long months and years, came to me the consciousness of a new being, new pulsations, sensories, throbbings, rooted in but differing widely from the old; and little Paul, the Paul of whom I have hitherto spoken, faded from my life.

So likewise must I let him fade with sorrow from this book. But before I part with him entirely, let me recall what else I can remember of him. Thus we shall be quit of him, and he will interfere with us no more.

Chief among the pictures that I see is that of my aunt Fan, crouching over the kitchen fire; her skirt and crinoline rolled up round her waist, leaving as sacrifice to custom only her petticoat. Up and down her body sways in rhythmic motion, her hands stroking affectionately her own knees; the while I, with paper knife for sword, or horse of broomstick, stand opposite her, flourishing and declaiming. Sometimes I am a knight and she a wicked ogre. She is slain, growling and swearing, and at once becomes the beautiful princess that I secure and bear away with me upon the prancing broomstick. So long as the princess is merely holding sweet converse with me from her high-barred window, the scene is realistic, at least, to sufficiency; but the bearing away has to be make-believe; for my aunt cannot be persuaded to leave her chair before the fire, and the everlasting rubbing of her knees.

At other times, with the assistance of the meat chopper, I am an Indian brave, and then she is Laughing Water or Singing Sunshine, and we go out scalping together; or in less bloodthirsty moods I am the Fairy Prince and she the Sleeping Beauty. But in such parts she is not at her best. Better, when seated in the centre of the up-turned table, I am Captain Cook, and she the Cannibal Chief.

"I shall skin him and hang him in the larder till Sunday week," says my aunt, smacking her lips, "then he'll be just in right condition; not too tough and not too high." She was always strong in detail, was my aunt Fan.

I do not wish to deprive my aunt of any credit due to her, but the more I exercise my memory for evidence, the more I am convinced that her compliance on these occasions was not conceived entirely in the spirit of self-sacrifice. Often would she suggest the game and even the theme; in such case, casting herself invariably for what, in old theatrical parlance, would have been termed the heavy lead, the dragons and the wicked uncles, the fussy necromancers and the uninvited fairies. As authoress of a new cookery book for use in giant-land, my aunt, I am sure, would have been successful. Most recipes that one reads are so monotonously meagre: "Boil him," "Put her on the spit and roast her for supper," "Cook 'em in a pie, with plenty of gravy;" but my aunt into the domestic economy of Ogredom introduced variety and daintiness.

"I think, my dear," my aunt would direct, "we'll have him stuffed with chestnuts and served on toast. And don't forget the giblets. They make such excellent sauce."

With regard to the diet of imprisoned maidens she would advise:

"Not too much fish, it spoils the flesh for roasting."

The things that she would turn people into, king's sons, rightful princesses, such sort of people, people who after a time, one would think, must have quite forgotten what they started as. To let her have her way was a lesson to me in natural history both present and pre-historic. The most beautiful damsel that ever lived she would without a moment's hesitation turn into a Glyptodon or a Hippocrepian. Afterwards, when I could guess at the spelling, I would look these creatures up in the illustrated dictionary, and feel that under no circumstances could I have loved the lady ever again. Warriors and kings she would delight in transforming into plaice or prawns, and haughty queens into Brussels sprouts.

With gusto would she plan a complicated slaughter, paying heed to every detail: the sharpening of the knives, the having ready of mops and pails of water for purposes of after cleaning up. As a writer she would have followed the realistic school.

Her death, with which we invariably wound up the afternoon, was another conscientious effort. Indeed, her groans and writhings would sometimes frighten me. I always welcomed the last gurgle. That finished, but not a moment before, my aunt would let down her skirt, in this way suggesting the fall of the curtain upon our play, and set to work to get the tea.

Another frequently recurring picture that I see is of myself in glazed-peaked cap explaining many things the while we walk through dingy streets to yet a smaller figure curly haired and open eyed. Still every now and then she runs ahead to turn and look admiringly into my face as on the day she first became captive to the praise and fame of me.

I was glad of her company for more reasons than she knew of. For one, she protected me against my baser self. With her beside me I should not have dared to flee from sudden foes. Indeed, together we courted adventure; for once you get used to it this standing hazard of attack adds a charm to outdoor exercise that older folk in districts better policed enjoy not. So possibly my dog feels when together we take the air. To me it is a simple walk, maybe a little tiresome, suggested rather by contemplation of my waistband than by desire for walking for mere walking's sake; to him an expedition full of danger and surprises: "The gentleman asleep with one eye open on The Chequer's doorstep! will he greet me with a friendly sniff or try to bite my head off? This cross-eyed, lop-eared loafer, lurching against the lamp-post! shall we pass with a careless wag and a 'how-do,' or become locked in a life and death struggle? Impossible to say. This coming corner, now, 'Ware! Is anybody waiting round there to kill me, or not?"

But the trusting face beside me nerved me. As reward in lonely places I would let her hold my hand.

A second advantage I derived from her company was that of being less trampled on, less walked over, less swept aside into doorway or gutter than when alone. A pretty, winsome face had this little maid, if Memory plays me not kindly false; but also she had a vocabulary; and when the blind idiot, male or female, instead of passing us by walking round us, would, after the custom of the blind idiot, seek to gain the other side of us by walking through us, she would use it.

"Now, then, where yer coming to, old glass-eye? We ain't sperrits. Can't yer see us?"

And if they attempted reply, her child's treble, so strangely at variance with her dainty appearance, would only rise more shrill.

"Garn! They'd run out of 'eads when they was making you. That's only a turnip wot you've got stuck on top of yer!" I offer but specimens.

Nor was it of the slightest use attempting personal chastisement, as sometimes an irate lady or gentleman would be foolish enough to do. As well might an hippopotamus attempt to reprove a terrier. The only result was to provide comedy for the entire street.

On these occasions our positions were reversed, I being the admiring spectator of her prowess. Yet to me she was ever meek, almost irritatingly submissive. She found out where I lived and would often come and wait for me for hours, her little face pressed tight against the iron railings, until either I came out or shook my head at her from my bedroom window, when she would run off, the dying away into silence of her pattering feet leaving me a little sad.

I think I cared for her in a way, yet she never entered into my day-dreams, which means that she existed for me only in the outer world of shadows that lay round about me and was not of my real life.

Also, I think she was unwise, introducing me to the shop, for children and dogs, one seems unconsciously to bracket them in one's thoughts, are snobbish little wretches. If only her father had been a dealer in firewood I could have soothed myself by imagining mistakes. It was a common occurrence, as I well knew, for children of quite the best families to be brought up by wood choppers. Fairies, the best intentioned in the world, but born muddlers, were generally responsible for these mishaps, which, however, always became righted in time for the wedding. Or even had he been a pork butcher, and there were many in the neighbourhood, I could have thought of him as a swineherd, and so found precedent for hope.

But a fishmonger, from six in the evening a fried fishmonger! I searched history in vain. Fried fishmongers were without the pale.

So gradually our meetings became less frequent, though I knew that every afternoon she waited in the quiet Stainsby Road, where dwelt in semi-detached, six-roomed villas the aristocracy of Poplar, and that after awhile, for arriving late at times I have been witness to the sad fact, tears would trace pathetic patterns upon her dust-besprinkled cheeks; and with the advent of the world-illuminating Barbara, to which event I am drawing near, they ceased altogether.

So began and ended my first romance. One of these days, some quiet summer's afternoon, when even the air of Pigott Street vibrates with tenderness beneath the whispered sighs of Memory, I shall walk into the little grocer's shop and boldly ask to see her. So far have I already gone as to trace her, and often have I tried to catch sight of her through the glass door, but hitherto in vain. I know she is the more or less troubled mother of a numerous progeny. I am told she has grown stout, and probable enough it is that her tongue has gained rather than lost in sharpness. Yet under all the unrealities the clumsy-handed world has built about her, I shall see, I know, the lithesome little maid with fond, admiring eyes. What help they were to me I never knew till I had lost them. How hard to gain such eyes I have learned since. Were we to write the truth in our confession books, should we not admit the quality we most admire in others is admiration of ourselves? And is it not a wise selection? If you would have me admirable, my friend, admire me, and speak your commendation without stint that in the sunshine of your praises I may wax. For indifference maketh an indifferent man, and contempt a contemptible man. Come, is it not true? Does not all that is worthy in us grow best by honour?

Chief among the remaining figures on my childhood's stage were the many servants of our house, the "generals," as they were termed. So rapid, as a rule, was their transit through our kitchen that only one or two, conspicuous by reason of their lingering, remain upon my view. It was a neighbourhood in which domestic servants were not much required. Those intending to take up the calling seriously went westward. The local ranks were recruited mainly from the discontented or the disappointed, from those who, unappreciated at home, hoped from the stranger more discernment; or from the love-lorn, the jilted and the jealous, who took the cap and apron as in an earlier age their like would have taken the veil. Maybe, to the comparative seclusion of our basement, as contrasted with the alternative frivolity of shop or factory, they felt in such mood more attuned. With the advent of the new or the recovery of the old young man they would plunge again into the vain world, leaving my poor mother to search afresh amid the legions of the cursed.

With these I made such comradeship as I could, for I had no child friends. Kind creatures were most of them, at least so I found them. They were poor at "making believe," but would always squeeze ten minutes from their work to romp with me, and that, perhaps, was healthier for me. What, perhaps, was not so good for me was that, staggered at the amount of "book-learning" implied by my conversation (for the journalistic instinct, I am inclined to think, was early displayed in me), they would listen open-mouthed to all my information, regarding me as a precocious oracle. Sometimes they would obtain permission to take me home with them to tea, generously eager that their friends should also profit by me. Then, encouraged by admiring, grinning faces, I would "hold forth," keenly enjoying the sound of my own proud piping.

"As good as a book, ain't he?" was the tribute most often paid to me.

"As good as a play," one enthusiastic listener, an old greengrocer, went so far as to say.

Already I regarded myself as among the Immortals.

One girl, a dear, wholesome creature named Janet, stayed with us for months and might have stayed years, but for her addiction to strong language. The only and well-beloved child of the captain of the barge "Nancy Jane," trading between Purfleet and Ponder's End, her conversation was at once my terror and delight.

"Janet," my mother would exclaim in agony, her hands going up instinctively to guard her ears, "how can you use such words?"

"What words, mum?"

"The things you have just called the gas man."

"Him! Well, did you see what he did, mum? Walked straight into my clean kitchen, without even wiping his boots, the" And before my mother could stop her, Janet had relieved her feelings by calling him it or rather them, again, without any idea that she had done aught else than express in fitting phraseology a natural human emotion.

We were good friends, Janet and I, and therefore it was that I personally undertook her reformation. It was not an occasion for mincing one's words. The stake at issue was, I felt, too important. I told her bluntly that if she persisted in using such language she would inevitably go to hell.

"Then where's my father going?" demanded Janet.

"Does he use language?"

I gathered from Janet that no one who had enjoyed the privilege of hearing her father could ever again take interest in the feeble efforts of herself.

"I am afraid, Janet," I explained, "that if he doesn't give it up"

"But it's the only way he can talk," interrupted Janet. "He don't mean anything by it."

I sighed, yet set my face against weakness. "You see, Janet, people who swear do go there."

But Janet would not believe.

"God send my dear, kind father to hell just because he can't talk like the gentlefolks! Don't you believe it of Him, Master Paul. He's got more sense."

I hope I pain no one by quoting Janet's common sense. For that I should be sorry. I remember her words because so often, when sinking in sloughs of childish despond, they afforded me firm foothold. More often than I can tell, when compelled to listen to the sententious voice of immeasurable Folly glibly explaining the eternal mysteries, has it comforted me to whisper to myself: "I don't believe it of Him. He's got more sense."

And about that period I had need of all the comfort I could get. As we descend the road of life, the journey, demanding so much of our attention, becomes of more importance than the journey's end; but to the child, standing at the valley's gate, the terminating hills are clearly visible. What lies beyond them is his constant wonder. I never questioned my parents directly on the subject, shrinking as so strangely we all do, both young and old, from discussion of the very matters of most moment to us; and they, on their part, not guessing my need, contented themselves with the vague generalities with which we seek to hide even from ourselves the poverty of our beliefs. But there were foolish voices about me less reticent; while the literature, illustrated and otherwise, provided in those days for serious-minded youth, answered all questionings with blunt brutality. If you did wrong you burnt in a fiery furnace forever and ever. Were your imagination weak you could turn to the accompanying illustration, and see at a glance how you yourself would writhe and shrink and scream, while cheerful devils, well organised, were busy stoking. I had been burnt once, rather badly, in consequence of live coals, in course of transit on a shovel, being let fall upon me. I imagined these burning coals, not confined to a mere part of my body, but pressing upon me everywhere, not snatched swiftly off by loving hands, the pain assuaged by applications of soft soap and the blue bag, but left there, eating into my flesh and veins. And this continued for eternity. You suffered for an hour, a day, a thousand years, and were no nearer to the end; ten thousand, a million years, and yet, as at the very first, it was forever, and forever still it would always be forever! I suffered also from insomnia about this period.

"Then be good," replied the foolish voices round me; "never do wrong, and so avoid this endless agony."

But it was so easy to do wrong. There were so many wrong things to do, and the doing of them was so natural.

"Then repent," said the voices, always ready.

But how did one repent? What was repentance? Did I "hate my sin," as I was instructed I must, or merely hate the idea of going to hell for it? Because the latter, even my child's sense told me, was no true repentance. Yet how could one know the difference?

Above all else there haunted me the fear of the "Unforgivable Sin." What this was I was never able to discover. I dreaded to enquire too closely, lest I should find I had committed it. Day and night the terror of it clung to me.

"Believe," said the voices; "so only shall you be saved." How believe? How know you did believe? Hours would I kneel in the dark, repeating in a whispered scream:

"I believe, I believe. Oh, I do believe!" and then rise with white knuckles, wondering if I really did believe.

Another question rose to trouble me. In the course of my meanderings I had made the acquaintance of an old sailor, one of the most disreputable specimens possible to find; and had learned to love him. Our first meeting had been outside a confectioner's window, in the Commercial Road, where he had discovered me standing, my nose against the glass, a mere palpitating Appetite on legs. He had seized me by the collar, and hauled me into the shop. There, dropping me upon a stool, he bade me eat. Pride of race prompted me politely to decline, but his language became so awful that in fear and trembling I obeyed. So soon as I was finished, it cost him two and fourpence, I remember, we walked down to the docks together, and he told me stories of the sea and land that made my blood run cold. Altogether, in the course of three weeks or a month, we met about half a dozen times, when much the same programme was gone through. I think I was a fairly frank child, but I said nothing about him at home, feeling instinctively that if I did there would be an end of our comradeship, which was dear to me: not merely by reason of the pastry, though I admit that was a consideration, but also for his wondrous tales. I believed them all implicitly, and so came to regard him as one of the most interesting criminals as yet unhanged: and what was sad about the case, as I felt myself, was that his recital of his many iniquities, instead of repelling, attracted me to him. If ever there existed a sinner, here was one. He chewed tobacco, one of the hundred or so deadly sins, according to my theological library, and was generally more or less drunk. Not that a stranger would have noticed this; the only difference being that when sober he appeared constrained, was less his natural, genial self. In a burst of confidence he once admitted to me that he was the biggest blackguard in the merchant service. Unacquainted with the merchant service, as at the time I was, I saw no reason to doubt him.

One night in a state of intoxication he walked over a gangway and was drowned. Our mutual friend, the confectioner, seeing me pass the window, came out to tell me so; and having heard, I walked on, heavy of heart, and pondering.

About his eternal destination there could be no question. The known facts precluded the least ray of hope. How could I be happy in heaven, supposing I eventually did succeed in slipping in, knowing that he, the lovable old scamp, was burning forever in hell?

How could Janet, taking it that she reformed and thus escaped damnation, be contented, knowing the father she loved doomed to torment? The heavenly hosts, so I argued, could be composed only of the callous and indifferent.

I wondered how people could go about their business, eat, drink and be merry, with tremendous fate hanging thus ever suspended over their heads. When for a little space I myself forgot it, always it fell back upon me with increased weight.

Nor was the contemplation of heaven itself particularly attractive to me, for it was a foolish paradise these foolish voices had fashioned out of their folly. You stood about and sang hymns forever! I was assured that my fear of finding the programme monotonous was due only to my state of original sin, that when I got there I should discover I liked it. But I would have given much for the hope of avoiding both their heaven and their hell.

Fortunately for my sanity I was not left long to brood unoccupied upon such themes. Our worldly affairs, under the sunshine of old Hasluck's round red face, prospered, for awhile; and one afternoon my father, who had been away from home since breakfast time, calling me into his office where also sat my mother, informed me that the long-talked-of school was become at last a concrete thing.

"The term commences next week," explained my father. "It is not exactly what I had intended, but it will do for the present. Later, of course, you will go to one of the big public schools; your mother and I have not yet quite decided which."

"You will meet other boys there, good and bad," said my mother, who sat clasping and unclasping her hands. "Be very careful, dear, how you choose your companions."

"You will learn to take your own part," said my father. "School is an epitome of the world. One must assert oneself, or one is sat upon."

I knew not what to reply, the vista thus opened out to me was so unexpected. My blood rejoiced, but my heart sank.

"Take one of your long walks," said my father, smiling, "and think it over."

"And if you are in any doubt, you know where to go for guidance, don't you?" whispered my mother, who was very grave.

Yet I went to bed, dreaming of quite other things that night: of Queens of Beauty bending down to crown my brows with laurel: of wronged Princesses for whose cause I rode to death or victory. For on my return home, being called into the drawing-room by my father, I stood transfixed, my cap in hand, staring with all my eyes at the vision that I saw.

No such wonder had I ever seen before, at all events, not to my remembrance. The maidens that one meets in Poplar streets may be fair enough in their way, but their millinery displays them not to advantage; and the few lady visitors that came to us were of a staid and matronly appearance. Only out of pictures hitherto had such witchery looked upon me; and from these the spell faded as one gazed.

I heard old Hasluck's smoky voice saying, "My little gell, Barbara," and I went nearer to her, moving unconsciously.

"You can kiss 'er," said the smoky voice again; "she won't bite." But I did not kiss her. Nor ever felt I wanted to, upon the mouth.

I suppose she must have been about fourteen, and I a little over ten, though tall for my age. Later I came to know she had that rare gold hair that holds the light, so that upon her face, which seemed of dainty porcelain, there ever fell a softened radiance as from some shining aureole; those blue eyes where dwell mysteries, shadow veiled. At the time I knew nothing, but that it seemed to me as though the fairy-tales had all come true.

She smiled, understanding and well pleased with my confusion. Child though I was little more than child though she was, it flattered her vanity.

Fair and sweet, you had but that one fault. Would it had been another, less cruel to you yourself.

CHAPTER V.

IN WHICH THERE COMES BY ONE BENT UPON PURSUING HIS OWN WAY.

"Correct" is, I think, the adjective by which I can best describe Doctor Florret and all his attributes. He was a large man, but not too large, just the size one would select for the head-master of an important middle-class school; stout, not fat, suggesting comfort, not grossness. His hands were white and well shaped. On the left he wore a fine diamond ring, but it shone rather than sparkled. He spoke of commonplace things in a voice that lent dignity even to the weather. His face, which was clean-shaven, radiated benignity tempered by discretion.

So likewise all about him: his wife, the feminine counterpart of himself. Seeing them side by side one felt tempted to believe that for his special benefit original methods had been reverted to, and she fashioned, as his particular helpmeet, out of one of his own ribs. His furniture was solid, meant for use, not decoration. His pictures, following the rule laid down for dress, graced without drawing attention to his walls. He ever said the correct thing at the correct time in the correct manner. Doubtful of the correct thing to do, one could always learn it by waiting till he did it; when one at once felt that nothing else could possibly have been correct. He held on all matters the correct views. To differ from him was to discover oneself a revolutionary.

In practice, as I learned at the cost of four more or less wasted years, he of course followed the methods considered correct by English schoolmen from the days of Edward VI. onwards.

Heaven knows I worked hard. I wanted to learn. Ambition, the all containing ambition of a boy that "has its centre everywhere nor cares to fix itself to form" stirred within me. Did I pass a speaker at some corner, hatless, perspiring, pointing Utopias in the air to restless hungry eyes, at once I saw myself, a Demosthenes swaying multitudes, a statesman holding the House of Commons spellbound, the Prime Minister of England, worshipped by the entire country. Even the Opposition papers, had I known of them, I should have imagined forced to reluctant admiration. Did the echo of a distant drum fall upon my ear, then before me rose picturesque fields of carnage, one figure ever conspicuous: Myself, well to the front, isolated. Promotion in the British army of my dream being a matter purely of merit, I returned Commander-in-Chief. Vast crowds thronged every flag-decked street. I saw white waving hands from every roof and window. I heard the dull, deep roar of welcome, as with superb seat upon my snow-white charger, or should it be coal-black? The point cost me much consideration, so anxious was I that the day should be without a flaw, I slowly paced at the head of my victorious troops, between wild waves of upturned faces: walked into a lamp-post or on to the toes of some irascible old gentleman, and awoke. A drunken sailor stormed from between swing doors and tacked tumultuously down the street: the factory chimney belching smoke became a swaying mast. The costers round about me shouted "Ay, ay, sir. 'Ready, ay, ready." I was Christopher Columbus, Drake, Nelson, rolled into one. Spurning the presumption of modern geographers, I discovered new continents. I defeated the French, those useful French! I died in the moment of victory. A nation mourned me and I was buried in Westminster Abbey. Also I lived and was created a Duke. Either alternative had its charm: personally I was indifferent. Boys who on November the ninth, as explained by letters from their mothers, read by Doctor Florret with a snort, were suffering from a severe toothache, told me on November the tenth of the glories of Lord Mayor's Shows. I heard their chatter fainter and fainter as from an ever-increasing distance. The bells of Bow were ringing in my ears. I saw myself a merchant prince, though still young. Nobles crowded my counting house. I lent them millions and married their daughters. I listened, unobserved in a corner, to discussion on some new book. Immediately I was a famous author. All men praised me: for of reviewers and their density I, in those days, knew nothing. Poetry, fiction, history, I wrote them all; and all men read, and wondered. Only here was a crumpled rose leaf in the pillow on which I laid my swelling head: penmanship was vexation to me, and spelling puzzled me, so that I wrote with sorrow and many blots and scratchings out. Almost I put aside the idea of becoming an author.

But along whichever road I might fight my way to the Elysian Fields of fame, education, I dimly but most certainly comprehended, was a necessary weapon to my hand. And so, with aching heart and aching head, I pored over my many books. I see myself now in my small bedroom, my elbows planted on the shaky, one-legged table, startled every now and again by the frizzling of my hair coming in contact with the solitary candle. On cold nights I wear my overcoat, turned up about the neck, a blanket round my legs, and often I must sit with my fingers in my ears, the better to shut out the sounds of life, rising importunately from below. "A song, Of a song, To a song, A song, 0! song!" "I love, Thou lovest, He she or it loves. I should or would love" over and over again, till my own voice seems some strange buzzing thing about me, while my head grows smaller and smaller till I put my hands up frightened, wondering if it still be entire upon my shoulders.

Was I more stupid than the average, or is a boy's brain physically incapable of the work our educational system demands of it?

"Latin and Greek" I hear repeating the suave tones of Doctor Florret, echoing as ever the solemn croak of Correctness, "are useful as mental gymnastics." My dear Doctor Florret and Co., cannot you, out of the vast storehouse of really necessary knowledge, select apparatus better fitted to strengthen and not overstrain the mental muscles of ten-to-fourteen? You, gentle reader, with brain fully grown, trained by years of practice to its subtlest uses, take me from your bookshelf, say, your Browning or even your Shakespeare. Come, you know this language well. You have not merely learned: it is your mother tongue. Construe for me this short passage, these few verses: parse, analyse, resolve into component parts! And now, will you maintain that it is good for Tommy, tear-stained, ink-bespattered little brat, to be given AEsop's Fables, Ovid's Metamorphoses to treat in like manner? Would it not be just as sensible to insist upon his practising his skinny little arms with hundred pounds dumb-bells?

We were the sons of City men, of not well-to-do professional men, of minor officials, clerks, shopkeepers, our roads leading through the workaday world. Yet quite half our time was taken up in studies utterly useless to us. How I hated them, these youth-tormenting Shades. Homer! how I wished the fishermen had asked him that absurd riddle earlier. Horace! why could not that shipwreck have succeeded: it would have in the case of any one but a classic.

Until one blessed day there fell into my hands a wondrous talisman.

Hearken unto me, ye heavy burdened little brethren of mine. Waste not your substance upon tops and marbles, nor yet upon tuck (Do ye still call it "tuck"?), but scrape and save. For in the neighbourhood of Paternoster

Row there dwells a good magician who for silver will provide you with a "Key" that shall open wide for you the gates of Hades.

By its aid, the Frogs of Aristophanes became my merry friends. With Ulysses I wandered eagerly through Wonderland. Doctor Florret was charmed with my progress, which was real, for now, at last, I was studying according to the laws of common sense, understanding first, explaining afterwards. Let Youth, that the folly of Age would imprison in ignorance, provide itself with "Keys."

But let me not seem to claim credit due to another. Dan it was, Dan of the strong arm and the soft smile, Dan the wise hater of all useless labour, sharp-witted, easy-going Dan, who made this grand discovery.

Dan followed me a term later into the Lower Fourth, but before he had been there a week was handling Latin verse with an ease and dexterity suggestive of unholy dealings with the Devil. In a lonely corner of Regent's Park, first making sure no one was within earshot, he revealed to me his magic.

"Don't tell the others," he commanded; "or it will get out, and then nobody will be any the better."

"But is it right?" I asked.

"Look here, young 'un," said Dan; "what are you here for, what's your father paying school fees for (it was the appeal to our conscientiousness most often employed by Dr. Florret himself), for you to play a silly game, or to learn something?

"Because if it's only a game, we boys against the masters," continued Dan, "then let's play according to rule. If we're here to learn, well, you've been in the class four months and I've just come, and I bet I know more Ovid than you do already." Which was true.

So I thanked Dan and shared with him his key; and all the Latin I remember, for whatever good it may be to me, I take it I owe to him.

And knowledge of yet greater value do I owe to the good fortune that his sound mother wit was ever at my disposal to correct my dreamy unfeasibility; for from first to last he was my friend; and to have been the chosen friend of Dan, shrewd judge of man and boy, I deem no unimportant feather in my cap. He "took to" me, he said, because I was so jolly green", "such a rummy little mug." No other reason would he ever give me, save only a sweet smile and a tumbling of my hair with his great hand; but I think I understood. And I loved him because he was big and strong and handsome and kind; no one but a little boy knows how brutal or how kind a big boy can be. I was still somewhat of an effeminate little chap, nervous and shy, with a pink and white face, and hair that no amount of wetting would make straight. I was growing too fast, which took what strength I had, and my journey every day, added to school work and home work, maybe was too much for my years. Every morning I had to be up at six, leaving the house before seven to catch the seven fifteen from Poplar station; and from Chalk Farm I had to walk yet another couple of miles. But that I did not mind, for at Chalk Farm station Dan was always waiting for me. In the afternoon we walked back together also; and when I was tired and my back ached, just as if someone had cut a piece out of it, I felt he would put his arm round me, for he always knew, and oh, how strong and restful it was to lean against, so that one walked as in an easy-chair.

It seems to me, remembering how I would walk thus by his side, looking up shyly into his face, thinking how strong and good he was, feeling so glad he liked me, I can understand a little how a woman loves. He was so solid. With his arm round me, it was good to feel weak.

At first we were in the same class, the Lower Third. He had no business there. He was head and shoulders taller than any of us and years older. It was a disgrace to him that he was not in the Upper Fourth. The Doctor would tell him so before us all twenty times a week. Old Waterhouse (I call him "Old Waterhouse" because "Mister Waterhouse, M.A.," would convey no meaning to me, and I should not know about whom I was speaking) who cordially liked him, was honestly grieved. We, his friends, though it was pleasant to have him among us, suffered in our pride of him. The only person quite contented was Dan himself. It was his way in all things. Others had their opinion of what was good for him. He had his own, and his own was the only opinion that ever influenced him. The Lower Third suited him. For him personally the Upper Fourth had no attraction.

And even in the Lower Third he was always at the bottom. He preferred it. He selected the seat and kept it, in spite of all allurements, in spite of all reproaches. It was nearest to the door. It enabled him to be first out and last in. Also it afforded a certain sense of retirement. Its occupant, to an extent screened from observation, became in the course of time almost forgotten. To Dan's philosophical temperament its practical advantages outweighed all sentimental objection.

Only on one occasion do I remember his losing it. As a rule, tiresome questions, concerning past participles, square roots, or meridians never reached him, being snapped up in transit by arm-waving lovers of such trifles. The few that by chance trickled so far he took no notice of. They possessed no interest for him, and he never pretended that they did. But one day, taken off his guard, he gave voice quite unconsciously to a correct reply, with the immediate result of finding himself in an exposed position on the front bench. I had never seen Dan out of temper before, but that moment had any of us ventured upon a whispered congratulation we would have had our head punched, I feel confident.

Old Waterhouse thought that here at last was reformation. "Come, Brian," he cried, rubbing his long thin hands together with delight, "after all, you're not such a fool as you pretend."

"Never said I was," muttered Dan to himself, with a backward glance of regret towards his lost seclusion; and before the day was out he had worked his way back to it again.

As we were going out together, old Waterhouse passed us on the stairs: "Haven't you any sense of shame, my boy?" he asked sorrowfully, laying his hand kindly on Dan's shoulder.

"Yes, sir," answered Dan, with his frank smile; "plenty. It isn't yours, that's all."

He was an excellent fighter. In the whole school of over two hundred boys, not half a dozen, and those only Upper Sixth boys, fellows who came in top hats with umbrellas, and who wouldn't out of regard to their own dignity, could have challenged him with any chance of success. Yet he fought very seldom, and then always in a bored, lazy fashion, as though he were doing it purely to oblige the other fellow.

One afternoon, just as we were about to enter Regent's Park by the wicket opposite Hanover Gate, a biggish boy, an errand boy carrying an empty basket, and supported by two smaller boys, barred our way.

"Can't come in here," said the boy with the basket.

"Why not?" inquired Dan.

"'Cos if you do I shall kick you," was the simple explanation.

Without a word Dan turned away, prepared to walk on to the next opening. The boy with the basket, evidently encouraged, followed us: "Now, I'm going to give you your coward's blow," he said, stepping in front of us; "will you take it quietly?" It is a lonely way, the Outer Circle, on a winter's afternoon.

"I'll tell you afterwards," said Dan, stopping short.

The boy gave him a slight slap on the cheek. It could not have hurt, but the indignity, of course, was great. No boy of honour, according to our code, could have accepted it without retaliating.

"Is that all?" asked Dan.

"That's all for the present," replied the boy with the basket.

"Good-bye," said Dan, and walked on.

"Glad he didn't insist on fighting," remarked Dan, cheerfully, as we proceeded; "I'm going to a party tonight."

Yet on another occasion, in a street off Lisson Grove, he insisted on fighting a young rough half again his own weight, who, brushing up against him, had knocked his hat off into the mud.

"I wouldn't have said anything about his knocking it off," explained Dan afterwards, tenderly brushing the poor bruised thing with his coat sleeve, "if he hadn't kicked it."

On another occasion I remember, three or four of us, Dan among the number, were on our way one broiling summer's afternoon to Hadley Woods. As we turned off from the highroad just beyond Barnet and struck into the fields, Dan drew from his pocket an enormous juicy-looking pear.

"Where did you get that from?" inquired one, Dudley.

"From that big greengrocer's opposite Barnet Church," answered Dan. "Have a bit?"

"You told me you hadn't any more money," retorted Dudley, in reproachful tones.

"No more I had," replied Dan, holding out a tempting slice at the end of his pocket-knife.

"You must have had some, or you couldn't have bought that pear," argued Dudley, accepting.

"Didn't buy it."

"Do you mean to say you stole it?"

"Yes."

"You're a thief," denounced Dudley, wiping his mouth and throwing away a pip.

"I know it. So are you."

"No, I'm not."

"What's the good of talking nonsense. You robbed an orchard only last Wednesday at Mill Hill, and gave yourself the stomach-ache."

"That isn't stealing."

"What is it?"

"It isn't the same thing."

"What's the difference?"

And nothing could make Dan comprehend the difference. "Stealing is stealing," he would have it, "whether you take it off a tree or out of a basket. You're a thief, Dudley; so am I. Anybody else say a piece?"

The thermometer was at that point where morals become slack. We all had a piece; but we were all of us shocked at Dan, and told him so. It did not agitate him in the least.

To Dan I could speak my inmost thoughts, knowing he would understand me, and sometimes from him I received assistance and sometimes confusion. The yearly examination was approaching. My father and mother said nothing, but I knew how anxiously each of them awaited the result; my father, to see how much I had accomplished; my mother, how much I had endeavoured. I had worked hard, but was doubtful, knowing that prizes depend less upon what you know than upon what you can make others believe you know; which applies to prizes beyond those of school.

"Are you going in for anything, Dan?" I asked him. We were discussing the subject, crossing Primrose Hill, one bright June morning.

I knew the question absurd. I asked it of him because I wanted him to ask it of me.

"They're not giving away anything I particularly want," murmured Dan, in his lazy drawl: looked at from that point of view, school prizes are, it must be confessed, not worth their cost.

"You're sweating yourself, young 'un, of course?" he asked next, as I expected.

"I mean to have a shot at the History," I admitted. "Wish I was better at dates."

"It's always two-thirds dates," Dan assured me, to my discouragement. "Old Florret thinks you can't eat a potato until you know the date that chap Raleigh was born."

"I've prayed so hard that I may win the History prize," I explained to him. I never felt shy with Dan. He never laughed at me.

"You oughtn't to have done that," he said. I stared. "It isn't fair to the other fellows. That won't be your winning the prize; that will be your getting it through favouritism."

"But they can pray, too," I reminded him.

"If you all pray for it," answered Dan, "then it will go, not to the fellow that knows most history, but to the fellow that's prayed the hardest. That isn't old Florret's idea, I'm sure."

"But we are told to pray for things we want," I insisted.

"Beastly mean way of getting 'em," retorted Dan. And no argument that came to me, neither then nor at any future time, brought him to right thinking on this point.

He would judge all matters for himself. In his opinion Achilles was a coward, not a hero.

"He ought to have told the Trojans that they couldn't hurt any part of him except his heel, and let them have a shot at that," he argued; "King Arthur and all the rest of them with their magic swords, it wasn't playing the game. There's no pluck in fighting if you know you're bound to win. Beastly cads, I call them all."

I won no prize that year. Oddly enough, Dan did, for arithmetic; the only subject studied in the Lower Fourth that interested him. He liked to see things coming right, he explained.

My father shut himself up with me for half an hour and examined me himself.

"It's very curious, Paul," he said, "you seem to know a good deal."

"They asked me all the things I didn't know. They seemed to do it on purpose," I blurted out, and laid my head upon my arm. My father crossed the room and sat down beside me.

"Spud!" he said, it was a long time since he had called me by that childish nickname, "perhaps you are going to be with me, one of the unlucky ones."

"Are you unlucky?" I asked.

"Invariably," answered my father, rumpling his hair. "I don't know why. I try hard, I do the right thing, but it turns out wrong. It always does."

"But I thought Mr. Hasluck was bringing us such good fortune," I said, looking up in surprise. "We're getting on, aren't we?"

"I have thought so before, so often," said my father, "and it has always ended in a, in a collapse."

I put my arms round his neck, for I always felt to my father as to another boy; bigger than myself and older, but not so very much.

"You see, when I married your mother," he went on, "I was a rich man. She had everything she wanted."

"But you will get it all back," I cried.

"I try to think so," he answered. "I do think so, generally speaking. But there are times, you would not understand, they come to you."

"But she is happy," I persisted; "we are all happy."

He shook his head.

"I watch her," he said. "Women suffer more than we do. They live more in the present. I see my hopes, but she, she sees only me, and I have always been a failure. She has lost faith in me.

I could say nothing. I understood but dimly.

"That is why I want you to be an educated man, Paul," he continued after a silence. "You can't think what a help education is to a man. I don't mean it helps you to get on in the world; I think for that it rather hampers you. But it helps you to bear adversity. To a man with a well-stored mind, life is interesting on a piece of bread and a cup of tea. I know. If it were not for you and your mother I should not trouble."

And yet at that time our fortunes were at their brightest, so far as I remember them; and when they were dark again he was full of fresh hope, planning, scheming, dreaming again. It was never acting. A worse actor never trod this stage on which we fret. His occasional attempts at a cheerfulness he did not feel inevitably resulted in our all three crying in one another's arms. No; it was only when things were going well that experience came to his injury. Child of misfortune, he ever rose, Antaeus-like, renewed in strength from contact with his mother.

Nor must it be understood that his despondent moods, even in time of prosperity, were oft recurring. Generally speaking, as he himself said, he was full of confidence. Already had he fixed upon our new house in Guilford Street, then still a good residential quarter; while at the same time, as he would explain to my mother, sufficiently central for office purposes, close as it was to Lincoln and Grey's Inn and Bedford Row, pavements long worn with the weary footsteps of the Law's sad courtiers.

"Poplar," said my father, "has disappointed me. It seemed a good idea, a rapidly rising district, singularly destitute of solicitors. It ought to have turned out well, and yet somehow it hasn't."

"There have been a few come," my mother reminded him.

"Of a sort," admitted my father; "a criminal lawyer might gather something of a practice here, I have no doubt. But for general work, of course, you must he in a central position. Now, in Guilford Street people will come to me."

"It should certainly be a pleasanter neighbourhood to live in," agreed my mother.

"Later on," said my father, "in case I want the whole house for offices, we could live ourselves in Regent's Park. It is quite near to the Park."

"Of course you have consulted Mr. Hasluck?" asked my mother, who of the two was by far the more practical.

"For Hasluck," replied my father, "it will be much more convenient. He grumbles every time at the distance."

"I have never been quite able to understand," said my mother, "why Mr. Hasluck should have come so far out of his way. There must surely be plenty of solicitors in the City."

"He had heard of me," explained my father. "A curious old fellow, likes his own way of doing things. It's not everyone who would care for him as a client. But I seem able to manage him."

Often we would go together, my father and I, to Guilford Street. It was a large corner house that had taken his fancy, half creeper covered, with a balcony, and pleasantly situated, overlooking the gardens of the Foundling Hospital. The wizened old caretaker knew us well, and having opened the door, would leave us to wander through the empty, echoing rooms at our own will. We furnished them handsomely in later Queen Anne style, of which my father was a connoisseur, sparing no necessary expense; for, as my father observed, good furniture is always worth its price, while to buy cheap is pure waste of money.

"This," said my father, on the second floor, stepping from the bedroom into the smaller room adjoining, "I shall make your mother's boudoir. We will have the walls in lavender and maple green, she is fond of soft tones, and the window looks out upon the gardens. There we will put her writing-table."

My own bedroom was on the third floor, a sunny little room.

"You will be quiet here," said my father, "and we can shut out the bed and the washstand with a screen."

Later, I came to occupy it; though its rent, eight and sixpence a week, including attendance, was somewhat more than at the time I ought to have afforded. Nevertheless, I adventured it, taking the opportunity of being an inmate of the house to refurnish it, unknown to my stout landlady, in later Queen Anne style, putting a neat brass plate with my father's name upon the door. "Luke Kelver, Solicitor. Office hours, 10 till 4." A medical student thought he occupied my mother's boudoir. He was a dull dog, full of tiresome talk. But I made acquaintanceship with him; and often of an evening would smoke my pipe there in silence while pretending to be listening to his monotonous brag.

The poor thing! he had no idea that he was only a foolish ghost; that his walls, seemingly covered with coarse-coloured prints of wooden-looking horses, simpering ballet girls and petrified prize-fighters, were in reality a delicate tone of lavender and maple green; that at her writing-table in the sunlit window sat my mother, her soft curls curtaining her quiet face.

CHAPTER VI.

OF THE SHADOW THAT CAME BETWEEN THE MAN IN GREY AND THE LADY OF THE LOVE-LIT EYES.

"There's nothing missing," said my mother, "so far as I can find out. Depend upon it, that's the explanation: she has got frightened and has run away.

"But what was there to frighten her?" said my father, pausing with a decanter in one hand and the bottle in the other.

"It was the idea of the thing," replied my mother. "She has never been used to waiting at table. She was actually crying about it only last night."

"But what's to be done?" said my father. "They will be here in less than an hour."

"There will be no dinner for them," said my mother, "unless I put on an apron and bring it up myself."

"Where does she live?" asked my father.

"At Ilford," answered my mother.

"We must make a joke of it," said my father.

My mother, sitting down, began to cry. It had been a trying week for my mother. A party to dinner, to a real dinner, beginning with anchovies and ending with ices from the confectioner's; if only they would remain ices and not, giving way to unaccustomed influences, present themselves as cold custard, was an extraordinary departure from the even tenor of our narrow domestic way; indeed, I recollect none previous. First there had been the house to clean and rearrange almost from top to bottom; endless small purchases to be made of articles that Need never misses, but which Ostentation, if ever you let her sneering nose inside the door, at once demands. Then the kitchen range, it goes without saying: one might imagine them all members of a stove union, controlled by some agitating old boiler out of work, had taken the opportunity to strike, refusing to bake another dish except under permanently improved conditions, necessitating weary days with plumbers. Fat cookery books, long neglected on their shelf, had been consulted, argued with and abused; experiments made, failures sighed over, successes noted; cost calculated anxiously; means and ways adjusted, hope finally achieved, shadowed by fear.

And now with victory practically won, to have the reward thus dashed from her hand at the last moment! Downstairs in the kitchen would be the dinner, waiting for the guests; upstairs round the glittering table would be the assembled guests, waiting for their dinner. But between the two yawned an impassable gulf. The bridge, without a word of warning, had bolted, was probably by this time well on its way to Ilford. There was excuse for my mother's tears.

"Isn't it possible to get somebody else?" asked my father.

"Impossible, in the time," said my mother. "I had been training her for the whole week. We had rehearsed it perfectly."

"Have it in the kitchen," suggested my aunt, who was folding napkins to look like ships, which they didn't in the least, "and call it a picnic." Really it seemed the only practical solution.

There came a light knock at the front door.

"It can't be anybody yet, surely," exclaimed my father in alarm, making for his coat.

"It's Barbara, I expect," explained my mother. "She promised to come round and help me dress. But now, of course, I shan't want her." My mother's nature was pessimistic.

But with the words Barbara ran into the room, for I had taken it upon myself to admit her, knowing that shadows slipped out through the window when Barbara came in at the door, in those days, I mean.

She kissed them all three, though it seemed but one movement, she was so quick. And at once they saw the humour of the thing.

"There's going to be no dinner," laughed my father. "We are going to look surprised and pretend that it was yesterday. It will be fun to see their faces."

"There will be a very nice dinner," smiled my mother, "but it will be in the kitchen, and there's no way of getting it upstairs." And they explained to her the situation.

She stood for an instant, her sweet face the gravest in the group. Then a light broke upon it.

"I'll get you someone," she said.

"My dear, you don't even know the neighbourhood," began my mother. But Barbara had snatched the latchkey from its nail and was gone.

With her disappearance, shadow fell again upon us. "If there were only an hotel in this beastly neighbourhood," said my father.

"You must entertain them by yourself, Luke," said my mother; "and I must wait, that's all."

"Don't be absurd, Maggie," cried my father, getting angry. "Can't cook bring it in?"

"No one can cook a dinner and serve it, too," answered my mother, impatiently. "Besides, she's not presentable."

"What about Fan?" whispered my father.

My mother merely looked. It was sufficient.

"Paul?" suggested my father.

"Thank you," retorted my mother. "I don't choose to have my son turned into a footman, if you do."

"Well, hadn't you better go and dress?" was my father's next remark.

"It won't take me long to put on an apron," was my mother's reply.

"I was looking forward to seeing you in that new frock," said my father. In the case of another, one might have attributed such a speech to tact; in the case of my father, one felt it was a happy accident.

My mother confessed, speaking with a certain indulgence, as one does of one's own follies when past, that she herself also had looked forward to seeing herself therein. Threatening discord melted into mutual sympathy.

"I so wanted everything to be all right, for your sake, Luke," said my mother; "I know you were hoping it would help on the business."

"I was only thinking of you, Maggie, dear," answered my father. "You are my business."

"I know, dear," said my mother. "It is hard."

The key turned in the lock, and we all stood quiet to listen.

"She's come back alone," said my mother. "I knew it was hopeless."

The door opened.

"Please, ma'am," said the new parlour-maid, "will I do?"

She stood there, framed by the lintel, in the daintiest of aprons, the daintiest of caps upon her golden hair; and every objection she swept aside with the wind of her merry wilfulness. No one ever had their way with her, nor wanted it.

"You shall be footman," she ordered, turning to me, but this time my mother only laughed. "Wait here till I come down again." Then to my mother: "Now, ma'am, are you ready?"

It was the first time I had seen my mother, or, indeed, any other flesh and blood woman, in evening dress, and to tell the truth I was a little shocked. Nay, more than a little, and showed it, I suppose; for my mother flushed and drew her shawl over the gleaming whiteness of her shoulders, pleading coldness. But Barbara cried out against this, saying it was a sin such beauty should be hid; and my father, filching a shawl with a quick hand, so dextrously indeed as to suggest some previous practice in the feat, dropped on one knee, as though the world were some sweet picture book, and raised my mother's hand with grave reverence to his lips; and Barbara, standing behind my mother's chair, insisted on my following suit, saying the Queen was receiving. So I knelt also, glancing up shyly as towards the gracious face of some fair lady hitherto unknown, thus Catching my first glimpse of the philosophy of clothes.

My memory lingers upon this scene by contrast with the sad, changed days that swiftly followed, when my mother's eyes would flash towards my father angry gleams, and her voice ring cruel and hard; though the moment he was gone her lips would tremble and her eyes grow soft again and fill with tears; when my father would sit with averted face and sullen lips tight pressed, or worse, would open them only to pour forth a rapid flood of savage speech; and fling out of the room, slamming the door behind him, and I would find him hours afterwards, sitting alone in the dark, with bowed head between his hands.

Wretched, I would lie awake, hearing through the flimsy walls their passionate tones, now rising high, now fiercely forced into cold whispers; and then their words to each other sounded even crueller.

In their estrangement from each other, so new to them, both clung closer to me, though they would tell me nothing, nor should I have understood if they had. When my mother was sobbing softly, her arms clasping me tighter and tighter with each quivering throb, then I hated my father, who I felt had inflicted this sorrow upon her. Yet when my father drew me down upon his knee, and I looked into his kind eyes so full of pain, then I felt angry with my mother, remembering her bitter tongue.

It seemed to me as though some cruel, unseen thing had crept into the house to stand ever between them, so that they might never look into each other's loving eyes but only into the eyes of this evil shadow. The idea grew upon me until at times I could almost detect its outline in the air, feel a chillness as it passed me. It trod silently through the pokey rooms, always alert to thrust its grinning face before them. Now beside my mother it would whisper in her ear; and the next moment, stealing across to my father, answer for him with his voice, but strangely different. I used to think I could hear it laughing to itself as it stepped back into enfolding space.

To this day I seem to see it, ever following with noiseless footsteps man and woman, waiting patiently its opportunity to thrust its face between them. So that I can read no love tale, but, glancing round, I see its mocking eyes behind my shoulder, reading also, with a silent laugh. So that never can I meet with boy and girl, whispering in the twilight, but I see it lurking amid the half lights, just behind them, creeping after them with stealthy tread, as hand in hand they pass me in quiet ways.

Shall any of us escape, or lies the road of all through this dark valley of the shadow of dead love? Is it Love's ordeal? testing the feeble-hearted from the strong in faith, who shall find each other yet again, the darkness passed?

Of the dinner itself, until time of dessert, I can give no consecutive account, for as footman, under the orders of this enthusiastic parlour-maid, my place was no sinecure, and but few opportunities of observation through the crack of the door were afforded me. All that was clear to me was that the chief guest was a Mr. Teidelmann or Tiedelmann, I cannot now remember which, a snuffy, mumbling old frump, with whose name then, however, I was familiar by reason of seeing it so often in huge letters, though with a Co. added, on dreary long blank walls, bordering the Limehouse reach. He sat at my mother's right hand; and I wondered, noticing him so ugly and so foolish seeming, how she could be so interested in him, shouting much and often to him; for added to his other disattractions he was very deaf, which necessitated his putting his hand up to his ear at every other observation made to him, crying querulously: "Eh, what? What are you talking about? Say it again,", smiling upon him and paying close attention to his every want. Even old Hasluck, opposite to him, and who, though pleasant enough in his careless way, was far from being a slave to politeness, roared himself purple, praising some new disinfectant of which this same Teidelmann appeared to be the proprietor.

"My wife swears by it," bellowed Hasluck, leaning across the table.

"Our drains!" chimed in Mrs. Hasluck, who was a homely soul; "well, you'd hardly know there was any in the house since I've took to using it."

"What are they talking about?" asked Teidelmann, appealing to my mother. "What's he say his wife does?"

"Your disinfectant," explained my mother; "Mrs. Hasluck swears by it."

"Who?"

"Mrs. Hasluck."

"Does she? Delighted to hear it," grunted the old gentleman, evidently bored.

"Nothing like it for a sick-room," persisted Hasluck; "might almost call it a scent."

"Makes one quite anxious to be ill," remarked my aunt, addressing no one in particular.

"Reminds me of cocoanuts," continued Hasluck.

Its proprietor appeared not to hear, but Hasluck was determined his flattery should not be lost.

"I say it reminds me of cocoanuts." He screamed it this time.

"Oh, does it?" was the reply.

"Doesn't it you?"

"Can't say it does," answered Teidelmann. "As a matter of fact, don't know much about it myself. Never use it."

Old Teidelmann went on with his dinner, but Hasluck was still full of the subject.

"Take my advice," he shouted, "and buy a bottle."

"Buy a what?"

"A bottle," roared the other, with an effort palpably beyond his strength.

"What's he say? What's he talking about now?" asked Teidelmann, again appealing to my mother.

"He says you ought to buy a bottle," again explained my mother.

"What of?"

"Of your own disinfectant."

"Silly fool!"

Whether he intended the remark to be heard and thus to close the topic (which it did), or whether, as deaf people are apt to, merely misjudged the audibility of an intended sotto vocalism, I cannot say. I only know that outside in the passage I heard the words distinctly, and therefore assume they reached round the table also.

A lull in the conversation followed, but Hasluck was not thin-skinned, and the next thing I distinguished was his cheery laugh.

"He's quite right," was Hasluck's comment; "that's what I am undoubtedly. Because I can't talk about anything but shop myself, I think everybody else is the same sort of fool."

But he was doing himself an injustice, for on my next arrival in the passage he was again shouting across the table, and this time Teidelmann was evidently interested.

"Well, if you could spare the time, I'd be more obliged than I can tell you," Hasluck was saying. "I know absolutely nothing about pictures myself, and Pearsall says you are one of the best judges in Europe."

"He ought to know," chuckled old Teidelmann. "He's tried often enough to palm off rubbish onto me."

"That last purchase of yours must have been a good thing for young" Hasluck mentioned the name of a painter since world famous; "been the making of him, I should say."

"I gave him two thousand for the six," replied Teidelmann, "and they'll sell for twenty thousand."

"But you'll never sell them?" exclaimed my father.

"No," grunted old Teidelmann, "but my widow will." There came a soft, low laugh from a corner of the table I could not see.

"It's Anderson's great disappointment," followed a languid, caressing voice (the musical laugh translated into prose, it seemed), "that he has never been able to educate me to a proper appreciation of art. He'll pay thousands of pounds for a child in rags or a badly dressed Madonna. Such a waste of money, it appears to me."

"But you would pay thousands for a diamond to hang upon your neck," argued my father's voice.

"It would enhance the beauty of my neck," replied the musical voice.

"An even more absolute waste of money," was my father's answer, spoken low. And I heard again the musical, soft laugh.

"Who is she?" I asked Barbara.

"The second Mrs. Teidelmann," whispered Barbara. "She is quite a swell. Married him for his money, I don't like her myself, but she's very beautiful."

"As beautiful as you?" I asked incredulously. We were sitting on the stairs, sharing a jelly.

"Oh, me!" answered Barbara. "I'm only a child. Nobody takes any notice of me, except other kids, like you." For some reason she appeared out of conceit with herself, which was not her usual state of mind.

"But everybody thinks you beautiful," I maintained.

"Who?" she asked quickly.

"Dr. Hal," I answered.

We were with our backs to the light, so that I could not see her face.

"What did he say?" she asked, and her voice had more of contentment in it.

I could not remember his exact words, but about the sense of them I was positive.

"Ask him what he thinks of me, as if you wanted to know yourself," Barbara instructed me, "and don't forget what he says this time. I'm curious." And though it seemed to me a foolish command, for what could he say of her more than I myself could tell her, I never questioned Barbara's wishes.

Yet if I am right in thinking that jealousy of Mrs. Teidelmann may have clouded for a moment Barbara's sunny nature, surely there was no reason for this, seeing that no one attracted greater attention throughout the dinner than the parlour-maid.

"Where ever did you get her from?" asked Mrs. Florret, Barbara having just descended the kitchen stairs.

"A neat-handed Phillis," commented Dr. Florret with approval.

"I'll take good care she never waits at my table," laughed the wife of our minister, the Rev. Cottle, a broad-built, breezy-voiced woman, mother of eleven, eight of them boys.

"To tell the truth," said my mother, "she's only here temporarily."

"As a matter of fact," said my father, "we have to thank Mrs. Hasluck for her."

"Don't leave me out of it," laughed Hasluck; "can't let the old girl take all the credit."

Later my father absent-mindedly addressed her as "My dear," at which Mrs. Cottle shot a swift glance towards my mother; and before that incident could have been forgotten, Hasluck, when no one was looking, pinched her elbow, which would not have mattered had not the unexpectedness of it drawn from her an involuntary "augh," upon which, for the reputation of the house, and the dinner being then towards its end; my mother deemed it better to take the whole company into her confidence. Naturally the story gained for Barbara still greater admiration, so that when with the dessert, discarding the apron but still wearing the dainty cap, which showed wisdom, she and the footman took their places among the guests, she was even more than before the centre of attention and remark.

"It was very nice of you," said Mrs. Cottle, thus completing the circle of compliments, "and, as I always tell my girls, that is better than being beautiful."

"Kind hearts," added Dr. Florret, summing up the case, "are more than coronets." Dr. Florret had ever ready for the occasion the correct quotation, but from him, somehow, it never irritated; rather it fell upon the ear as a necessary rounding and completing of the theme; like the Amen in church.

Only to my aunt would further observations have occurred.

"When I was a girl," said my aunt, breaking suddenly upon the passing silence, "I used to look into the glass and say to myself: 'Fanny, you've got to be amiable,' and I was amiable," added my aunt, challenging contradiction with a look; "nobody can say that I wasn't, for years."

"It didn't pay?" suggested Hasluck.

"It attracted," replied my aunt, "no attention whatever."

Hasluck had changed places with my mother, and having after many experiments learned the correct pitch for conversation with old Teidelmann, talked with him as much aside as the circumstances of the case would permit. Hasluck never wasted time on anything else than business. It was in his opera box on the first night of Verdi's Aida (I am speaking of course of days then to come) that he arranged the details of his celebrated deal in guano; and even his very religion, so I have been told and can believe, he varied to suit the enterprise of the moment, once during the protracted preliminaries of a cocoa scheme becoming converted to Quakerism.

But for the most of us interest lay in a discussion between Washburn and Florret concerning the superior advantages attaching to residence in the East End.

As a rule, incorrect opinion found itself unable to exist in Dr. Florret's presence. As no bird, it is said, can continue its song once looked at by an owl, so all originality grew silent under the cold stare of his disapproving eye. But Dr. "Fighting Hal" was no gentle warbler of thought. Vehement, direct, indifferent, he swept through all polite argument as a strong wind through a murmuring wood, carrying his partisans with him further than they meant to go, and quite unable to turn back; leaving his opponents clinging desperately, upside down, anyhow, to their perches, angry, their feathers much ruffled.

"Life!" flung out Washburn, Dr. Florret had just laid down unimpeachable rules for the conduct of all mankind on all occasions, "what do you respectable folk know of life? You are not men and women, you are marionettes. You don't move to your natural emotions implanted by God; you dance according to the latest book of etiquette. You live and love, laugh and weep and sin by rule. Only one moment do you come face to face with life; that is in the moment when you die, leaving the other puppets to be dressed in black and make believe to cry."

It was a favourite subject of denunciation with him, the artificiality of us all.

"Little doll," he had once called me, and I had resented the term.

"That's all you are, little Paul," he had persisted, "a good little hard-working doll, that does what it's made to do, and thinks what it's made to think. We are all dolls. Your father is a gallant-hearted, soft-headed little doll; your mother the sweetest and primmest of dolls. And I'm a silly, dissatisfied doll that longs to be a man, but hasn't the pluck. We are only dolls, little Paul."

"He's a trifle, a trifle whimsical on some subjects," explained my father, on my repeating this conversation.

"There are a certain class of men," explained my mother, "you will meet with them more as you grow up, who talk for talking's sake. They don't know what they mean. And nobody else does either."

"But what would you have?" argued Dr. Florret, "that every man should do that which is right in his own eyes?"

"Far better than, like the old man in the fable, he should do what every other fool thinks right," retorted Washburn. "The other day I called to see whether a patient of mine was still alive or not. His wife was washing clothes in the front room. 'How's your husband?' I asked. 'I think he's dead,' replied the woman. Then, without leaving off her work, 'Jim,' she shouted, 'are you there?' No answer came from the inner room. 'He's a goner,' she said, wringing out a stocking."

"But surely," said Dr. Florret, "you don't admire a woman for being indifferent to the death of her husband?"

"I don't admire her for that," replied Washburn, "and I don't blame her. I didn't make the world and I'm not responsible for it. What I do admire her for is not pretending a grief she didn't feel. In Berkeley Square she'd have met me at the door with an agonised face and a handkerchief to her eyes."

"Assume a virtue, if you have it not," murmured Dr. Florret.

"Go on," said Washburn. "How does it run? 'That monster, custom, who all sense doth eat, of devil's habit, is angel yet in this, that to the use of actions fair and good he gives a frock that aptly is put on.' So was the lion's skin by the ass, but it showed him only the more an ass. Here asses go about as asses, but there are lions also. I had a woman under my hands only a little while ago. I could have cured her easily. Why she got worse every day instead of better I could not understand. Then by accident learned the truth: instead of helping me she was doing all she could to kill herself. 'I must, Doctor,' she cried. 'I must. I have promised. If I get well he will only leave me, and if I die now he has sworn to be good to the children.' Here, I tell you, they live, think their thoughts, work their will, kill those they hate, die for those they love; savages if you like, but savage men and women, not bloodless dolls."

"I prefer the dolls," concluded Dr. Florret.

"I admit they are pretty," answered Washburn.

"I remember," said my father, "the first masked ball I ever went to when I was a student in Paris. It struck me just as you say, Hal; everybody was so exactly alike. I was glad to get out into the street and see faces."

"But I thought they always unmasked at midnight," said the second Mrs. Teidelmann in her soft, languid tones.

"I did not wait," explained my father.

"That was a pity," she replied. "I should have been interested to see what they were like, underneath."

"I might have been disappointed," answered my father. "I agree with Dr. Florret that sometimes the mask is an improvement."

Barbara was right. She was a beautiful woman, with a face that would have been singularly winning if one could have avoided the hard cold eyes ever restless behind the half-closed lids.

Always she was very kind to me. Moreover, since the disappearance of Cissy she was the first to bestow again upon me a good opinion of my small self. My mother praised me when I was good, which to her was the one thing needful; but few of us, I fear, child or grown-up, take much pride in our solid virtues, finding them generally hindrances to our desires: like the oyster's pearl, of more comfort to the world than to ourselves. If others there were who admired me, very guardedly must they have kept the secret I would so gladly have shared with them. But this new friend of ours, or had I not better at once say enemy, made me feel when in her presence a person of importance. How it was accomplished I cannot explain. No word of flattery nor even of mere approval ever passed her lips. Her charm to me was not that she admired me, but that she led me by some mysterious process to admire myself.

And yet in spite of this and many lesser kindnesses she showed to me, I never really liked her; but rather feared her, dreading always the sudden raising of those ever half-closed eyelids.

She sat next to my father at the corner of the table, her chin resting on her long white hands, her sweet lips parted, and as often as his eyes were turned away from her, her soft low voice would draw them back again. Once she laid her hand on his, laughing the while at some light jest of his, and I saw that he flushed; and following his quick glance, saw that my mother's eyes were watching also.

I have spoken of my father only as he then appeared to me, a child, an older chum with many lines about his mobile mouth, the tumbled hair edged round with grey; but looking back with older eyes, I see him a slightly stooping, yet still tall and graceful man, with the face of a poet, the face I mean a poet ought to possess but rarely does, nature apparently abhorring the obvious, with the shy eyes of a boy, and a voice tender as a woman's. Never the dingiest little drab that entered the kitchen but adored him, speaking always of "the master" in tones of fond proprietorship, for to the most slatternly his "orders" had ever the air of requests for favours. Women, I so often read, can care for only masterful men. But may there not be variety in women as in other species? Or perhaps, if the suggestion be not over-daring, the many writers, deeming themselves authorities upon this subject of woman, may in this one particular have erred? I only know my father spoke to few women whose eyes did not brighten. Yet hardly should I call him a masterful man.

"I think it's all right," whispered Hasluck to my father in the passage, they were the last to go. "What does she think of it, eh?"

"I think she'll be with us," answered my father.

"Nothing like food for bringing people together," said Hasluck. "Good-night."

The door closed, but Something had crept into the house. It stood between my father and mother. It followed them silently up the narrow creaking stairs.

CHAPTER VII.

OF THE PASSING OF THE SHADOW.

Better is little, than treasure and trouble therewith. Better a dinner of herbs where love is, than a stalled ox and hatred therewith. None but a great man would have dared to utter such a glaring commonplace as that. Not only on Sundays now, but all the week, came the hot joint to table, and on every day there was pudding, till a body grew indifferent to pudding; thus a joy-giving luxury of life being lost and but another item added to the long list of uninteresting needs. Now we could eat and drink without stint. No need now to organise for the morrow's hash. No need now to cut one's bread instead of breaking it, thinking of Saturday's bread pudding. But there the saying fails, for never now were we merry. A silent unseen guest sat with us at the board, so that no longer we laughed and teased as over the half pound of sausages or the two sweet-scented herrings; but talked constrainedly of empty things that lay outside us.

Easy enough would it have been for us to move to Guilford Street. Occasionally in the spiritless tones in which they now spoke on all subjects save the one, my mother and father would discuss the project; but always into the conversation would fall, sooner or later, some loosened thought to stir it to anger, and so the aching months went by, and the cloud grew.

Then one day the news came that old Teidelmann had died suddenly in his counting house.

"You are going to her?" said my mother.

"I have been sent for," said my father; "I must, it may mean business."

My mother laughed bitterly; why, at the time, I could not understand; and my father flung out of the house. During the many hours that he was away my mother remained locked in her room, and, stealing sometimes to the door, I was sure I heard her crying; and that she should grieve so at old Teidelmann's death puzzled me.

She came oftener to our house after that. Her mourning added, I think, to her beauty, softening, or seeming to soften, the hardness of her eyes. Always she was very sweet to my mother, who by contrast beside her appeared witless and ungracious; and to me, whatever her motive, she was kindness itself; hardly ever arriving without some trifling gift or plan for affording me some childish treat. By instinct she understood exactly what I desired and liked, the books that would appeal to me as those my mother gave me never did, the pleasures that did please me as opposed to the pleasures that should have pleased me. Often my mother, talking to me, would chill me with the vista of the life that lay before me: a narrow, viewless way between twin endless walls of "Must" and "Must not." This soft-voiced lady set me dreaming of life as of sunny fields through which one wandered laughing, along the winding path of Will; so that, although as I have said, there lurked at the bottom of my thoughts a fear of her; yet something within me I seemed unable to control went out to her, drawn by her subtle sympathy and understanding of it.

"Has he ever seen a pantomime?" she asked of my father one morning, looking at me the while with a whimsical screwing of her mouth.

My heart leaped within me. My father raised his eyebrows: "What would your mother say, do you think?" he asked. My heart sank.

"She thinks," I replied, "that theatres are very wicked places." It was the first time that any doubt as to the correctness of my mother's judgments had ever crossed my mind.

Mrs. Teidelmann's smile strengthened my doubt. "Dear me," she said, "I am afraid I must be very wicked. I have always regarded a pantomime as quite a moral entertainment. All the bad people go down so very straight to, well, to the fit and proper place for them. And we could promise to leave before the Clown stole the sausages, couldn't we, Paul?"

My mother was called and came; and I could not help thinking how insignificant she looked with her pale face and plain dark frock, standing stiffly beside this shining lady in her rustling clothes.

"You will let him come, Mrs. Kelver," she pleaded in her soft caressing tones; "it's Dick Whittington, you know, such an excellent moral."

My mother had stood silent, clasping and unclasping her hands, a childish trick she had when troubled; and her lips were trembling. Important as the matter loomed before my own eyes, I wondered at her agitation.

"I am very sorry," said my mother, "it is very kind of you. But I would rather he did not go."

"Just this once," persisted Mrs. Teidelmann. "It is holiday time."

A ray of sunlight fell into the room, lighting upon her coaxing face, making where my mother stood seem shadow.

"I would rather he did not go," repeated my mother, and her voice sounded harsh and grating. "When he is older others must judge for him, but for the present he must be guided by me alone."

"I really don't think there could be any harm, Maggie," urged my father. "Things have changed since we were young."

"That may be," answered my mother, still in the same harsh voice; "it is long ago since then."

"I didn't intend it that way," said my father with a short laugh.

"I merely meant that I may be wrong," answered my mother. "I seem so old among you all, so out of place. I have tried to change, but I cannot."

"We will say no more about it," said Mrs. Teidelmann, sweetly. "I merely thought it would give him pleasure; and he has worked so hard this last term, his father tells me."

She laid her hand caressingly on my shoulder, drawing me a little closer to her; and it remained there.

"It was very kind of you," said my mother, "I would do anything to give him pleasure, anything-I could. He knows that. He understands."

My mother's hand, I knew, was seeking mine, but I was angry and would not see; and without another word she left the room.

My mother did not allude again to the subject; but the very next afternoon she took me herself to a hall in the neighbourhood, where we saw a magic-lantern, followed by a conjurer. She had dressed herself in a prettier frock than she had worn for many a long day, and was brighter and gayer in herself than had lately been her wont, laughing and talking merrily. But I, nursing my wrongs, remained moody and sulky. At any other time such rare amusement would have overjoyed me; but the wonders of the great theatre that from other boys I had heard so much of, that from gaudy-coloured posters I had built up for myself, were floating vague and undefined before me in the air; and neither the open-mouthed sleeper, swallowing his endless chain of rats; nor even the live rabbit found in the stout old gentleman's hat, the last sort of person in whose hat one would have expected to find such a thing, could draw away my mind from the joy I had caught a glimpse of only to lose.

So we walked home through the muddy, darkening streets, speaking but little; and that night, waking, or rather half waking, as children do, I thought I saw a figure in white crouching at the foot of my bed. I must have gone to sleep again; and later, though I cannot say whether the intervening time was short or long, I opened my eyes to see it still there; and frightened, I cried out; and my mother rose from her knees.

She laughed, a curious broken laugh, in answer to my questions. "It was a silly dream I had," she explained "I must have been thinking of the conjurer we saw. I dreamt that a wicked Magician had spirited you away from me. I could not find you and was all alone in the world."

She put her arms around me, so tight as almost to hurt me. And thus we remained until again I must have fallen asleep.

It was towards the close of these same holidays that my mother and I called upon Mrs. Teidelmann in her great stone-built house at Clapton. She had sent a note round that morning, saying she was suffering from terrible headaches that quite took her senses away, so that she was unable to come out. She would be leaving England in a few days to travel. Would my mother come and see her, she would like to say good-bye to her before she went. My mother handed the letter across the table to my father.

"Of course you will go," said my father. "Poor girl, I wonder what the cause can be. She used to be so free from everything of the kind."

"Do you think it well for me to go?" said my mother. "What can she have to say to me?"

"Oh, just to say good-bye," answered my father. "It would look so pointed not to go."

It was a dull, sombre house without, but one entered through its commonplace door as through the weed-grown rock into Aladdin's cave. Old Teidelmann had been a great collector all his life, and his treasures, now scattered through a dozen galleries, were then heaped there in curious confusion. Pictures filled every inch of wall, stood propped against the wonderful old furniture, were even stretched unframed across the ceilings. Statues gleamed from every corner (a few of the statues were, I remember, the only things out of the entire collection that Mrs. Teidelmann kept for herself), carvings, embroideries, priceless china, miniatures framed in gems, illuminated missals and gorgeously bound books crowded the room. The ugly little thick-lipped man had surrounded himself with the beauty of every age, brought from every land. He himself must have been the only thing cheap and uninteresting to be found within his own walls; and now he lay shrivelled up in his coffin, under a monument by means of which an unknown cemetery became quite famous.

Instructions had been given that my mother was to be shown up into Mrs. Teidelmann's boudoir. She was lying on a sofa near the fire when we entered, asleep, dressed in a loose lace robe that fell away, showing her thin but snow-white arms, her rich dark hair falling loose about her. In sleep she looked less beautiful: harder and with a suggestion of coarseness about the face, of which at other times it showed no trace. My mother said she would wait, perhaps Mrs. Teidelmann would awake; and the servant, closing the door softly, left us alone with her.

An old French clock standing on the mantelpiece, a heart supported by Cupids, ticked with a muffled, soothing sound. My mother, choosing a chair by the window, sat with her eyes fixed on the sleeping woman's face, and it seemed to me, though this may have been but my fancy born of after-thought, that a faint smile relaxed for a moment the sleeping woman's pained, pressed lips. Neither I nor my mother spoke, the only sound in the room being the hushed ticking of the great gilt clock. Until the other woman after a few slight movements of unrest began to talk in her sleep.

Only confused murmurs escaped her at first, and then I heard her whisper my father's name. Very low, hardly more than breathed, were the words, but upon the silence each syllable struck clear and distinct: "Ah no, we must not. Luke, my darling."

My mother rose swiftly from her chair, but she spoke in quite matter-of-fact tones.

"Go, Paul," she said, "wait for me downstairs;" and noiselessly opening the door, she pushed me gently out, and closed it again behind me.

It was half an hour or more before she came down, and at once we left the house, letting ourselves out. All the way home my mother never once spoke, but walked as one in a dream with eyes that saw not. With her hand upon the lock of our gate she came back to life.

"You must say nothing, Paul, do you understand?" she said. "When people are delirious they use strange words that have no meaning. Do you understand, Paul; you must never breathe a word, never."

I promised, and we entered the house; and from that day my mother's whole manner changed. Not another angry word ever again escaped her lips, never an angry flash lighted up again her eyes. Mrs. Teidelmann remained away three months. My father, of course, wrote to her often, for he was managing all her affairs. But my mother wrote to her also, though this my father, I do not think, knew, long letters that she would go away by herself to pen, writing them always in the twilight, close to the window.

"Why do you choose this time, just when it's getting dark, to write your letters," my father would expostulate, when by chance he happened to look into the room. "Let me ring for the lamp, you will strain your eyes." But my mother would always excuse herself, saying she had only a few lines to finish.

"I can think better in this light," she would explain.

And when Mrs. Teidelmann returned, it was my mother who was the first to call upon her; before even my father knew that she was back. And from thence onward one might have thought them the closest of friends, my mother visiting her often, speaking of her to all in terms of praise and liking.

In this way peace returned unto the house, and my father was tender again in all his words and actions towards my mother, and my mother thoughtful as before of all his wants and whims, her voice soft and low, the sweet smile ever lurking around her lips as in the old days before this evil thing had come to dwell among us; and I might have forgotten it had ever cast its blight upon our life but that every day my mother grew feebler, the little ways that had seemed a part of her gone from her.

The summer came and went, that time in towns of panting days and stifling nights, when through the open window crawls to one's face the hot foul air, heavy with reeking odours drawn from a thousand streets; when lying awake one seems to hear the fitful breathing of the myriad mass around, as of some over-laboured beast too tired to even rest; and my mother moved about the house ever more listlessly.

"There's nothing really the matter with her," said Dr. Hal, "only weakness. It is the place. Cannot you get her away from it?"

"I cannot leave myself," said my father, "just yet; but there is no reason why you and the boy should not take a holiday. This year I can afford it, and later I might possibly join you."

My mother consented, as she did to all things now, and so it came about that again of afternoons we climbed, though more slowly and with many pauses, the steep path to the ruined tower old Jacob in his happy foolishness had built upon the headland, rested once again upon its topmost platform, sheltered from the wind that ever blew about its crumbling walls, saw once more the distant mountains, faint like spectres, and the silent ships that came and vanished, and about our feet the pleasant farm lands, and the grave, sweet river.

We had taken lodgings in the village: smaller now it seemed than previously; but wonderful its sunny calm, after the turmoil of the fierce dark streets. Mrs. Fursey was there still, but quite another than the Mrs. Fursey of my remembrance, a still angular but cheery dame, bent no longer on suppressing me, but rather on drawing me out before admiring neighbours, as one saying: "The material was unpromising, as you know. There were times when I almost despaired. But with patience, and, may I say, a natural gift that way, you see what can be accomplished!" And Anna, now a buxom wife and mother, with an uncontrollable desire to fall upon and kiss me at most unexpected moments, necessitating a never sleeping watchfulness on my part, and a choosing of positions affording means of ready retreat. And old Chumbley, still cobbling shoes in his tiny cave. On the bench before him in a row they sat and watched him while he tapped and tapped and hammered: pert little shoes piping "Be quick, be quick, we want to be toddling. You seem to have no idea, my good man, how much toddling there is to be done." Dapper boots, sighing: "Oh, please make haste, we are waiting to dance and to strut. Jack walks in the lane, Jill waits by the gate. Oh, deary, how slowly he taps." Stout sober boots, saying: "As soon as you can, old friend. Remember we've work to do." Flat-footed old boots, rusty and limp, mumbling: "We haven't much time, Mr. Chumbley. Just a patch, that is all, we haven't much further to go." And old Joe, still peddling his pack, with the help of the same old jokes. And Tom Pinfold, still puzzled and scratching his head, the rejected fish still hanging by its tail from his expostulating hand; one might almost have imagined it the same fish. Grown-up folks had changed but little. Only the foolish children had been playing tricks; parties I had left mere sucking babes now swaggering in pinafore or knickerbocker; children I had known now mincing it as men and women; such affectation annoyed me.

One afternoon, it was towards the close of the last week of our stay, my mother and I had climbed, as was so often our wont, to the upper platform of old Jacob's tower. My mother leant upon the parapet, her eyes fixed dreamingly upon the distant mountains, and a smile crept to her lips.

"What are you thinking of?" I asked.

"Oh, only of things that happened over there", she nodded her head towards the distant hills as to some old crony with whom she shares secrets, "when I was a girl."

"You lived there, long ago, didn't you, when you were young?" I asked. Boys do not always stop to consider whether their questions might or might not be better expressed.

"You're very rude," said my mother, it was long since a tone of her old self had rung from her in answer to any touch; "it was a very little while ago."

Suddenly she raised her head and listened. Perhaps some twenty seconds she remained so with her lips parted, and then from the woods came a faint, long-drawn "Coo-ee." We ran to the side of the tower commanding the pathway from the village, and waited until from among the dark pines my father emerged into the sunlight.

Seeing us, he shouted again and waved his stick, and from the light of his eyes and his gallant bearing, and the spring of his step across the heathery turf, we knew instinctively that trouble had come upon him. He always rose to meet it with that look and air. It was the old Norse blood in his veins, I suppose. So, one imagines, must those godless old Pirates have sprung to their feet when the North wind, loosed as a hawk from the leash, struck at the beaked prow.

We heard his quick step on the rickety stair, and the next moment he was between us, breathing a little hard, but laughing.

He stood for awhile beside my mother without speaking, both of them gazing at the distant hills among which, as my mother had explained, things had happened long ago. And maybe, "over there," their memories met and looked upon each other with kind eyes.

"Do you remember," said my father, "we climbed up here, it was the first walk we took together after coming here. We discussed our plans for the future, how we would retrieve our fortunes."

"And the future," answered my mother, "has a way of making plans for us instead."

"It would seem so," replied my father, with a laugh. "I am an unlucky beggar, Maggie. I dropped all your money as well as my own down that wretched mine."

"It was the will, it was Fate, or whatever you call it," said my mother. "You could not help that, Luke."

"If only that damned pump hadn't jambed," said my father.

"Do you remember that Mrs. Tharand?" asked my mother.

"Yes, what of her?"

"A worldly woman, I always thought her. She called on me the morning we were leaving; I don't think you saw her. 'I've been through more worries than you would think, to look at me,' she said to me, laughing. I've always remembered her words: 'and of all the troubles that come to us in this world, believe me, Mrs. Kelver, money troubles are the easiest to bear.'"

"I wish I could think so," said my father.

"She rather irritated me at the time," continued my mother. "I thought it one of those commonplaces with which we console ourselves for other people's misfortunes. But now I know she spoke the truth."

There was silence between them for awhile. Then said my father in a cheery tone:

"I've broken with old Hasluck."

"I thought you would be compelled to sooner or later," answered my mother.

"Hasluck," exclaimed my father, with sudden vehemence, "is little better than a thief; I told him so."

"What did he say?" asked my mother.

"Laughed, and said that was better than some people."

My father laughed himself.

I wish to do the memory of Noel Hasluck no injustice. Ever was he a kind friend to me; not only then, but in later years, when, having come to learn that kindness is rarer in the world than I had dreamt, I was glad of it. Added to which, if only for Barbara's sake, I would prefer to write of him throughout in terms of praise. Yet even were his good-tempered, thick-skinned ghost (and unless it were good-tempered and thick-skinned it would be no true ghost of old Noel Hasluck) to be reading over my shoulder the words as I write them down, I think it would agree with me, I do not think it would be offended with me (forever in his life he was an admirer and a lover of the Truth, being one of those good fighters capable of respecting even his foe, his enemy, against whom from ten to four, occasionally a little later, he fought right valiantly) for saying that of all the men who go down into the City each day in a cab or 'bus or train, he was perhaps one of the most unprincipled: and whether that be saying much or little I leave to those with more knowledge to decide.

To do others, as it was his conviction, right or wrong, that they would do him if ever he gave them half a chance, was his notion of "business;" and in most of his transactions he was successful. "I play a game," he would argue, "where cheating is the rule. Nine out of every ten men round the table are sharpers like myself, and the tenth man is a fool who has no business to be there. We prey upon each other, and the cutest of us is the winner."

"But the innocent people, lured by your fine promises," I ventured once to suggest to him, "the widows and the orphans?"

"My dear lad," he said, with a laugh, laying his fat hand upon my shoulder, "I remember one of your widows writing me a pathetic letter about some shares she had taken in a Silver Company of mine. Lord knows where the mine is now, somewhere in Spain, I think. It looked as though all her savings were gone. She had an only son, and it was nearly all they possessed in the world, etc., etc., you know the sort of thing. Well, I did what I've often been numskull enough to do in similar cases, wrote and offered to buy her out at par. A week later she answered, thanking me, but saying it did not matter. There had occurred a momentary rise, and she had sold out at a profit, to her own brother-in-law, as I discovered, happening to come across the transfers. You can find widows and orphans round the Monte Carlo card tables, if you like to look for them; they are no more deserving of consideration than the rest of the crowd. Besides, if it comes to that, I'm an orphan myself;" and he laughed again, one of his deep, hearty, honest laughs. No one ever possessed a laugh more suggestive in its every cadence of simple, transparent honesty. He used to say himself it was worth thousands to him.

Better from the Moralists' point of view had such a man been an out-and-out rogue. Then might one have pointed, crying: "Behold: Dishonesty, as you will observe in the person of our awful example, to be hated, needs but to be seen." But the duty of the Chronicler is to bear witness to what he knows, leaving Truth with the whole case before her to sum up and direct the verdict. In the City, old Hasluck had a bad reputation and deserved it; in Stoke-Newington, then a green suburb, containing many fine old houses, standing in great wooded gardens, he was loved and respected. In his business, he was a man void of all moral sense, without bowels of compassion for any living thing; in retirement, a man with a strong sense of duty and a fine regard for the rights and feelings of others, never happier than when planning to help or give pleasure. In his office, he would have robbed his own mother. At home, he would have spent his last penny to add to her happiness or comfort. I make no attempt to explain. I only know that such men do exist, and that Hasluck was one of them. One avoids difficulties by dismissing them as a product of our curiously complex civilisation, a convenient phrase; let us hope the recording angel may be equally impressed by it.

Casting about for some reason of excuse to myself for my liking of him, I hit upon the expedient of regarding him as a modern Robin Hood, whom we are taught to admire without shame, a Robin Hood up to date, adapted to the changed conditions of modern environment; making his living relieving the rich; taking pleasure relieving the poor.

"What will you do?" asked my mother.

"I shall have to give up the office," answered my father. "Without him there's not enough to keep it going. He was quite good-tempered about the matter, offered to divide the work, letting me retain the straightforward portion for whatever that might be worth. But I declined. Now I know, I feel I would rather have nothing more to do with him."

"I think you were quite right," agreed my mother.

"What I blame myself for," said my father, "is that I didn't see through him before. Of course he has been making a mere tool of me from the beginning. I ought to have seen through him. Why didn't I?"

They discussed the future, or, rather, my father discussed, my mother listening in silence, stealing a puzzled look at him from time to time, as though there were something she could not understand.

He would take a situation in the City. One had been offered him. It might sound poor, but it would be a steady income on which we must contrive to live. The little money he had saved must be kept for investments, nothing speculative, judicious "dealings," by means of which a cool, clear-headed man could soon accumulate capital. Here the training acquired by working for old Hasluck would serve him well. One man my father knew, quite a dull, commonplace man, starting a few years ago with only a few hundreds, was now worth tens of thousands. Foresight was the necessary qualification. You watched the "tendency" of things. So often had my father said to himself: "This is going to be a big thing. That other, it is no good," and in every instance his prognostications had been verified. He had "felt it;" some men had that gift. Now was the time to use it for practical purposes.

"Here," said my father, breaking off, and casting an approving eye upon the surrounding scenery, "would be a pleasant place to end one's days. The house you had was very pretty and you liked it. We might enlarge it, the drawing-room might be thrown out, perhaps another wing." I felt that our good fortune as from this day was at last established.

But my mother had been listening with growing impatience, her puzzled glances giving place gradually to flashes of anger; and now she turned her face full upon him, her question written plainly thereon, demanding answer.

Some idea of it I had even then, watching her; and since I have come to read it word for word: "But that woman, that woman that loves you, that you love. Ah, I know, why do you play with me? She is rich. With her your life will be smooth. And the boy, it will be better far for him. Cannot you three wait a little longer? What more can I do? Cannot you see that I am surely dying, dying as quickly as I can, dying as that poor creature your friend once told us of; knowing it was the only thing she could do for those she loved. Be honest with me: I am no longer jealous. All that is past: a man is ever younger than a woman, and a man changes. I do not blame you. It is for the best. She and I have talked; it is far better so. Only be honest with me, or at least silent. Will you not honour me enough for even that?"

My father did not answer, having that to speak of that put my mother's question out of her mind for all time; so that until the end no word concerning that other woman passed again between them. Twenty years later, nearly, I myself happened to meet her, and then long physical suffering had chased the wantonness away for ever from the pain-worn mouth; but in that hour of waning voices, as some trouble of the fretful day when evening falls, so she faded from their life; and if even the remembrance of her returned at times to either of them, I think it must have been in those moments when, for no seeming reason, shyly their hands sought one another.

So the truth of the sad ado, how far my mother's suspicions wronged my father; for the eye of jealousy (and what loving woman ever lived that was not jealous?) has its optic nerve terminating not in the brain but in the heart, which was not constructed for the reception of true vision, I never knew. Later, long after the curtain of green earth had been rolled down upon the players, I spoke once on the matter with Doctor Hal, who must have seen something of the play and with more understanding eyes than mine, and who thereupon delivered to me a short lecture on life in general, a performance at which he excelled.

"Flee from temptation and pray that you may be delivered from evil," shouted the Doctor (his was not the Socratic method) "but remember this: that as sure as the sparks fly upward there will come a time when, however fast you run, you will be overtaken, cornered, no one to deliver you but yourself, the gods sitting round interested. It is a grim fight, for the Thing, you may be sure, has chosen its right moment. And every woman in the world will sympathise with you and be just to you, not even despising you should you be overcome; for however they may talk, every woman in the world knows that male and female cannot be judged by the same standard. To woman, Nature and the Law speak with one voice: 'Sin not, lest you be cursed of your sex!' It is no law of man: it is the law of creation. When the woman sins, she sins not only against her conscience, but against her every instinct. But to the man Nature whispers: 'Yield.' It is the Law alone that holds him back. Therefore every woman in the world, knowing this, will be just to you, every woman in the world but one, the woman that loves you. From her, hope for no sympathy, hope for no justice."

"Then you think" I began.

"I think," said the Doctor, "that your father loved your mother devotedly; but he was one of those fighters that for the first half-dozen rounds or so cause their backers much anxiety. It is a dangerous method."

"Then you think my mother"

"I think your mother was a good woman, Paul; and the good woman will never be satisfied with man till the Lord lets her take him to pieces and put him together herself."

My father had been pacing to and fro the tiny platform. Now he came to a halt opposite my mother, placing his hands upon her shoulders.

"I want you to help me, Maggie, help me to be brave. I have only a year or two longer to live, and there's a lot to be done in that time."

Slowly the anger died out of my mother's face.

"You remember that fall I had when the cage broke," my father went on. "Andrews, as you know, feared from the first it might lead to that. But I always laughed at him."

"How long have you known?" my mother asked.

"Oh, about six months. I felt it at the beginning of the year, but I didn't say anything to Washburn till a month later. I thought it might be only fancy."

"And he is sure?"

My father nodded.

"But why have you never told me?"

"Because," replied my father, with a laugh, "I didn't want you to know. If I could have done without you, I should not have told you now."

And at this there came a light into my mother's face that never altogether left it until the end.

She drew him down beside her on the seat. I had come nearer; and my father, stretching out his hand, would have had me with them. But my mother, putting her arms about him, held him close to her, as though in that moment she would have had him to herself alone.

CHAPTER VIII.

HOW THE MAN IN GREY MADE READY FOR HIS GOING.

The eighteen months that followed, for the end came sooner than we had expected, were, I think, the happiest days my father and mother had ever known; or if happy be not altogether the right word, let me say the most beautiful, and most nearly perfect. To them it was as though God in His sweet thoughtfulness had sent death to knock lightly at the door, saying: "Not yet. You have still a little longer to be together. In a little while."

In those last days all things false and meaningless they laid aside. Nothing was of real importance to them but that they should love each other, comforting each other, learning to understand each other. Again we lived poorly; but there was now no pitiful straining to keep up appearances, no haunting terror of what the neighbours might think. The petty cares and worries concerning matters not worth a moment's thought, the mean desires and fears with which we disfigure ourselves, fell from them. There came to them broader thought, a wider charity, a deeper pity. Their love grew greater even than their needs, overflowing towards at things. Sometimes, recalling these months, it has seemed to me that we make a mistake seeking to keep Death, God's go-between, ever from our thoughts. Is it not closing the door to a friend who would help us would we let him (for who knows life so well), whispering to us: "In a little while. Only a little longer that you have to be together. Is it worth taking so much thought for self? Is it worth while being unkind?"

From them a graciousness emanated pervading all around. Even my aunt Fan decided for the second time in her career to give amiability a trial. This intention she announced publicly to my mother and myself one afternoon soon after our return from Devonshire.

"I'm a beast of an old woman," said my aunt, suddenly.

"Don't say that, Fan," urged my mother.

"What's the good of saying 'Don't say it' when I've just said it," snapped back my aunt.

"It's your manner," explained my mother; "people sometimes think you disagreeable."

"They'd be daft if they didn't," interrupted my aunt. "Of course you don't really mean it," continued my mother.

"Stuff and nonsense," snorted my aunt; "does she think I'm a fool. I like being disagreeable. I like to see 'em squirming."

My mother laughed.

"I can be agreeable," continued my aunt, "if I choose. Nobody more so."

"Then why not choose?" suggested my mother. "I tried it once," said my aunt, "and it fell flat. Nothing could have fallen flatter."

"It may not have attracted much attention," replied my mother, with a smile, "but one should not be agreeable merely to attract attention."

"It wasn't only that," returned my aunt, "it was that it gave no satisfaction to anybody. It didn't suit me. A disagreeable person is at their best when they are disagreeable."

"I can hardly agree with you there," answered my mother.

"I could do it again," communed my aunt to herself. There was a suggestion of vindictiveness in her tones. "It's easy enough. Look at the sort of fools that are agreeable."

"I'm sure you could be if you tried," urged my mother.

"Let 'em have it," continued my aunt, still to herself; "that's the way to teach 'em sense. Let 'em have it."

And strange though it may seem, my aunt was right and my mother altogether wrong. My father was the first to notice the change.

"Nothing the matter with poor old Fan, is there?" he asked. It was one evening a day or two after my aunt had carried her threat into effect. "Nothing happened, has there?"

"No," answered my mother, "nothing that I know of."

"Her manner is so strange," explained my father, "so, so weird."

My mother smiled. "Don't say anything to her. She's trying to be agreeable."

My father laughed and then looked wistful. "I almost wish she wouldn't," he remarked; "we were used to it, and she was rather amusing."

But my aunt, being a woman of will, kept her way; and about the same time that occurred tending to confirm her in her new departure. This was the introduction into our small circle of James Wellington Gadley. Properly speaking, it should have been Wellington James, that being the order in which he had been christened in the year 1815. But in course of time, and particularly during his school career, it had been borne in upon him that Wellington is a burdensome name for a commonplace mortal to bear, and very wisely he had reversed the arrangement. He was a slightly pompous but simpleminded little old gentleman, very proud of his position as head clerk to Mr. Stillwood, the solicitor to whom my father was now assistant. Stillwood, Waterhead and Royal dated back to the Georges, and was a firm bound up with the history, occasionally shady, of aristocratic England. True, in these later years its glory was dwindling. Old Mr. Stillwood, its sole surviving representative, declined to be troubled with new partners, explaining frankly, in answer to all applications, that the business was a dying one, and that attempting to work it up again would be but putting new wine into worn-out skins. But though its clientele was a yearly diminishing quantity, much business yet remained to it, and that of a good class, its name being still a synonym for solid respectability; and my father had deemed himself fortunate indeed in securing such an appointment. James Gadley had entered the firm as office boy in the days of its pride, and had never awakened to the fact that it was not still the most important legal firm within the half mile radius from Lombard Street. Nothing delighted him more than to discuss over and over again the many strange affairs in which Stillwood, Waterhead and Royal had been concerned, all of which he had at his tongue's tip. Could he find a hearer, these he would reargue interminably, but with professional reticence, personages becoming Mr. Y. and Lady X.; and places, "the capital of, let us say, a foreign country," or "a certain town not a thousand miles from where we are now sitting." The majority of his friends, his methods being somewhat forensic, would seek to discourage him, but my aunt was a never wearied listener, especially if the case were one involving suspicion of mystery and crime. When, during their very first conversation, he exclaimed: "Now why, why, after keeping away from his wife for nearly eighteen years, never even letting her know whether he was alive or dead, why this sudden resolve to return to her? That is what I want explained to me!" he paused, as was his wont, for sympathetic comment, my aunt, instead of answering as others, with a yawn: "Oh, I'm sure I don't know. Felt he wanted to see her, I suppose," replied with prompt intelligence:

"To murder her, by slow poison."

"To murder her! But why?"

"In order to marry the other woman."

"What other woman?"

"The woman he had just met and fallen in love with. Before that it was immaterial to him what had become of his wife. This woman had said to him: 'Come back to me a free man or never see my face again.'"

"Dear me! Now that's very curious."

"Nothing of the sort. Plain common sense."

"I mean, it's curious because, as a matter of fact, his wife did die a little later, and he did marry again."

"Told you so," remarked my aunt.

In this way every case in the Stillwood annals was reviewed, and light thrown upon it by my aunt's insight into the hidden springs of human action. Fortunate that the actors remained mere Mr. X. and Lady Y., for into the most innocent seeming behaviour my aunt read ever dark criminal intent.

"I think you are a little too severe," Mr. Gadley would now and then plead.

"We're all of us miserable sinners," my aunt would cheerfully affirm; "only we don't all get the same chances."

An elderly maiden lady, a Miss Z., residing in "a western town once famous as the resort of fashion, but which we will not name," my aunt was convinced had burnt down a house containing a will, and forged another under which her children, should she ever marry and be blessed with such, would inherit among them on coming of age a fortune of seven hundred pounds.

The freshness of her views on this, his favourite topic, always fascinated Mr. Gadley.

"I have to thank you, ma'am," he would remark on rising, "for a most delightful conversation. I may not be able to agree with your conclusions, but they afford food for reflection."

To which my aunt would reply, "I hate talking to any one who agrees with me. It's like taking a walk to see one's own looking-glass. I'd rather talk to somebody who didn't, even if he were a fool," which for her was gracious.

He was a stout little gentleman with a stomach that protruded about a foot in front of him, and of this he appeared to be quite unaware. Nor would it have mattered had it not been for his desire when talking to approach as close to his listener as possible. Gradually in the course of conversation, his stomach acting as a gentle battering ram, he would in this way drive you backwards round the room, sometimes, unless you were artful, pinning you hopelessly into a corner, when it would surprise him that in spite of all his efforts he never succeeded in getting any nearer to you. His first evening at our house he was talking to my aunt from the corner of his chair. As he grew more interested so he drew his chair nearer and nearer, till at length, having withdrawn inch by inch to avoid his encroachments, my aunt was sitting on the extreme edge of her own. His next move sent her on to the floor. She said nothing, which surprised me; but on the occasion of his next visit she was busy darning stockings, an unusual occupation for her. He approached nearer and nearer as before; but this time she sat her ground, and it was he who in course of time sprang back with an exclamation foreign to the subject under discussion.

Ever afterwards my aunt met him with stockings in her hand, and they talked with a space between their chairs.

Nothing further came of it, though his being a widower added to their intercourse that spice of possibility no woman is ever too old to relish; but that he admired her intellectually was evident. Once he even went so far as to exclaim: "Miss Davies, you should have been a solicitor's wife!" to his thinking the crown of feminine ambition. To which my aunt had replied: "Chances are I should have been if one had ever asked me." And warmed by appreciation, my aunt's amiability took root and flourished, though assuming, as all growth developed late is apt to, fantastic shape.

There came to her the idea, by no means ill-founded, that by flattery one can most readily render oneself agreeable; so conscientiously she set to work to flatter in season and out. I am sure she meant to give pleasure, but the effect produced was that of thinly veiled sarcasm.

My father would relate to us some trifling story, some incident noticed during the day that had seemed to him amusing. At once she would break out into enthusiasm, holding up her hands in astonishment.

"What a funny man he is! And to think that it comes to him naturally without an effort. What a gift it is!"

On my mother appearing in a new bonnet, or an old one retrimmed, an event not unfrequent; for in these days my mother took more thought than ever formerly for her appearance (you will understand, you women who have loved), she would step back in simulated amazement.

"Don't tell me it's a married woman with a boy getting on for fourteen. It's a girl. A saucy, tripping girl. That's what it is."

Persons have been known, I believe, whose vanity, not checked in time, has grown into a hopeless disease. But I am inclined to think that a dose of my aunt, about this period, would have cured the most obstinate case.

So also, and solely for our benefit, she assumed a vivacity and spriteliness that ill suited her, that having regard to her age and tendency towards rheumatism must have cost her no small effort. From these experiences there remains to me the perhaps immoral opinion that Virtue, in common with all other things, is at her best when unassuming.

Occasionally the old Adam, or should one say Eve, would assert itself in my aunt, and then, still thoughtful for others, she would descend into the kitchen and be disagreeable to Amy, our new servitor, who never minded it. Amy was a philosopher who reconciled herself to all things by the reflection that there were only twenty-four hours in a day. It sounds a dismal theory, but from it Amy succeeded in extracting perpetual cheerfulness. My mother would apologise to her for my aunt's interference.

"Lord bless you, mum, it don't matter. If I wasn't listening to her something else worse might be happening. Everything's all the same when it's over."

Amy had come to us merely as a stop gap, explaining to my mother that she was about to be married and desired only a temporary engagement to bridge over the few weeks between then and the ceremony.

"It's rather unsatisfactory," had said my mother. "I dislike changes."

"I can quite understand it, mum," had replied Amy; "I dislike 'em myself. Only I heard you were in a hurry, and I thought maybe that while you were on the lookout for somebody permanent"

So on that understanding she came. A month later my mother asked her when she thought the marriage would actually take place.

"Don't think I'm wishing you to go," explained my mother, "indeed I'd like you to stop. I only want to know in time to make my arrangements."

"Oh, some time in the spring, I expect," was Amy's answer.

"Oh!" said my mother, "I understood it was coming off almost immediately."

Amy appeared shocked.

"I must know a little bit more about him before I go as far as that," she said.

"But I don't understand," said my mother; "you told me when you came to me that you were going to be married in a few weeks."

"Oh, that one!" Her tone suggested that an unfair strain was being put upon her memory. "I didn't feel I wanted him as much as I thought I did when it came to the point."

"You had meantime met the other one?" suggested my mother, with a smile.

"Well, we can't help our feelings, can we, mum?" admitted Amy, frankly, "and what I always say is", she spoke as one with experience even then, "better change your mind before it's too late afterwards."

Amiable, sweet-faced, broad-hearted Amy! most faithful of friends, but oh! most faithless of lovers. Age has not withered nor custom staled her liking for infinite variety. Butchers, bakers, soldiers, sailors, Jacks of all trades! Does the sighing procession never pass before you, Amy, pointing ghostly fingers of reproach! Still Amy is engaged. To whom at the particular moment I cannot say, but I fancy to an early one who has lately become a widower. After more exact knowledge I do not care to enquire; for to confess ignorance on the subject, implying that one has treated as a triviality and has forgotten the most important detail of a matter that to her is of vital importance, is to hurt her feelings; while to angle for information is but to entangle oneself. To speak of Him as "Tom," when Tom has belonged for weeks to the dead and buried past, to hastily correct oneself to "Dick" when there hasn't been a Dick for years, clearly not to know that he is now Harry, annoys her even more. In my mother's time we always referred to him as "Dearest." It was the title with which she herself distinguished them all, and it avoided confusion.

"Well, and how's Dearest?" my mother would enquire, opening the door to Amy on the Sunday evening.

"Oh, very well indeed, mum, thank you, and he sends you his respects," or, "Well, not so nicely as I could wish. I'm a little anxious about him, poor dear!"

"When you are married you will be able to take good care of him."

"That's really what he wants, someone to take care of him. It's what they all want, the poor dears."

"And when is it coming off?"

"In the spring, mum." She always chose the spring when possible.

Amy was nice to all men, and to Amy all men were nice. Could she have married a dozen, she might have settled down, with only occasional regrets concerning those left without in the cold. But to ask her to select only one out of so many "poor dears" was to suggest shameful waste of affection.

We had meant to keep our grim secret to ourselves; but to hide one's troubles long from Amy was like keeping cold hands from the fire. Very soon she knew everything that was to be known, drawing it all from my mother as from some overburdened child. Then she put my mother down into a chair and stood over her.

"Now you leave the house and everything connected with it to me, mum," commanded Amy; "you've got something else to do."

And from that day we were in the hands of Amy, and had nothing else to do but praise the Lord for His goodness.

Barbara also found out (from Washburn, I expect), though she said nothing, but came often. Old Hasluck would have come himself, I am sure, had he thought he would be welcome. As it was, he always sent kind messages and presents of fruit and flowers by Barbara, and always welcomed me most heartily whenever she allowed me to see her home.

She brought, as ever, sunshine with her, making all trouble seem far off and shadowy. My mother tended to the fire of love, but Barbara lit the cheerful lamp of laughter.

And with the lessening days my father seemed to grow younger, life lying lighter on him.

One summer's night he and I were walking with Barbara to Poplar station, for sometimes, when he was not looking tired, she would order him to fetch his hat and stick, explaining to him with a caress, "I like them tall and slight and full grown. The young ones, they don't know how to flirt! We will take the boy with us as gooseberry;" and he, pretending to be anxious that my mother did not see, would kiss her hand, and slip out quietly with her arm linked under his. It was admirable the way he would enter into the spirit of the thing.

The last cloud faded from before the moon as we turned the corner, and even the East India Dock Road lay restful in front of us.

"I have always regarded myself," said my father, "as a failure in life, and it has troubled me." I felt him pulled the slightest little bit away from me, as though Barbara, who held his other arm, had drawn him towards her with a swift pressure. "But do you know the idea that has come to me within the last few months? That on the whole I have been successful. I am like a man," continued my father, "who in some deep wood has been frightened, thinking he has lost his way, and suddenly coming to the end of it, finds that by some lucky chance he has been guided to the right point after all. I cannot tell you what a comfort it is to me.

"What is the right point?" asked Barbara.

"Ah, that I cannot tell you," answered my father, with a laugh. "I only know that for me it is here where I am. All the time I thought I was wandering away from it I was drawing nearer to it. It is very wonderful. I am just where I ought to be. If I had only known I never need have worried."

Whether it would have troubled either him or my mother very much even had it been otherwise I cannot say, for Life, so small a thing when looked at beside Death, seemed to have lost all terror for them; but be that as it may, I like to remember that Fortune at the last was kind to my father, prospering his adventures, not to the extent his sanguine nature had dreamt, but sufficiently: so that no fear for our future marred the peaceful passing of his tender spirit.

Or should I award thanks not to Fate, but rather to sweet Barbara, and behind her do I not detect shameless old Hasluck, grinning good-naturedly in the background?

"Now, Uncle Luke, I want your advice. Dad's given me this cheque as a birthday present. I don't want to spend it. How shall I invest it?"

"My dear, why not consult your father?"

"Now, Uncle Luke, dad's a dear, especially after dinner, but you and I know him. Giving me a present is one thing, doing business for me is another. He'd unload on me. He'd never be able to resist the temptation."

My father would suggest, and Barbara would thank him. But a minute later would murmur: "You don't know anything about Argentinos."

My father did not, but Barbara did; to quite a remarkable extent for a young girl.

"That child has insisted on leaving this cheque with me and I have advised her to buy Argentinos," my father would observe after she was gone. "I am going to put a few hundreds into them myself. I hope they will turn out all right, if only for her sake. I have a presentiment somehow that they will."

A month later Barbara would greet him with: "Isn't it lucky we bought Argentinos!"

"Yes; they haven't turned out badly, have they? I had a feeling, you know, for Argentinos."

"You're a genius, Uncle Luke. And now we will sell out and buy Calcuttas, won't we?"

"Sell out? But why?"

"You said so. You said, 'We will sell out in about a month and be quite safe.'"

"My dear, I've no recollection of it."

But Barbara had, and before she had done with him, so had he. And the next day Argentinos would be sold, not any too soon, and Calcuttas bought.

Could money so gained bring a blessing with it? The question would plague my father.

"It's very much like gambling," he would mutter uneasily to himself at each success, "uncommonly like gambling."

"It is for your mother," he would impress upon me. "When she is gone, Paul, put it aside, Keep it for doing good; that may make it clean. Start your own life without any help from it."

He need not have troubled. It went the road that all luck derived however indirectly from old Hasluck ever went. Yet it served good purpose on its way.

But the most marvellous feat, to my thinking, ever accomplished by Barbara was the bearing off of my father and mother to witness "A Voice from the Grave, or the Power of Love, New and Original Drama in five acts and thirteen tableaux."

They had been bred in a narrow creed, both my father and my mother. That Puritan blood flowed in their veins that throughout our land has drowned much harmless joyousness; yet those who know of it only from hearsay do foolishly to speak but ill of it. If ever earnest times should come again, not how to enjoy but how to live being the question, Fate demanding of us to show not what we have but what we are, we may regret that they are fewer among us than formerly, those who trained themselves to despise all pleasure, because in pleasure they saw the subtlest foe to principle and duty. No graceful growth, this Puritanism, for its roots are in the hard, stern facts of life; but it is strong, and from it has sprung all that is worth preserving in the Anglo-Saxon character. Its men feared and its women loved God, and if their words were harsh their hearts were tender. If they shut out the sunshine from their lives it was that their eyes might see better the glory lying beyond; and if their view be correct, that earth's threescore years and ten are but as preparation for eternity, then who shall call them even foolish for turning away their thoughts from its allurements.

"Still, I think I should like to have a look at one, just to see what it is like," argued my father; "one cannot judge of a thing that one knows nothing about."

I imagine it was his first argument rather than his second that convinced my mother.

"That is true," she answered. "I remember how shocked my poor father was when he found me one night at the bedroom window reading Sir Walter Scott by the light of the moon."

"What about the boy?" said my father, for I had been included in the invitation.

"We will all be wicked together," said my mother.

So an evening or two later the four of us stood at the corner of Pigott Street waiting for the 'bus.

"It is a close evening," said my father; "let's go the whole hog and ride outside."

In those days for a lady to ride outside a 'bus was as in these days for a lady to smoke in public. Surely my mother's guardian angel must have betaken himself off in a huff.

"Will you keep close behind and see to my skirt?" answered my mother, commencing preparations. If you will remember that these were the days of crinolines, that the "knife-boards" of omnibuses were then approached by a perpendicular ladder, the rungs two feet apart, you will understand the necessity for such precaution.

Which of us was the most excited throughout that long ride it would be difficult to say. Barbara, feeling keenly her responsibility as prompter and leader of the dread enterprise, sat anxious, as she explained to us afterwards, hoping there would be nothing shocking in the play, nothing to belie its innocent title; pleased with her success so far, yet still fearful of failure, doubtful till the last moment lest we should suddenly repent, and stopping the 'bus, flee from the wrath to come. My father was the youngest of us all. Compared with him I was sober and contained. He fidgeted: people remarked upon it. He hummed. But for the stern eye of a thin young man sitting next to him trying to read a paper, I believe he would have broken out into song. Every minute he would lean across to enquire of my mother: "How are you feeling, all right?" To which my mother would reply with a nod and a smile, She sat very silent herself, clasping and unclasping her hands. As for myself, I remember feeling so sorry for the crowds that passed us on their way home. It was sad to think of the long dull evening that lay before them. I wondered how they could face it.

Our seats were in the front row of the upper circle. The lights were low and the house only half full when we reached them.

"It seems very orderly and, and respectable," whispered my mother. There seemed a touch of disappointment in her tone.

"We are rather early," replied Barbara; "it will be livelier when the band comes in and they turn up the gas."

But even when this happened my mother was not content. "There is so little room for the actors," she complained.

It was explained to her that the green curtain would go up, that the stage lay behind.

So we waited, my mother sitting stiffly on the extreme edge of her seat, holding me tightly by the hand; I believe with some vague idea of flight, should out of that vault-scented gloom the devil suddenly appear to claim us for his own. But before the curtain was quite up she had forgotten him.

You poor folk that go to the theatre a dozen times a year, perhaps oftener, what do you know of plays? You see no drama, you see but middle-aged Mr. Brown, churchwarden, payer of taxes, foolishly pretending to be a brigand; Miss Jones, daughter of old Jones the Chemist, making believe to be a haughty Princess. How can you, a grown man, waste money on a seat to witness such tomfoolery! What we saw was something very different. A young and beautiful girl, true, not a lady by birth, being merely the daughter of an honest yeoman, but one equal in all the essentials of womanhood to the noblest in the land, suffered before our very eyes an amount of misfortune that, had one not seen it for oneself, one would never have believed Fate could have accumulated upon the head of any single individual. Beside her woes our own poor troubles sank into insignificance. We had used to grieve, as my mother in a whisper reminded my father, if now and again we had not been able to afford meat for dinner. This poor creature, driven even from her wretched attic, compelled to wander through the snow without so much as an umbrella to protect her, had not even a crust to eat; and yet never lost her faith in Providence. It was a lesson, as my mother remarked afterwards, that she should never forget. And virtue had been triumphant, let shallow cynics say what they will. Had we not proved it with our own senses? The villain, I think his Christian name, if one can apply the word "Christian" in connection with such a fiend, was Jasper, had never really loved the heroine. He was incapable of love. My mother had felt this before he had been on the stage five minutes, and my father, in spite of protests from callous people behind who appeared to be utterly indifferent to what was going on under their very noses, had agreed with her. What he was in love with was her fortune, the fortune that had been left to her by her uncle in Australia, but about which nobody but the villain knew anything. Had she swerved a hair's breadth from the course of almost supernatural rectitude, had her love for the hero ever weakened, her belief in him, in spite of damning evidence to the contrary, for a moment wavered, then wickedness might have triumphed. How at times, knowing all the facts but helpless to interfere, we trembled, lest deceived by the cruel lies the villain told her; she should yield to importunity. How we thrilled when, in language eloquent though rude, she flung his false love back into his teeth. Yet still we feared. We knew well that it was not the hero who had done the murder. "Poor dear," as Amy would have called him, he was quite incapable of doing anything requiring one-half as much smartness. We knew that it was not he, poor innocent lamb! who had betrayed the lady with the French accent; we had heard her on the subject and had formed a very shrewd conjecture. But appearances, we could not help admitting, were terribly to his disfavour. The circumstantial evidence against him would have hanged an Archbishop. Could she in face of it still retain her faith? There were moments when my mother restrained with difficulty her desire to rise and explain.

Between the acts Barbara would whisper to her that she was not to mind, because it was only a play, and that everything would be sure to come right in the end.

"I know, my dear," my mother would answer, laughing, "it is very foolish of me; I forget. Paul, when you see me getting excited, you must remind me."

But of what use was I in such case! I, who only by holding on to the arms of my seat could keep myself from swarming down on to the stage to fling myself between this noble damsel and her persecutor, this fair-haired, creamy angel in whose presence for the time being I had forgotten even Barbara.

The end came at last. The uncle from Australia was not dead. The villain, bungler as well as knave, had killed the wrong man, somebody of no importance whatever. As a matter of fact, the comic man himself was the uncle from Australia, had been so all along. My mother had had a suspicion of this from the very first. She told us so three times, to make up, I suppose, for not having mentioned it before. How we cheered and laughed, in spite of the tears in our eyes.

By pure accident it happened to be the first night of the piece, and the author, in response to much shouting and whistling, came before the curtain. He was fat and looked commonplace; but I deemed him a genius, and my mother said he had a good face, and waved her handkerchief wildly; while my father shouted "Bravo!" long after everybody else had finished; and people round about muttered "packed house," which I didn't understand at the time, but came to later.

And stranger still, it happened to be before that very same curtain that many years later I myself stepped forth to make my first bow as a playwright. I saw the house but dimly, for on such occasion one's vision is apt to be clouded. All that I saw clearly was in the front row of the second circle, a sweet face laughing though the tears were in her eyes; and she waved to me a handkerchief. And on one side of her stood a gallant gentleman with merry eyes who shouted "Bravo!" and on the other a dreamy-looking lad; but he appeared disappointed, having expected better work from me. And the fourth face I could not see, for it was turned away from me.

Barbara, determined on completeness, insisted upon supper. In those days respectability fed at home; but one resort possible there was, an eating-house with some pretence to gaiety behind St. Clement Danes, and to that she led us. It was a long, narrow room, divided into wooden compartments, after the old coffee-house plan, a gangway down the centre. Now we should call it a dismal hole, and closing the door hasten away. But to Adam, Eve in her Sunday fig-leaves was a stylishly dressed woman; and to my eyes, with its gilded mirrors and its flaring gas, the place seemed a palace.

Barbara ordered oysters, a fish that familiarity with its empty shell had made me curious concerning. Truly no spot on the globe is so rich in oyster shells as the East End of London. A stranger might be led to the impression (erroneous) that the customary lunch of the East End labourer consists of oysters. How they collect there in such quantities is a mystery, though Washburn, to whom I once presented the problem, found no difficulty in solving it to his own satisfaction: "To the rich man the oyster; to the poor man the shell; thus are the Creator's gifts divided among all His creatures; none being sent empty away." For drink the others had stout and I had ginger beer. The waiter, who called me "Sir," advised against this mixture; but among us all the dominating sentiment by this time was that nothing really mattered very much. Afterwards my father called for a cigar and boldly lighted it, though my mother looked anxious; and fortunately perhaps it would not draw. And then it came out that he himself had once written a play.

"You never told me of that," complained my mother.

"It was a long while ago," replied my father; "nothing came of it."

"It might have been a success," said my mother; "you always had a gift for writing."

"I must look it over again," said my father; "I had quite forgotten it. I have an impression it wasn't at all bad."

"It can be of much help," said my mother, "a good play. It makes one think."

We put Barbara into a cab and rode home ourselves inside a 'bus. My mother was tired, so my father slipped his arm round her, telling her to lean against him, and soon she fell asleep with her head upon his shoulder. A coarse-looking wench sat opposite, her man's arm round her likewise, and she also fell asleep, her powdered face against his coat.

"They can do with a bit of nursing, can't they?" said the man with a grin to the conductor.

"Ah, they're just kids," agreed the conductor, sympathetically, "that's what they are, all of 'em, just kids."

So the day ended. But oh, the emptiness of the morrow! Life without a crime, without a single noble sentiment to brighten it! no comic uncles, no creamy angels! Oh, the barrenness and dreariness of life! Even my mother at moments was quite irritable.

We were much together again, my father and I, about this time. Often, making my way from school into the City, I would walk home with him, he leaning on each occasion a little heavier upon my arm. To this day I can always meet and walk with him down the Commercial Road. And on Saturday afternoons, crossing the river to Greenwich, we would climb the hill and sit there talking, or sometimes merely thinking together, watching the dim vast city so strangely still and silent at our feet.

At first I did not grasp the fact that he was dying. The "year to two" of life that Washburn had allowed to him had somehow become converted in my mind to vague years, a fate with no immediate meaning; the meanwhile he himself appeared to grow from day to day in buoyancy. How could I know it was his great heart rising to his need.

The comprehension came to me suddenly. It was one afternoon in early spring. I was on my way to the City to meet him. The Holborn Viaduct was then in building, and the traffic round about was in consequence always much disorganised. The 'bus on which I was riding became entangled in a block at the corner of Snow Hill, and for ten minutes we had been merely crawling, one joint of a long, sinuous serpent moving by short, painful jerks. It came to me while I was sitting there with a sharp spasm of physical pain. I jumped from the 'bus and began to run, and the terror and the hurt of it grew with every step. I ran as if I feared he might be dead before I could reach the office. He was waiting for me with a smile as usual, and I flung myself sobbing into his arms.

I think he understood, though I could explain nothing, but that I had had a fear something had happened to him, for from that time forward he dropped all reserve with me, and talked openly of our approaching parting.

"It might have come to us earlier, my dear boy," he would say with his arm round me, "or it might have been a little later. A year or so one way or the other, what does it matter? And it is only for a little while, Paul. We shall meet again."

But I could not answer him, for clutch them to me as I would, all my beliefs, the beliefs in which I had been bred, the beliefs that until then I had never doubted, in that hour of their first trial, were falling from me. I could not even pray. If I could have prayed for anything, it would have been for my father's life. But if prayer were all powerful, as they said, would our loved ones ever die? Man has not faith enough, they would explain; if he had there would be no parting. So the Lord jests with His creatures, offering with the one hand to snatch back with the other. I flung the mockery from me. There was no firm foothold anywhere. What were all the religions of the word but narcotics with which Humanity seeks to dull its pain, drugs in which it drowns its terrors, faith but a bubble that death pricks.

I do not mean my thoughts took this form. I was little more than a lad, and to the young all thought is dumb, speaking only with a cry. But they were there, vague, inarticulate. Thoughts do not come to us as we grow older. They are with us all our lives. We learn their language, that is all.

One fair still evening it burst from me. We had lingered in the Park longer than usual, slowly pacing the broad avenue leading from the Observatory to the Heath. I poured forth all my doubts and fears, that he was leaving me for ever, that I should never see him again, I could not believe. What could I do to believe?

"I am glad you have spoken, Paul," he said, "it would have been sad had we parted not understanding each other. It has been my fault. I did not know you had these doubts. They come to all of us sooner or later. But we hide them from one another. It is foolish."

"But tell me," I cried, "what can I do? How can I make myself believe?"

"My dear lad," answered my father, "how can it matter what we believe or disbelieve? It will not alter God's facts. Would you liken Him to some irritable schoolmaster, angry because you cannot understand him?"

"What do you believe," I asked, "father, really I mean."

The night had fallen. My father put his arm round me and drew me to him.

"That we are God's children, little brother," he answered, "that what He wills for us is best. It may be life, it may be sleep; it will be best. I cannot think that He will let us die: that were to think of Him as without purpose. But His uses may not be our desires. We must trust Him. 'Though He slay me yet will I trust in Him.'"

We walked awhile in silence before my father spoke again.

"'Now abideth these three, Faith, Hope and Charity', you remember the verse, Faith in God's goodness to us, Hope that our dreams may be fulfiled. But these concern but ourselves, the greatest of all is Charity."

Out of the night-shrouded human hive beneath our feet shone here and there a point of light.

"Be kind, that is all it means," continued my father. "Often we do what we think right, and evil comes of it, and out of evil comes good. We cannot understand, maybe the old laws we have misread. But the new Law, that we love one another, all creatures He has made; that is so clear. And if it be that we are here together only for a little while, Paul, the future dark, how much the greater need have we of one another."

I looked up into my father's face, and the peace that shone from it slid into my soul and gave me strength.

CHAPTER IX.

OF THE FASHIONING OF PAUL.

Loves of my youth, whither are ye vanished? Tubby of the golden locks; Langley of the dented nose; Shamus stout of heart but faint of limb, easy enough to "down," but utterly impossible to make to cry: "I give you best;" Neal the thin; and Dicky, "dicky Dick" the fat; Ballett of the weeping eye; Beau Bunnie lord of many ties, who always fought in black kid gloves; all ye others, ye whose names I cannot recollect, though I well remember ye were very dear to me, whither are ye vanished, where haunt your creeping ghosts? Had one told me then there would come a day I should never see again your merry faces, never hear your wild, shrill whoop of greeting, never feel again the warm clasp of your inky fingers, never fight again nor quarrel with you, never hate you, never love you, could I then have borne the thought, I wonder?

Once, methinks, not long ago, I saw you, Tubby, you with whom so often I discovered the North Pole, probed the problem of the sources of the Nile, (Have you forgotten, Tubby, our secret camping ground beside the lonely waters of the Regent's Park canal, where discussing our frugal meal of toasted elephant's tongue, by the uninitiated mistakable for jumbles, there would break upon our trained hunters' ear the hungry lion or tiger's distant roar, mingled with the melancholy, long-drawn growling of the Polar Bear, growing ever in volume and impatience until half-past four precisely; and we would snatch our rifles, and with stealthy tread and every sense alert make our way through the jungle, until stopped by the spiked fencing round the Zoological Gardens?) I feel sure it was you, in spite of your side whiskers and the greyness and the thinness of your once clustering golden locks. You were hurrying down Throgmorton Street chained to a small black bag. I should have stopped you, but that I had no time to spare, having to catch a train at Liverpool Street and to get shaved on the way. I wonder if you recognised me: you looked at me a little hard, I thought. Gallant, kindly hearted Shamus, you who fought once for half an hour to save a frog from being skinned; they tell me you are now an Income Tax assessor; a man, it is reported, with power of disbelief unusual among even Inland Revenue circles; of little faith, lacking in the charity that thinketh no evil. May Providence direct you to other districts than to mine.

So Time, Nature's handy-man, bustles to and fro about the many rooms, making all things tidy, covers with sweet earth the burnt volcanoes, turns to use the debris of the ages, smoothes again the ground above the dead, heals again the beech bark marred by lovers.

In the beginning I was far from being a favourite with my schoolmates, and this was the first time trouble came to dwell with me. Later, we men and women generally succeed in convincing ourselves that whatever else we may have missed in life, popularity in a greater or less degree we have at all events secured, for without it altogether few of us, I think, would care to face existence. But where the child suffers keener than the man is in finding himself exposed to the cold truth without the protecting clothes of self-deception. My ostracism was painfully plain to me, and, as was my nature, I brooded upon it in silence.

"Can you run?" asked of me one day a most important personage whose name I have forgotten. He was head of the Lower Fourth, a tall youth with a nose like a beak, and the manner of one born to authority. He was the son of a draper in the Edgware Road, and his father failing, he had to be content for a niche in life with a lower clerkship in the Civil Service. But to us youngsters he always appeared a Duke of Wellington in embryo, and under other circumstances might, perhaps, have become one.

"Yes," I answered. As a matter of fact it was my one accomplishment, and rumour of it maybe had reached him.

"Run round the playground twice at your fastest," he commanded; "let me see you."

I clinched my fists and charged off. How grateful I was to him for having spoken to me, the outcast of the class, thus publicly, I could only show by my exertions to please him. When I drew up before him I was panting hard, but I could see that he was satisfied.

"Why don't the fellows like you?" he asked bluntly.

If only I could have stepped out of my shyness, spoken my real thoughts! "0 Lord of the Lower Fourth! You upon whom success, the only success in life worth having, has fallen as from the laps of the gods! You to whom all Lower Fourth hearts turn! tell me the secret of this popularity. How may I acquire it? No price can be too great for me to pay for it. Vain little egoist that I am, it is the sum of my desires, and will be till the long years have taught me wisdom. The want of it embitters all my days. Why does silence fall upon their chattering groups when I draw near? Why do they drive me from their games? What is it shuts me out from them, repels them from me? I creep into the corners and shed scalding tears of shame. I watch with envious eyes and ears all you to whom the wondrous gift is given. What is your secret? Is it Tommy's swagger? Then I will swagger, too, with anxious heart, with mingled fear and hope. But why, why, seeing that in Tommy they admire it, do they wait for me with imitations of cock-a-doodle-do, strut beside me mimicking a pouter pigeon? Is it Dicky's playfulness? Dicky, who runs away with their balls, snatches their caps from off their heads, springs upon their backs when they are least expecting it?

Why should Dicky's reward be laughter, and mine a bloody nose and a widened, deepened circle of dislike? I am no heavier than Dicky; if anything a pound or two lighter. Is it Billy's friendliness? I too would fling my arms about their necks; but from me they angrily wrench themselves free. Is indifference the best plan? I walk apart with step I try so hard to render careless; but none follows, no little friendly arm is slipped through mine. Should one seek to win one's way by kind offices? Ah, if one could! How I would fag for them. I could do their sums for them, I am good at sums, write their impositions for them, gladly take upon myself their punishments, would they but return my service with a little love and, more important still, a little admiration."

But all I could find to say was, sulkily: "They do like me, some of them." I dared not, aloud, acknowledge the truth.

"Don't tell lies," he answered; "you know they don't, none of them." And I hung my head.

"I'll tell you what I'll do," he continued in his lordly way; "I'll give you a chance. We're starting hare and hounds next Saturday; you can be a hare. You needn't tell anybody. Just turn up on Saturday and I'll see to it. Mind, you'll have to run like the devil."

He walked away without waiting for my answer, leaving me to meet Joy running towards me with outstretched hands. The great moment comes to all of us; to the politician, when the Party whip slips from confabulation with the Front Bench to congratulate him, smiling, on his really admirable little speech; to the youthful dramatist, reading in his bed-sitting-room the managerial note asking him to call that morning at eleven; to the subaltern, beckoned to the stirrup of his chief, the moment when the sun breaks through the morning mists, and the world lies stretched before us, our way clear.

Obeying orders, I gave no hint in school of the great fortune that had come to me; but hurrying home, I exploded in the passage before the front door could be closed behind me.

"I am to be a hare because I run so fast. Anybody can be a hound, but there's only two hares, and they all want me. And can I have a jersey? We begin next Saturday. He saw me run. I ran twice round the playground. He said I was splendid! Of course, it's a great honour to be a hare. We start from Hampstead Heath. And may I have a pair of shoes?"

The jersey and the shoes my mother and I purchased that very day, for the fear was upon me that unless we hastened, the last blue and white striped jersey in London might be sold, and the market be empty of running shoes. That evening, before getting into bed, I dressed myself in full costume to admire myself before the glass; and from then till the end of the week, to the terror of my mother, I practised leaping over chairs, and my method of descending stairs was perilous and roundabout. But, as I explained to them, the credit of the Lower Fourth was at stake, and banisters and legs equally of small account as compared with fame and honour; and my father, nodding his head, supported me with manly argument; but my mother added to her prayers another line.

Saturday came. The members of the hunt were mostly boys who lived in the neighbourhood; so the arrangement was that at half-past two we should meet at the turnpike gate outside the Spaniards. I brought my lunch with me and ate it in Regent's Park, and then took the 'bus to the Heath. One by one the others came up. Beyond mere glances, none of them took any notice of me. I was wearing my ordinary clothes over my jersey. I knew they thought I had come merely to see them start, and I hugged to myself the dream of the surprise that was in store for them, and of which I should be the hero. He came, one of the last, our leader and chief, and I sidled up behind him and waited, while he busied himself organising and constructing.

"But we've only got one hare," cried one of them. "We ought to have two, you know, in case one gets blown."

"We've got two," answered the Duke. "Think I don't know what I'm about? Young Kelver's going to be the other one."

Silence fell upon the meet.

"Oh, I say, we don't want him," at last broke in a voice. "He's a muff."

"He can run," explained the Duke.

"Let him run home," came another voice, which was greeted with laughter.

"You'll run home in a minute yourself," threatened the Duke, "if I have any of your cheek. Who's captain here, you or me? Now, young 'un, are you ready?"

I had commenced unbuttoning my jacket, but my hands fell to my side. "I don't want to come," I answered, "if they don't want me."

"He'll get his feet wet," suggested the boy who had spoken first. "Don't spoil him, he's his mother's pet."

"Are you coming or are you not?" shouted the Duke, seeing me still motionless. But the tears were coming into my eyes and would not go back. I turned my face away without speaking.

"All right, stop then," cried the Duke, who, like all authoritative people, was impatient above all things of hesitation. "Here, Keefe, you take the bag and be off. It'll be dark before we start."

My substitute snatched eagerly at the chance, and away went the hares, while I, still keeping my face hid, moved slowly off.

"Cry-baby!" shouted a sharp-eyed youngster.

"Let him alone," growled the Duke; and I went on to where the cedars grew.

I heard them start off a few minutes later with a whoop. How could I go home, confess my disappointment, my shame? My father would be expecting me with many questions, my mother waiting for me with hot water and blankets. What explanation could I give that would not betray my miserable secret?

It was a chill, dismal afternoon, the Heath deserted, a thin rain commencing. I slipped off my shirt and jacket, and rolling them under my arm, trotted off alone, hare and hounds combined in one small carcass, to chase myself sadly by myself.

I see it still, that pathetically ridiculous little figure, jogging doggedly over the dank fields. Mile after mile it runs, the little idiot; jumping, sometimes falling into the muddy ditches: it seems anxious rather than otherwise to get itself into a mess; scrambling through the dripping hedges; swarming over tarry fence and slimy paling. On, on it pants, through Bishop's Wood, by tangled Churchyard Bottom, where now the railway shrieks; down sloppy lanes, bordering Muswell Hill, where now stand rows of jerry-built, prim villas. At intervals it stops an instant to dab its eyes with its dingy little rag of a handkerchief, to rearrange the bundle under its arm, its chief anxiety to keep well out of sight of chance wanderers, to dodge farmhouses, to dart across highroads when nobody is looking. And so tear-smeared and mud-bespattered up the long rise of darkening Crouch End Lane, where to-night the electric light blazes from a hundred shops, and dead beat into the Seven Sisters Road station, there to tear off its soaked jersey; and then home to Poplar, with shameless account of the jolly afternoon that it has spent, of the admiration and the praise that it has won.

You poor, pitiful little brat! Popularity? it is a shadow. Turn your eyes towards it, and it shall ever run before you, escaping you. Turn your back upon it, walk joyously towards the living sun, and it shall follow you. Am I not right? Why, then, do you look at me, your little face twisted into that quizzical grin?

When one takes service with Deceit, one signs a contract that one may not break but under penalty. Maybe it was good for my health, those lonely runs; but oh, they were dreary! By a process of argument not uncommon I persuaded myself that truth was a matter of mere words, that so long as I had actually gone over the ground I described I was not lying. To further satisfy my conscience, I bought a big satchel and scattered from it torn-up paper as I ran.

"And they never catch you?" asked my mother.

"Oh, no, never; they never even get within sight of me."

"Be careful, dear," would advise my mother; "don't overstrain yourself." But I could see that she was proud of me.

And after awhile imagination came to my help, so that often I could hear behind me the sound of pursuing feet, catch through gaps in the trees a sight of a merry, host upon my trail, and would redouble my speed.

Thus, but for Dan, my loneliness would have been unbearable. His friendship was always there for me to creep to, the shadow of a great rock in a weary land. To this day one may always know Dan's politics: they are those of the Party out of power. Always without question one may know the cause that he will champion, the unpopular cause; the man he will defend, the man who is down.

"You are such an un-understandable chap," complained a fellow Clubman to him once in my hearing. "I sometimes ask myself if you have any opinions at all."

"I hate a crowd," was Dan's only confession of faith.

He never claimed anything from me in return for his affection; he was there for me to hold to when I wanted him. When, baffled in all my attempts to win the affections of others, I returned to him for comfort, he gave it me, without even relieving himself of friendly advice. When at length childish success came to me and I needed him less, he was neither hurt nor surprised. Other people, their thoughts, their actions, even when these concerned himself, never troubled him. He loved to bestow, but as to response was strangely indifferent; indeed, if anything, it bored him. His nature appeared to be that of the fountain, which fulfils itself by giving, but is unable to receive.

My popularity came to me unexpectedly after I had given up hoping for it; surprising me, annoying me. Gradually it dawned upon me that my company was being sought.

"Come along, Kelver," would say the spokesman of one group; "we're going part of your way home. You can walk with us."

Maybe I would go with them, but more often, before we reached the gate, the delight of my society would be claimed by a rival troop.

"He's coming with us this afternoon. He promised."

"No, he didn't."

"Yes, he did."

"Well, he ain't, anyhow. See?"

"Oh, isn't he? Who says he isn't?"

"I do."

"Punch his head, Dick!"

"Yes, you do, Jimmy Blake, and I'll punch yours. Come, Kelver."

I might have been some Queen of Beauty offered as prize for knightly contest. Indeed, more than once the argument concluded thus primitively, I being carried off in triumph by the victorious party.

For a period it remained a mystery to me, until I asked explanation of Norval, we called him "Norval," he being one George Grampian: it was our wit. From taking joy in teasing me, Norval had suddenly become one of my greatest admirers. This by itself was difficult enough to understand. He was in the second eleven, and after Dan the best fighter in the lower school. If I could understand Norval's change of attitude all would be plain to me; so when next time, bounding upon me in the cloakroom and slipping his arm into mine, he clamoured for my company to Camden Town, I put the question to him bluntly.

"Why should I walk home with you? Why do you want me?"

"Because we like you."

"But why do you like me?"

"Why! Why, because you're such a funny chap. You say such funny things."

It struck me like a slap in the face. I had thought to reach popularity upon the ladder of heroic qualities. In all the school books I had read,

Leonard or Marmaduke (we had a Marmaduke in the Lower Fifth, they called him Marmalade: in the school books these disasters are not contemplated), won love and admiration by reason of integrity of character, nobility of sentiment, goodness of heart, brilliance of intellect; combined maybe with a certain amount of agility, instinct in the direction of bowling, or aptitude for jumping; but such only by the way. Not one of them had ever said a funny thing, either consciously or unconsciously.

"Don't be disagreeable, Kelver. Come with us and we will let you into the team as an extra. I'll teach you batting."

So I was to be their Fool, I, dreamer of knightly dreams, aspirant to hero's fame! I craved their wonder; I had won their laughter. I had prayed for popularity; it had been granted to me in this guise. Were the gods still the heartless practical jokers poor Midas had found them?

Had my vanity been less I should have flung their gift back in their faces. But my thirst for approbation was too intense. I had to choose: Cut capers and be followed, or walk in dignity, ignored. I chose to cut the capers. As time wore on I found myself striving to cut them quicker, quainter, thinking out funny stories, preparing ingenuous impromptus, twisting all ideas into odd expression.

I had my reward. Before long my company was desired by all the school. But I was never content. I would rather have been the Captain of their football club, even his deputy Vice; would have given all my meed of laughter for stuttering Jerry's one round of applause when in our match against Highbury he knocked up his century, and so won the victory for us by just three.

Till the end I never quite abandoned hope of exchanging my vine leaves for the laurels. I would rise an hour earlier in the morning to practise throwing at broomsticks set up in waste places. At another time, the sport coming into temporary fashion, I wearied body and mind for weeks in vain attempts to acquire skill on stilts. That even fat Tubby could out-distance me upon them saddened my life for months.

A lad there was, a Sixth Form boy, one Wakeham by name, if I remember rightly, who greatly envied me my gift of being able to amuse. He was of the age when the other sex begins to be of importance to a fellow, and the desire had come to him to be regarded as a star of wit among the social circles of Gospel Oak. Need I say that by nature he was a ponderously dull boy.

One afternoon I happened to be the centre of a small group in the playground. I had been holding forth and they had been laughing. Whether I had delivered myself of anything really entertaining or not I cannot say. It made no difference; they had got into the habit of laughing when I talked. Sometimes I would say quite serious things on purpose; they would laugh just the same. Wakeham was among them, his eyes fixed on me, watching me as boys watch a conjurer in the hope of finding out "how he does it." Later in the afternoon he slipped his arm through mine, and drew me away into an empty corner of the ground.

"I say, Kelver," he broke out, the moment we were beyond hearing, "you really are funny!"

It gave me no pleasure. If he had told me that he admired my bowling I might not have believed him, but should have loved him for it.

"So are you," I answered savagely, "only you don't know it."

"No, I'm not," he replied. "Wish I was. I say, Kelver", he glanced round to see that no one was within earshot, "do you think you could teach me to be funny?"

I was about to reply with conviction in the negative when an idea occurred to me. Wakeham was famous among us for one thing; he could, inserting two fingers in his mouth, produce a whistle capable of confusing dogs a quarter of a mile off, and of causing people near at hand to jump from six to eighteen inches into the air.

This accomplishment of his I envied him as keenly as he envied me mine. I did not admire it; I could not see the use of it. Generally speaking, it called forth irritation rather than affection. A purple-faced old gentleman, close to whose ear he once performed, promptly cuffed his head for it; and for so doing was commended by the whole street as a public benefactor. Drivers of vehicles would respond by flicking at him, occasionally with success. Even youth, from whom sympathy might have been expected, appeared impelled, if anything happened to be at all handy, to take it up and throw it at him. My own social circle would, I knew, regard it as a vulgar accomplishment, and even Wakeham himself dared not perform it in the hearing of his own classmates. That any human being should have desired to acquire it seems incomprehensible. Yet for weeks in secret I had wrestled to produce the hideous sound. Why? For three reasons, so far as I can analyse this youngster of whom I am writing:

Firstly, here was a means of attracting attention; secondly, it was something that somebody else could do and that he couldn't; thirdly, it was a thing for which he evidently had no natural aptitude whatever, and therefore a thing to acquire which his soul yearned the more. Had a boy come across his path, clever at walking on his hands with his heels in the air, Master Paul Kelver would in all probability have broken his neck in attempts to copy and excel. I make no apologies for the brat: I merely present him as a study for the amusement of a world of wiser boys and men.

I struck a bargain with young Wakeham; I undertook to teach him to be funny in return for his teaching me this costermonger's whistle.

Each of us strove conscientiously to impart knowledge. Neither of us succeeded. Wakeham tried hard to be funny; I tried hard to whistle. He did all I told him; I followed his instructions implicitly. The result was the feeblest of wit and the feeblest of whistles.

"Do you think anybody would laugh at that?" Wakeham would pathetically enquire at the termination of his supremest effort. And honestly I would have to confess I did not think any living being would.

"How far off do you think anyone could hear that?" I would demand anxiously, on recovering sufficient breath to speak at all.

"Well, it would depend upon whether you knew it was coming," Wakeham would reply kindly, not wishing to discourage me.

We abandoned the scheme by mutual consent at about the end of a fortnight.

"I suppose it's something that you've got to have inside you," I suggested to Wakeham in consolation.

"I don't think the roof of your mouth can be quite the right shape for it," concluded Wakeham.

My success as story-teller, commentator, critic, jester, revived my childish ambition towards authorship. My first stirrings in this direction I cannot rightly place. I remember when very small falling into a sunk dust-bin, a deep hole, rather, into which the gardener shot his rubbish. The fall twisted my ankle so that I could not move; and the time being evening and my prison some distance from the house, my predicament loomed large before me. Yet one consolation remained with me: the incident would be of value to me in the autobiography upon which I was then engaged. I can distinctly recollect lying on my back among decaying leaves and broken glass, framing my account. "On this day a strange adventure befell me. Walking in the garden, all unheeding, I suddenly", I did not want to add the truth, "tumbled into a dust-hole, six feet square, that anyone but a moon calf might have seen." I puzzled to evolve a more dignified situation. The dust-bin became a cavern, the entrance to which had been artfully concealed; the six or seven feet I had really fallen, "an endless descent, terminating in a vast and gloomy chamber." I was divided between opposing desires: One, for rescue followed by sympathy and supper; the other, for the alarming experience of a night of terror where I lay. Nature conquering Art, I yelled; and the episode terminated prosaically with a warm bath and arnica. But from it I judge that desire for the woes and perils of authorship was with me somewhat early.

Of my many other dreams I would speak freely, discussing them at length with sympathetic souls, but concerning this one ambition I was curiously reticent. Only to two, my mother and a grey-bearded Stranger, did I ever breathe a word of it. Even from my father I kept it a secret, close comrades in all else though we were. He would have talked of it much and freely, dragged it into the light of day; and from this I shrank.

My talk with the Stranger came about in this wise. One evening I had taken a walk to Victoria Park, a favourite haunt of mine at summer time. It was a fair and peaceful evening, and I fell a-wandering there in pleasant reverie, until the waning light hinted to me the question of time. I looked about me. Only one human being was in sight, a man with his back towards me, seated upon a bench overlooking the ornamental water.

I drew nearer. He took no notice of me, and interested, though why, I could not say, I seated myself beside him at the other end of the bench. He was a handsome, distinguished-looking man, with wonderfully bright, clear eyes and iron-grey hair and beard. I might have thought him a sea captain, of whom many were always to be met with in that neighbourhood, but for his hands, which were crossed upon his stick, and which were white and delicate as a woman's. He turned his face and glanced at me. I fancied that his lips beneath the grey moustache smiled; and instinctively I edged a little nearer to him.

"Please, sir," I said, after awhile, "could you tell me the right time?"

"Twenty minutes to eight," he answered, looking at his watch. And his voice drew me towards him even more than had his beautiful strong face. I thanked him, and we fell back into silence.

"Where do you live?" he turned and suddenly asked me.

"Oh, only over there," I answered, with a wave of my arm towards the chimney-fringed horizon behind us. "I needn't be in till half-past eight. I like this Park so much," I added, "I often come and sit here of an evening.'

"Why do you like to come and sit here?" he asked. "Tell me."

"Oh, I don't know," I answered. "I think."

I marvelled at myself. With strangers generally I was shy and silent; but the magic of his bright eyes seemed to have loosened my tongue.

I told him my name; that we lived in a street always full of ugly sounds, so that a gentleman could not think, not even in the evening time, when Thought goes a-visiting.

"Mamma does not like the twilight time," I confided to him. "It always makes her cry. But then mamma is not very young, you know, and has had a deal of trouble; and that makes a difference, I suppose."

He laid his hand upon mine. We were sitting nearer to each other now. "God made women weak to teach us men to be tender," he said. "But you, Paul, like this 'twilight time'?"

"Yes," I answered, "very much. Don't you?"

"And why do you like it?" he asked.

"Oh," I answered, "things come to you."

"What things?"

"Oh, fancies," I explained to him. "I am going to be an author when I grow up, and write books."

He took my hand in his and shook it gravely, and then returned it to me. "I, too, am a writer of books," he said.

And then I knew what had drawn me to him.

So for the first time I understood the joy of talking "shop" with a fellow craftsman. I told him my favourite authors, Scott, and Dumas, and Victor Hugo; and to my delight found they were his also; he agreeing with me that real stories were the best, stories in which people did things.

"I used to read silly stuff once," I confessed, "Indian tales and that sort of thing, you know. But mamma said I'd never be able to write if I read that rubbish."

"You will find it so all through life, Paul," he replied. "The things that are nice are rarely good for us. And what do you read now?"

"I am reading Marlowe's Plays and De Quincey's Confessions just now," I confided to him.

"And do you understand them?"

"Fairly well," I answered. "Mamma says I'll like them better as I go on. I want to learn to write very, very well indeed," I admitted to him; "then I'll be able to earn heaps of money."

He smiled. "So you don't believe in Art for Art's sake, Paul?"

I was puzzled. "What does that mean?" I asked.

"It means in our case, Paul," he answered, "writing books for the pleasure of writing books, without thinking of any reward, without desiring either money or fame."

It was a new idea to me. "Do many authors do that?" I asked.

He laughed outright this time. It was a delightful laugh. It rang through the quiet Park, awaking echoes; and caught by it, I laughed with him.

"Hush!" he said; and he glanced round with a whimsical expression of fear, lest we might have been overheard. "Between ourselves, Paul," he continued, drawing me more closely towards him and whispering, "I don't think any of us do. We talk about it. But I'll tell you this, Paul; it is a trade secret and you must remember it: No man ever made money or fame but by writing his very best. It may not be as good as somebody else's best, but it is his best. Remember that, Paul."

I promised I would.

"And you must not think merely of the money and the fame, Paul," he added the next moment, speaking more seriously. "Money and fame are very good things, and only hypocrites pretend to despise them. But if you write books thinking only of money, you will be disappointed. It is earned easier in other ways. Tell me, that is not your only idea?"

I pondered. "Mamma says it is a very noble calling, authorship," I remembered, "and that any one ought to be very proud and glad to be able to write books, because they give people happiness and make them forget things; and that one ought to be very good if one is going to be an author, so as to be worthy to help and teach others."

"And do you try to be good, Paul?" he enquired.

"Yes," I answered; "but it's very hard to be quite good, until of course you're grown up."

He smiled, but more to himself than to me. "Yes," he said, "I suppose it is difficult to be good until you are grown up. Perhaps we shall all of us be good when we're quite grown up." Which, from a gentleman with a grey beard, appeared to me a puzzling observation.

"And what else does mamma say about literature?" he asked. "Can you remember?"

Again I pondered, and her words came back to me. "That he who can write a great book is greater than a king; that the gift of being able to write is given to anybody in trust; that an author should never forget he is God's servant."

He sat for awhile without speaking, his chin resting on his folded hands supported by his gold-topped cane. Then he turned and laid a hand upon my shoulder, and his clear, bright eyes were close to mine.

"Your mother is a wise lady, Paul," he said. "Remember her words always. In later life let them come back to you; they will guide you better than the chatter of the Clubs."

"And what modern authors do you read?" he asked after a silence: "any of them, Thackeray, Bulwer Lytton, Dickens?"

"I have read 'The Last of the Barons,'" I told him; "I like that. And I've been to Barnet and seen the church. And some of Mr. Dickens'."

"And what do you think of Mr. Dickens?" he asked. But he did not seem very interested in the subject. He had picked up a few small stones, and was throwing them carefully into the water.

"I like him very much," I answered; "he makes you laugh."

"Not always?" he asked. He stopped his stone-throwing, and turned sharply towards me.

"Oh, no, not always," I admitted; "but I like the funny bits best. I like so much where Mr. Pickwick"

"Oh, damn Mr. Pickwick!" he said.

"Don't you like him?" I asked.

"Oh, yes, I like him well enough, or used to," he replied; "I'm a bit tired of him, that's all. Does your mamma like Mr., Mr. Dickens?"

"Not the funny parts," I explained to him. "She thinks he is occasionally"

"I know," he interrupted, rather irritably, I thought; "a trifle vulgar."

It surprised me that he should have guessed her exact words. "I don't think mamma has much sense of humour," I explained to him. "Sometimes she doesn't even see papa's jokes."

At that he laughed again. "But she likes the other parts?" he enquired, "the parts where Mr. Dickens isn't vulgar?"

"Oh, yes," I answered. "She says he can be so beautiful and tender, when he likes."

Twilight was deepening. It occurred to me to enquire of him again the time.

"Just over the quarter," he answered, looking at his watch.

"I'm so sorry," I said. "I must go now."

"So am I sorry, Paul," he answered. "Perhaps we shall meet again. Good-bye." Then as our hands touched: "You have never asked me my name, Paul," he reminded me.

"Oh, haven't I?" I answered.

"No, Paul," he replied, "and that makes me think of your future with hope. You are an egotist, Paul; and that is the beginning of all art."

And after that he would not tell me his name. "Perhaps next time we meet," he said. "Good-bye, Paul. Good luck to you!"

So I went my way. Where the path winds out of sight I turned. He was still seated upon the bench, but his face was towards me, and he waved his hand to me. I answered with a wave of mine. And then the intervening boughs and bushes gradually closed in around me. And across the rising mist there rose the hoarse, harsh cry:

"All out! All out!"

CHAPTER X.

IN WHICH PAUL IS SHIPWRECKED, AND CAST INTO DEEP WATERS.

My father died, curiously enough, on the morning of his birthday. We had not expected the end to arrive for some time, and at first did not know that it had come.

"I have left him sleeping," said my mother, who had slipped out very quietly in her dressing-gown. "Washburn gave him a draught last night. We won't disturb him."

So we sat round the breakfast table, speaking in low tones, for the house was small and flimsy, all sound easily heard through its thin partitions. Afterwards my mother crept upstairs, I following, and cautiously opened the door a little way.

The blinds were still down, and the room dark. It seemed a long time that my mother stood there listening, her ear against the jar. The first costermonger, a girl's voice, it sounded, passed, crying shrilly: "Watercreases, fine fresh watercreases with your breakfast-a'penny a bundle watercreases;" and further off a hoarse youth was wailing: "Mee-ilk-mee-ilk-oi."

Inch by inch my mother opened the door wider and we stole in. He was lying with his eyes still closed, the lips just slightly parted. I had never seen death before, and could not realise it. All that I could see was that he looked even younger than I had ever seen him look before. By slow degrees only, it came home to me, the knowledge that he was gone away from us. For days, for weeks, I would hear his step behind me in the street, his voice calling to me, see his face among the crowds, and hastening to meet him, stand bewildered because it had mysteriously disappeared. But at first I felt no pain whatever.

To my mother it was but a short parting. Into her placid faith had never fallen fear nor doubt. He was waiting for her. In God's good time they would meet again. What need of sorrow! Without him the days passed slowly: the house must ever be a little dull when the good man's away. But that was all. So my mother would speak of him always, of his dear, kind ways, of his oddities and follies we loved so to recall, not through tears, but smiles, thinking of him not as of one belonging to the past, but as of one beckoning to her from the future.

We lived on still in the old house though ever planning to move, for the great brick monster had crept closer round about us year by year, devouring in his progress all things fair. Field and garden, tree and cottage, time-mellowed house suggesting story, kind hedgerow hiding hideousness beyond, the few spots yet in that doomed land lingering to remind one of the sunshine, one by one had he scrunched them between his ugly teeth. A world apart, this east end of London, this ghetto of the poor for ever growing, dreariness added year by year to dreariness, hopelessness stretching ever farther its long, shrivelled arms, these endless rows of reeking cells where London herds her slaves. Often of a misty afternoon when we knew that without this city of the dead life was stirring in the sunshine, we would fare forth to house-hunt in pleasant suburbs, now themselves added to the weary catacomb of narrow streets, to Highgate, then a tiny town connected by a coach with leafy Holloway; to Hampstead with its rows of ancient red-brick houses, from whose wind-blown heath one saw beyond the woods and farms, far London's domes and spires, to Wood Green among the pastures, where smock-coated labourers discussed their politics and ale beneath wide-spreading elms; to Hornsey, then a village consisting of an ivy-covered church and one grass-bordered way. But though we often saw "the very thing for us" and would discuss its possibilities from every point of view and find them good, we yet delayed.

"We must think it over," would say my mother; "there is no hurry; for some reasons I shall be sorry to leave Poplar."

"For what reasons, mother?"

"Oh, well, no particular reason, Paul. Only we have lived there so long, you know. It will be a wrench leaving the old house."

To the making of man go all things, even to the instincts of the clinging vine. We fling our tendrils round what is the nearest castle-keep or pig-stye wall, rain and sunshine fastening them but firmer. Dying Sir Walter Scott, do you remember? hastening home from Italy, fearful lest he might not be in time to breathe again the damp mists of the barren hills. An ancient dame I knew, they had carried her from her attic in slumland that she might be fanned by the sea breezes, and the poor old soul lay pining for what she called her "home." Wife, mother, widow, she had lived there till the alley's reek smelt good to her nostrils, till its riot was the voices of her people. Who shall understand us save He who fashioned us?

So the old house held us to its dismal bosom; and not until within its homely but unlovely arms, first my aunt, and later on my mother had died, and I had said good-bye to Amy, crying in the midst of littered emptiness, did I leave it.

My aunt died as she had lived, grumbling.

"You will be glad to get rid of me, all of you!" she said, dropping for the first and last time I can recollect into the retort direct; "and I can't say I shall be very sorry to go myself. It hasn't been my idea of life."

Poor old lady! That was only a couple of weeks before the end. I do not suppose she guessed it was so certain or perhaps she might have been more sentimental.

"Don't be foolish," said my mother, "you're not going to die!"

"What's the use of talking like an idiot," retorted my aunt, "I've got to do it some time. Why not now, when everything's all ready for it. It isn't as if I was enjoying myself."

"I am sure we do all we can for you," said my mother. "I know you do," replied my aunt. "I'm a burden to you. I always have been."

"Not a burden," corrected my mother.

"What does the woman call it then," snapped back my aunt. "Does she reckon I've been a sunbeam in the house? I've been a trial to everybody. That's what I was born for; it's my metier."

My mother put her arms about the poor old soul and kissed her. "We should miss you very much," she said.

"I'm sure I hope they all will!" answered my aunt. "It's the only thing I've got to leave 'em, worth having."

My mother laughed.

"Maybe it's been a good thing for you, Maggie," grumbled my aunt; "if it wasn't for cantankerous, disagreeable people like me, gentle, patient people like you wouldn't get any practice. Perhaps, after all, I've been a blessing to you in disguise."

I cannot honestly say we ever wished her back; though we certainly did miss her, missed many a joke at her oddities, many a laugh at her cornery ways. It takes all sorts, as the saying goes, to make a world. Possibly enough if only we perfect folk were left in it we would find it uncomfortably monotonous.

As for Amy, I believe she really regretted her.

"One never knows what's good for one till one's lost it," sighed Amy.

"I'm glad to think you liked her," said my mother.

"You see, mum," explained Amy, "I was one of a large family; and a bit of a row now and again cheers one up, I always think. I'll be losing the power of my tongue if something doesn't come along soon."

"Well, you are going to be married in a few weeks now," my mother reminded her.

But Amy remained despondent. "They're poor things, the men, at a few words, the best of them," she replied. "As likely as not just when you're getting interested you turn round to find that they've put on their hat and gone out."

My mother and I were very much alone after my aunt's death. Barbara had gone abroad to put the finishing touches to her education, to learn the tricks of the Nobs' trade, as old Hasluck phrased it; and I had left school and taken employment with Mr. Stillwood, without salary, the idea being that I should study for the law.

"You are in luck's way, my boy, in luck's way," old Mr. Gadley had assured me. "To have commenced your career in the office of Stillwood, Waterhead and Royal will be a passport for you anywhere. It will stamp you, my boy."

Mr. Stillwood himself was an extremely old and feeble gentleman, so old and feeble it seemed strange that he, a wealthy man, had not long ago retired.

"I am always meaning to," he explained to me one day soon after my advent in his office. "When your poor father came to me he told me very frankly the sad fact, that he had only a few more years to live. 'Mr. Kelver,' I answered him, 'do not let that trouble you, so far as I am concerned. There are one or two matters in the office I should like to see cleared up, and in these you can help me. When they are completed I shall retire! Yet, you see, I linger on. I am like the old hackney coach horse, Mr. Weller, or is it Mr. Jingle, tells us of; if the shafts were drawn away I should probably collapse. So I jog on, I jog on.'"

He had married late in life a common woman much younger than himself, who had brought to him a horde of needy and greedy relatives, and no doubt, as a refuge from her noisy neighbourhood, the daily peace of Lombard Street was welcome to him. We saw her occasionally. She was one of those blustering, "managing" women who go through life under the impression that making a disturbance is somehow "putting things to rights." Ridiculously ashamed of her origin, she sought to hide it under what her friends assured her was the air of a duchess, but which, as a matter of fact, resembled rather the Sunday manners of an elderly barmaid. Mr. Gadley alone was not afraid of her; but, on the contrary, kept her always very much in fear of him, often speaking to her with refreshing candour. He had known her in the days it was her desire should be buried in oblivion, and had always resented as a personal insult her entry into the old established aristocratic firm of Stillwood & Co.

Her history was peculiar. Mr. Stillwood, when a blase man about town, verging on forty, had first seen her, then a fair-haired, ethereal-looking child, in spite of her dirt, playing in the gutter. To his lasting self-reproach it was young Gadley himself, accompanying his employer home from Westminster, who had drawn Mr. Stillwood's attention to the girl by boxing her ears for having, as he passed, slapped his face with a convenient sprat. Stillwood, acting on the impulse of the moment, had taken the child by the hand and dragged her, unwilling, to her father's place of business, a small coal shed in the Horseferry Road. The arrangement he there made amounted practically to the purchase of the child. She was sent abroad to school and the coal shed closed. On her return, ten years later, a big, handsome young woman, he married her, and learned at leisure the truth of the old saying, "what's bred in the bone will come out in the flesh," scrub it and paint it and hide it away under fine clothes as you will.

Her constant complaint against her husband was that he was only a solicitor, a profession she considered vulgar; and nothing "riled" old Gadley more than hearing her views upon this point.

"It's not fair to the gals," I once heard her say to him. I was working in the next room, with the door not quite closed, added to which she talked at the top of her voice on all subjects. "What real gentleman, I should like to know, is going to marry the daughter of a City attorney? As I told him years ago, he ought to have retired and gone into the House."

"The very thing your poor father used to talk of doing whenever things were going a bit queer in the retail coal and potato business," grunted old Gadley.

Mrs. Stillwood called him a "low beast" in her most aristocratic tones, and swept out of the room.

Not that old Stillwood himself ever expressed fondness for the law.

"I am not at all sure, Kelver," I remember his saying to me on one occasion, "that you have done wisely in choosing the law. It makes one regard humanity morally as the medical profession regards it physically: as universally unsound. You suspect everybody of being a rogue. When people are behaving themselves, we lawyers hear nothing of them. All we hear of is roguery, trickery and hypocrisy. It deteriorates the character, Kelver. We live in a perpetual atmosphere of transgression. I sometimes fancy it may be infectious."

"It does not seem to have infected you, sir," I replied; for, as I think I have already mentioned, the firm of Stillwood, Waterhead and Royal was held in legal circles as the synonym for rectitude of dealing quite old-fashioned.

"I hope not, Kelver, I hope not," the old gentleman replied; "and yet, do you know, I sometimes suspect myself, wonder if I may not perhaps be a scamp without realising it. A rogue, you know, Kelver, can always explain himself into an honest man to his own satisfaction. A scamp is never a scamp to himself."

His words for the moment alarmed me, for, acting on old Gadley's advice, I had persuaded my mother to put all her small capital into Mr. Stillwood's hands for re-investment, a transaction that had resulted in substantial increase of our small income. But, looking into his smiling eyes, my momentary fear vanished.

Laughing, he laid his hand upon my shoulder. "One person always be suspicious of, Kelver, yourself. Nobody can do you so much harm as yourself."

Of Washburn we saw more and more. "Hal" we both called him now, for removing with his gentle, masterful hands my mother's shyness from about her, he had established himself almost as one of the family, my mother regarding him as she might some absurdly bearded boy entrusted to her care without his knowing it, I looking up to him as to some wonderful elder brother.

"You rest me, Mrs. Kelver," he would say, lighting his pipe and sinking down into the deep leathern chair that always waited for him in our parlour. "Your even voice, your soft eyes, your quiet hands, they soothe me."

"It is good for a man," he would say, looking from one to the other of us through the hanging smoke, "to test his wisdom by two things: the face of a good woman, and the ear of a child, I beg your pardon, Paul, of a young man. A good woman's face is the white sunlight. Under the gas-lamps who shall tell diamond from paste? Bring it into the sunlight: does it stand that test? Then it is good. And the children! they are the waiting earth on which we fling our store. Is it chaff and dust or living seed? Wait and watch. I shower my thoughts over our Paul, Mrs. Kelver. They seem to me brilliant, deep, original. The young beggar swallows them, forgets them. They were rubbish. Then I say something that dwells with him, that grows. Ah, that was alive, that was a seed. The waiting earth, it can make use only of what is true."

"You should marry, Hal," my mother would say. It was her panacea for all mankind.

"I would, Mrs. Kelver," he answered her on one occasion, "I would to-morrow if I could marry half a dozen women. I should make an ideal husband for half a dozen wives. One I should neglect for five days, and be a burden to upon the sixth."

From any other than Hal my mother would have taken such a remark, made even in jest, as an insult to her sex. But Hal's smile was a coating that could sugar any pill.

"I am not one man, Mrs. Kelver, I am half a dozen. If I were to marry one wife she would be married to six husbands. It is too many for any woman to manage."

"Have you never fallen in love?" asked my mother.

"Three of me have, but on each occasion the other five of me out-voted him."

"You're sure six would be sufficient?" queried my mother, smiling.

"Just the right number, Mrs. Kelver. There is one of me must worship, adore a woman madly, abjectly; grovel before her like the Troubadour before his Queen of Song, eat her slipper, drink the water she has washed in, scourge himself before her window, die for a kiss of her glove flung down with a laugh. She must be scornful, contemptuous, cruel. There is another I would cherish, a tender, yielding creature, one whose face would light at my coming, cloud at my going; one to whom I should be a god. There is a third I, a child of Pan, an ugly little beast, Mrs. Kelver; horns on head and hoofs on feet, leering through the wood, seeking its fit mate. And a fourth would wed a wholesome, homely wench, deep of bosom, broad of hip; fit mother of a sturdy brood. A fifth could only be content with a true friend, a comrade wise and witty, a sharer and understander of all joys and thoughts and feelings. And a last, Mrs. Kelver, yearns for a woman pure and sweet, clothed in love and crowned with holiness. Shouldn't we be a handful, Mrs. Kelver, for any one woman in an eight-roomed house?"

But my mother was not to be discouraged. "You will find the woman one day, Hal, who will be all of them to you, all of them that are worth having, that is. And your eight-roomed house will be a kingdom!"

"A man is many, and a woman but one," answered Hal.

"That is what men say who are too blind to see more than one side of a woman," retorted my mother, a little sharply; for the honour and credit of her own sex in all things was very dear to my mother. And indeed this I have learned, that the flag of Womanhood you shall ever find upheld by all true women, flouted only by the false. For a judge in petticoats is ever but a witness in a wig.

Hal laid aside his pipe and leant forward in his chair. "Now tell us, Mrs. Kelver, for our guidance, we two young bachelors, what must the lover of a young girl be?"

Always very serious on this subject of love, my mother answered gravely: "She asks for the whole of a man, Hal, not merely for a sixth, nor any other part of him. She is a child asking for a lover to whom she can look up, who will teach her, guide her, protect her. She is a queen demanding homage, and yet he is her king whom it is her joy to serve. She asks to be his partner, his fellow-worker, his playmate, and at the same time she loves to think of him as her child, her big baby she must take care of. Whatever he has to give she has also to respond with. You need not marry six wives, Hal; you will find your six in one."

"'As the water to the vessel, woman shapes herself to man;' an old heathen said that three thousand years ago, and others have repeated him; that is what you mean."

"I don't like that way of putting it," answered my mother. "I mean that as you say of man, so in every true woman is contained all women. But to know her completely you must love her with all love."

Sometimes the talk would be of religion, for my mother's faith was no dead thing that must be kept ever sheltered from the air, lest it crumble.

One evening "Who are we that we should live?" cried Hal. "The spider is less cruel; the very pig less greedy, gluttonous and foul; the tiger less tigerish; our cousin ape less monkeyish. What are we but savages, clothed and ashamed, nine-tenths of us?"

"But Sodom and Gomorrah," reminded him my mother, "would have been spared for the sake of ten just men."

"Much more sensible to have hurried the ten men out, leaving the remainder to be buried with all their abominations under their own ashes," growled Hal.

"And we shall be purified," continued my mother, "the evil in us washed away."

"Why have made us ill merely to mend us? If the Almighty were so anxious for our company, why not have made us decent in the beginning?" He had just come away from a meeting of Poor Law Guardians, and was in a state of dissatisfaction with human nature generally.

"It is His way," answered my mother. "The precious stone lies hid in clay. He has His purpose."

"Is the stone so very precious?"

"Would He have taken so much pains to fashion it if it were not? You see it all around you, Hal, in your daily practice, heroism, self-sacrifice, love stronger than death. Can you think He will waste it, He who uses again even the dead leaf?"

"Shall the new leaf remember the new flower?"

"Yes, if it ever knew it. Shall memory be the only thing to die?"

Often of an evening I would accompany Hal upon his rounds. By the savage tribe he both served and ruled he had come to be regarded as medicine man and priest combined. He was both their tyrant and their slave, working for them early and late, yet bullying them unmercifully, enforcing his commands sometimes with vehement tongue, and where that would not suffice with quick fists; the counsellor, helper, ruler, literally of thousands. Of income he could have made barely enough to live upon; but few men could have enjoyed more sense of power; and that I think it was that held him to the neighbourhood.

"Nature laid me by and forgot me for a couple of thousand years," was his own explanation of himself. "Born in my proper period, I should have climbed to chieftainship upon uplifted shields. I might have been an Attila, an Alaric. Among the civilised one can only climb by crawling, and I am too impatient to crawl. Here I am king at once by force of brain and muscle." So in Poplar he remained, poor in fees but rich in honour.

The love of justice was a passion with him. The oppressors of the poor knew and feared him well. Injustice once proved before him, vengeance followed sure. If the law would not help, he never hesitated to employ lawlessness, of which he could always command a satisfactory supply. Bumble might have the Board of Guardians at his back, Shylock legal support for his pound of flesh; but sooner or later the dark night brought punishment, a ducking in dock basin or canal, "Brutal Assault Upon a Respected Resident" (according to the local papers), the "miscreants" always making and keeping good their escape, for he was an admirable organiser.

One night it seemed to him necessary that a child should go at once into the Infirmary.

"It ain't no use my taking her now," explained the mother, "I'll only get bullyragged for disturbing 'em. My old man was carried there three months ago when he broke his leg, but they wouldn't take him in till the morning."

"Oho! oho! oho!" sang Hal, taking the child up in his arms and putting on his hat. "You follow me; we'll have some sport. Tally ho! tally ho!" And away we went, Hal heading our procession through the streets, shouting a rollicking song, the baby staring at him openmouthed.

"Now ring," cried Hal to the mother on our reaching the Workhouse gate. "Ring modestly, as becomes the poor ringing at the gate of Charity." And the bell tinkled faintly.

"Ring again!" cried Hal, drawing back into the shadow; and at last the wicket opened.

"Oh, if you please, sir, my baby"

"Blast your baby!" answered a husky voice, "what d'ye mean by coming here this time of night?"

"Please, sir, I'm afraid it's dying, and the Doctor"

The man was no sentimentalist, and to do him justice made no hypocritical pretence of being one. He consigned the baby and its mother and the doctor to Hell, and the wicket would have closed but for the point of Hal's stick.

"Open the gate!" roared Hal. It was idle pretending not to hear Hal anywhere within half a mile of him when he filled his lungs for a cry. "Open it quick, you blackguard! You gross vat-load of potato spirit, you"

That the Governor should speak a language familiar to the governed was held by the Romans, born rulers of men, essential to authority. This theory Hal also maintained. His command of idiom understood by his people was one of his rods of power. In less time than it took the trembling porter to loosen the bolts, Hal had presented him with a word picture of himself, as seen by others, that must have lessened his self-esteem.

"I didn't know as it was you, Doctor," explained the man.

"No, you thought you had only to deal with some helpless creature you could bully. Stir your fat carcass, you ugly cur! I'm in a hurry."

The House Surgeon was away, but an attendant or two were lounging about, unfortunately for themselves, for Hal, being there, took it upon himself to go round the ward setting crooked things straight; and a busy and alarming time they had of it. Not till a couple of hours later did he fling himself forth again, having enjoyed himself greatly.

A gentleman came to reside in the district, a firm believer in the wisdom of the couplet: "A woman, a spaniel and a walnut tree, The more you beat them the better they be." The spaniel and the walnut tree he did not possess, so his wife had the benefit of his undivided energies. Whether his treatment had improved her morally, one cannot say; her evident desire to do her best may have been natural or may have been assisted; but physically it was injuring her. He used to beat her about the head with his strap, his argument being that she always seemed half asleep, and that this, for the time being, woke her up. Sympathisers brought complaint to Hal, for the police in that neighbourhood are to keep the streets respectable. With the life in the little cells that line them they are no more concerned than are the scavengers of the sewers with the domestic arrangements of the rats.

"What's he like?" asked Hal.

"He's a big 'un," answered the woman who had come with the tale, "and he's good with his fists, I've seen him. But there's no getting at him. He's the sort to have the law on you if you interfere with him, and she's the sort to help him."

"Any likely time to catch him at it?" asked Hal.

"Saturdays it's as regular as early closing," answered the woman, "but you might have to wait a bit."

"I'll wait in your room, granny, next Saturday," suggested Hal.

"All right," agreed the woman, "I'll risk it, even if I do get a bloody head for it."

So that week end we sat very still on two rickety chairs listening to a long succession of sharp, cracking sounds that, had one not known, one might have imagined produced by some child monotonously exploding percussion caps, each one followed by an answering groan. Hal never moved, but sat smoking his pipe, an ugly smile about his mouth. Only once he opened his lips, and then it was to murmur to himself: "And God blessed them and said unto them, Be fruitful and multiply."

The horror ceased at last, and later we heard the door unlock and a man's foot upon the landing above. Hal beckoned to me, and swiftly we slipped out and down the creaking stairs. He opened the front door, and we waited in the evil-smelling little passage. The man came towards us whistling. He was a powerfully built fellow, rather good-looking, I remember. He stopped abruptly upon catching sight of Hal, who stood crouching in the shadow of the door.

"What are you doing here?" he demanded.

"Waiting to pull your nose!" answered Hal, suiting the action to the word. And then laughing he ran down the street, I following.

The man gave chase, calling to us with a string of imprecations to stop. But Hal only ran the faster, though after a street or two he slackened, and the man gained on us a little.

So we continued, the distance between us and our pursuer now a little more, now a little less. People turned and stared at us. A few boys, scenting grim fun, followed shouting for awhile; but these we soon out-paced, till at last in deserted streets, winding among warehouses bordering the river, we three ran alone, between long, lifeless walls. I looked into Hal's face from time to time, and he was laughing; but every now and then he would look over his shoulder at the man behind him still following doggedly, and then his face would be twisted into a comically terrified grimace. Turning into a narrow cul-de-sac, Hal suddenly ducked behind a wide brick buttress, and the man, still running, passed us. And then Hal stood up and called to him, and the man turned, looked into Hal's eyes, and understood.

He was not a coward. Besides, even a rat when cornered will fight for its life. He made a rush at Hal, and Hal made no attempt to defend himself. He stood there laughing, and the man struck him full in the face, and the blood spurted out and flowed down into his mouth. The man came on again, though terror was in every line of his face, all his desire being to escape. But this time Hal drove him back again. They fought for awhile, if one can call it fighting, till the man, mad for air, reeled against the wall, stood there quivering convulsively, his mouth wide open, resembling more than anything else some huge dying fish. And Hal drew away and waited.

I have no desire to see again the sight I saw that quiet, still evening, framed by those high, windowless walls, from behind which sounded with ceaseless regularity the gentle swish of the incoming tide. All sense of retribution was drowned in the sight of Hal's evident enjoyment of his sport. The judge had disappeared, leaving the work to be accomplished by a savage animal loosened for the purpose.

The wretched creature flung itself again towards its only door of escape, fought with the vehemence of despair, to be flung back again, a hideous, bleeding mass of broken flesh. I tried to cling to Hal's arm, but one jerk of his steel muscles flung me ten feet away.

"Keep off, you fool!" he cried. "I won't kill him. I'm keeping my head. I shall know when to stop." And I crept away and waited.

Hal joined me a little later, wiping the blood from his face. We made our way to a small public-house near the river, and from there Hal sent a couple of men on whom he could rely with instructions how to act. I never heard any more of the matter. It was a subject on which I did not care to speak to Hal. I can only hope that good came of it.

There was a spot, it has been cleared away since to make room for the approach to Greenwich Tunnel, it was then the entrance to a grain depot in connection with the Milwall Docks. A curious brick well it resembled, in the centre of which a roadway wound downward, corkscrew fashion, disappearing at the bottom into darkness under a yawning arch. The place possessed the curious property of being ever filled with a ceaseless murmur, as though it were some aerial maelstrom, drawing into its silent vacuum all wandering waves of sound from the restless human ocean flowing round it. No single tone could one ever distinguish: it was a mingling of all voices, heard there like the murmur of a sea-soaked shell.

We passed through it on our return. Its work for the day was finished, its strange, weary song uninterrupted by the mighty waggons thundering up and down its spiral way. Hal paused, leaning against the railings that encircled its centre, and listened.

"Hark, do you not hear it, Paul?" he asked. "It is the music of Humanity. All human notes are needful to its making: the faint wail of the new-born, the cry of the dying thief; the beating of the hammers, the merry trip of dancers; the clatter of the teacups, the roaring of the streets; the crooning of the mother to her babe, the scream of the tortured child; the meeting kiss of lovers, the sob of those that part. Listen! prayers and curses, sighs and laughter; the soft breathing of the sleeping, the fretful feet of pain; voices of pity, voices of hate; the glad song of the strong, the foolish complaining of the weak. Listen to it, Paul! Right and wrong, good and evil, hope and despair, it is but one voice, a single note, drawn by the sweep of the Player's hand across the quivering strings of man. What is the meaning of it, Paul? Can you read it? Sometimes it seems to me a note of joy, so full, so endless, so complete, that I cry: 'Blessed be the Lord whose hammers have beaten upon us, whose fires have shaped us to His ends!' And sometimes it sounds to me a dying note, so that I could curse Him who in wantonness has wrung it from the anguish of His creatures, till I would that I could fling myself, Prometheus like, between Him and His victims, calling: "My darkness, but their light; my agony, O God; their hope!'"

The faint light from a neighbouring gas-lamp fell upon his face that an hour before I had seen the face of a wild beast. The ugly mouth was quivering, tears stood in his great, tender eyes. Could his prayer in that moment have been granted, could he have pressed against his bosom all the pain of the world, he would have rejoiced.

He shook himself together with a laugh. "Come, Paul, we have had a busy afternoon, and I'm thirsty. Let us drink some beer, my boy, good sound beer, and plenty of it."

My mother fell ill that winter. Mountain born and mountain bred, the close streets had never agreed with her, and scolded by all of us, she promised, "come the fine weather," to put sentiment behind her, and go away from them.

"I'm thinking she will," said Hal, gripping my shoulder with his strong hand, "but it'll be by herself that she'll go, lad. My wonder is," he continued, "that she has held out so long. If anything, it is you that have kept her alive. Now that you are off her mind to a certain extent, she is worrying about your father, I expect. These women, they never will believe a man can take care of himself, even in Heaven. She's never quite trusted the Lord with him, and never will till she's there to give an eye to things herself."

Hal's prophecy fell true. She left "come the fine weather," as she had promised: I remember it was the first day primroses were hawked in the street. But another death had occurred just before; which, concerning me closely as it does, I had better here dispose of; and that was the death of old Mr. Stillwood, who passed away rich in honour and regret, and was buried with much ostentation and much sincere sorrow; for he had been to many of his clients, mostly old folk, rather a friend than a mere man of business, and had gained from all with whom he had come in contact, respect, and from many real affection.

In conformity with the old legal fashions that in his life he had so fondly clung to, his will was read aloud by Mr. Gadley after the return from the funeral, and many were the tears its recital called forth. Written years ago by himself and never altered, its quaint phraseology was full of kindly thought and expression. No one had been forgotten. Clerks, servants, poor relations, all had been treated with even-handed justice, while for those with claim upon him, ample provision had been made. Few wills, I think, could ever have been read less open to criticism.

Old Gadley slipped his arm into mine as we left the house. "If you've nothing to do, young 'un," he said, "I'll get you to come with me to the office. I have got all the keys in my pocket, and we shall be quiet. It will be sad work for me, and I had rather we were alone. A couple of hours will show us everything."

We lighted the wax candles, old Stillwood could never tolerate gas in his own room, and opening the safe took out the heavy ledgers one by one, and from them Gadley dictated figures which I wrote down and added up.

"Thirty years I have kept these books for him," said old Gadley, as we laid by the last of them, "thirty years come Christmas next, he and I together. No other hands but ours have ever touched them, and now people to whom they mean nothing but so much business will fling them about, drop greasy crumbs upon them, I know their ways, the brutes! scribble all over them. And he who always would have everything so neat and orderly!"

We came to the end of them in less than the time old Gadley had thought needful: in such perfect order had everything been maintained. I was preparing to go, but old Gadley had drawn a couple of small keys from his pocket, and was shuffling again towards the safe.

"Only one more," he explained in answer to my look, "his own private ledger. It will merely be in the nature of a summary, but we'll just glance through it."

He opened an inner drawer and took from it a small thick volume bound in green leather and closed with two brass locks. An ancient volume, it appeared, its strong binding faded and stained. Old Gadley sat down with it at the dead man's own desk, and snuffing the two shaded candles, unlocked and opened it. I was standing opposite, so that the book to me was upside down, but the date on the first page, "1841," caught my eye, as also the small neat writing now brown with age.

"So neat, so orderly he always was," murmured old Gadley again, smoothing the page affectionately with his hand, and I waited for his dictation.

But no glib flow of figures fell from him. His eyebrows suddenly contracted, his body stiffened itself. Then for the next quarter of an hour nothing sounded in the quiet room but his turning of the creakling pages. Once or twice he glanced round swiftly over his shoulder, as though haunted by the idea of some one behind him; then back to the neat, closely written folios, his little eyes, now exhibiting a comical look of horror, starting out of his round red face. First slowly, then quickly with trembling hands he turned the pages, till the continual ratling of the leaves sounded like strange, mocking laughter through the silent, empty room; almost one could imagine it coming from some watching creature hidden in the shadows.

The end reached, he sat staring before him, his whole body quivering, great beads of sweat upon his shiny bald head.

"Am I mad?" was all he could find to say. "Kelver, am I mad?"

He handed me the book. It was a cynically truthful record of fraud, extending over thirty years. Every client, every friend, every relative that had fallen into his net he had robbed: the fortunate ones of a part, the majority of their all. Its very first entry debited him with the proceeds of his own partner's estate. Its last ran "Re Kelver, various sales of stock." To his credit were his payments year after year of imaginary interests on imaginary securities, the surplus accounted for with simple brevity: "Transferred to own account." No record could have been more clear, more frank. Beneath each transaction was written its true history; the actual investments, sometimes necessary, carefully distinguished from the false. In neat red ink would occur here and there a note for his own guidance: "Eldest child comes of age August, '73. Be prepared for trustees desiring production." Turning to "August, '73," one found that genuine investment had been made, to be sold again a few months later on. From beginning to end not a single false step had he committed. Suspicious clients had been ear-marked: the trusting discriminated with gratitude, and milked again and again to meet emergency.

As a piece of organisation it was magnificent. No one but a financial genius could have picked a dozen steps through such a network of chicanery. For half a lifetime he had moved among it, dignified, respected and secure.

Whether even he could have maintained his position for another month was doubtful. Suicide, though hinted at, was proved to have been impossible. It seemed as though with his amazing audacity he had tricked even Death into becoming his accomplice.

"But it is impossible, Kelver!" cried Gadley, "this must be some dream. Stillwood, Waterhead and Royal! What is the meaning of it?"

He took the book into his hands again, then burst into tears. "You never knew him," wailed the poor little man. "Stillwood, Waterhead and Royal! I came here as office boy fifty years ago. He was more like a friend to me than, " and again the sobs shook his little fat body.

I locked the books away and put him into his hat and coat. But I had much difficulty in getting him out of the office.

"I daren't, young 'un," he cried, drawing back. "Fifty years I have walked out of this office, proud of it, proud of being connected with it. I daren't face the street!"

All the way home his only idea was: Could it not be hidden? Honest, kindly little man that he was, he seemed to have no thought for the unfortunate victims. The good name of his master, of his friend, gone! Stillwood, Waterhead and Royal, a by-word! To have avoided that I believe he would have been willing for yet another hundred clients to be ruined.

I saw him to his door, then turned homeward; and to my surprise in a dark by-street heard myself laughing heartily. I checked myself instantly, feeling ashamed of my callousness, of my seeming indifference to the trouble even of myself and my mother. Yet as there passed before me the remembrance of that imposing and expensive funeral with its mournful following of tearful faces; the hushed reading of the will with its accompaniment of rustling approval; the picture of the admirably sympathetic clergyman consoling with white hands Mrs. Stillwood, inclined to hysteria, but anxious concerning her two hundred pounds' worth of crape which by no possibility of means could now be paid for, recurred to me the obituary notice in "The Chelsea Weekly Chronicle": the humour of the thing swept all else before it, and I laughed again, I could not help it, loud and long. It was my first introduction to the comedy of life, which is apt to be more brutal than the comedy of fiction.

But nearing home, the serious side of the matter forced itself uppermost. Fortunately, our supposed dividends had been paid to us by Mr. Stillwood only the month before. Could I keep the thing from troubling my mother's last days? It would be hard work. I should have to do it alone, for a perhaps foolish pride prevented my taking Hal into my confidence, even made his friendship a dread to me, lest he should come to learn and offer help. There is a higher generosity, it is said, that can receive with pleasure as well as bestow favour; but I have never felt it. Could I be sure of acting my part, of not betraying myself to her sharp eyes, of keeping newspapers and chance gossip away from her? Good shrewd Amy I cautioned, but I shrank from even speaking on the subject to Hal, and my fear was lest he should blunder into the subject, which for the usual nine days occupied much public attention. But fortunately he appeared not even to have heard of the scandal.

Possibly had the need lasted longer I might have failed, but as it was, a few weeks saw the end.

"Don't leave me to-day, Paul," whispered my mother to me one morning. So I stayed, and in the evening my mother put her arms around my neck and I lay beside her, my head upon her breast, as I used to when a little boy. And when the morning came I was alone.

BOOK II.

CHAPTER I

DESCRIBES THE DESERT ISLAND TO WHICH PAUL WAS DRIFTED.

"Room to let for a single gentleman." Sometimes in an idle hour, impelled by foolishness, I will knock at the door. It is opened after a longer or shorter interval by the "slavey", in the morning, slatternly, her arms concealed beneath her apron; in the afternoon, smart in dirty cap and apron. How well I know her! Unchanged, not grown an inch, her round bewildered eyes, her open mouth, her touzled hair, her scored red hands. With an effort I refrain from muttering: "So sorry, forgot my key," from pushing past her and mounting two at a time the narrow stairs, carpeted to the first floor, but bare beyond. Instead, I say, "Oh, what rooms have you to let?" when, scuttling to the top of the kitchen stairs, she will call over the banisters: "A gentleman to see the rooms." There comes up, panting, a harassed-looking, elderly female, but genteel in black. She crushes past the little "slavey," and approaching, eyes me critically.

"I have a very nice room on the first floor," she informs me, "and one behind on the third."

I agree to see them, explaining that I am seeking them for a young friend of mine. We squeeze past the hat and umbrella stand: there is just room, but one must keep close to the wall. The first floor is rather an imposing apartment, with a marble-topped sideboard measuring quite three feet by two, the doors of which will remain closed if you introduce a wad of paper between them. A green table-cloth, matching the curtains, covers the loo-table. The lamp is perfectly safe so long as it stands in the exact centre of the table, but should not be shifted. A paper fire-stove ornament in some mysterious way bestows upon the room an air of chastity. Above the mantelpiece is a fly-blown mirror, between the once gilt frame and glass of which can be inserted invitation cards; indeed, one or two so remain, proving that the tenants even of "bed-sitting-rooms" are not excluded from social delights. The wall opposite is adorned by an oleograph of the kind Cheap Jacks sell by auction on Saturday nights in the Pimlico Road, and warrant as "hand-made." Generally speaking, it is a Swiss landscape. There appears to be more "body" in a Swiss landscape than in scenes from less favoured localities. A dilapidated mill, a foaming torrent, a mountain, a maiden and a cow can at the least be relied upon. An easy chair (I disclaim all responsibility for the adjective), stuffed with many coils of steel wire, each possessing a "business end" in admirable working order, and covered with horsehair, highly glazed, awaits the uninitiated. There is one way of sitting upon it, and only one: by using the extreme edge, and planting your feet firmly on the floor. If you attempt to lean back in it you inevitably slide out of it. When so treated it seems to say to you: "Excuse me, you are very heavy, and you would really be much more comfortable upon the floor. Thank you so much." The bed is behind the door, and the washstand behind the bed. If you sit facing the window you can forget the bed. On the other hand, if more than one friend come to call on you, you are glad of it. As a matter of fact, experienced visitors prefer it, make straight for it, refusing with firmness to exchange it for the easy chair.

"And this room is?"

"Eight shillings a week, sir, with attendance, of course."

"Any extras?"

"The lamp, sir, is eighteenpence a week; and the kitchen fire, if the gentleman wishes to dine at home, two shillings."

"And fire?"

"Sixpence a scuttle, sir, I charge for coals."

"It's rather a small scuttle."

The landlady bridles a little. "The usual size, I think, sir." One presumes there is a special size in coal-scuttles made exclusively for lodging-house keepers.

I agree that while I am about it I may as well see the other room, the third floor back. The landlady opens the door for me, but remains herself on the landing. She is a stout lady, and does not wish to dwarf the apartment by comparison. The arrangement here does not allow of your ignoring the bed. It is the life and soul of the room, and it declines to efface itself. Its only possible rival is the washstand, straw-coloured; with staring white basin and jug, together with other appurtenances. It glares defiantly from its corner. "I know I'm small," it seems to say; "but I'm very useful; and I won't be ignored." The remaining furniture consists of a couple of chairs, there is no hypocrisy about them: they are not easy and they do not pretend to be easy; a small chest of light-painted drawers before the window, with white china handles, upon which is a tiny looking-glass; and, occupying the entire remaining space, after allowing three square feet for the tenant, when he arrives, an attenuated four-legged table apparently home-made. The only ornament in the room is, suspended above the fireplace, a funeral card, framed in beer corks. As the corpse introduced by the ancient Egyptians into their banquets, it is hung there perhaps to remind the occupant of the apartment that the luxuries and allurements of life have their end; or maybe it consoles him in despondent moments with the reflection that after all he might be worse off.

The rent of this room is three-and-sixpence a week, also including attendance; lamp, as for the first floor, eighteen-pence; but kitchen fire a shilling.

"But why should kitchen fire for the first floor be two shillings, and for this only one?"

"Well, as a rule, sir, the first floor wants more cooking done."

You are quite right, my dear lady, I was forgetting. The gentleman in the third floor back! cooking for him is not a great tax upon the kitchen fire. His breakfast, it is what, madam, we call plain, I think. His lunch he takes out. You may see him, walking round the quiet square, up and down the narrow street that, leading to nowhere in particular, is between twelve and two somewhat deserted. He carries a paper bag, into which at intervals, when he is sure nobody is looking, his mouth disappears. From studying the neighbourhood one can guess what it contains. Saveloys hereabouts are plentiful and only twopence each. There are pie shops, where meat pies are twopence and fruit pies a penny. The lady behind the counter, using deftly a broad, flat knife, lifts the little dainty with one twist clean from its tiny dish: it is marvellous, having regard to the thinness of the pastry, that she never breaks one. Roley-poley pudding, sweet and wonderfully satisfying, more especially when cold, is but a penny a slice. Peas pudding, though this is an awkward thing to eat out of a bag, is comforting upon cold days. Then with his tea he takes two eggs or a haddock, the fourpenny size; maybe on rare occasions, a chop or steak; and you fry it for him, madam, though every time he urges on you how much he would prefer it grilled, for fried in your one frying-pan its flavour becomes somewhat confused. But maybe this is the better for him, for, shutting his eyes and trusting only to smell and flavour, he can imagine himself enjoying variety. He can begin with herrings, pass on to liver and bacon, opening his eyes again for a moment perceive that he has now arrived at the joint, and closing them again, wind up with distinct suggestion of toasted cheese, thus avoiding monotony. For dinner he goes out again. Maybe he is not hungry, late meals are a mistake; or, maybe, putting his hand into his pocket and making calculations beneath a lamp-post, appetite may come to him. Then there are places cheerful with the sound of frizzling fat, where fried plaice brown and odorous may be had for three halfpence, and a handful of sliced potatoes for a penny; where for fourpence succulent stewed eels may be discussed; vinegar ad lib.; or for sevenpence, but these are red-letter evenings, half a sheep's head may be indulged in, which is a supper fit for any king, who happened to be hungry.

I explain that I will discuss the matter with my young friend when he arrives. The landlady says, "Certainly, sir:" she is used to what she calls the "wandering Christian;" and easing my conscience by slipping a shilling into the "slavey's" astonished, lukewarm hand, I pass out again into the long, dreary street, now echoing maybe to the sad cry of "Muffins!"

Or sometimes of an evening, the lamp lighted, the remnants of the meat tea cleared away, the flickering firelight cosifying the dingy rooms, I go a-visiting. There is no need for me to ring the bell, to mount the stairs. Through the thin transparent walls I can see you plainly, old friends of mine, fashions a little changed, that is all. We wore bell-shaped trousers; eight-and-six to measure, seven-and-six if from stock; fastened our neckties in dashing style with a horseshoe pin. I think in the matter of waistcoats we had the advantage of you; ours were gayer, braver. Our cuffs and collars were of paper: sixpence- halfpenny the dozen, three-halfpence the pair. On Sunday they were white and glistening; on Monday less aggressively obvious; on Tuesday morning decidedly dappled. But on Tuesday evening, when with natty cane, or umbrella neatly rolled in patent leather case, we took our promenade down Oxford Street, fashionable hour nine to ten p.m., we could shoot our arms and cock our chins with the best. Your india-rubber linen has its advantages. Storm does not wither it; it braves better the heat and turmoil of the day. The passing of a sponge! and your "Dicky" is itself again. We had to use bread-crumbs, and so sacrifice the glaze. Yet I cannot help thinking that for the first few hours, at all events, our paper was more dazzling.

For the rest I see no change in you, old friends. I wave you greeting from the misty street. God rest you, gallant gentlemen, lonely and friendless and despised; making the best of joyless lives; keeping yourselves genteel on twelve, fifteen, or eighteen (ah, but you are plutocrats!) shillings a week; saving something even of that, maybe, to help the old mother in the country, so proud of her "gentleman" son who has book learning and who is "something in the City." May nothing you dismay. Bullied, and badgered, and baited from nine to six though you may be, from then till bedtime you are rorty young dogs. The half-guinea topper, "as worn by the Prince of Wales" (ah, how many a meal has it not cost!), warmed before the fire, brushed and polished and coaxed, shines resplendent. The second pair of trousers are drawn from beneath the bed; in the gaslight, with well-marked crease from top to toe, they will pass for new. A pleasant evening to you! May your cheap necktie make all the impression your soul can desire! May your penny cigar be mistaken for Havana! May the barmaid charm your simple heart by addressing you as "Baby!" May some sweet shop-girl throw a kindly glance at you, inviting you to walk with her! May she snigger at your humour; may other dogs cast envious looks at you, and may no harm come of it!

You dreamers of dreams, you who while your companions play and sleep will toil upward in the night! You have read Mr. Smiles' "Self-Help," Longfellow's "Psalm of Life," and so strengthened attack with confidence "French Without a Master," "Bookkeeping in Six Lessons." With a sigh to yourselves you turn aside from the alluring streets, from the bright, bewitching eyes, into the stuffy air of Birkbeck Institutions, Polytechnic Schools. May success compensate you for your youth devoid of pleasure! May the partner's chair you seen in visions be yours before the end! May you live one day in Clapham in a twelve-roomed house!

And, after all, we have our moments, have we not? The Saturday night at the play. The hours of waiting, they are short. We converse with kindred souls of the British Drama, its past and future: we have our views. We dream of Florence This, Kate That; in a little while we shall see her. Ah, could she but know how we loved her! Her photo is on our mantelpiece, transforming the dismal little room into a shrine. The poem we have so often commenced! when it is finished we will post it to her. At least she will acknowledge its receipt; we can kiss the paper her hand has rested on. The great doors groan, then quiver. Ah, the wild thrill of that moment! Now push for all you are worth: charge, wriggle, squirm! It is an epitome of life. We are through, collarless, panting, pummelled from top to toe: but what of that? Upward, still upward; then downward with leaps at risk of our neck, from bench to bench through the gloom. We have gained the front row! Would we exchange sensations with the stallite, strolling languidly to his seat? The extravagant dinner once a week! We banquet a la Francais, in Soho, for one-and-six, including wine. Does Tortoni ever give his customers a repast they enjoy more? I know not.

My first lodging was an attic in a square the other side of Blackfriars Bridge. The rent of the room, if I remember rightly, was three shillings a week with cooking, half-a-crown without. I purchased a methylated spirit stove with kettle and frying-pan, and took it without.

Old Hasluck would have helped me willingly, and there were others to whom I might have appealed, but a boy's pride held me back. I would make my way alone, win my place in the world by myself. To Hal, knowing he would sympathise with me, I confided the truth.

"Had your mother lived," he told me, "I should have had something to say on the subject. Of course, I knew what had happened, but as it is, well, you need not be afraid, I shall not offer you help; indeed, I should refuse it were you to ask. Put your Carlyle in your pocket: he is not all voices, but he is the best maker of men I know. The great thing to learn of life is not to be afraid of it."

"Look me up now and then," he added, "and we'll talk about the stars, the future of Socialism, and the Woman Question, anything you like except about yourself and your twopenny-half-penny affairs."

From another it would have sounded brutal, but I understood him. And so we shook hands and parted for longer than either of us at the time expected. The Franco-German War broke out a few weeks later on, and Hal, the love of adventure always strong within him, volunteered his services, which were accepted. It was some years before we met again.

On the door-post of a house in Farringdon Street, not far from the Circus, stood in those days a small brass plate, announcing that the "Ludgate News Rooms" occupied the third and fourth floors, and that the admission to the same was one penny. We were a seedy company that every morning crowded into these rooms: clerks, shopmen, superior artisans, travellers, warehousemen, all of us out of work. Most of us were young, but with us was mingled a sprinkling of elder men, and these latter were always the saddest and most silent of this little whispering army of the down-at-heel. Roughly speaking, we were divided into two groups: the newcomers, cheery, confident. These would flit from newspaper to newspaper with buzz of pleasant anticipation, select their advertisement as one choosing some dainty out of a rich and varied menu card, and replying to it as one conferring favour.

"Dear Sir, in reply to your advertisement in to-day's Standard, I shall be pleased to accept the post vacant in your office. I am of good appearance and address. I am an excellent" It was really marvellous the quality and number of our attainments. French! we wrote and spoke it fluently, a la Ahn. German! of this we possessed a slighter knowledge, it was true, but sufficient for mere purposes of commerce. Bookkeeping! arithmetic! geometry! we played with them. The love of work! it was a passion with us. Our moral character! it would have adorned a Free Kirk Elder. "I could call on you to-morrow or Friday between eleven and one, or on Saturday any time up till two. Salary required, two guineas a week. An early answer will oblige. Yours truly."

The old stagers did not buzz. Hour after hour they sat writing, steadily, methodically, with day by day less hope and heavier fears:

"Sir, Your advt. in to-day's D. T. I am" of such and such an age. List of qualifications less lengthy, set forth with more modesty; object desired being air of verisimilitude. "If you decide to engage me I will endeavour to give you every satisfaction. Any time you like to appoint I will call on you. I should not ask a high salary to start with. Yours obediently."

Dozens of the first letter, hundreds of the second, I wrote with painful care, pen carefully chosen, the one-inch margin down the left hand side of the paper first portioned off with dots. To three or four I received a curt reply, instructing me to call. But the shyness that had stood so in my way during the earlier half of my school days had now, I know not why, returned upon me, hampering me at every turn. A shy child grown-up folks at all events can understand and forgive; but a shy young man is not unnaturally regarded as a fool. I gave the impression of being awkward, stupid, sulky. The more I strove against my temperament the worse I became. My attempts to be at my ease, to assert myself, resulted, I could see it myself, only in rudeness.

"Well, I have got to see one or two others. We will write and let you know," was the conclusion of each interview, and the end, as far as I was concerned, of the enterprise.

My few pounds, guard them how I would, were dwindling rapidly. Looking back, it is easy enough to regard one's early struggles from a humorous point of view. One knows the story, it all ended happily. But at the time there is no means of telling whether one's biography is going to be comedy or tragedy. There were moments when I felt confident it was going to be the latter. Occasionally, when one is feeling well, it is not unpleasant to contemplate with pathetic sympathy one's own death-bed. One thinks of the friends and relations who at last will understand and regret one, be sorry they had not behaved themselves better. But myself, there was no one to regret. I felt very small, very helpless. The world was big. I feared it might walk over me, trample me down, never seeing me. I seemed unable to attract its attention.

One morning I found waiting for me at the Reading Room another of the usual missives. It ran: "Will Mr. P. Kelver call at the above address to-morrow morning between ten-thirty and eleven. The paper was headed: "Lott and Co., Indian Commission Agents, Aldersgate Street." Without much hope I returned to my lodgings, changed my clothes, donned my silk hat, took my one pair of gloves, drew its silk case over my holey umbrella; and so equipped for fight with Fate made my way to Aldersgate Street. For a quarter of an hour or so, being too soon, I walked up and down the pavement outside the house, gazing at the second-floor windows, behind which, so the door-plate had informed me, were the offices of Lott & Co. I could not recall their advertisement, nor my reply to it. The firm was evidently not in a very flourishing condition. I wondered idly what salary they would offer. For a moment I dreamt of a Cheeryble Brother asking me kindly if I thought I could do with thirty shillings a week as a beginning; but the next I recalled my usual fate, and considered whether it was even worthwhile to climb the stairs, go through what to me was a painful ordeal, merely to be impressed again with the sense of my own worthlessness.

A fine rain began to fall. I did not wish to unroll my umbrella, yet felt nervous for my hat. It was five minutes to the half hour. Listlessly I crossed the road and mounted the bare stairs to the second floor. Two doors faced me, one marked "Private." I tapped lightly at the second. Not hearing any response, after a second or two I tapped again. A sound reached me, but it was unintelligible. I knocked yet again, still louder. This time I heard a reply in a shrill, plaintive tone:

"Oh, do come in."

The tone was one of pathetic entreaty. I turned the handle and entered. It was a small room, dimly lighted by a dirty window, the bottom half of which was rendered opaque by tissue paper pasted to its panes. The place suggested a village shop rather than an office. Pots of jam, jars of pickles, bottles of wine, biscuit tins, parcels of drapery, boxes of candles, bars of soap, boots, packets of stationery, boxes of cigars, tinned provisions, guns, cartridges, things sufficient to furnish a desert island littered every available corner. At a small desk under the window sat a youth with a remarkably small body and a remarkably large head; so disproportionate were the two I should hardly have been surprised had he put up his hands and taken it off. Half in the room and half out, I paused.

"Is this Lott & Co.?" I enquired.

"No," he answered; "it's a room." One eye was fixed upon me, dull and glassy; it never blinked, it never wavered. With the help of the other he continued his writing.

"I mean," I explained, coming entirely into the room, "are these the offices of Lott & Co.?"

"It's one of them," he replied; "the back one. If you're really anxious for a job, you can shut the door."

I complied with his suggestion, and then announced that I was Mr. Kelver, Mr. Paul Kelver.

"Minikin's my name," he returned, "Sylvanus Minikin. You don't happen by any chance to know what you've come for, I suppose?"

Looking at his body, my inclination was to pick my way among the goods that covered the floor and pull his ears for him. From his grave and massive face, he might, for all I knew, be the head clerk.

"I have called to see Mr. Lott," I replied, with dignity; "I have an appointment." I produced the letter from my pocket, and leaning across a sewing-machine, I handed it to him for his inspection. Having read it, he suddenly took from its socket the eye with which he had been hitherto regarding me, and proceeding to polish it upon his pocket handkerchief, turned upon me his other. Having satisfied himself, he handed me back my letter.

"Want my advice?" he asked.

I thought it might be useful to me, so replied in the affirmative.

"Hook it," was his curt counsel.

"Why?" I asked. "Isn't he a good employer?"

Replacing his glass eye, he turned again to his work. "If employment is what you want," answered Mr. Minikin, "you'll get it. Best employer in London. He'll keep you going for twenty-four hours a day, and then offer you overtime at half salary."

"I must get something to do," I confessed.

"Sit down then," suggested Mr. Minikin. "Rest while you can."

I took the chair; it was the only chair in the room, with the exception of the one Minikin was sitting on.

"Apart from his being a bit of a driver," I asked, "what sort of a man is he? Is he pleasant?"

"Never saw him put out but once," answered Minikin.

It sounded well. "When was that?" I asked.

"All the time I've known him."

My spirits continued to sink. Had I been left alone with Minikin much longer, I might have ended by following his advice, "hooking it" before Mr. Lott arrived. But the next moment I heard the other door open, and some one entered the private office. Then the bell rang, and Minikin disappeared, leaving the communicating door ajar behind him. The conversation that I overheard was as follows:

"Why isn't Mr. Skeat here?"

"Because he hasn't come."

"Where are the letters?"

"Under your nose."

"How dare you answer me like that?"

"Well, it's the truth. They are under your nose."

"Did you give Thorneycroft's man my message?"

"Yes."

"What did he answer?"

"Said you were a liar."

"Oh, he did, did he! What did you reply?"

"Asked him to tell me something I didn't know."

"Thought that clever, didn't you?"

"Not bad."

Whatever faults might be laid to Mr. Lott's door, he at least, I concluded, possessed the virtue of self-control.

"Anybody been here?"

"Yes."

"Who?"

"Mr. Kelver, Mr. Paul Kelver."

"Kelver, Kelver. Who's Kelver?"

"Know what he is, a fool."

"What do you mean?"

"He's come after the place."

"Is he there?"

"Yes."

"What's he like?"

"Not bad looking; fair"

"Idiot! I mean is he smart?"

"Just at present, got all his Sunday clothes on."

"Send him in to me. Don't go, don't go."

"How can I send him in to you if I don't go?"

"Take these. Have you finished those bills of lading?"

"No."

"Good God! when will you have finished them?"

"Half an hour after I have begun them."

"Get out, get out! Has that door been open all the time?"

"Well, I don't suppose it's opened itself."

Minikin re-entered with papers in his hand. "In you go," he said. "Heaven help you!" And I passed in and closed the door behind me.

The room was a replica of the one I had just left. If possible, it was more crowded, more packed with miscellaneous articles. I picked my way through these and approached the desk. Mr. Lott was a small, dingy-looking man, with very dirty hands, and small, restless eyes. I was glad that he was not imposing, or my shyness might have descended upon me; as it was, I felt better able to do myself justice. At once he plunged into the business by seizing and waving in front of my eyes a bulky bundle of letters tied together with red tape.

"One hundred and seventeen answers to an advertisement," he cried with evident satisfaction, "in one day! That shows you the state of the labour market!"

I agreed it was appalling.

"Poor devils, poor devils!" murmured Mr. Lott "what will become of them? Some of them will starve. Terrible death, starvation, Kelver; takes such a long time, especially when you're young."

Here also I found myself in accord with him.

"Living with your parents?"

I explained to him my situation.

"Any friends?"

I informed him I was entirely dependent upon my own efforts.

"Any money? Anything coming in?"

I told him I had a few pounds still remaining to me, but that after that was gone I should be penniless.

"And to think, Kelver, that there are hundreds, thousands of young fellows precisely in your position! How sad, how very sad! How long have you been looking for a berth?"

"A month," I answered him.

"I thought as much. Do you know why I selected your letter out of the whole batch?"

I replied I hoped it was because he judged from it I should prove satisfactory.

"Because it's the worst written of them all." He pushed it across to me. "Look at it. Awful, isn't it?"

I admitted that handwriting was not my strong point.

"Nor spelling either," he added, and with truth. "Who do you think will engage you if I don't?"

"Nobody," he continued, without waiting for me to reply. "A month hence you will still be looking for a berth, and a month after that. Now, I'm going to do you a good turn; save you from destitution; give you a start in life."

I expressed my gratitude.

He waived it aside. "That is my notion of philanthropy: help those that nobody else will help. That young fellow in the other room, he isn't a bad worker, he's smart, but he's impertinent."

I murmured that I had gathered so much.

"Doesn't mean to be, can't help it. Noticed his trick of looking at you with his glass eye, keeping the other turned away from you?"

I replied that I had.

"Always does it. Used to irritate his last employer to madness. Said to him one day: 'Do turn that signal lamp of yours off, Minikin, and look at me with your real eye.' What do you think he answered? That it was the only one he'd got, and that he didn't want to expose it to shocks. Wouldn't have mattered so much if it hadn't been one of the ugliest men in London."

I murmured my indignation.

"I put up with him. Nobody else would. The poor fellow must live."

I expressed admiration at Mr. Lott's humanity.

"You don't mind work? You're not one of those good-for-nothings who sleep all day and wake up when it's time to go home?"

I assured him that in whatever else I might fail I could promise him industry.

"With some of them," complained Mr. Lott, in a tone of bitterness, "it's nothing but play, girls, gadding about the streets. Work, business, oh, no. I may go bankrupt; my wife and children may go into the workhouse. No thought for me, the man that keeps them, feeds them, clothes them. How much salary do you want?"

I hesitated. I gathered this was not a Cheeryble Brother; it would be necessary to be moderate in one's demands. "Five-and-twenty shillings a week," I suggested.

He repeated the figure in a scream. "Five-and-twenty shillings for writing like that! And can't spell commission! Don't know anything about the business. Five-and-twenty! Tell you what I'll do: I'll give you twelve."

"But I can't live on twelve," I explained.

"Can't live on twelve! Do you know why? Because you don't know how to live. I know you all. One veal and ham pie, one roley-poley, one Dutch cheese and a pint of bitter."

His recital made my mouth water.

"You overload your stomachs, then you can't work. Half the diseases you young fellows suffer from are brought about by overeating."

"Now, you take my advice," continued Mr. Lott; "try vegetarianism. In the morning, a little oatmeal. Wonderfully strengthening stuff, oatmeal: look at the Scotch. For dinner, beans. Why, do you know there's more nourishment in half a pint of lentil beans than in a pound of beefsteak, more gluten. That's what you want, more gluten; no corpses, no dead bodies. Why, I've known young fellows, vegetarians, who have lived like fighting cocks on sevenpence a day. Seven times seven are forty-nine. How much do you pay for your room?"

I told him.

"Four-and-a-penny and two-and-six makes six-and-seven. That leaves you five and fivepence for mere foolery. Good God! what more do you want?"

"I'll take eighteen, sir," I answered. "I can't really manage on less."

"Very well, I won't beat you down," he answered. "Fifteen shillings a week."

"I said eighteen," I persisted.

"Well, and I said fifteen," he retorted, somewhat indignant at the quibbling. "That's splitting the difference, isn't it? I can't be fairer than that."

I dared not throw away the one opportunity that had occurred. Anything was better than return to the Reading Rooms, and the empty days full of despair. I accepted, and it was agreed that I should come the following Monday morning.

"Nabbed?" was Minikin's enquiry on my return to the back office for my hat.

I nodded.

"What's he wasting on you?"

"Fifteen shillings a week," I whispered.

"Felt sure somehow that he'd take a liking to you," answered Minikin. "Don't be ungrateful and look thin on it."

Outside the door I heard Mr. Lott's shrill voice demanding to know where postage stamps were to be found.

"At the Post-office," was Minikin's reply.

The hours were long, in fact, we had no office hours; we got away when we could, which was rarely before seven or eight, but my work was interesting. It consisted of buying for unfortunate clients in India or the Colonies anything they might happen to want, from a stage coach to a pot of marmalade; packing it and shipping it across to them. Our "commission" was anything they could be persuaded to pay over and above the value of the article. I was not much interfered with. There was that to be said for Lott & Co., so long as the work was done he was quite content to leave one to one's own way of doing it. And hastening through the busy streets, bargaining in shop or warehouse, bustling important in and out the swarming docks, I often thanked my stars that I was not as some poor two-pound-a-week clerk chained to a dreary desk.

The fifteen shillings a week was a tight fit; but that was not my trouble. Reduce your denominator, you know the quotation. I found it no philosophical cant, but a practical solution of life. My food cost me on the average a shilling a day. If more of us limited our commissariat bill to the same figure, there would be less dyspepsia abroad. Generally I cooked my own meals in my own frying-pan; but occasionally I would indulge myself with a more orthodox dinner at a cook shop, or tea with hot buttered toast at a coffee-shop; and but for the greasy table-cloth and the dirty-handed waiter, such would have been even greater delights. The shilling a week for amusements afforded me at least one, occasionally two, visits to the theatre, for in those days there were Paradises where for sixpence one could be a god. Fourpence a week on tobacco gave me half-a-dozen cigarettes a day; I have spent more on smoke and derived less satisfaction. Dress was my greatest difficulty. One anxiety in life the poor man is saved: he knows not the haunting sense of debt. My tailor never dunned me. His principle was half-a-crown down on receipt of order, the balance on the handing over of the goods. No system is perfect; the method avoided friction, it is true; yet on the other hand it was annoying to be compelled to promenade, come Sundays, in shiny elbows and frayed trousers, knowing all the while that finished, waiting, was a suit in which one might have made one's mark, had only one shut one's eyes passing that pastry-cook's window on pay-day. Surely there should be a sumptuary law compelling pastry-cooks to deal in cellars or behind drawn blinds.

Were it because of its mere material hardships that to this day I think of that period of my life with a shudder, I should not here confess to it. I was alone. I knew not a living soul to whom I dared to speak, who cared to speak to me. For those first twelve months after my mother's death I lived alone, thought alone, felt alone. In the morning, during the busy day, it was possible to bear; but in the evenings the sense of desolation gripped me like a physical pain. The summer evenings came again, bringing with them the long, lingering light so laden with melancholy. I would walk into the Parks and, sitting there, watch with hungry eyes the men and women, boys and girls, moving all around me, talking, laughing, interested in one another; feeling myself some speechless ghost, seeing but not seen, crying to the living with a voice they heard not. Sometimes a solitary figure would pass by and glance back at me; some lonely creature like myself longing for human sympathy. In the teeming city must have been thousands such, young men and women to whom a friendly ear, a kindly voice, would have been as the water of life. Each imprisoned in his solitary cell of shyness, we looked at one another through the grating with condoling eyes; further than that was forbidden to us. Once, in Kensington Gardens, a woman turned, then slowly retracing her steps, sat down beside me on the bench. Neither of us spoke; had I done so she would have risen and moved away; yet there was understanding between us. To each of us it was some comfort to sit thus for a little while beside the other. Had she poured out her heart to me, she could have told me nothing more than I knew: "I, too, am lonely, friendless; I, too, long for the sound of a voice, the touch of a hand. It is hard for you, it is harder still for me, a girl; shut out from the bright world that laughs around me; denied the right of youth to joy and pleasure; denied the right of womanhood to love and tenderness."

The footsteps to and fro grew fewer. She moved to rise. Stirred by an impulse, I stretched out my hand, then seeing the flush upon her face, drew it back hastily. But the next moment, changing her mind, she held hers out to me, and I took it. It was the first clasp of a hand I had felt since six months before I had said good-bye to Hal. She turned and walked quickly away. I stood watching her; she never looked round, and I never saw her again.

I take no credit to myself for keeping straight, as it is termed, during these days. For good or evil, my shyness prevented my taking part in the flirtations of the streets. Whether inviting eyes were ever thrown to me as to others, I cannot say. Sometimes, fancying so, hoping so, I would follow. Yet never could I summon up sufficient resolution to face the possible rebuff before some less timid swain would swoop down upon the quarry. Then I would hurry on, cursing myself for the poorness of my spirit, fancying mocking contempt in the laughter that followed me.

On a Sunday I would rise early and take long solitary walks into the country. One winter's day, I remember it was on the road between Edgware and Stanmore, there issued from a by-road a little ahead of me a party of boys and girls, young people about my own age, bound evidently on a skating expedition. I could hear the musical ring of their blades, clattering as they walked, and the sound of their merry laughter so clear and bell-like through the frosty air. And an aching anguish fell upon me. I felt a mad desire to run after them, to plead with them to let me walk with them a little way, to let me laugh and talk with them. Every now and then they would pirouette to cry some jest to one another. I could see their faces: the girls' so sweetly alluring, framed by their dainty hats and furs, the bright colour in their cheeks, the light in their teasing eyes. A little further on they turned aside into a by-lane, and I stood at the corner listening till the last echo of their joyous voices died away, and on a stone that still remains standing there I sat down and sobbed.

I would walk about the streets always till very late. I dreaded the echoing clang of the little front door when I closed it behind me, the climbing of the silent stairs, the solitude that waited for me in my empty room. It would rise and come towards me like some living thing, kissing me with cold lips. Often, unable to bear the closeness of its presence, I would creep out into the streets. There, even though it followed me, I was not alone with it. Sometimes I would pace them the whole night, sharing them with the other outcasts while the city slept.

Occasionally, during these nightly wanderings would come to me moments of exaltation when fear fell from me and my blood would leap with joy at prospect of the fierce struggle opening out before me. Then it was the ghostly city sighing round me that seemed dead, I the only living thing real among a world of shadows. In long, echoing streets I would laugh and shout. Misunderstanding policemen would turn their bull's-eyes on me, gruffly give me practical advice: they knew not who I was! I stood the centre of a vast galanty-show: the phantom houses came and went; from some there shone bright lights; the doors were open, and little figures flitted in and out, the tiny coaches glided to and fro, manikins grotesque but pitiful crept across the star-lit curtain.

Then the mood would change. The city, grim and vast, stretched round me endless. I crawled, a mere atom, within its folds, helpless, insignificant, absurd. The houseless forms that shared my vigil were my fellows. What were we? Animalcule upon its bosom, that it saw not, heeded not. For company I would mingle with them: ragged men, frowsy women, ageless youths, gathered round the red glow of some coffee stall.

Rarely would we speak to one another. More like animals we browsed there, sipping the halfpenny cup of hot water coloured with coffee grounds (at least it was warm), munching the moist slab of coarse cake; looking with dull, indifferent eyes each upon the wretchedness of the others. Perhaps some two would whisper to each other in listless, monotonous tone, broken here and there by a short, mirthless laugh; some shivering creature, not yet case-hardened to despair, seek, perhaps, the relief of curses that none heeded. Later, a faint chill breeze would shake the shadows loose, a thin, wan light streak the dark air with shade, and silently, stealthily, we would fade away and disappear.

CHAPTER II.

PAUL, ESCAPING FROM HIS SOLITUDE, FALLS INTO STRANGE COMPANY. AND BECOMES CAPTIVE TO ONE OF HAUGHTY MIEN.

All things pass, even the self-inflicted sufferings of shy young men, condemned by temperament to solitude. Came the winter evenings, I took to work: in it one may drown much sorrow for oneself. With its handful of fire, its two candles lighted, my "apartment" was more inviting. I bought myself paper, pens and ink. Great or small, what more can a writer do? He is but the would-be medium: will the spirit voices employ him or reject him?

London, with its million characters, grave and gay; its ten thousand romances, its mysteries, its pathos, and its humour, lay to my hand. It stretched before me, asking only intelligent observation, more or less truthful report. But that I could make a story out of the things I really knew never occurred to me. My tales were of cottage maidens, of bucolic yeomen. My scenes were laid in windmills, among mountains, or in moated granges. I fancy this phase of folly is common to most youthful fictionists.

A trail of gentle melancholy lay over them. Sentiment was more popular then than it is now, and, as do all beginners, I scrupulously followed fashion. Generally speaking, to be a heroine of mine was fatal. However naturally her hair might curl, and curly hair, I believe, is the hall-mark of vitality; whatever other indications of vigorous health she might exhibit in the first chapter, such as "dancing eyes," "colour that came and went," "ringing laughter," "fawn-like agility," she was tolerably certain, poor girl, to end in an untimely grave. Snowdrops and early primroses (my botany I worked up from a useful little volume, "Our Garden Favourites, Illustrated") grew there as in a forcing house; and if in the neighbourhood of the coast, the sea-breezes would choose that particular churchyard, somewhat irreverently, for their favourite playground. Years later a white-haired man would come there leading little children by the hand,

and to them he would tell the tale anew, which must have been a dismal entertainment for them.

Now and then, by way of change, it would be the gentleman who would fall a victim of the deadly atmosphere of my literature. It was of no particular consequence, so he himself would conclude in his last soliloquy; "it was better so." Snowdrops and primroses, for whatever consolation they might have been to him, it was hopeless for him to expect; his grave, marked by a rude cross, being as a rule situate in an exceptionally unfrequented portion of the African veldt or amid burning sands. For description of final scenery on these occasions a visit to the British Museum reading-room would be necessary.

Dismal little fledgelings! And again and again would I drive them from the nest; again and again they fluttered back to me, soiled, crumpled, physically damaged. Yet one person had admired them, cried over them myself.

All methods I tried. Sometimes I would send them forth accompanied by a curt business note of the take-it-or-leave-it order. At other times I would attach to it pathetic appeals for its consideration. Sometimes I would give value to it, stating that the price was five guineas and requesting that the cheque should be crossed; at other times seek to tickle editorial cupidity by offering this, my first contribution to their pages, for nothing, my sample packet, so to speak, sent gratis, one trial surely sufficient. Now I would write sarcastically, enclosing together with the stamped envelope for return a brutally penned note of rejection. Or I would write frankly, explaining elaborately that I was a beginner, and asking to be told my faults, if any.

Not one found a resting place for its feet. A month, a week, a couple of days, they would remain away from me, then return. I never lost a single one. I wished I had. It would have varied the monotony.

I hated the poor little slavey who, bursting joyously into the room, would hold them out to me from between her apron-hidden thumb and finger; her chronic sniff I translated into contempt. If flying down the stairs at the sound of the postman's knock I secured it from his hands, it seemed to me he smiled. Tearing them from their envelopes, I would curse them, abuse them, fling them into the fire sometimes; but before they were more than scorched I would snatch them out, smooth them, reread them. The editor himself could never have seen them; it was impossible; some jealous underling had done this thing. I had sent them to the wrong paper. They had arrived at the inopportune moment. Their triumph would come. Rewriting the first and last sheets, I would send them forth again with fresh hope.

Meanwhile, understanding that the would-be happy warrior must shine in camp as well as field, I sought to fit myself also for the social side of life. Smoking and drinking were the twin sins I found most difficulty in acquiring. I am not claiming a mental excellence so much as confessing a bodily infirmity. The spirit had always been willing, but my flesh was weak. Fired by emulation, I had at school occasionally essayed a cigarette. The result had been distinctly unsatisfactory, and after some two or three attempts, I had abandoned, for the time being, all further endeavour; excusing my faint-heartedness by telling myself with sanctimonious air that smoking was bad for growing boys; attempting to delude myself by assuming, in presence of contemporaries of stronger stomach, fine pose of disapproval; yet in my heart knowing myself a young hypocrite, disguising physical cowardice in the robes of moral courage: a self-deception to which human nature is prone.

So likewise now and again I had tasted the wine that was red, and that stood year in, year out, decanted on our sideboard. The true inwardness of St. Paul's prescription had been revealed to me; the attitude, sometimes sneered at, of those who drink it under doctor's orders, regarding it purely as a medicine, appeared to me reasonable. I had noticed also that others, some of them grown men even, making wry faces, when drinking my mother's claret, and had concluded therefrom that taste for strong liquor was an accomplishment less easily acquired than is generally supposed. The lack of it in a young man could be no disgrace, and accordingly effort in that direction also had I weakly postponed.

But now, a gentleman at large, my education could no longer be delayed. To the artist in particular was training, and severe training, an absolute necessity. Recently fashion has changed somewhat, but a quarter of a century ago a genius who did not smoke and drink, and that more than was good for him, would have been dismissed without further evidence as an impostor. About the genius I was hopeful, but at no time positively certain. As regarded the smoking and drinking, so much at least I could make sure of. I set to work methodically, conscientiously. Smoking, experience taught me, was better practised on Saturday nights, Sunday affording me the opportunity of walking off the effects. Patience and determination were eventually crowned with success: I learned to smoke a cigarette to all appearance as though I were enjoying it. Young men of less character might here have rested content, but attainment of the highest has always been with me a motive force. The cigarette conquered, I next proceeded to attack the cigar. My first one I remember well: most men do. It was at a smoking concert held in the Islington Drill Hall, to which Minikin had invited me. Not feeling sure whether my growing dizziness were due solely to the cigar, or in part to the hot, over-crowded room, I made my excuses and slipped out. I found myself in a small courtyard, divided from a neighbouring garden by a low wall. The cause of my trouble was clearly the cigar. My inclination was to take it from my mouth and see how far I could throw it. Conscience, on the other hand, urged me to persevere. It occurred to me that if climbing on to the wall I could walk along it from end to end, there would be no excuse for my not heeding the counsels of perfection. If, on the contrary, try as I might, the wall proved not wide enough for my footsteps, then I should be entitled to lose the beastly thing, and, as best I could, make my way home to bed. I attained the wall with some difficulty and commenced my self-inflicted ordeal. Two yards further I found myself lying across the wall, my legs hanging down one side, my head overhanging the other. The position proving suitable to my requirements, I maintained it. Inclination, again seizing its opportunity, urged me then and there to take a solemn vow never to smoke again. I am proud to write that through that hour of temptation I remained firm; strengthening myself by whispering to myself: "Never despair. What others can do, so can you. Is not all victory won through suffering?"

A liking for drink I had found, if possible, even yet more difficult of achievement. Spirits I almost despaired of. Once, confusing bottles, I drank some hair oil in mistake for whiskey, and found it decidedly less nauseous. But twice a week I would force myself to swallow a glass of beer, standing over myself insisting on my draining it to the bitter dregs. As reward afterwards, to take the taste out of my mouth, I would treat myself to chocolates; at the same time comforting myself by assuring myself that it was for my good, that there would come a day when I should really like it, and be grateful to myself for having been severe with myself.

In other and more sensible directions I sought also to progress. Gradually I was overcoming my shyness. It was a slow process. I found the best plan was not to mind being shy, to accept it as part of my temperament, and with others laugh at it. The coldness of an indifferent world is of service in hardening a too sensitive skin. The gradual rubbings of existence were rounding off my many corners. I became possible to my fellow creatures, and they to me. I began to take pleasure in their company.

By directing me to this particular house in Nelson Square, Fate had done to me a kindness. I flatter myself we were an interesting menagerie gathered together under its leaky roof. Mrs. Peedles, our landlady, who slept in the basement with the slavey, had been an actress in Charles Keane's company at the old Princess's. There, it is true, she had played only insignificant parts. London, as she would explain to us was even then but a poor judge of art, with prejudices. Besides an actor-manager, hampered by a wife, we understood. But previously in the Provinces there had been a career of glory: Juliet, Amy Robsart, Mrs. Haller in "The Stranger", almost the entire roll of the "Legitimates". Showed we any signs of disbelief, proof was forthcoming: handbills a yard long, rich in notes of exclamation: "On Tuesday Evening! By Special Desire!!! Blessington's Theatre! In the Meadow, adjoining the Falcon Arms!", "On Saturday! Under the Patronage of Col. Sir William and the Officers of the 74th!!!! In the Corn Exchange!" Maybe it would convince us further were she to run through a passage here and there, say Lady Macbeth's sleep-walking scene, or from Ophelia's entrance in the fourth act? It would be no trouble; her memory was excellent. We would hasten to assure her of our perfect faith.

Listening to her, it was difficult, as she herself would frankly admit, to imagine her the once "arch Miss Lucretia Barry;" looking at her, to remember there had been an evening when she had been "the cynosure of every eye." One found it necessary to fortify oneself with perusal of underlined extracts from ancient journals, much thumbed and creased, thoughtfully lent to one for the purpose. Since those days Fate had woven round her a mantle of depression. She was now a faded, watery-eyed little woman, prone on the slightest provocation to sit down suddenly On the nearest chair and at once commence a history of her troubles. Quite unconscious of this failing, it was an idea of hers that she was an exceptionally cheerful person.

"But there, fretting's no good. We must grin and bear things in this world," she would conclude, wiping her eyes upon her apron. "It's better to laugh than to cry, I always say." And to prove that this was no mere idle sentiment, she would laugh then and there upon the spot.

Much stair-climbing had bestowed upon her a shortness of breath, which no amount of panting in her resting moments was able to make good.

"You don't know 'ow to breathe," explained our second floor front to her on one occasion, a kindly young man; "you don't swallow it, you only gargle with it. Take a good draught and shut your mouth; don't be frightened of it; don't let it out again till it's done something: that's what it's 'ere for."

He stood over her with his handkerchief pressed against her mouth to assist her; but it was of no use.

"There don't seem any room for it inside me," she explained.

Bells had become to her the business of life; she lived listening for them. Converse to her was a filling in of time while waiting for interruptions.

A bottle of whiskey fell into my hands that Christmas time, a present from a commercial traveller in the way of business. Not liking whiskey myself, it was no sacrifice for me to reserve it for the occasional comfort of Mrs.

Peedles, when, breathless, with her hands to her side, she would sink upon the chair nearest to my door. Her poor, washed-out face would lighten at the suggestion.

"Ah, well," she would reply, "I don't mind if I do. It's a poor heart that never rejoices."

And then, her tongue unloosened, she would sit there and tell me stories of my predecessors, young men lodgers who like myself had taken her bed-sitting-rooms, and of the woes and misfortunes that had overtaken them. I gathered that a more unlucky house I could not have selected. A former tenant of my own room, of whom I strangely reminded her, had written poetry on my very table. He was now in Portland doing five years for forgery. Mrs. Peedles appeared to regard the two accomplishments as merely different expressions of the same art. Another of her young men, as she affectionately called us, had been of studious ambition. His career up to a point appeared to have been brilliant. "What he mightn't have been," according to Mrs. Peedles, there was practically no saying; what he happened to be at the moment of conversation was an unpromising inmate of the Hanwell lunatic asylum.

"I've always noticed it," Mrs. Peedles would explain; "it's always the most deserving, those that try hardest, to whom trouble comes. I'm sure I don't know why."

I was glad on the whole when that bottle of whiskey was finished. A second might have driven me to suicide.

There was no Mr. Peedles, at least, not for Mrs. Peedles, though as an individual he continued to exist. He had been "general utility" at the Princess's, the old terms were still in vogue at that time, a fine figure of a man in his day, so I was given to understand, but one easily led away, especially by minxes. Mrs. Peedles spoke bitterly of general utilities as people of not much use.

For working days Mrs. Peedles had one dress and one cap, both black and void of ostentation; but on Sundays and holidays she would appear metamorphosed. She had carefully preserved the bulk of her stage wardrobe, even to the paste-decked shoes and tinsel jewellery. Shapeless in classic garb as Hermia, or bulgy in brocade and velvet as Lady Teazle, she would receive her few visitors on Sunday evenings, discarded puppets like herself, with whom the conversation was of gayer nights before their wires had been cut; or, her glory hid from the ribald street beneath a mackintosh, pay her few calls. Maybe it was the unusual excitement that then brought colour into her furrowed cheeks, that straightened and darkened her eyebrows, at other times so singularly unobtrusive. Be this how it may, the change was remarkable, only the thin grey hair and the work-worn hands remaining for purposes of identification. Nor was the transformation merely one of surface. Mrs. Peedles hung on her hook behind the kitchen door, dingy, limp, discarded; out of the wardrobe with the silks and satins was lifted down to be put on as an undergarment Miss Lucretia Barry, like her costumes somewhat aged, somewhat withered, but still distinctly "arch."

In the room next to me lived a law-writer and his wife. They were very old and miserably poor. The fault was none of theirs. Despite copy-books maxims, there is in this world such a thing as ill-luck-persistent, monotonous, that gradually wears away all power of resistance. I learned from them their history: it was hopelessly simple, hopelessly uninstructive. He had been a schoolmaster, she a pupil teacher; they had married young, and for a while the world had smiled upon them. Then came illness, attacking them both: nothing out of which any moral could be deduced, a mere case of bad drains resulting in typhoid fever. They had started again, saddled by debt, and after years of effort had succeeded in clearing themselves, only to fall again, this time in helping a friend. Nor was it even a case of folly: a poor man who had helped them in their trouble, hardly could they have done otherwise without proving themselves ungrateful. And so on, a tedious tale, commonplace, trivial. Now listless, patient, hard working, they had arrived at an animal-like indifference to their fate, content so long as they could obtain the bare necessities of existence, passive when these were not forthcoming, their interest in life limited to the one luxury of the poor, an occasional glass of beer or spirits. Often days would go by without his obtaining any work, and then they would more or less starve. Law documents are generally given out to such men in the evening, to be returned finished the next morning. Waking in the night, I would hear through the thin wooden partition that divided our rooms the even scratching of his pen.

Thus cheek by jowl we worked, I my side of the screen, he his: youth and age, hope and realisation.

Out of him my fears fashioned a vision of the future. Past his door I would slink on tiptoe, dread meeting him upon the stairs. Once had not he said to himself: "The world's mine oyster?" May not the voices of the night have proclaimed him also king? Might I not be but an idle dreamer, mistaking desire for power? Would not the world prove stronger than I? At such times I would see my life before me: the clerkship at thirty shillings a week rising by slow instalments, it may be, to one hundred and fifty a year; the four-roomed house at Brixton; the girl wife, pretty, perhaps, but sinking so soon into the slatternly woman; the squalling children. How could I, unaided, expect to raise myself from the ruck? Was not this the more likely picture?

Our second floor front was a young fellow in the commercial line. Jarman was Young London personified, blatant yet kind-hearted; aggressively self-assertive, generous to a fault; cunning, yet at the same time frank; shrewd, cheery, and full of pluck. "Never say die" was his motto, and anything less dead it would be difficult to imagine. All day long he was noisy, and all night long he snored. He woke with a start, bathed like a porpoise, sang while dressing, roared for his boots, and whistled during his breakfast. His entrance and exit were always to an orchestration of banging doors, directions concerning his meals shouted at the top of his voice as he plunged up or down the stairs, the clattering and rattling of brooms and pails flying before his feet. His departure always left behind it the suggestion that the house was now to let; it came almost as a shock to meet a human being on the landing. He would have conveyed an atmosphere of bustle to the Egyptian pyramids.

Sometimes carrying his own supper-tray, arranged for two, he would march into my room. At first, resenting his familiarity, I would hint at my desire to be alone, would explain that I was busy.

"You fire away, Shakespeare Redivivus," he would reply. "Don't delay the tragedy. Why should London wait? I'll keep quiet."

But his notion of keeping quiet was to retire into a corner and there amuse himself by enacting a tragedy of his own in a hoarse whisper, accompanied by appropriate gesture.

"Ah, ah!" I would hear him muttering to himself, "I 'ave killed 'er good old father; I 'ave falsely accused 'er young man of all the crimes that I 'ave myself committed; I 'ave robbed 'er of 'er ancestral estates. Yet she loves me not! It is streeange!" Then changing his bass to a shrill falsetto: "It is a cold and dismal night: the snow falls fast. I will leave me 'at and umbrella be'ind the door and go out for a walk with the chee-ild. Aha! who is this? 'E also 'as forgotten 'is umbrella. Ah, now I know 'im in the pitch dark by 'is cigarette! Villain, murderer, silly josser! it is you!" Then with lightning change of voice and gesture: "Mary, I love yer!" "Sir Jasper Murgatroyd, let me avail myself of this opportunity to tell you what I think of you" "No, no; the 'ouses close in 'alf an hour; there is not tee-ime. Fly with me instead!" "Never! Un'and me!" "'Ear me! Ah, what 'ave I done? I 'ave slipped upon a piece of orange peel and broke me 'ead! If you will kindly ask them to turn off the snow and give me a little moonlight, I will confess all."

Finding it (much to Jarman's surprise) impossible to renew the thread of my work, I would abandon my attempts at literature, and instead listen to his talk, which was always interesting. His conversation was, it is true, generally about himself, but it was none the less attractive on that account. His love affairs, which appeared to be numerous, formed his chief topic. There was no reserve about Jarman: his life contained no secret chambers. What he "told her straight," what she "up and said to him" in reply was for all the world that cared to hear. So far his search after the ideal had met with but ill success.

"Girls," he would say, "they're all alike, till you know 'em. So long as they're trying to palm themselves off on yer, they'll persuade you there isn't such another article in all the market. When they've got yer order, ah, then yer find out what they're really made of. And you take it from me, 'Omer Junior, most of 'em are put together cheap. Bah! it sickens me sometimes to read the way you paper-stainers talk about 'em-angels, goddesses, fairies! They've just been getting at yer. You're giving 'em just the price they're asking without examining the article. Girls ain't a special make, like what you seem to think 'em. We're all turned out of the same old slop shop."

"Not that I say, mind yer," he would continue, "that there are none of the right sort. They're to be 'ad, real good 'uns. All I say is, taking 'em at their own valuation ain't the way to do business with 'em."

What he was on the look out for, to quote his own description, was a really first class article, not something from which the paint would come off almost before you got it home.

"They're to be found," he would cheerfully affirm, "but you've got to look for 'em. They're not the sort that advertises."

Behind Jarman in the second floor back resided one whom Jarman had nicknamed "The Lady 'Ortensia." I believe before my arrival there had been love passages between the two; but neither of them, so I gathered, had upon closer inspection satisfied the other's standard. Their present attitude towards each other was that of insult thinly veiled under exaggerated politeness. Miss Rosina Sellars was, in her own language, a "lady assistant," in common parlance, a barmaid at the Ludgate Hill Station refreshment room. She was a large, flabby young woman. With less powder, her complexion might by admirers have been termed creamy; as it was, it presented the appearance rather of underdone pastry. To be on all occasions "quite the lady" was her pride. There were those who held the angle of her dignity to be exaggerated. Jarman would beg her for her own sake to be more careful lest one day she should fall down backwards and hurt herself. On the other hand, her bearing was certainly calculated to check familiarity. Even stockbrokers' clerks, young men as a class with the bump of reverence but poorly developed, would in her presence falter and grow hesitating. She had cultivated the art of not noticing to something approaching perfection. She could draw the noisiest customer a glass of beer, which he had never ordered; exchange it for three of whiskey, which he had; take his money and return him his change without ever seeing him, hearing him, or knowing he was there. It shattered the self-assertion of the youngest of commercial travellers. Her tone and manner, outside rare moments of excitement, were suggestive of an offended but forgiving iceberg. Jarman invariably passed her with his coat collar turned up to his ears, and even thus protected might have been observed to shiver. Her stare, in conjunction with her "I beg your pardon!" was a moral douche that would have rendered apologetic and explanatory Don Juan himself.

To me she was always gracious, which by contrast to her general attitude towards my sex of studied disdain, I confess flattered me. She was good enough to observe to Mrs. Peedles, who repeated it to me, that I was the only gentleman in the house who knew how to behave himself.

The entire first floor was occupied by an Irishman and they never minced the matter themselves, so hardly is there need for me to do so. She was a charming little dark-eyed woman, an ex-tight-rope dancer, and always greatly offended Mrs. Peedles by claiming Miss Lucretia Barry as a sister artiste.

"Of course I don't know how it may be now," would reply Mrs. Peedles, with some slight asperity; "but in my time we ladies of the legitimate stage used to look down upon dancers and such sort. Of course, no offence to you, Mrs. O'Kelly."

Neither of them was in the least offended.

"Sure, Mrs. Peedles, ye could never have looked down upon the Signora," the O'Kelly would answer laughing. "Ye had to lie back and look up to her. Why, I've got the crick in me neck to this day!"

"Ah! my dear, and you don't know how nervous I was when glancing down I'd see his handsome face just underneath me, thinking that with one false step I might spoil it for ever," would reply the Signora.

"Me darling! I'd have died happy, just smothered in loveliness!" would return the O'Kelly; and he and the Signora would rush into each other's arms, and the sound of their kisses would quite excite the little slavey sweeping down the stairs outside.

He was a barrister attached in theory to the Western Circuit; in practice, somewhat indifferent to it, much more attached to the lower strata of Bohemia and the Signora. At the present he was earning all sufficient for the simple needs of himself and the Signora as a teacher of music and singing. His method was simple and suited admirably the locality. Unless specially requested, he never troubled his pupils with such tiresome things as scales and exercises. His plan was to discover the song the young man fancied himself singing, the particular jingle the young lady yearned to knock out of the piano, and to teach it to them. Was it "Tom Bowling?" Well and good. Come on; follow your leader. The O'Kelly would sing the first line.

"Now then, try that. Don't be afraid. Just open yer mouth and gave it tongue. That's all right. Everything has a beginning. Sure, later on, we'll get the time and tune, maybe a little expression."

Whether the system had any merit in it, I cannot answer. Certain it was that as often as not it achieved success. Gradually, say, by the end of twelve eighteen-penny lessons, out of storm and chaos "Tom Bowling" would emerge, recognisable for all men to hear. Had the pupil any voice to start with, the O'Kelly improved it; had he none, the O'Kelly would help him to disguise the fact.

"Take it easy, now; take it easy," the O'Kelly would counsel. "Sure, it's a delicate organ, yer voice. Don't ye strain it now. Ye're at yer best when ye're just low and sweet."

So also with the blushing pianiste. At the end of a month a tune was distinctly discernible; she could hear it herself, and was happy. His repute spread.

Twice already had he eloped with the Signora (and twice again was he to repeat the operation, before I finally lost sight of him: to break oneself of habit is always difficult) and once by well-meaning friends had he been induced to return to home, if not to beauty. His wife, who was considerably older than himself, possessed, so he would inform me with tears in his eyes, every moral excellence that should attract mankind. Upon her goodness and virtue, her piety and conscientiousness he would descant to me by the half hour. His sincerity it was impossible to question. It was beyond doubt that he respected her, admired her, honoured her. She was a saint, an angel, a wretch, a villain such as he, was not fit to breathe the same pure air. To do him justice, it must be admitted he showed no particular desire to do so. As an aunt or grandmother, I believe he would have suffered her gladly. He had nothing to say against her, except that he found himself unable to live with her.

That she must have been a lady of exceptional merit one felt convinced. The Signora, who had met her only once, and then under somewhat trying conditions, spoke her praises with equal enthusiasm. Had she, the Signora, enjoyed the advantage of meeting such a model earlier, she, the Signora, might have been a better woman. It seemed a pity the introduction could not have taken place sooner and under different circumstances. Could they both have adopted her as a sort of mutual mother-in-law, it would have given them, I am positive, the greatest satisfaction. On her occasional visits they would have vied with each other in showing her affectionate attention. For the deserted lady I tried to feel sorry, but could not avoid the reflection that it would have been better for all parties had she been less patient and forgiving. Her husband was evidently much more suited to the Signora.

Indeed, the relationship between these two was more a true marriage than one generally meets with. No pair of love-birds could have been more snug together. In their virtues and failings alike they fitted each other. When sober the immorality of their behaviour never troubled them; in fact, when sober nothing ever troubled them. They laughed, joked, played through life, two happy children. To be shocked at them was impossible. I tried it and failed.

But now and again there came an evening when they were not sober. It happened when funds were high. On such occasion the O'Kelly would return laden with bottles of a certain sweet champagne, of which they were both extremely fond; and a friend or two would be invited to share in the festivity. Whether any exceptional quality resided in this particular brand of champagne I am not prepared to argue; my own personal experience of it has prompted me to avoid it for the rest of my life. Its effect upon them was certainly unique. Instead of intoxicating them, it sobered them: there is no other way of explaining it. With the third or fourth glass they began to take serious views of life. Before the end of the second bottle they would be staring at each other, appalled at contemplation of their own transgression. The Signora, the tears streaming down her pretty face, would declare herself a wicked, wicked woman; she had dragged down into shame the most blameless, the most virtuous of men. Emptying her glass, she would bury her face in her hands, and with her elbows on her knees, in an agony of remorse, sit rocking to and fro. The O'Kelly, throwing himself at her feet, would passionately abjure her to "look up." She had, it appeared, got hold of the thing at the wrong end; it was he who had dragged her down.

At this point metaphor would become confused. Each had been dragged down by the other one and ruined; also each one was the other one's good angel. All that was commendable in the Signora, she owed to the O'Kelly. Whatever was not discreditable about the O'Kelly was in the nature of a loan from the Signora. With the help of more champagne the right course would grow plain to them. She would go back broken-hearted but repentant to the tight-rope; he would return a better but a blighted man to Mrs. O'Kelly and the Western Circuit. This would be their last evening together on earth. A fresh bottle would be broached, and the guest or guests called upon to assist in the ceremony of renunciation; glasses full to the brim this time.

So much tragedy did they continue to instil into the scene that on the first occasion of my witnessing it I was unable to refrain from mingling my tears with theirs. As, however, the next morning they had forgotten all about it, and as nothing came of it, nor of several subsequent repetitions, I should have believed a separation between them impossible but that even while I was an inmate of the house the thing actually happened.

It came about in this wise. His friends, having discovered him, had pointed out to him again his duty. The Signora, a really excellent little woman so far as intention was concerned, had seconded their endeavours, with the result that on a certain evening in autumn we of the house assembled all of us on the first floor to support them on the occasion of their final, so we all deemed it then, leave-taking. For eleven o'clock two four-wheeled cabs had been ordered, one to transport the O'Kelly with his belongings to Hampstead and respectability; in the other the Signora would journey sorrowfully to the Tower Basin, there to join a circus company sailing for the Continent.

I knocked at the door some quarter of an hour before the appointed hour of the party. I fancy the idea had originated with the Signora.

"Dear Willie has something to say to you," she had informed me that morning on the stairs. "He has taken a sincere liking to you, and it is something very important."

They were sitting one each side the fireplace, looking very serious; a bottle of the sobering champagne stood upon the table. The Signora rose and kissed me gravely on the brow; the O'Kelly laid both hands upon my shoulders, and sat me down on a chair between them.

"Mr. Kelver," said the Signora, "you are very young."

I hinted, it was one of those rare occasions upon which gallantry can be combined with truth, that I found myself in company.

The Signora smiled sadly, and shook her head.

"Age," said the O'Kelly, "is a matter of feeling. Kelver, may ye never be as old as I am feeling now."

"As we are feeling," corrected the Signora. "Kelver," said the O'Kelly, pouring out a third glass of champagne, "we want ye to promise us something."

"It will make us both happier," added the Signora.

"That ye will take warning," continued the O'Kelly, "by our wretched example. Paul, in this world there is only one path to possible happiness. The path of strict" he paused.

"Propriety," suggested the Signora.

"Of strict propriety," agreed the O'Kelly. "Deviate from it," continued the O'Kelly, impressively, "and what is the result?"

"Unutterable misery," supplied the Signora.

"Ye think we two have been happy here together," said the O'Kelly.

I replied that such was the conclusion to which observation had directed me.

"We tried to appear so," explained the Signora; "it was merely on the outside. In reality all the time we hated each other. Tell him, Willie, dear, how we have hated each other."

"It is impossible," said the O'Kelly, finishing and putting down his glass, "to give ye any idea, Kelver, how we have hated each other."

"How we have quarrelled!" said the Signora. "Tell him, dear, how we have quarrelled."

"All day long and half the night," concluded the O'Kelly.

"Fought," added the Signora. "You see, Mr. Kelver, people in, in our position always do. If it had been otherwise, if, if everything had been proper, then of course we should have loved each other. As it is, it has been a cat and dog existence. Hasn't it been a cat and dog existence, Willie?"

"It's been just hell upon earth," murmured the O'Kelly, with his eyes fixed gloomily upon the fire-stove ornament. Deadly in earnest though they both were, I could not repress a laugh, their excellent intention was so obvious. The Signora burst into tears.

"He doesn't believe us," she wailed.

"Me dear," replied the O'Kelly, throwing up his part with promptness and satisfaction, "how could ye expect it? How could he believe that any man could look at ye and hate ye?"

"It's all my fault," cried the little woman; "I am such a wicked creature. I cannot even be miserable when I am doing wrong. A decent woman in my place would have been wretched and unhappy, and made everybody about her wretched and unhappy, and so have set a good example and have been a warning. I don't seem to have any conscience, and I do try." The poor little lady was sobbing her heart out.

When not shy I could be sensible, and of the O'Kelly and the Signora one could be no more shy than of a pair of robin redbreasts. Besides, I was really fond of them; they had been very good to me.

"Dear Miss Beltoni," I answered, "I am going to take warning by you both."

She pressed my hand. "Oh, do, please do," she murmured. "We really have been miserable, now and then."

"I am never going to be content," I assured her, "until I find a lady as charming and as amiable as you, and if ever I get her I'll take good care never to run any risk of losing her."

It sounded well and pleased us all. The O'Kelly shook me warmly by the hand, and this time spoke his real feelings.

"Me boy," he said, "all women are good for somebody. But the woman that is good for yerself is better for ye than a better woman who's the best for somebody else. Ye understand?"

I said I did.

At eight o'clock precisely Mrs. Peedles arrived, as Flora MacDonald, in green velvet jacket and twelve to fifteen inches of plaid stocking. As a topic fitting the occasion we discussed the absent Mr. Peedles and the subject of deserted wives in general.

"A fine-looking man," allowed Mrs. Peedles, "but weak, weak as water."

The Signora agreed that unfortunately there did exist such men: 'twas pitiful but true.

"My dear," continued Mrs. Peedles, "she wasn't even a lady."

The Signora expressed astonishment at the deterioration in Mr. Peedles' taste thus implied.

"I won't go so far as to say we never had a difference," continued Mrs. Peedles, whose object appeared to be an impartial statement of the whole case. "There may have been incompatability of temperament, as they say. Myself, I have always been of a playful disposition, frivolous, some might call me."

The Signora protested; the O'Kelly declined to listen to such aspersion on her character even from Mrs. Peedles herself.

Mrs. Peedles, thus corrected, allowed that maybe frivolous was too sweeping an accusation: say sportive.

"But a good wife to him I always was," asserted Mrs. Peedles, with a fine sense of justice; "never flighty, like some of them. I challenge any one to accuse me of having been flighty."

We felt we should not believe anyone who did, and told her so.

Mrs. Peedles, drawing her chair closer to the Signora, assumed a confidential attitude. "If they want to go, let 'em go, I always say," she whispered loudly into the Signora's ear. "Ten to one they'll find they've only jumped out of the frying-pan into the fire. One can always comfort oneself with that."

There seemed to be confusion in the mind of Mrs. Peedles. Her virtuous sympathies, I gathered, were with the Signora. Mr. O'Kelly's return to Mrs. O'Kelly evidently manifested itself in the light of a shameful desertion. Having regard to the fact, patent to all who knew him, that the poor fellow was sacrificing every inclination to stern sense of duty, such view of the matter was rough on him. But philosophers from all ages have agreed that our good deeds are the whips with which Fate punishes us for our bad.

"My dear," continued Mrs. Peedles, "when Mr. Peedles left me I thought that I should never smile again. Yet here you see me laughing away through life, just as ever. You'll get over it all right." And Mrs. Peedles wiped away her tears and smiled upon the Signora; upon which the Signora commenced to cry again.

Happily, timely diversion was made at this point by the bursting into the room of Jarman, who upon perceiving Mrs. Peedles, at once gave vent to a hoot, supposed to be expressive of Scottish joy, and without a moment's hesitation commenced to dance a reel.

My neighbours of the first floor knocked at the door a little while afterwards; and genteelly late arrived Miss Rosina Sellars, coldly gleaming in a decollete but awe-inspiring costume of mingled black and scarlet, out of which her fair, if fleshy, neck and arms shone luxuriant.

We did not go into supper; instead, supper came into us from the restaurant at the corner of the Blackfriars Road. I cannot say that at first it was a festive meal. The O'Kelly and the Signora made effort, as in duty bound, to be cheerful, but for awhile were somewhat unsuccessful. The third floor front wasted no time in speech, but ate and drank copiously. Miss Sellars, retaining her gloves, which was perhaps wise, her hands being her weak point, signalled me out, much to my embarrassment, as the recipient of her most polite conversation. Mrs. Peedles became reminiscent of parties generally. Seeing that most of Mrs. Peedles' former friends and acquaintances were either dead or in more or less trouble, her efforts did not tend to enliven the table. One gathering, of which the present strangely reminded her, was a funeral, chiefly remarkable from discovery of the romantic fact, late in the proceedings, that the gentleman in whose honour the whole affair had been organised was not dead at all; but instead, having taken advantage of an error arising out of a railway accident, was at the moment eloping with the wife of his own chief mourner. As Mrs. Peedles explained, and as one could well credit, it had been an awkward position for all present. Nobody had quite known whether to feel glad or sorry, with the exception of the chief mourner, upon whose personal undertaking that the company might regard the ceremony as merely postponed, festivities came to an end.

Our prop and stay from a convivial point of view was Jarman. As a delicate attention to Mrs. Peedles and her costume he sunk his nationality and became for the evening, according to his own declaration, "a braw laddie." With her, his "sonsie lassie," so he termed her, he flirted in the broadest, if not purest, Scotch. The O'Kelly for him became "the Laird;" the third floor "Jamie o' the Ilk;" Miss Sellars, "the bonnie wee rose;" myself, "the chiel." Periods of silence were dispersed by suggestions that we should "hoot awa'," Jarman himself setting us the example.

With the clearance away of the eatables, making room for the production of a more varied supply of bottles, matters began to mend. Mrs. Peedles became more arch, Jarman's Scotch more striking and extensive, the Lady 'Ortensia's remarks less depressingly genteel, her aitches less accentuated.

Jarman rose to propose the health of the O'Kelly, coupled with that of the Signora. To the O'Kelly, in a burst of generosity, Jarman promised our united patronage. To Jarman it appeared that by employing the O'Kelly to defend us whenever we got into trouble with the police, and by recommending him to our friends, a steady income should be assured to him.

The O'Kelly replied feelingly to the effect that Nelson Square, Blackfriars, would ever remain engraved upon his memory as the fairest and brightest spot on earth. Personally, nothing would have given him greater pleasure than to die among the dear friends who now surrounded him. But there was such a thing as duty, and he and the Signora had come to the conclusion that true happiness could only be obtained by acting according to one's conscience, even if it made one miserable.

Jarman, warming to his work, then proposed the health of Mrs. Peedles, as true-hearted and hard-breathing a lady as ever it had been his privilege to know. Her talent for cheery conversation was familiar to us all, upon it he need not enlarge; all he would say was that personally never did she go out of his room without leaving him more cheerful than when she entered it.

After that, I forget in what, we drank the health of the Lady 'Ortensia. Persons there were, Jarman would not attempt to disguise the fact, who complained that the Lady 'Ortensia was too distant, "too stand-offish." With such complaint he himself had no sympathy; but tastes differed. If the Lady 'Ortensia were inclined to be exclusive, who should blame her? Everybody knew their own business best. For use in a second floor front he could not honestly recommend the Lady 'Ortensia; it would not be giving her a fair chance, and it would not be giving the second floor a fair chance. But for any gentleman fitting up marble halls, for any one on the lookout for a really "toney article," Jarman would say: Inquire for Miss Rosina Sellars, and see that you get her.

There followed my turn. There had been literary chaps in the past, Jarman admitted so much. Against them he had nothing to say. They had no doubt done their best. But the gentleman whose health Jarman wished the company now to drink had this advantage over them: that they were dead, and he wasn't. Some of this gentleman's work Jarman had read, in manuscript; but that was a distinction purely temporary. He, Jarman, claimed to be no judge of literature, but this he could and would say, it took a good deal to make him miserable, yet this the literary efforts of Mr. Kelver invariably accomplished.

Mrs. Peedles, speaking without rising, from personal observation in the daytime, which she hoped would not be deemed a liberty; literature, even in manuscript, being, so to speak, public property, found herself in a position to confirm all that Mr. Jarman had remarked. Speaking as one not entirely without authority on the subject of literature and the drama, Mrs. Peedles could say that passages she had read had struck her as distinctly not half bad. Some of the love-scenes, in particular, had made her to feel quite a girl again. How he had acquired such knowledge was not for her to say. Cries of "Naughty!" from Jarman, and "Oh, Mr. Kelver, I shall be quite afraid of you," roguishly from Miss Sellars.

The O'Kelly, who, having abandoned his favourite champagne for less sobering liquor, had since supper-time become rapidly more cheerful, felt sure there was a future before me. That he had not seen any of my work, so he assured me, in no way lessened his opinion of it. One thing only would he impress upon me: that the best work was the result of strict attention to virtue. His advice to me was to marry young and be happy.

My persevering efforts of the last few months towards the acquisition of convivial habits appeared this evening to be receiving their reward. The O'Kelly's sweet champagne I had drunk with less dislike than hitherto; a white, syrupy sort of stuff, out of a fat and artistic-looking bottle, I had found distinctly grateful to the palate. Dimly the quotation about taking things at the flood, and so getting on quickly, floated through my brain, coupled with another one about fortune favouring the bold. It had seemed to me a good occasion to try for the second time in my life a full flavoured cigar. I had selected with the caution of a connoisseur one of mottled green complexion from the O'Kelly's largest box. And so far all had gone well. An easy self-confidence, delightful by reason of its novelty, had replaced my customary shyness; a sense of lightness, of positive airiness, emanating from myself, pervaded all things. Tossing off another glass of the champagne, I rose to reply.

Modesty in my present mood would have been affectation. To such dear and well-beloved friends I had no hesitation in admitting the truth, that I was a clever fellow, a damned clever fellow. I knew it, they knew it, in a short time everybody would know it. But they need not fear that in the hour of my pride, when it arrived, I should prove ungrateful. Never should I forget their kindness to me, a lonely young man, alone in a lonely - Here the pathos of my own situation overcame me; words seemed weak. "Jarman" I meant, putting my hand upon his head, to have blessed him for his goodness to me; but he being not exactly where he looked to be, I just missed him, and sat down on the edge of my chair, which was a hard one. I had not intended this to be the end of my speech, by a long one; but Jarman, whispering to me: "Ended at exactly the right moment; shows the born orator," strong inclination to remain seated, now that I was down seconding his counsel, and the company being clearly satisfied, I decided to leave things where they were.

A delightful dreaminess was stealing over me. Everything and everybody appeared to be a long way off, but, whether because of this or in spite of it, exceedingly attractive. Never had I noticed the Signora so bewitching; in a motherly sort of way even the third floor front was good to look upon; Mrs. Peedles I could almost have believed to be the real Flora MacDonald sitting in front of me. But the vision of Miss Rosina Sellars made literally my head to swim. Never before had I dared to cast upon female loveliness the satisfying gaze with which I now boldly regarded her every movement. Evidently she noticed it, for she turned away her eyes. I had heard that exceptionally strong-minded people merely by concentrating their will could make other, ordinary people, do just whatever they, the exceptionally strong-minded people, wished. I willed that Miss Rosina Sellars should turn her eyes again towards me. Victory crowned my efforts. Evidently I was one of these exceptionally strong-minded persons. Slowly her eyes came round and met mine with a smile, a helpless, pathetic smile that said, so I read it: "You know no woman can resist you: be merciful!"

Inflamed by the brutal lust of conquest, I suppose I must have willed still further, for the next thing I remember is sitting with Miss Sellars on the sofa, holding her hand, the while the O'Kelly sang a sentimental ballad, only one line of which comes back to me: "For the angels must have told him, and he knows I love him now," much stress upon the "now." The others had their backs towards us. Miss Sellars, with a look that pierced my heart, dropped her somewhat large head upon my shoulder, leaving, as I observed the next day, a patch of powder on my coat.

Miss Sellars observed that one of the saddest things in the world was unrequited love.

I replied gallantly, "Whateryou know about it?"

"Ah, you men, you men," murmured Miss Sellars; "you're all alike."

This suggested a personal aspersion on my character. "Not allus," I murmured.

"You don't know what love is," said Miss Sellars. "You're not old enough."

The O'Kelly had passed on to Sullivan's "Sweethearts," then in its first popularity.

"Oh, love for a year, a week, a day! But oh for the love that loves al-wa-ay[s]!" Miss Sellars' languishing eyes were fixed upon me; Miss Sellars' red lips pouted and twitched; Miss Sellars' white bosom rose and fell. Never, so it seemed to me, had so large an amount of beauty been concentrated in one being.

"Yeserdo," I said. "I love you."

I stooped to kiss the red lips, but something was in my way. It turned out to be a cold cigar. Miss Sellars thoughtfully removed it, and threw it away. Our lips met. Her large arms closed about my neck and held me tight.

"Well, I'm sure!" came the voice of Mrs. Peedles, as from afar. "Nice goings on!"

I have vague remembrance of a somewhat heated discussion, in which everybody but myself appeared to be taking extreme interest, of Miss Sellars in her most ladylike and chilling tones defending me against the charge of "being no gentleman," which Mrs. Peedles was explaining nobody had said I wasn't. The argument seemed to be of the circular order. No gentleman had ever kissed Miss Sellars who had not every right to do so, nor ever would. To kiss Miss Sellars without such right was to declare oneself no gentleman. Miss Sellars appealed to me to clear my character from the aspersion of being no gentleman. I was trying to understand the situation, when Jarman, seizing me somewhat roughly by the arm, suggested my going to bed. Miss Sellars, seizing my other arm, suggested my refusing to go to bed. So far I was with Miss Sellars. I didn't want to go to bed, and said so. My desire to sit up longer was proof positive to Miss Sellars that I was a gentleman, but to no one else. The argument shifted, the question being now as to whether Miss Sellars were a lady. To prove the point it was, according to Miss Sellars, necessary that I should repeat I loved her. I did repeat it, adding, with faint remembrance of my own fiction, that if a life's devotion was likely to be of the slightest further proof, my heart's blood was at her service. This cleared the air, Mrs. Peedles observing that under such circumstances it only remained for her to withdraw everything she had said; to which Miss Sellars replied graciously that she had always known Mrs. Peedles to be a good sort at the bottom.

Nevertheless, gaiety was gone from among us, and for this, in some way I could not understand, I appeared to be responsible. Jarman was distinctly sulky. The O'Kelly, suddenly thinking of the time, went to the door and discovered that the two cabs were waiting. The third floor recollected that work had to be finished. I myself felt sleepy.

Our host and hostess departed; Jarman again suggested bed, and this time I agreed with him. After a slight misunderstanding with the door, I found myself upon the stairs. I had never noticed before that they were quite perpendicular. Adapting myself to the changed conditions, I climbed them with the help of my hands. I accomplished the last flight somewhat quickly, and feeling tired, sat down the moment I was within my own room. Jarman knocked at the door. I told him to come in; but he didn't. It occurred to me that the reason was I was sitting on the floor with my back against the door. The discovery amused me exceedingly and I laughed; and Jarman, baffled, descended to his own floor. I found getting into bed a difficulty, owing to the strange behaviour of the room. It spun round and round. Now the bed was just in front of me, now it was behind me. I managed at last to catch it before it could get past me, and holding on by the ironwork, frustrated its efforts to throw me out again on to the floor.

But it was some time before I went to sleep, and over my intervening experiences I draw a veil.

GOOD FRIENDS SHOW PAUL THE ROAD TO FREEDOM. BUT BEFORE SETTING OUT, HE WILL GO A-VISITING.

The sun was streaming into my window when I woke in the morning. I sat up and listened. The roar of the streets told me plainly that the day had begun without me. I reached out my hand for my watch; it was not in its usual place upon the rickety dressing-table. I raised myself still higher and looked about me. My clothes lay scattered on the floor. One boot, in solitary state, occupied the chair by the fireplace; the other I could not see anywhere.

During the night my head appeared to have grown considerably. I wondered idly for the moment whether I had not made a mistake and put on Minikin's; if so, I should be glad to exchange back for my own. This thing I had got was a top-heavy affair, and was aching most confoundedly.

Suddenly the recollection of the previous night rushed at me and shook me awake. From a neighbouring steeple rang chimes: I counted with care. Eleven o'clock. I sprang out of bed, and at once sat down upon the floor.

I remembered how, holding on to the bed, I had felt the room waltzing wildly round and round. It had not quite steadied itself even yet. It was still rotating, not whirling now, but staggering feebly, as though worn out by its all-night orgie. Creeping to the wash-stand, I succeeded, after one or two false plunges, in getting my head inside the basin. Then, drawing on my trousers with difficulty and reaching the easy-chair, I sat down and reviewed matters so far as I was able, commencing from the present and working back towards the past.

I was feeling very ill. That was quite clear. Something had disagreed with me.

"That strong cigar," I whispered feebly to myself; "I ought never to have ventured upon it. And then the little room with all those people in it. Besides, I have been working very hard. I must really take more exercise.

It gave me some satisfaction to observe that, shuffling and cowardly though I might be, I was not a person easily bamboozled.

"Nonsense," I told myself brutally; "don't try to deceive me. You were drunk."

"Not drunk," I pleaded; "don't say drunk; it is such a coarse expression. Some people cannot stand sweet champagne, so I have heard. It affected my liver. Do please make it a question of liver."

"Drunk," I persisted unrelentingly, "hopelessly, vulgarly drunk, drunk as any 'Arry after a Bank Holiday."

"It is the first time," I murmured.

"It was your first opportunity," I replied.

"Never again," I promised.

"The stock phrase," I returned.

"How old are you?"

"Nineteen."

"So you have not even the excuse of youth. How do you know that it will not grow upon you; that, having thus commenced a downward career, you will not sink lower and lower, and so end by becoming a confirmed sot?"

My heavy head dropped into my hands, and I groaned. Many a temperance tale perused on Sunday afternoons came back to me. Imaginative in all directions, I watched myself hastening toward a drunkard's grave, now heroically struggling against temptation, now weakly yielding, the craving growing upon me. In the misty air about me I saw my father's white face, my mother's sad eyes. I thought of Barbara, of the scorn that could quiver round that bewitching mouth; of Hal, with his tremendous contempt for all forms of weakness. Shame of the present and terror of the future between them racked my mind.

"It shall be never again!" I cried aloud. "By God, it shall!" (At nineteen one is apt to be vehement.) "I will leave this house at once," I continued to myself aloud; "I will get away from its unwholesome atmosphere. I will wipe it out of my mind, and all connected with it. I will make a fresh start. I will"

Something I had been dimly conscious of at the back of my brain came forward and stood before me: the flabby figure of Miss Rosina Sellars. What was she doing here? What right had she to step between me and my regeneration?

"The right of your affianced bride," my other half explained, with a grim smile to myself.

"Did I really go so far as that?"

"We will not go into details," I replied; "I do not wish to dwell upon them. That was the result."

"I was, I was not quite myself at the time. I did not know what I was doing."

"As a rule, we don't when we do foolish things; but we have to abide by the consequences, all the same. Unfortunately, it happened to be in the presence of witnesses, and she is not the sort of lady to be easily got rid of. You will marry her and settle down with her in two small rooms. Her people will be your people. You will come to know them better before many days are passed. Among them she is regarded as 'the lady,' from which you can judge of them. A nice commencement of your career, is it not, my ambitious young friend? A nice mess you have made of it!"

"What am I to do?" I asked.

"Upon my word, I don't know," I answered.

I passed a wretched day. Ashamed to face Mrs. Peedles or even the slavey, I kept to my room, with the door locked. At dusk, feeling a little better, or, rather, less bad, I stole out and indulged in a simple meal, consisting of tea without sugar and a kippered herring, at a neighbouring coffee-house. Another gentleman, taking his seat opposite to me and ordering hot buttered toast, I left hastily.

At eight o'clock in the evening Minikin called round from the office to know what had happened. Seeking help from shame, I confessed to him the truth.

"Thought as much," he answered. "Seems to have been an A1 from the look of you."

"I am glad it has happened, now it is over," I said to him. "It will be a lesson I shall never forget."

"I know," said Minikin. "Nothing like a fair and square drunk for making you feel real good; better than a sermon."

In my trouble I felt the need of advice; and Minikin, though my junior, was, I knew, far more experienced in worldly affairs than I was.

"That's not the worst," I confided to him. "What do you think I've done?"

"Killed a policeman?" suggested Minikin.

"Got myself engaged."

"No one like you quiet fellows for going it when you do begin," commented Minikin. "Nice girl?"

"I don't know," I answered. "I only know I don't want her. How can I get out of it?"

Minikin removed his left eye and commenced to polish it upon his handkerchief, a habit he had when in doubt. From looking into it he appeared to derive inspiration.

"Take-her-own-part sort of a girl?"

I intimated that he had diagnosed Miss Rosina Sellars correctly.

"Know how much you're earning?"

"She knows I live up here in this attic and do my own cooking," I answered.

Minikin glanced round the room. "Must be fond of you."

"She thinks I'm clever," I explained, "and that I shall make my way."

"And she's willing to wait?"

I nodded.

"Well, I should let her wait," replied Minikin, replacing his eye. "There's plenty of time before you."

"But she's a barmaid, and she'll expect me to walk with her, to take her out on Sundays, to go and see her friends. I can't do it. Besides, she's right: I mean to get on. Then she'll stick to me. It's awful!"

"How did it happen?" asked Minikin.

"I don't know," I replied. "I didn't know I had done it till it was over."

"Anybody present?"

"Half-a-dozen of them," I groaned.

The door opened, and Jarman entered; he never troubled to knock anywhere. In place of his usual noisy greeting, he crossed in silence and shook me gravely by the hand.

"Friend of yours?" he asked, indicating Minikin.

I introduced them to each other.

"Proud to meet you," said Jarman.

"Glad to hear it," said Minikin. "Don't look as if you'd got much else to be stuck up about."

"Don't mind him," I explained to Jarman. "He was born like it."

"Wonderful gift" replied Jarman. "D'ye know what I should do if I 'ad it?" He did not wait for Minikin's reply. "'Ire myself out to break up evening parties. Ever thought of it seriously?"

Minikin replied that he would give the idea consideration.

"Make your fortune going round the suburbs," assured him Jarman. "Pity you weren't 'ere last night," he continued; "might 'ave saved our young friend 'ere a deal of trouble. Has 'e told you the news?"

I explained that I had already put Minikin in possession of all the facts.

"Now you've got a good, steady eye," said Jarman, upon whom Minikin, according to his manner, had fixed his glass orb; "'ow d'ye think 'e is looking?"

"As well as can be expected under the circumstances, don't you think?" answered Minikin.

"Does 'e know the circumstances? Has 'e seen the girl?" asked Jarman.

I replied he had not as yet enjoyed that privilege. "Then 'e don't know the worst," said Jarman. "A hundred and sixty pounds of 'er, and still growing! Bit of a load for 'im, ain't it?"

"Some of 'em do have luck," was Minikin's rejoinder. Jarman leant forward and took further stock for a few seconds of his new acquaintance.

"That's a fine 'ead of yours," he remarked; "all your own? No offence," continued Jarman, without giving Minikin time for repartee. "I was merely thinking there must be room for a lot of sense in it. Now, what do you, as a practical man, advise 'im: dose of poison, or Waterloo Bridge and a brick?"

"I suppose there's no doubt," I interjected, "that we are actually engaged?"

"Not a blooming shadow," assured me Jarman, cheerfully, "so far as she's concerned."

"I shall tell her plainly," I explained, "that I was drunk at the time."

"And 'ow are you going to convince 'er of it?" asked Jarman. "You think your telling 'er you loved 'er proves it.   So it would to anybody else, but not to 'er. You can't expect it. Besides, if every girl is going to give up 'er catch just because the fellow 'adn't all 'is wits about 'im at the time, well, what do you think?" He appealed to Minikin.

To Minikin it appeared that if such contention were allowed girls might as well shut up shop.

Jarman, who now that he had "got even" with Minikin, was more friendly disposed towards that young man, drew his chair closer to him and entered upon a private and confidential argument, from which I appeared to be entirely excluded.

"You see," explained Jarman, "this ain't an ordinary case. This chap's going to be the future Poet Laureate. Now, when the Prince of Wales invites him to dine at Marlborough 'ouse, 'e don't want to go there tacked on to a girl that carries aitches with her in a bag, and don't know which end of the spoon out of which to drink 'er soup."

"It makes a difference, of course," agreed Minikin.

"What we've got to do," said Jarman, "is to get 'im out of it. And upon my sivvy, blessed if I see 'ow to do it!"

"She fancies him?" asked Minikin.

"What she fancies," explained Jarman, "is that nature intended 'er to be a lady. And it's no good pointing out to 'er the mistake she's making, because she ain't got sense enough to see it."

"No good talking straight to her," suggested Minikin, "telling her that it can never be?"

"That's our difficulty," replied Jarman; "it can be. This chap", I listened as might a prisoner in the dock to the argument of counsel, interested but impotent, "don't know enough to come in out of the rain, as the saying is. 'E's just the sort of chap this sort of thing does 'appen to."

"But he don't want her," urged Minikin. "He says he don't want her."

"Yes, to you and me," answered Jarman; "and of course 'e don't. I'm not saying 'e's a natural born idiot. But let 'er come along and do a snivel, tell 'im that 'e's breaking 'er 'eart, and appeal to 'im to be'ave as a gentleman, and all that sort of thing, and what do you think will be the result?"

Minikin agreed that the problem presented difficulties.

"Of course, if 'twas you or me, we should just tell 'er to put 'erself away somewhere where the moth couldn't get at 'er and wait till we sent round for 'er; and there'd be an end of the matter. But with 'im it's different."

"He is a bit of a soft," agreed Minikin.

"'Tain't 'is fault," explained Jarman; "'twas the way 'e was brought up. 'E fancies girls are the sort of things one sees in plays, going about saying 'Un'and me!' 'Let me pass!' Maybe some of 'em are, but this ain't one of 'em."

"How did it happen?" asked Minikin.

"'Ow does it 'appen nine times out of ten?" returned Jarman. "'E was a bit misty, and she was wide awake. 'E gets a bit spoony, and, well, you know."

"Artful things, girls," commented Minikin.

"Can't blame 'em," returned Jarman, with generosity; "it's their business. Got to dispose of themselves somehow. Oughtn't to be binding without a written order dated the next morning; that'd make it all right."

"Couldn't prove a prior engagement?" suggested Minikin.

"She'd want to see the girl first before she'd believe it only natural," returned Jarman.

"Couldn't get a girl?" urged Minikin.

"Who could you trust?" asked the cautious Jarman. "Besides, there ain't time. She's letting 'im rest to-day; to-morrow evening she'll be down on 'im."

"Don't see anything for it," said Minikin, "but for him to do a bunk."

"Not a bad idea that," mused Jarman; "only where's 'e to bunk to?"

"Needn't go far," said Minikin.

"She'd find 'im out and follow 'im," said Jarman. "She can look after herself, mind you. Don't you go doing 'er any injustice."

"He could change his name," suggested Minikin.

"'Ow could 'e get a crib?" asked Jarman; "no character, no references."

"I've got it," cried Jarman, starting up; "the stage!"

"Can he act?" asked Minikin.

"Can do anything," retorted my supporter, "that don't want too much sense. That's 'is sanctuary, the stage. No questions asked, no character wanted. Lord! why didn't I think of it before?"

"Wants a bit of getting on to, doesn't it?" suggested Minikin.

"Depends upon where you want to get," replied Jarman. For the first time since the commencement of the discussion he turned to me. "Can you sing?" he asked me.

I replied that I could a little, though I had never done so in public.

"Sing something now," demanded Jarman; "let's 'ear you. Wait a minute!" he cried.

He slipped out of the room. I heard him pause upon the landing below and knock at the door of the fair Rosina's room. The next minute he returned.

"It's all right," he explained; "she's not in yet. Now, sing for all you're worth. Remember, it's for life and freedom."

I sang "Sally in Our Alley," not with much spirit, I am inclined to think. With every mention of the lady's name there rose before me the abundant form and features of my fiancee, which checked the feeling that should have trembled through my voice. But Jarman, though not enthusiastic, was content.

"It isn't what I call a grand opera voice," he commented, "but it ought to do all right for a chorus where economy is the chief point to be considered. Now, I'll tell you what to do. You go to-morrow straight to the O'Kelly, and put the whole thing before 'im. 'E's a good sort; 'e'll touch you up a bit, and maybe give you a few introductions. Lucky for you, this is just the right time. There's one or two things comin' on, and if Fate ain't dead against you, you'll lose your amorita, or whatever it's called, and not find 'er again till it's too late."

I was not in the mood that evening to feel hopeful about anything; but I thanked both of them for their kind intentions and promised to think the suggestion over on the morrow, when, as it was generally agreed, I should be in a more fitting state to bring cool judgment to bear upon the subject; and they rose to take their departure.

Leaving Minikin to descend alone, Jarman returned the next minute. "Consols are down a bit this week," he whispered, with the door in his hand. "If you want a little of the ready to carry you through, don't go sellin' out. I can manage a few pounds. Suck a couple of lemons and you'll be all right in the morning. So long."

I followed his advice regarding the lemons, and finding it correct, went to the office next morning as usual. Lott & Co., in consideration of my agreeing to a deduction of two shillings on the week's salary, allowed himself to overlook the matter. I had intended acting on Jarman' S advice, to call upon the O'Kelly at his address of respectability in Hampstead that evening, and had posted him a note saying I was coming. Before leaving the office, however, I received a reply to the effect that he would be out that evening, and asking me to make it the following Friday instead. Disappointed, I returned to my lodgings in a depressed state of mind. Jarman 's scheme, which had appeared hopeful and even attractive during the daytime, now loomed shadowy and impossible before me. The emptiness of the first floor parlour as I passed its open door struck a chill upon me, reminding me of the disappearance of a friend to whom, in spite of moral disapproval, I had during these last few months become attached. Unable to work, the old pain of loneliness returned upon me. I sat for awhile in the darkness, listening to the scratching of the pen of my neighbour, the old law-writer, and the sense of despair that its sound always communicated to me encompassed me about this evening with heavier weight than usual.

After all, was not the sympathy of the Lady 'Ortensia, stimulated for personal purposes though it might be, better than nothing? At least, here was some living creature to whom I belonged, to whom my existence or nonexistence was of interest, who, if only for her own sake, was bound to share my hopes, my fears.

It was in this mood that I heard a slight tap at the door. In the dim passage stood the small slavey, holding out a note. I took it, and returning, lighted my candle. The envelope was pink and scented. It was addressed, in handwriting not so bad as I had expected, to "Paul Kelver, Esquire." I opened it and read:

"Dr mr. Paul, I herd as how you was took hill hafter the party. I feer you are not strong. You must not work so hard or you will be hill and then I shall be very cros with you. I hop you are well now. If so I am going for a wark and you may come with me if you are good. With much love. From your affechonat ROSIE."

In spite of the spelling, a curious, tingling sensation stole over me as I read this my first love-letter. A faint mist swam before my eyes. Through it, glorified and softened, I saw the face of my betrothed, pasty yet alluring, her large white fleshy arms stretched out invitingly toward me. Moved by a sudden hot haste that seized me, I dressed myself with trembling hands; I appeared to be anxious to act without giving myself time for thought. Complete, with a colour in my cheeks unusual to them, and a burning in my eyes, I descended and knocked with a nervous hand at the door of the second floor back.

"Who's that?" came in answer Miss Sellars' sharp tones.

"It is I, Paul."

"Oh, wait a minute, dear." The tone was sweeter. There followed the sound of scurried footsteps, a rustling of clothes, a banging of drawers, a few moments' dead silence, and then:

"You can come in now, dear."

I entered. It was a small, untidy room, smelling of smoky lamp; but all I saw distinctly at the moment was Miss Sellars with her arms above her head, pinning her hat upon her straw-coloured hair.

With the sight of her before me in the flesh, my feelings underwent a sudden revulsion. During the few minutes she had kept me waiting outside the door I had suffered from an almost uncontrollable desire to turn the handle and rush in. Now, had I acted on impulse, I should have run out. Not that she was an unpleasant-looking girl by any means; it was the atmosphere of coarseness, of commonness, around her that repelled me. The fastidiousness, finikinness; if you will, that would so often spoil my rare chop, put before me by a waitress with dirty finger-nails, forced me to disregard the ample charms she no doubt did possess, to fasten my eyes exclusively upon her red, rough hands and the one or two warts that grew thereon.

"You're a very naughty boy," told me Miss Sellars, finishing the fastening of her hat. "Why didn't you come in and see me in the dinner-hour? I've a great mind not to kiss you."

The powder she had evidently dabbed on hastily was plainly visible upon her face; the round, soft arms were hidden beneath ill-fitting sleeves of some crapey material, the thought of which put my teeth on edge. I wished her intention had been stronger. Instead, relenting, she offered me her flowery cheek, which I saluted gingerly, the taste of it reminding me of certain pale, thin dough-cakes manufactured by the wife of our school porter and sold to us in playtime at four a penny, and which, having regard to their satisfying quality, had been popular with me in those days.

At the top of the kitchen stairs Miss Sellars paused and called down shrilly to Mrs. Peedles, who in course of time appeared, panting.

"Oh, me and Mr. Kelver are going out for a short walk, Mrs. Peedles. I shan't want any supper. Good night."

"Oh, good night, my dear," replied Mrs. Peedles. "Hope you'll enjoy yourselves. Is Mr. Kelver there?"

"He's round the corner," I heard Miss Sellars explain in a lower voice; and there followed a snigger.

"He's a bit shy, ain't he?" suggested Mrs. Peedles in a whisper.

"I've had enough of the other sort," was Miss Sellars' answer in low tones.

"Ah, well; it's the shy ones that come out the strongest after a bit, leastways, that's been my experience."

"He'll do all right. So long."

Miss Sellars, buttoning a burst glove, rejoined me.

"I suppose you've never had a sweetheart before?" asked Miss Sellars, as we turned into the Blackfriars Road.

I admitted that this was my first experience.

"I can't a-bear a flirty man," explained Miss Sellars. "That's why I took to you from the beginning. You was so quiet."

I began to wish that nature had bestowed upon me a noisier temperament.

"Anybody could see you was a gentleman," continued Miss Sellars. "Heaps and heaps of hoffers I've had, hundreds you might almost say. But what I've always told 'em is, 'I like you very much indeed as a friend, but I'm not going to marry anyone but a gentleman.' Don't you think I was right?"

I murmured it was only what I should have expected of her.

"You may take my harm, if you like," suggested Miss Sellars, as we crossed St. George's Circus; and linked, we pursued our way along the Kennington Park Road.

Fortunately, there was not much need for me to talk. Miss Sellars was content to supply most of the conversation herself, and all of it was about herself.

I learned that her instincts since childhood had been toward gentility. Nor was this to be wondered at, seeing that her family on her mother's side, at all events, were connected distinctly with "the highest in the land." Mesalliances, however, are common in all communities, and one of them, a particularly flagrant specimen, her "Mar" had, alas! contracted, having married, what did I think? I should never guess, a waiter! Miss Sellars, stopping in the act of crossing Newington Butts to shudder at the recollection of her female parent's shame, was nearly run down by a tramcar.

Mr. and Mrs. Sellars did not appear to have "hit it off" together. Could one wonder: Mrs. Sellars with an uncle on the Stock Exchange, and Mr. Sellars with one on Peckham Rye? I gathered his calling to have been, chiefly, "three shies a penny." Mrs. Sellars was now, however, happily dead; and if no other good thing had come out of the catastrophe, it had determined Miss Sellars to take warning by her mother's error and avoid connection with the lowly born. She it was who, with my help, would lift the family back again to its proper position in society.

"It used to be a joke against me," explained Miss Sellars, "heven when I was quite a child. I never could tolerate anything low. Why, one day when I was only seven years old, what do you think happened?"

I confessed my inability to guess.

"Well, I'll tell you," said Miss Sellars; "it'll just show you. Uncle Joseph, that was father's uncle, you understand?"

I assured Miss Sellars that the point was fixed in my mind.

"Well, one day when he came to see us he takes a cocoanut out of his pocket and offers it to me. 'Thank you,' I says; 'I don't heat cocoanuts that have been shied at by just anybody and missed!' It made him so wild. After that," explained Miss Sellars, "they used to call me at home the Princess of Wales."

I murmured it was a pretty fancy.

"Some people," replied Miss Sellars, with a giggle, "says it fits me; but, of course, that's only their nonsense."

Not knowing what to reply, I remained silent, which appeared to somewhat disappoint Miss Sellars.

Out of the Clapham Road we turned into a by-street of two-storeyed houses.

"You'll come in and have a bit of supper?" suggested Miss Sellars. "Mar's quite hanxious to see you."

I found sufficient courage to say I was not feeling well, and would much rather return home.

"Oh, but you must just come in for five minutes, dear. It'll look so funny if you don't. I told 'em we was coming."

"I would really rather not," I urged; "some other evening." I felt a presentiment, I confided to her, that on this particular evening I should not shine to advantage.

"Oh, you mustn't be so shy," said Miss Sellars. "I don't like shy fellows, not too shy. That's silly." And Miss Sellars took my arm with a decided grip, making it clear to me that escape could be obtained only by an unseemly struggle in the street; not being prepared for which, I meekly yielded.

We knocked at the door of one of the small houses, Miss Sellars retaining her hold upon me until it had been opened to us by a lank young man in his shirt-sleeves and closed behind us.

"Don't gentlemen wear coats of a hevening nowadays?" asked Miss Sellars, tartly, of the lank young man. "New fashion just come in?"

"I don't know what gentlemen wear in the evening or what they don't," retorted the lank young man, who appeared to be in an aggressive mood. "If I can find one in this street, I'll ast him and let you know."

"Mother in the droaring-room?" enquired Miss Sellars, ignoring the retort.

"They're all of 'em in the parlour, if that's what you mean," returned the lank young man, "the whole blooming shoot. If you stand up against the wall and don't breathe, there'll just be room for you."

Sweeping by the lank young man, Miss Sellars opened the parlour door, and towing me in behind her, shut it.

"Well, Mar, here we are," announced Miss Sellars. An enormously stout lady, ornamented with a cap that appeared to have been made out of a bandanna handkerchief, rose to greet us, thus revealing the fact that she had been sitting upon an extremely small horsehair-covered easy-chair, the disproportion between the lady and her support being quite pathetic.

"I am charmed, Mr. "

"Kelver," supplied Miss Sellars.

"Kelver, to make your ac-quain-tance," recited Mrs. Sellars in the tone of one repeating a lesson.

I bowed, and murmured that the honour was entirely mine.

"Don't mention it," replied Mrs. Sellars. "Pray be seated."

Mrs. Sellars herself set the example by suddenly giving way and dropping down into her chair, which thus again became invisible. It received her with an agonised groan.

Indeed, the insistence with which this article of furniture throughout the evening called attention to its sufferings was really quite distracting. With every breath that Mrs. Sellars took it moaned wearily. There were moments when it literally shrieked. I could not have accepted Mrs. Sellars' offer had I wished, there being no chair vacant and no room for another. A young man with watery eyes, sitting just behind me between a fat young lady and a lean one, rose and suggested my taking his place. Miss Sellars introduced me to him as her cousin Joseph something or other, and we shook hands.

The watery-eyed Joseph remarked that it had been a fine day between the showers, and hoped that the morrow would be either wet or dry;

upon which the lean young lady, having slapped him, asked admiringly of the fat young lady if he wasn't a "silly fool;" to which the fat young lady replied, with somewhat unnecessary severity, I thought, that no one could help being what they were born. To this the lean young lady retorted that it was with precisely similar reflection that she herself controlled her own feelings when tempted to resent the fat young lady's "nasty jealous temper."

The threatened quarrel was nipped in the bud by the discretion of Miss Sellars, who took the opportunity of the fat young lady's momentary speechlessness to introduce me promptly to both of them. They also, I learned, were cousins. The lean girl said she had "erd on me," and immediately fell into an uncontrollable fit of giggles; of which the watery-eyed Joseph requested me to take no notice, explaining that she always went off like that at exactly three-quarters to the half-hour every evening, Sundays and holidays excepted; that she had taken everything possible for it without effect, and that what he himself advised was that she should have it off.

The fat girl, seizing the chance afforded her, remarked genteelly that she too had "heard hof me," with emphasis upon the "hof." She also remarked it was a long walk from Blackfriars Bridge.

"All depends upon the company, eh? Bet they didn't find it too long."

This came from a loud-voiced, red-faced man sitting on the sofa beside a somewhat melancholy-looking female dressed in bright green. These twain I discovered to be Uncle and Aunt Gutton. From an observation dropped later in the evening concerning government restrictions on the sale of methylated spirit, and hastily smothered, I gathered that their line was oil and colour.

Mr. Gutton's forte appeared to be badinage. He it was who, on my explaining my heightened colour as due to the closeness of the evening, congratulated his niece on having secured so warm a partner.

"Will be jolly handy," shouted Uncle Gutton, "for Rosina, seeing she's always complaining of her cold feet."

Here the lank young man attempted to squeeze himself into the room, but found his entrance barred by the square, squat figure of the watery-eyed young man.

"Don't push," advised the watery-eyed young man. "Walk over me quietly."

"Well, why don't yer get out of the way," growled the lank young man, now coated, but still aggressive.

"Where am I to get to?" asked the watery-eyed young man, with some reason. "Say the word and I'll 'ang myself up to the gas bracket."

"In my courting days," roared Uncle Gutton, "the girls used to be able to find seats, even if there wasn't enough chairs to go all round."

The sentiment was received with varying degrees of approbation. The watery-eyed young man, sitting down, put the lean young lady on his knee, and in spite of her struggles and sounding slaps, heroically retained her there.

"Now, then, Rosie," shouted Uncle Gutton, who appeared to have constituted himself master of the ceremonies, "don't stand about, my girl; you'll get tired."

Left to herself, I am inclined to think my fiancee would have spared me; but Uncle Gutton, having been invited to a love comedy, was not to be cheated of any part of the performance, and the audience clearly being with him, there was nothing for it but compliance. I seated myself, and amid plaudits accommodated the ample and heavy Rosina upon my knee.

"Good-bye," called out to me the watery-eyed young man, as behind the fair Rosina I disappeared from his view. "See you again later on."

"I used to be a plump girl myself before I married," observed Aunt Gutton. "Plump as butter I was at one time."

"It isn't what one eats," said the maternal Sellars. "I myself don't eat enough to keep a fly, and my legs"

"That'll do, Mar," interrupted the filial Sellars, tartly.

"I was only going to say, my dear"

"We all know what you was going to say, Mar," retorted Miss Sellars. "We've heard it before, and it isn't interesting."

Mrs. Sellars relapsed into silence.

"'Ard work and plenty of it keeps you thin enough, I notice," remarked the lank young man, with bitterness. To him I was now introduced, he being Mr. George Sellars. "Seen 'im before," was his curt greeting.

At supper, referred to by Mrs. Sellars again in the tone of one remembering a lesson, as a cold col-la-tion, with the accent on the "tion", I sat between Miss Sellars and the lean young lady, with Aunt and Uncle Gutton opposite to us. It was remarked with approval that I did not appear to be hungry.

"Had too many kisses afore he started," suggested Uncle Gutton, with his mouth full of cold roast pork and pickles. "Wonderfully nourishing thing, kisses, eh? Look at mother and me. That's all we live on."

Aunt Gutton sighed, and observed that she had always been a poor feeder.

The watery-eyed young man, observing he had never tasted them himself, at which sally there was much laughter, said he would not mind trying a sample if the lean young lady would kindly pass him one.

The lean young lady opined that, not being used to high living, it might disagree with him.

"Just one," pleaded the watery-eyed young man, "to go with this bit of cracklin'."

The lean young lady, amid renewed applause, first thoughtfully wiping her mouth, acceded to his request.

The watery-eyed young man turned it over with the air of a gourmet.

"Not bad," was his verdict. "Reminds me of onions." At this there was another burst of laughter.

"Now then, ain't Paul goin' to have one?" shouted Uncle Gutton, when the laughter had subsided.

Amid silence, feeling as wretched as perhaps I have ever felt in my life before or since, I received one from the gracious Miss Sellars, wet and sounding.

"Looks better for it already," commented the delighted Uncle Gutton. "He'll soon get fat on 'em."

"Not too many at first," advised the watery-eyed young man. "Looks to me as if he's got a weak stomach."

I think, had the meal lasted much longer, I should have made a dash for the street; the contemplation of such step was forming in my mind. But Miss Sellars, looking at her watch, declared we must be getting home at once, for the which I could have kissed her voluntarily; and, being a young lady of decision, at once rose and commenced leave-taking. Polite protests were attempted, but these, with enthusiastic assistance from myself, she swept aside.

"Don't want anyone to walk home with you?" suggested Uncle Gutton. "Sure you won't feel lonely by yourselves, eh?"

"We shan't come to no harm," assured him Miss Sellars.

"P'raps you're right," agreed Uncle Gutton. "There don't seem to be much of the fiery and untamed about him, so far as I can see."

"'Slow waters run deep,'" reminded us Aunt Gutton, with a waggish shake of her head.

"No question about the slow," assented Uncle Gutton. "If you don't like him" observed Miss Sellars, speaking with dignity.

"To be quite candid with you, my girl, I don't," answered Uncle Gutton, whose temper, maybe as the result of too much cold pork and whiskey, seemed to have suddenly changed.

"Well, he happens to be good enough for me," recommenced Miss Sellars.

"I'm sorry to hear a niece of mine say so," interrupted Uncle Gutton. "If you want my opinion of him"

"If ever I do I'll call round some time when you're sober and ast you for it," returned Miss Sellars. "And as for being your niece, you was here when I came, and I don't see very well as how I could have got out of it. You needn't throw that in my teeth."

The gust was dispersed by the practical remark of brother George to the effect that the last tram for Walworth left the Oval at eleven-thirty; to which he further added the suggestion that the Clapham Road was wide and well adapted to a row.

"There ain't going to be no rows," replied Uncle Gutton, returning to amiability as suddenly as he had departed from it. "We understand each other, don't we, my girl?"

"That's all right, uncle. I know what you mean," returned Miss Sellars, with equal handsomeness.

"Bring him round again when he's feeling better," added Uncle Gutton, "and we'll have another look at him."

"What you want," advised the watery-eyed young man on shaking hands with me, "is complete rest and a tombstone."

I wished at the time I could have followed his prescription.

The maternal Sellars waddled after us into the passage, which she completely blocked. She told me she was delight-ted to have met me, and that she was always at home on Sundays.

I said I would remember it, and thanked her warmly for a pleasant evening, at Miss Sellars' request calling her Ma.

Outside, Miss Sellars agreed that my presentiment had proved correct, that I had not shone to advantage. Our journey home on a tramcar was a somewhat silent proceeding. At the door of her room she forgave me, and kissed me good night. Had I been frank with her, I should have thanked her for that evening's experience. It had made my course plain to me.

The next day, which was Thursday, I wandered about the streets till two o'clock in the morning, when I slipped in quietly, passing Miss Sellars' door with my boots in my hand.

After Mr. Lott's departure on Friday, which, fortunately, was pay-day, I set my desk in order and confided to Minikin written instructions concerning all matters unfinished.

"I shall not be here to-morrow," I told him. "Going to follow your advice."

"Found anything to do?" he asked.

"Not yet," I answered.

"Suppose you can't get anything?"

"If the worst comes to the worst," I replied, "I can hang myself."

"Well, you know the girl. Maybe you are right," he agreed.

"Hope it won't throw much extra work on you," I said.

"Well, I shan't be catching it if it does," was his answer. "That's all right."

He walked with me to the "Angel," and there we parted.

"If you do get on to the stage," he said, "and it's anything worth seeing, and you send me an order, and I can find the time, maybe I'll come and see you."

I thanked him for his promised support and jumped upon the tram.

The O'Kelly's address was in Belsize Square. I was about to ring and knock, as requested by a highly-polished brass plate, when I became aware of pieces of small coal falling about me on the doorstep. Looking up, I perceived the O'Kelly leaning out of an attic window. From signs I gathered I was to retire from the doorstep and wait. In a few minutes the door opened and his hand beckoned me to enter.

"Walk quietly," he whispered; and on tip-toe we climbed up to the attic from where had fallen the coal. "I've been waiting for ye," explained the O'Kelly, speaking low. "Me wife, a good woman, Paul; sure, a better woman never lived; ye'll like her when ye know her, later on, she might not care about ye're calling. She'd want to know where I met ye, and ye understand? Besides," added the O'Kelly, "we can smoke up here;" and seating himself where he could keep an eye upon the door, near to a small cupboard out of which he produced a pipe still alight, the O'Kelly prepared himself to listen.

I told him briefly the reason of my visit.

"It was my fault, Paul," he was good enough to say; "my fault entirely. Between ourselves, it was a damned silly idea, that party, the whole thing altogether. Don't ye think so?"

I replied that I was naturally prejudiced against it myself.

"Most unfortunate for me," continued the O'Kelly; "I know that. Me cabman took me to Hammersmith instead of Hampstead; said I told him Hammersmith. Didn't get home here till three o'clock in the morning. Most unfortunate, under the circumstances."

I could quite imagine it.

"But I'm glad ye've come," said the O'Kelly. "I had a notion ye did something foolish that evening, but I couldn't remember precisely what. It's been worrying me."

"It's been worrying me also, I can assure you," I told him; and I gave him an account of my Wednesday evening's experience.

"I'll go round to-morrow morning," he said, "and see one or two people. It's not a bad idea, that of Jarman's. I think I may be able to arrange something for ye."

He fixed a time for me to call again upon him the next day, when Mrs. O'Kelly would be away from home. He instructed me to walk quietly up and down on the opposite side of the road with my eye on the attic window, and not to come across unless he waved a handkerchief.

Rising to go, I thanked him for his kindness. "Don't put it that way, me dear Paul," he answered. "If I don't get ye out of this scrape I shall never forgive meself. If we damned silly fools don't help one another," he added, with his pleasant laugh, "who is to help us?"

We crept downstairs as we had crept up. As we reached the first floor, the drawing-room door suddenly opened.

"William!" cried a sharp voice.

"Me dear," answered the O'Kelly, snatching his pipe from his mouth and thrusting it, still alight, into his trousers pocket. I made the rest of the descent by myself, and slipping out, closed the door behind me as noiselessly as possible.

Again I did not return to Nelson Square until the early hours, and the next morning did not venture out until I had heard Miss Sellars, who appeared to be in a bad temper, leave the house. Then running to the top of the kitchen stairs, I called for Mrs. Peedles. I told her I was going to leave her, and, judging the truth to be the simplest explanation, I told her the reason why.

"My dear," said Mrs. Peedles, "I am only too glad to hear it. It wasn't for me to interfere, but I couldn't help seeing you were making a fool of yourself. I only hope you'll get clear off, and you may depend upon me to do all I can to help you."

"You don't think I'm acting dishonourably, do you, Mrs. Peedles?" I asked.

"My dear," replied Mrs. Peedles, "it's a difficult world to live in, leastways, that's been my experience of it."

I had just completed my packing, it had not taken me long, when I heard upon the stairs the heavy panting that always announced to me the up-coming of Mrs. Peedles. She entered with a bundle of old manuscripts under her arm, torn and tumbled booklets of various shapes and sizes. These she plumped down upon the rickety table, and herself upon the nearest chair.

"Put them in your box, my dear," said Mrs. Peedles. "They'll come in useful to you later on."

I glanced at the bundle. I saw it was a collection of old plays in manuscript-prompt copies, scored, cut and interlined. The top one I noticed was "The Bloodspot: Or the Maiden, the Miser and the Murderer;" the second, "The Female Highwayman."

"Everybody's forgotten 'em," explained Mrs. Peedles, "but there's some good stuff in all of them."

"But what am I to do with them?" I enquired.

"Just whatever you like, my dear," explained Mrs. Peedles. "It's quite safe. They're all of 'em dead, the authors of 'em. I've picked 'em out most carefully. You just take a scene from one and a scene from the other. With judgment and your talent you'll make a dozen good plays out of that little lot when your time comes."

"But they wouldn't be my plays, Mrs. Peedles," I suggested.

"They will if I give them to you," answered Mrs. Peedles. "You put 'em in your box. And never mind the bit of rent," added Mrs. Peedles; "you can pay me that later on."

I kissed the kind old soul good-bye and took her gift with me to my new lodgings in Camden Town. Many a time have I been hard put to it for plot or scene, and more than once in weak mood have I turned with guilty intent the torn and crumpled pages of Mrs. Peedles's donation to my literary equipment. It is pleasant to be able to put my hand upon my heart and reflect that never yet have I yielded to the temptation. Always have I laid them back within their drawer, saying to myself, with stern reproof:

"No, no, Paul. Stand or fall by your own merits. Never plagiarise, in any case, not from this 'little lot.'"

CHAPTER IV.

LEADS TO A MEETING.

"Don't be nervous," said the O'Kelly, "and don't try to do too much. You have a very fair voice, but it's not powerful. Keep cool and open your mouth."

It was eleven o'clock in the morning. We were standing at the entrance of the narrow court leading to the stage door. For a fortnight past the O'Kelly had been coaching me. It had been nervous work for both of us, but especially for the O'Kelly. Mrs. O'Kelly, a thin, acid-looking lady, of whom I once or twice had caught a glimpse while promenading Belsize Square awaiting the O'Kelly's signal, was a serious-minded lady, with a conscientious objection to all music not of a sacred character. With the hope of winning the O'Kelly from one at least of his sinful tendencies, the piano had been got rid of, and its place in the drawing-room filled by an American organ of exceptionally lugubrious tone. With this we had had to make shift, and though the O'Kelly, a veritable musical genius, had succeeded in evolving from it an accompaniment to "Sally in Our Alley" less misleading and confusing than might otherwise have been the case, the result had not been to lighten our labours. My rendering of the famous ballad had, in consequence, acquired a dolefulness not intended by the composer. Sung as I sang it, the theme became, to employ a definition since grown hackneyed as applied to Art, a problem ballad. Involuntarily one wondered whether the marriage would turn out as satisfactorily as the young man appeared to anticipate. Was there not, when one came to think of it, a melancholy, a pessimism ingrained within the temperament of the complainful hero that would ill assort with those instincts toward frivolity the careful observer could not avoid discerning in the charming yet nevertheless somewhat shallow character of Sally.

"Lighter, lighter. Not so soulful," would demand the O'Kelly, as the solemn notes rolled jerkily from the groaning instrument beneath his hands.

Once we were nearly caught, Mrs. O'Kelly returning from a district visitors' committee meeting earlier than was expected. Hastily I was hidden in a small conservatory adjutting from the first floor landing, where, crouching behind flower-pots, I listened in fear and trembling to the severe cross-examination of the O'Kelly.

"William, do not prevaricate. It was not a hymn."

"Me dear, so much depends upon the time. Let me give ye an example of what I mean."

"William, pray in my presence not to play tricks with sacred melodies. If you have no respect for religion, please remember that I have. Besides, why should you be playing hymns in any time at ten o'clock in the morning? It is not like you, William, and I do not credit your explanation. And you were singing. I distinctly heard the word 'Sally' as I opened the door."

"Salvation, me dear," corrected the O'Kelly.

"Your enunciation, William, is not usually so much at fault."

"A little hoarseness, me dear," explained the O'Kelly.

"Your voice did not sound hoarse. Perhaps it will be better if we do not pursue the subject further."

With this the O'Kelly appeared to agree.

"A lady a little difficult to get on with when ye're feeling well and strong," so the O'Kelly would explain her; "but if ye happen to be ill, one of the kindest, most devoted of women. When I was down with typhoid three years ago, a tenderer nurse no man could have had. I shall never forget it. And so she would be again to-morrow, if there was anything serious the matter with me."

I murmured the well-known quotation.

"Mrs. O'Kelly to a T," concurred the O'Kelly. "I sometimes wonder if Lady Scott may not have been the same sort of woman."

"The unfortunate part of it is," continued the O'Kelly, "that I'm such a healthy beggar; it don't give her a chance. If I were only a chronic invalid, now, there's nothing that woman would not do to make me happy. As it is" The O'Kelly struck a chord. We resumed our studies.

But to return to our conversation at the stage door.

"Meet me at the Cheshire Cheese at one o'clock," said the O'Kelly, shaking hands. "If ye don't get on here, we'll try something else; but I've spoken to Hodgson, and I think ye will. Good luck to ye!"

He went his way and I mine. In a glass box just behind the door a curved-nose, round-eyed little man, looking like an angry bird in a cage, demanded of me my business. I showed him my letter of appointment.

"Up the passage, across the stage, along the corridor, first floor, second door on the right," he instructed me in one breath, and shut the window with a snap.

I proceeded up the passage. It somewhat surprised me to discover that I was not in the least excited at the thought of this, my first introduction to "behind the scenes."

I recall my father's asking a young soldier on his return from the Crimea what had been his sensations at the commencement of his first charge.

"Well," replied the young fellow, "I was worrying all the time, remembering I had rushed out leaving the beer tap running in the canteen, and I could not forget it."

So far as the stage I found my way in safety. Pausing for a moment and glancing round, my impression was not so much disillusionment concerning all things theatrical as realisation of my worst forebodings. In that one moment all glamour connected with the stage fell from me, nor has it since ever returned to me. From the tawdry decorations of the auditorium to the childish make-believe littered around on the stage, I saw the Theatre a painted thing of shreds and patches, the grown child's doll's-house. The Drama may improve us, elevate us, interest and teach us. I am sure it does; long may it flourish! But so likewise does the dressing and undressing of dolls, the opening of the front of the house, and the tenderly putting of them away to bed in rooms they completely fill, train our little dears to the duties and the joys of motherhood. Toys! what wise child despises them? Art, fiction, the musical glasses: are they not preparing us for the time, however distant, when we shall at last be grown up?

In a maze of ways beyond the stage I lost myself, but eventually, guided by voices, came to a large room furnished barely with many chairs and worn settees, and here I found some twenty to thirty ladies and gentlemen already seated. They were of varying ages, sizes and appearance, but all of them alike in having about them that impossible-to-define but impossible-to-mistake suggestion of theatricality. The men were chiefly remarkable for having no hair on their faces, but a good deal upon their heads; the ladies, one and all, were blessed with remarkably pink and white complexions and exceptionally bright eyes. The conversation, carried on in subdued but penetrating voices, was chiefly of "him" and "her." Everybody appeared to be on an affectionate footing with everybody else, the terms of address being "My dear," "My love," "Old girl," "Old chappie," Christian names, when name of any sort was needful, alone being employed. I hesitated for a minute with the door in my hand, fearing I had stumbled upon a family gathering. As, however, nobody seemed disconcerted at my entry, I ventured to take a vacant seat next to an extremely small and boyish-looking gentleman and to ask him if this was the room in which I, an applicant for a place in the chorus of the forthcoming comic opera, ought to be waiting.

He had large, fishy eyes, with which he looked me up and down. For such a length of time he remained thus regarding me in silence that a massive gentleman sitting near, who had overheard, took it upon himself to reply in the affirmative, adding that from what he knew of Butterworth we would all of us be waiting here a damned sight longer than any gentleman should keep other ladies and gentlemen waiting for no reason at all.

"I think it exceedingly bad form," observed the fishy-eyed gentleman, in deep contralto tones, "for any gentleman to take it upon himself to reply to a remark addressed to quite another gentleman."

"I beg your pardon," retorted the large gentleman. "I thought you were asleep."

"I think it very ill manners," remarked the small gentlemen in the same slow and impressive tones, "for any gentleman to tell another gentleman, who happens to be wide awake, that he thought he was asleep."

"Sir," returned the massive gentleman, assuming with the help of a large umbrella a quite Johnsonian attitude, "I decline to alter my manners to suit your taste."

"If you are satisfied with them," replied the small gentleman, "I cannot help it. But I think you are making a mistake."

"Does anybody know what the opera is about?" asked a bright little woman at the other end of the room.

"Does anybody ever know what a comic opera is about?" asked another lady, whose appearance suggested experience.

"I once asked the author," observed a weary-looking gentleman, speaking from a corner. "His reply was: 'Well, if you had asked me at the beginning of the rehearsals I might have been able to tell you, but damned if I could now![']"

"It wouldn't surprise me," observed a good-looking gentleman in a velvet coat, "if there occurred somewhere in the proceedings a drinking chorus for male voices."

"Possibly, if we are good," added a thin lady with golden hair, "the heroine will confide to us her love troubles, which will interest us and excite us."

The door at the further end of the room opened and a name was cal[l]ed. An elderly lady rose and went out.

"Poor old Gertie!" remarked sympathetically the thin lady with the golden hair. "I'm told that she really had a voice once."

"When poor young Bond first came to London," said the massive gentleman who was sitting on my left, "I remember his telling me he applied to Lord Barrymore's 'tiger,' Alexander Lee, I mean, of course, who was then running the Strand Theatre, for a place in the chorus. Lee heard him sing two lines, and then jumped up. 'Thanks, that'll do; good morning,' says Lee. Bond knew he had got a good voice, so he asked Lee what was wrong. 'What's wrong?' shouts Lee. 'Do you think I hire a chorus to show up my principals?'"

"Having regard to the company present," commented the fishy-eyed gentleman, "I consider that anecdote as distinctly lacking in tact."

The feeling of the company appeared to be with the fish-eyed young man.

For the next half hour the door at the further end of the room continued to open and close, devouring, ogre-fashion, each time some dainty human morsel, now chorus gentleman, now chorus lady. Conversation among our thinning ranks became more fitful, a growing anxiety making for silence.

At length, "Mr. Horace Moncrieff" called the voice of the unseen Charon. In common with the rest, I glanced round languidly to see what sort of man "Mr. Horace Moncrieff" might be. The door was pushed open further. Charon, now revealed as a pale-faced young man with a drooping moustache, put his head into the room and repeated impatiently his invitation to the apparently coy Moncrieff. It suddenly occurred to me that I was Mr. Horace Moncrieff.

"So glad you've found yourself," said the pale-faced young man, as I joined him at the door. "Please don't lose yourself again; we're rather pressed for time."

I crossed with him through a deserted refreshment bar, one of the saddest of sights, into a room beyond. A melancholy-looking gentleman was seated at the piano. Beside him stood a tall, handsome man, who was opening and reading rapidly from a bundle of letters he held in his hand. A big, burly, bored-looking gentleman was making desperate efforts to be amused at the staccato conversation of a sharp-faced, restless-eyed gentleman, whose peculiarity was that he never by any chance looked at the person to whom he was talking, but always at something or somebody else.

"Moncrieff?" enquired the tall, handsome man, whom I later discovered to be Mr. Hodgson, the manager, without raising his eyes from his letters.

The pale-faced gentleman responded for me.

"Fire away," said Mr. Hodgson.

"What is it?" asked of me wearily the melancholy gentleman at the piano.

"'Sally in Our Alley,'" I replied.

"What are you?" interrupted Mr. Hodgson. He had never once looked at me, and did not now.

"A tenor," I replied. "Not a full tenor," I added, remembering the O'Kelly's instructions.

"Utterly impossible to fill a tenor," remarked the restless-eyed gentleman, looking at me and speaking to the worried-looking gentleman. "Ever tried?"

Everybody laughed, with the exception of the melancholy gentleman at the piano, Mr. Hodgson throwing in his contribution without raising his eyes from his letters. Throughout the proceedings the restless-eyed gentleman continued to make humorous observations of this nature, at which everybody laughed, excepting always the melancholy pianist, a short, sharp, mechanical laugh, devoid of the least suggestion of amusement. The restless-eyed gentleman, it appeared, was the leading low comedian of the theatre.

"Go on," said the melancholy gentleman, and commenced the accompaniment.

"Tell me when he's going to begin," remarked Mr. Hodgson at the conclusion of the first verse.

"He has a fair voice," said my accompanist. "He's evidently nervous."

"There is a prejudice throughout theatrical audiences," observed Mr. Hodgson, "in favour of a voice they can hear. That is all I am trying to impress upon him."

The second verse, so I imagined, I sang in the voice of a trumpet. The burly gentleman, the translator of the French libretto, as he turned out to be; the author of the English version, as he preferred to be called, acknowledged to having distinctly detected a sound. The restless-eyed comedian suggested an announcement from the stage requesting strict silence during my part of the performance.

The sickness of fear was stealing over me. My voice, so it seemed to me, disappointed at the effect it had produced, had retired, sulky, into my boots, whence it refused to emerge.

"Your voice is all right, very good," whispered the musical conductor. "They want to hear the best you can do, that's all."

At this my voice ran up my legs and out of my mouth. "Thirty shillings a week, half salary for rehearsals. If that's all right, Mr. Catchpole will give you your agreement. If not, very much obliged. Good morning," said Mr. Hodgson, still absorbed in his correspondence.

With the pale-faced young man I retired to a desk in the corner, where a few seconds sufficed for the completion of the business. Leaving, I sought to catch the eye of my melancholy friend, but he appeared too sunk in dejection to notice anything. The restless-eyed comedian, looking at the author of the English version and addressing me as Boanerges, wished me good morning, at which the everybody laughed; and, informed as to the way out by the pale-faced Mr. Catchpole, I left.

The first "call" was for the following Monday at two o'clock. I found the theatre full of life and bustle. The principals, who had just finished their own rehearsal, were talking together in a group. We ladies and gentlemen of the chorus filled the centre of the stage. I noticed the lady I had heard referred to as Gertie; as also the thin lady with the golden hair. The massive gentleman and the fishy-eyed young man were again in close proximity; so long as I knew them they always were together, possessed, apparently, of a sympathetic antipathy for each other. The fishy-eyed young gentleman was explaining the age at which he thought decayed chorus singers ought, in justice to themselves and the public, to retire from the profession; the massive gentleman, the age and size at which he thought parcels of boys ought to be learning manners across their mother's knee.

Mr. Hodgson, still reading letters exactly as I had left him four days ago, stood close to the footlights. My friend, the musical director, armed with a violin and supported by about a dozen other musicians, occupied the orchestra. The adapter and the stage manager, a Frenchman whom I found it good policy to mistake for a born Englishman, sat deep in confabulation at a small table underneath a temporary gas jet. Quarter of an hour or so passed by, and then the stage manager, becoming suddenly in a hurry, rang a small bell furiously.

"Clear, please; all clear," shouted a small boy, with important air suggestive of a fox terrier; and, following the others, I retreated to the wings.

The comedian and the leading lady, whom I knew well from the front, but whom I should never have recognised, severed themselves from their companions and joined Mr. Hodgson by the footlights. As a preliminary we were sorted out, according to our sizes, into loving couples.

"Ah," said the stage manager, casting an admiring gaze upon the fishy-eyed young man, whose height might have been a little over five feet two, "I have the very girl for you, a beauty!" Darting into the group of ladies, he returned with quite the biggest specimen, a lady of magnificent proportions, whom, with the air of the virtuous uncle of melodrama, he bestowed upon the fishy-eyed young man. To the massive gentleman was given a sharp-faced little lady, who at a distance appeared quite girlish. Myself I found mated to the thin lady with the golden hair.

At last complete, we took our places in the then approved semi-circle, and the attenuated orchestra struck up the opening chorus. My music, which had been sent me by post, I had gone over with the O'Kelly, and about that I felt confident; but for the rest, ill at ease.

"I am afraid," said the thin lady, "I must ask you to put your arm round my waist. It's very shocking, I know, but, you see, our salary depends upon it. Do you think you could manage it?"

I glanced into her face. A whimsical expression of fun replied to me and drove away my shyness. I carried out her instructions to the best of my ability.

The indefatigable stage manager ran in and out among us while we sang, driving this couple back a foot or so, this other forward, herding this group closer together, throughout another making space, suggesting the idea of a sheep-dog at work.

"Very good, very good indeed," commented Mr. Hodgson at the conclusion. "We will go over it once more, and this time in tune."

"And we will make love," added the stage manager; "not like marionettes, but like ladies and gentlemen all alive." Seizing the lady nearest to him, he explained to us by object lesson how the real peasant invariably behaves when under influence of the grand passion, standing gracefully with hands clasped upon heart, head inclined at an angle of forty-five, his whole countenance eloquent with tender adoration.

"If he expects" remarked the massive gentleman sotto voce to an experienced-looking young lady, "a performance of Romeo thrown in, I, for one, shall want an extra ten shillings a week."

Casting the lady aside and seizing upon a gentleman, our stage manager then proceeded to show the ladies how a village maiden should receive affectionate advances: one shoulder a trifle higher than the other, body from the waist upward gently waggling, roguish expression in left eye.

"Ah, he's a bit new to it," replied the experienced young lady. "He'll get over all that."

Again we started. Whether others attempted to follow the stage manager's directions I cannot say, my whole attention being centred upon the fishy-eyed young man, who did, implicitly. Soon it became apparent that the whole of us were watching the fishy-eyed young man to the utter neglect of our own business. Mr. Hodgson even looked up from his letters; the orchestra was playing out of time; the author of the English version and the leading lady exchanged glances. Three people only appeared not to be enjoying themselves: the chief comedian, the stage manager and the fishy-eyed young gentleman himself, who pursued his labours methodically and conscientiously. There was a whispered confabulation between the leading low comedian, Mr. Hodgson and the stage manager. As a result, the music ceased and the fishy-eyed young gentleman was requested to explain what he was doing.

"Only making love," replied the fishy-eyed young gentleman.

"You were playing the fool, sir," retorted the leading low comedian, severely.

"That is a very unkind remark," replied the fishy-eyed young gentleman, evidently hurt, "to make to a gentleman who is doing his best."

Mr. Hodgson behind his letters was laughing. "Poor fellow," he murmured; "I suppose he can't help it. Go on."

"We are not producing a pantomime, you know," urged our comedian.

"I want to give him a chance, poor devil," explained Mr. Hodgson in a lower voice. "Only support of a widowed mother."

Our comedian appeared inclined to argue; but at this point Mr. Hodgson's correspondence became absorbing.

For the chorus the second act was a busy one. We opened as soldiers and vivandieres, every warrior in this way possessing his own private travelling bar. Our stage manager again explained to us by example how a soldier behaves, first under stress of patriotic emotion, and secondly under stress of cheap cognac, the difference being somewhat subtle: patriotism displaying itself by slaps upon the chest, and cheap cognac by slaps upon the forehead. A little later we were conspirators; our stage manager, with the help of a tablecloth, showed us how to conspire. Next we were a mob, led by the sentimental baritone; our stage manager, ruffling his hair, expounded to us how a mob led by a sentimental baritone would naturally behave itself. The act wound up with a fight. Our stage manager, minus his coat, demonstrated to us how to fight and die, the dying being a painful and dusty performance, necessitating, as it did, much rolling about on the stage. The fishy-eyed young gentleman throughout the whole of it was again the centre of attraction. Whether he were solemnly slapping his chest and singing about glory, or solemnly patting his head and singing about grapes, was immaterial: he was the soldier for us. What the plot was about did not matter, so long as he was in it. Who led the mob one did not care; one's desire was to see him lead. How others fought and died was matter of no moment; to see him slaughtered was sufficient. Whether his unconsciousness was assumed or natural I cannot say; in either case it was admirable. An earnest young man, over-anxious, if anything, to do his duty by his employers, was the extent of the charge that could be brought against him. Our chief comedian frowned and fumed; our stage manager was in despair. Mr. Hodgson and the author of the English version, on the contrary, appeared kindly disposed towards the gentleman. In addition to the widowed mother, Mr. Hodgson had invented for him five younger brothers and sisters utterly destitute but for his earnings. To deprive so exemplary a son and brother of the means of earning a livelihood for dear ones dependent upon him was not in Mr. Hodgson's heart. Our chief comedian dissociated himself from all uncharitable feelings, would subscribe towards the subsistence of the young man out of his own pocket, his only concern being the success of the opera. The author of the English version was convinced the young man would not accept a charity; had known him for years, was a most sensitive creature.

The rehearsal proceeded. In the last act it became necessary for me to kiss the thin lady.

"I am very sorry," said the thin lady, "but duty is duty. It has to be done."

Again I followed directions. The thin lady was good enough to congratulate me on my performance.

The last three or four rehearsals we performed in company with the principals. Divided counsels rendered them decidedly harassing. Our chief comedian had his views, and they were decided; the leading lady had hers, and was generous with them. The author of the English version possessed his also, but of these nobody took much notice. Once every twenty minutes the stage manager washed his hands of the whole affair and left the theatre in despair, and anybody's hat that happened to be handy, to return a few minutes later full of renewed hope. The sentimental baritone was sarcastic, the tenor distinctly rude to everybody.

Mr. Hodgson's method was to agree with all and listen to none. The smaller fry of the company, together with the more pushing of the chorus, supported each in turn, when the others were not looking. Up to the dress rehearsal it was anybody's opera.

About one thing, and about one thing, only, had the principals fallen into perfect agreement, and that was that the fishy-eyed young gentleman was out of place in a romantic opera. The tenor would be making impassioned love to the leading lady. Perception would come to both of them that, though they might be occupying geographically the centre of the stage, dramatically they were not. Without a shred of evidence, yet with perfect justice, they would unhesitatingly blame for this the fishy-eyed young man.

"I wasn't doing anything," he would explain meekly. "I was only looking." It was perfectly true; that was all he was doing.

"Then don't look," would comment the tenor.

The fishy-eyed young gentleman obediently would turn his face away from them; and in some mysterious manner the situation would thereupon become even yet more hopelessly ridiculous.

"My scene, I think, sir!" would thunder our chief comedian, a little later on.

"I am only doing what I was told to do," answered the fishy-eyed young gentleman; and nobody could say that he was not.

"Take a circus, and run him as a side-show," counselled our comedian.

"I am afraid he would never be any good as a side-show," replied Mr. Hodgson, who was reading letters.

On the first night, passing the gallery entrance on my way to the stage door, the sight of the huge crowd assembled there waiting gave me my first taste of artistic joy. I was a part of what they had come to see, to praise or to condemn, to listen to, to watch. Within the theatre there was an atmosphere of suppressed excitement, amounting almost to hysteria. The bird-like gentleman in his glass cage was fluttering, agitated. The hands of the stage carpenters putting the finishing touches to the scenery were trembling, their voices passionate with anxiety; the fox-terrier-like call-boy was pale with sense of responsibility.

I made my way to the dressing-room, a long, low, wooden corridor, furnished from end to end with a wide shelf that served as common dressing-table, lighted by a dozen flaring gas-jets, wire-shielded. Here awaited us gentlemen of the chorus the wigmaker's assistant, whose duty it was to make us up. From one to another he ran, armed with his hare's foot, his box of paints and his bundle of crepe hair. My turn arriving, he seized me by the head, jabbed a wig upon me, and in less than a couple of minutes I left his hands the orthodox peasant of the stage, white of forehead and pink of cheek, with curly moustache and lips of coral. Glancing into the glass, I could not help feeling pleased with myself; a moustache, without doubt, suited me.

The chorus ladies, when I met them on the stage, were a revelation to me. Paint and powder though I knew their appearance to consist of chiefly, yet in that hot atmosphere of the theatre, under that artificial glare, it seemed fit and fascinating. The close approximation to so much bare flesh, its curious, subtle odour was almost intoxicating. Dr. Johnson's excuse to Garrick for the rarity of his visits to the theatre recurred to me with understanding.

"How do you like my costume?" asked the thin lady with the golden hair.

"I think you" We were standing apart behind a piece of projecting scenery. She laid her hand upon my mouth, laughing.

"How old are you?" she asked me.

"Isn't that a rude question?" I answered. "I don't ask your age.

"Mine," she replied, "entitles me to talk to you as I should to a boy of my own, I had one once. Get out of this life if you can. It's bad for a woman; it's worse still for a man. To you especially it will be harmful."

"Why to me in particular?"

"Because you are an exceedingly foolish little boy," she answered, with another laugh, "and are rather nice."

She slipped away and joined the others. The chorus was now entirely assembled on the stage. The sound of the rapidly-filling house reached us, softened through the thick baize curtain, a dull, continuous droning, as of water pouring into some huge cistern. Suddenly there fell upon our ears a startling crash; the overture had commenced. The stage manager, more suggestive of a sheep-dog than ever, but lacking the calm dignity, the self-possession born of conscious capability distinctive of his prototype; a fussy, argumentative sheep-dog, rushed into the midst of us and worried us into our positions, where the more experienced continued to converse in whispers, the rest of us waiting nervously, trying to remember our words. The chorus master, taking his stand with his back to the proscenium, held his white-gloved hand in readiness. The curtain rushed up, the house, a nightmare of white faces, appearing to run towards us. The chorus-master's white-gloved hand flung upward. A roar of voices struck upon my ear, but whether my own were of them I could not say; if I were singing at all it was unconsciously, mechanically. Later, I found myself standing in the wings beside the thin lady; the stage was in the occupation of the principals. On my next entrance my senses were more with me; I was able to look about me. Here and there a strongly-marked face among the audience stood out, but the majority were as indistinguishable as so many blades of grass. Looked at from the stage, the house seemed no more real than from the front do the painted faces upon a black cloth.

The curtain fell amid the usual applause, sounding to us behind it like the rattle of tiny stones against a window-pane. Three times it rose and fell, like the opening and shutting of a door; and then followed a scamper for the dressing-rooms, the long corridors being filled with the rustling of skirts and the scurrying of feet.

It was in the second act that the fishy-eyed young gentleman came into his own. The chorus had lingered till it was quite apparent that the tenor and the leading lady were in love with each other; then, with the exquisite delicacy so characteristic of a chorus, foreseeing that its further presence might be embarrassing, it turned to go, half to the east, the other half to the west. The fishy-eyed young man, starting from the centre, was the last to leave the stage. In another moment he would have disappeared from view. There came a voice from the gallery, clear, distinct, pathetic with entreaty:

"Don't go. Get behind a tree."

The request was instantly seconded by a roar of applause from every part of the house, followed by laughter. From that point onward the house was chiefly concerned with the fortunes of the fishy-eyed young gentleman. At his next entrance, disguised as a conspirator, he was welcomed with enthusiasm, his passing away regretted loudly. At the fall of the curtain, the tenor, furious, rushed up to him, and, shaking a fist in his face, demanded what he meant by it.

"I wasn't doing anything," explained the fishy-eyed young man.

"You went off sideways!" roared the tenor.

"Well, you told me not to look at you," explained meekly the fishy-eyed young gentleman. "I must go off somehow. I regard you as a very difficult man to please."

At the final fall of the curtain the house appeared divided as regarded the merits of the opera; but for "Goggles" there was a unanimous and enthusiastic call, and the while we were dressing a message came for "Goggles" that Mr. Hodgson wished to see him in his private room.

"He can make a funny face, no doubt about it," commented one gentleman, as "Goggles" left the room.

"I defy him to make a funnier one than God Almighty's made for him," responded the massive gentleman.

"There's a deal in luck," observed, with a sigh, another, a tall, handsome young gentleman possessed of a rich bass voice.

Leaving the stage door, I encountered a group of gentlemen waiting upon the pavement outside. Not interested in them myself, I was hurrying past, when one laid a hand upon my shoulder. I turned. He was a big, broad-shouldered fellow, with a dark Vandyke beard and soft, dreamy eyes.

"Dan!" I cried.

"I thought it was you, young 'un, in the first act," he answered. "In the second, when you came on without a moustache, I knew it. Are you in a hurry?"

"Not at all," I answered. "Are you?"

"No," he replied; "we don't go to press till Thursday, so I can write my notice to-morrow. Come and have supper with me at the Albion and we will talk. You look tired, young 'un."

"No," I assured him, "only excited, partly at meeting you."

He laughed, and drew my arm through his.

CHAPTER V.

HOW ON A SWEET GREY MORNING THE FUTURE CAME TO PAUL.

Over our supper Dan and I exchanged histories. They revealed points of similarity. Leaving school some considerable time earlier than myself, Dan had gone to Cambridge; but two years later, in consequence of the death of his father, of a wound contracted in the Indian Mutiny and never cured, had been compelled to bring his college career to an untimely termination.

"You might not have expected that to grieve me," said Dan, with a smile, "but, as a matter of fact, it was a severe blow to me. At Cambridge I discovered that I was by temperament a scholar. The reason why at school I took no interest in learning was because learning was, of set purpose, made as uninteresting as possible. Like a Cook's tourist party through a picture gallery, we were rushed through education; the object being not that we should see and understand, but that we should be able to say that we had done it. At college I chose my own subjects, studied them in my own way. I fed on knowledge, was not stuffed with it like a Strassburg goose."

Returning to London, he had taken a situation in a bank, the chairman of which had been an old friend of his father. The advantage was that while earning a small income he had time to continue his studies; but the deadly monotony of the work had appalled him, and upon the death of his mother he had shaken the cloying dust of the City from his brain and joined a small "fit-up" theatrical company. On the stage he had remained for another eighteen months; had played all roles, from "Romeo" to "Paul Pry," had helped to paint the scenery, had assisted in the bill-posting. The latter, so he told me, he had found one of the most difficult of accomplishments, the paste-laden poster having an innate tendency to recoil upon the amateur's own head, and to stick there. Wearying of the stage proper, he had joined a circus company, had been "Signor Ricardo, the daring bare-back rider," also one of the "Brothers Roscius in their marvellous trapeze act;" inclining again towards respectability, had been a waiter for three months at Ostend; from that, a footman.

"One never knows," remarked Dan. "I may come to be a society novelist; if so, inside knowledge of the aristocracy will give me decided advantage over the majority of my competitors."

Other callings he had sampled: had tramped through Ireland with a fiddle; through Scotland with a lecture on Palestine, assisted by dissolving views; had been a billiard-marker; next a schoolmaster. For the last three months he had been a journalist, dramatic and musical critic to a Sunday newspaper. Often had I dreamt of such a position for myself.

"How did you obtain it?" I asked.

"The idea occurred to me," replied Dan, "late one afternoon, sauntering down the Strand, wondering what I should do next. I was on my beam ends, with only a few shillings in my pocket; but luck has always been with me. I entered the first newspaper office I came to, walked upstairs to the first floor, and opening the first door without knocking, passed through a small, empty room into a larger one, littered with books and papers. It was growing dark. A gentleman of extremely youthful figure was running round and round, cursing to himself because of three things: he had upset the ink, could not find the matches, and had broken the bell-pull. In the gloom, assuming him to be the office boy, I thought it would be fun to mistake him for the editor. As a matter of fact, he turned out to be the editor. I lit the gas for him, and found him another ink-pot. He was a slim young man with the voice and manner of a schoolboy. I don't suppose he is any more than five or six-and-twenty. He owes his position to the fact of his aunt's being the proprietress. He asked me if he knew me. Before I could tell him that he didn't, he went on talking. He appeared to be labouring under a general sense of injury.

"'People come into this office,' he said; 'they seem to look upon it as a shelter from the rain, people I don't know from Adam. And that damned fool downstairs lets them march straight up, anybody, men with articles on safety valves, people who have merely come to kick up a row about something or another. Half my work I have to do on the stairs.

"I recommended to him that he should insist upon strangers writing their business upon a slip of paper. He thought it a good idea.

"'For the last three-quarters of an hour,' he said, 'have I been trying to finish this one column, and four times have I been interrupted.'

"At that precise moment there came another knock at the door.

"'I won't see him!' he cried. 'I don't care who he is; I won't see him. Send him away! Send everybody away!'

"I went to the door. He was an elderly gentleman. He made to sweep by me; but I barred his way, and closed the editorial door behind me. He seemed surprised; but I told him it was impossible for him to see the editor that afternoon, and suggested his writing his business on a sheet of paper, which I handed to him for the purpose. I remained in that ante-room for half an hour, and during that time I suppose I must have sent away about ten or a dozen people. I don't think their business could have been important, or I should have heard about it afterwards. The last to come was a tired-looking gentleman, smoking a cigarette. I asked him his name.

"He looked at me in surprise, and then answered, 'Idiot!'

"I remained firm, however, and refused to let him pass.

"'It's a bit awkward,' he retorted. 'Don't you think you could make an exception in favour of the sub-editor on press night?'

"I replied that such would be contrary to my instructions.

"'Oh, all right,' he answered. 'I'd like to know who's going to the Royalty to-night, that's all. It's seven o'clock already.'

"An idea occurred to me. If the sub-editor of a paper doesn't know whom to send to a theatre, it must mean that the post of dramatic critic on that paper is for some reason or another vacant.

"'Oh, that's all right,' I told him. 'I shall be in time enough.'

"He appeared neither pleased nor displeased. 'Have you arranged with the Guv'nor?' he asked me.

"'I'm just waiting to see him again for a few minutes,' I returned. 'It'll be all right. Have you got the ticket?'

"'Haven't seen it,' he replied.

"'About a column?' I suggested.

"'Three-quarters,' he preferred, and went.

"The moment he was gone, I slipped downstairs and met a printer's boy coming up.

"'What's the name of your sub?' I asked him. 'Tall man with a black moustache, looks tired.'

"'Oh, you mean Penton,' explained the boy.

"'That's the name,' I answered; 'couldn't think of it.'

"I walked straight into the editor; he was still irritable. 'What is it? What is it now?' he snapped out.

"'I only want the ticket for the Royalty Theatre,' I answered. 'Penton says you've got it.'

"'I don't know where it is,' he growled.

"I found it after some little search upon his desk.

"'Who's going?' he asked.

"'I am,' I said. And I went.

"They have never discovered to this day that I appointed myself. Penton thinks I am some relation of the proprietress, and in consequence everybody treats me with marked respect. Mrs. Wallace herself, the proprietress, thinks I am the discovery of Penton, in whose judgment she has great faith; and with her I get on admirably. The paper I don't think is doing too well, and the salary is small, but sufficient. Journalism suits my temperament, and I dare say I shall keep to it."

"You've been somewhat of a rolling stone hitherto," I commented.

He laughed. "From the stone's point of view," he answered, "I never could see the advantage of being smothered in moss. I should always prefer remaining the stone, unhidden, able to move and see about me. But now, to speak of other matters, what are your plans for the immediate future? Your opera, thanks to the gentlemen, the gods have dubbed 'Goggles,' will, I fancy, run through the winter. Are you getting any salary?"

"Thirty shillings a week," I explained to him, "with full salary for matinees."

"Say two pounds," he replied. "With my three we could set up an establishment of our own. I have an idea that is original. Shall we work it out together?"

I assured him with fervour that nothing would please me better.

"There are four delightful rooms in Queen's Square," he continued. "They are charmingly furnished: a fine sitting-room in the front, with two bedrooms and a kitchen behind. Their last tenant was a Polish Revolutionary, who, three months ago, poor fellow, was foolish enough to venture back to Russia, and who is now living rent free. The landlord of the house is an original old fellow, Deleglise the engraver. He occupies the rest of the house himself. He has told me I can have the rooms for anything I like to offer, and I should suggest thirty shillings a week, though under ordinary circumstances they would be worth three or four pounds. But he will only let us have them on the understanding that we 'do for' ourselves. He is quite an oddity. He hates petticoats, especially elderly petticoats. He has one servant, an old Frenchwoman, who, I believe, was housekeeper to his mother, and he and she do the housework together, most of their time quarrelling over it. Nothing else of the genus domestic female will he allow inside the door; not even an occasional charwoman would be permitted to us. On the other hand, it is a beautiful old Georgian house, with Adams mantelpieces, a stone staircase, and oak-panelled rooms; and our portion would be the entire second floor: no pianos and no landlady. He is a widower with one child, a girl of about fourteen or maybe a little older. Now, what do you say? I am a very fair cook; will you be house-and-parlour-maid?"

I needed no pressing. A week later we were installed there, and for nearly two years we lived there. At the risk of offending an adorable but somewhat touchy sex, convinced that man, left to himself, is capable of little more than putting himself to bed, and that only in a rough-and-ready fashion, truth compels me to record the fact that without female assistance or supervision of any kind we passed through those two years, and yet exist to tell the tale. Dan had not idly boasted. Better plain cooking I never want to taste; so good a cup of coffee, omelette, or devilled kidney I rarely have tasted. Had he always confined his efforts within the boundaries of his abilities, there would be little to record beyond continuous and monotonous success. But stirred into dangerous ambition at the call of an occasional tea or supper party, lured out of his depths by the example of old Deleglise, our landlord, a man who for twenty years had made cooking his hobby, Dan would at intervals venture upon experiment. Pastry, it became evident, was a thing he should never have touched: his hand was heavy and his temperament too serious. There was a thing called lemon sponge, necessitating much beating of eggs. In the cookery-book, a remarkably fat volume, luscious with illustrations of highly-coloured food, it appeared an airy and graceful structure of dazzling whiteness. Served as Dan sent it to table, it suggested rather in form and colour a miniature earthquake. Spongy it undoubtedly was. One forced it apart with the assistance of one's spoon and fork; it yielded with a gentle tearing sound. Another favourite dainty of his was manna-cake. Concerning it I would merely remark that if it in any way resembled anything the Children of Israel were compelled to eat, then there is explanation for that fretfulness and discontent for which they have been, perhaps, unjustly blamed, some excuse even for their backward-flung desires in the direction of the Egyptian fleshpots. Moses himself may have been blessed with exceptional digestion. It was substantial, one must say that for it. One slice of it, solid, firm, crusty on the outside, towards the centre marshy, satisfied most people to a sense of repletion. For supper parties Dan would essay trifles, by no means open to the criticism of being light as air, souffle's that guests, in spite of my admonishing kicks, would persist in alluding to as pudding; and in winter-time, pancakes. Later, as regards these latter, he acquired some skill; but at first the difficulty was the tossing. I think myself a safer plan would have been to turn them by the aid of a knife and fork; it is less showy, but more sure. At least, you avoid all danger of catching the half-baked thing upon your head instead of in the pan, of dropping it into the fire, or among the cinders. But "Thorough" was always Dan's motto; and after all, small particles of coal or a few hairs can always be detected by the careful feeder, and removed.

A more even-tempered man than Dan for twenty-three hours out of every twenty-four surely never breathed. It was a revelation to me to discover that for the other he could be uncertain, irritable, even ungrateful. At first, in a spirit of pure good nature, I would offer him counsel and advice; explain to him why, as it seemed to me, the custard was pimply, the mayonnaise sauce suggestive of hair oil. What was my return? Sneers, insult and abuse, followed, if I did not clear out quickly, by spoilt tomatoes, cold coffee grounds, anything that happened to be handy. Pained, saddened, I would withdraw, he would kick the door to after me. His greatest enemy appeared to be the oven. The oven it was that set itself to thwart his best wrought schemes. Always it was the oven's fault that the snowy bun appeared to have been made of red sandstone, the macaroni cheese of Cambrian clay. One might have sympathised with him more had his language been more restrained. As it was, the virulence of his reproaches almost inclined one to take the part of the oven.

Concerning our house-maid, I can speak in terms of unqualified praise. There are, alas, fussy house-maids, who has not known and suffered them? who overdo the thing, have no repose, no instinct telling them when to ease up and let the place alone. I have always held the perpetual stirring up of dust a scientific error; left to itself, it is harmless, may even be regarded as a delicate domestic bloom, bestowing a touch of homeliness upon objects that without it gleam cold and unsympathetic. Let sleeping dogs lie. Why be continually waking up the stuff, filling the air with all manner of unhealthy germs? Nature in her infinite wisdom has ordained that upon table, floor, or picture frame it shall sink and settle. There it remains, quiet and inoffensive; there it will continue to remain so long as nobody interferes with it: why worry it? So also with crumbs, odd bits of string, particles of egg-shell, stumps of matches, ends of cigarettes: what fitter place for such than under the nearest mat? To sweep them up is tiresome work. They cling to the carpet, you get cross with them, curse them for their obstinacy, and feel ashamed of yourself for your childishness. For every one you do persuade into the dust-pan, two jump out again. You lose your temper, feel bitter towards the man that dropped them. Your whole character becomes deteriorated. Under the mat they are always willing to go. Compromise is true statesmanship. There will come a day when you will be glad of an excuse for not doing something else that you ought to be doing. Then you can take up the mats and feel quite industrious, contemplating the amount of work that really must be done, some time or another.

To differentiate between the essential and the non-essential, that is where woman fails. In the name of common sense, what is the use of washing a cup that half an hour later is going to be made dirty again? If the cat be willing and able to so clean a plate that not one speck of grease remain upon it, why deprive her of pleasure to inflict toil upon yourself? If a bed looks made and feels made, then for all practical purposes it is made; why upset it merely to put it straight again? It would surprise most women the amount of labour that can be avoided in a house.

For needlework, I confess, I never acquired skill. Dan had learnt to handle a thimble, but my own second finger was ever reluctant to come forward when wanted. It had to be found, all other fingers removed out of its way. Then, feebly, nervously, it would push, slip, get itself pricked badly with the head of the needle, and, thoroughly frightened, remain incapable of further action. More practical I found it to push the needle through by help of the door or table.

The opera, as Dan had predicted, ran far into the following year. When it was done with, another, in which "Goggles" appeared as one of the principals, took its place, and was even more successful. After the experience of Nelson Square, my present salary of thirty-five shillings, occasionally forty shillings, a week seemed to me princely. There floated before my eyes the possibility of my becoming a great opera singer. On six hundred pounds a week, I felt I could be content. But the O'Kelly set himself to dispel this dream.

"Ye'd be making a mistake, me boy," explained the O'Kelly. "Ye'd be just wasting ye're time. I wouldn't tell ye so if I weren't convinced of it."

"I know it is not powerful," I admitted.

"Ye might almost call it thin," added the O'Kelly.

"It might be good enough for comic opera," I argued. "People appear to succeed in comic opera without much voice.

"Sure, there ye're right," agreed the O'Kelly, with a sigh. "An' of course if ye had an exceptionally fine presence and were strikingly handsome"

"One can do a good deal with make-up," I suggested.

The O'Kelly shook his head. "It's never quite the same thing. It would depend upon your acting."

I dreamt of becoming a second Kean, of taking Macready's place. It need not interfere with my literary ambition. I could combine the two: fill Drury Lane in the evening, turn out epoch-making novels in the morning, write my own plays.

Every day I studied in the reading-room of the British Museum. Wearying of success in Art, I might eventually go into Parliament: a Prime Minister with a thorough knowledge of history: why not? With Ollendorf for guide, I continued French and German. It might be the diplomatic service that would appeal to me in my old age. An ambassadorship! It would be a pleasant termination to a brilliant career.

There was excuse for my optimistic mood about this period. All things were going well with me. A story of mine had been accepted. I forget for the moment the name of the journal: it is dead now. Most of the papers in which my early efforts appeared are dead. My contributions might be likened to their swan songs. Proofs had been sent me, which I had corrected and returned. But proofs are not facts. This had happened to me once before, and I had been lifted to the skies only to fall the more heavily. The paper had collapsed before my story had appeared. (Ah, why had they delayed? It might have saved them!) This time I remembered the proverb, and kept my own counsel, slipping out early each morning on the day of publication to buy the paper, to scan eagerly its columns. For weeks I suffered hope deferred. But at last, one bright winter's day in January, walking down the Harrow Road, I found myself standing still, suddenly stunned, before a bill outside a small news-vendor's shop. It was the first time I had seen my real name in print: "The Witch of Moel Sarbod: a legend of Mona, by Paul Kelver." (For this I had even risked discovery by the Lady 'Ortensia.) My legs trembling under me, I entered the shop. A ruffianly-looking man in dirty shirt-sleeves, who appeared astonished that any one should want a copy, found one at length on the floor underneath the counter. With it in my pocket, I retraced my footsteps as in a dream. On a seat in Paddington Green I sat down and read it. The hundred best books! I have waded through them all; they have never charmed me as charmed me that one short story in that now forgotten journal. Need I add it was a sad and sentimental composition. Once upon a time there lived a mighty King; one, but with the names I will not bore you; they are somewhat unpronounceable. Their selection had cost me many hours of study in the British Museum reading-rooms, surrounded by lexicons of the Welsh language, gazetteers, translations from the early Celtic poets, with footnotes. He loved and was beloved by a beautiful Princess, whose name, being translated, was Purity. One day the King, hunting, lost his way, and being weary, lay down and fell asleep. And by chance the spot whereon he lay was near to a place which by infinite pains, with the aid of a magnifying glass, I had discovered upon the map, and which means in English the Cave of the Waters, where dwelt a wicked Sorceress, who, while he slept, cast her spells upon him, so that he awoke to forget his kingly honour and the good of all his people, his only desire being towards the Witch of Moel Sarbod.

Now, there lived in this Kingdom by the sea a great Magician; and Purity, who loved the King far better than herself, bethought her of him, and of all she had heard concerning his power and wisdom; and went to him and besought his aid that she might save the King. There was but one way to accomplish this: with bare feet Purity must climb the rocky path leading to the Witch's dwelling, go boldly up to her, not fearing her sharp claws nor her strong teeth, and kiss her upon the mouth. In this way the spirit of Purity would pass into the Witch's soul, and she would become a woman. But the form and spirit of the Witch would pass into Purity, transforming her, and in the Cave of the Waters she must forever abide. Thus Purity gave herself that the King might live. With bleeding feet she climbed the rocky path, clasped the Witch's form within her arms, kissed her on the mouth. And the Witch became a woman and reigned with the King over his people, wisely and helpfully. But Purity became a hideous witch, and to this day abides on Moel Sarbod, where is the Cave of the Waters. And they who climb the mountain's side still hear above the roaring of the cataract the sobbing of Purity, the King's betrothed. But many liken it rather to a joyous song of love triumphant.

No writer worth his salt was ever satisfied with anything he ever wrote, so I have been told, and so I try to believe. Evidently I am not worth my salt. Candid friends, and others, to whom in my salad days I used to show my work, asking for a frank opinion, meaning, of course, though never would they understand me, their unadulterated praise, would assure me for my good, that this, my first to whom the gods gave life, was but a feeble, ill-shaped child: its attempted early English a cross between "The Pilgrim's Progress" and "Old Moore's Almanac;" its scenery, which had cost me weeks of research, an apparent attempt to sum up in the language of a local guide book the leading characteristics of the Garden of Eden combined with Dante's Inferno; its pathos of the penny-plain and two-penny-coloured order. Maybe they were right. Much have I written since that at the time appeared to me good, that I have read later with regret, with burning cheek, with frowning brow. But of this, my first-born, the harbinger of all my hopes, I am no judge. Touching the yellowing, badly-printed pages, I feel again the deep thrill of joy with which I first unfolded them and read. Again I am a youngster, and life opens out before me, inmeasurable, no goal too high. This child of my brain, my work: it shall spread my name throughout the world. It shall be a household world in lands that I shall never see. Friends whose voices I shall never hear will speak of me. I shall die, but it shall live, yield fresh seed, bear fruit I know not of. Generations yet unborn shall read it and remember me. My thoughts, my words, my spirit: in it I shall live again; it shall keep my memory green.

The long, long thoughts of boyhood! We elders smile at them. The little world spins round; the little voices of an hour sink hushed. The crawling generations come and go. The solar system drops from space. The eternal mechanism reforms and shapes itself anew. Time, turning, ploughs another furrow. So, growing sleepy, we murmur with a yawn. Is it that we see clearer, or that our eyes are growing dim? Let the young men see their visions, dream their dreams, hug to themselves their hopes of enduring fame; so shall they serve the world better.

I brushed the tears from my eyes and looked up. Half-a-dozen urchins, male and female, were gaping at me open-mouthed. They scattered shouting, whether compliment or insult I know not: probably the latter. I flung them a handful of coppers, which for the moment silenced them; and went upon my way. How bright, how fair the bustling streets, golden in the winter sunshine, thronged with life, with effort! Laughter rang around me. Sweet music rolled from barrel-organs. The strenuous voices of the costermongers called invitation to the fruitful earth. Errand boys passed me whistling shrilly joyous melodies. Perspiring tradesmen shouted generous offers to the needy. Men and women hurried by with smiling faces. Sleek cats purred in sheltered nooks, till merry dogs invited them to sport. The sparrows, feasting in the roadway, chirped their hymn of praise.

At the Marble Arch I jumped upon a 'bus. I mentioned to the conductor in mounting that it was a fine day. He replied that he had noticed it himself. The retort struck me as a brilliant repartee. Our coachman, all but run into by a hansom cab driven by a surly old fellow of patriarchal appearance, remarked upon the danger of allowing horses out in charge of bits of boys. How full the world of wit and humour!

Almost without knowing it, I found myself in earnest conversation with a young man sitting next to me. We conversed of life, of love. Not until afterwards, reflecting upon the matter, did it surprise me that to a mere chance acquaintance of the moment he had spoken of the one thing dearest to his heart: a sweet but clearly wayward maiden, the Hebe of a small, old-fashioned coffee-shop the 'bus was at that moment passing. Hitherto I had not been the recipient of confidences. It occurred to me that as a rule not even my friends spoke much to me concerning their own affairs; generally it was I who spoke to them of mine. I sympathised with him, advised him, how, I do not recollect. He said, however, he thought that I was right; and at Regent Street he left me, expressing his determination to follow my counsel, whatever it may have been.

Between Berners Street and the Circus I lent a shilling to a couple of young ladies who had just discovered with amusement, quickly swallowed by despair, that they neither of them had any money with them. (They returned it next day in postage stamps, with a charming note.) The assurance with which I tendered the slight service astonished me myself. At any other time I should have hesitated, argued with my fears, offered it with an appearance of sulky constraint, and been declined. For a moment they were doubtful, then, looking at me, accepted with a delightful smile. They consulted me as to the way to Paternoster Row. I instructed them, adding a literary anecdote, which seemed to interest them. I even ventured on a compliment, neatly phrased, I am inclined to think. Evidently it pleased, a result hitherto unusual in the case of my compliments. At the corner of Southampton Row I parted from them with regret. Why had I never noticed before how full of pleasant people this sweet and smiling London?

At the corner of Queen's Square a decent-looking woman stopped me to ask the way to the Children's Hospital at Chelsea, explaining she had made a mistake, thinking it was the one in Great Ormond Street where her child lay. I directed her, then glancing into her face, noticed how tired she looked, and a vista of the weary pavements she would have to tramp flashed before me. I slipped some money into her hand and told her to take a 'bus. She flushed, then thanked me. I turned a few yards further on; she was starting after me, amazement on her face. I laughed and waved my hand to her. She smiled back in return, and went her way.

A rain began to fall. I paused upon the doorstep for a minute, enjoying the cool drops upon by upturned face, the tonic sharpness of the keen east wind; then slipped my key into the lock and entered.

The door of old Deleglise's studio on the first floor happened to he open. Hitherto, beyond the usual formal salutations, when by chance we met upon the stairs, I had exchanged but few words with my eccentric landlord; but remembering his kindly face, the desire came upon me to tell him my good fortune. I felt sure his eyes would lighten with delight. By instinct I knew him for a young man's man.

I tapped lightly; no answer came. Someone was talking; it sounded like a girl's voice. I pushed the door further open and walked in; such was the custom of the house. It was a large room, built over the yard, lighted by one high window, before which was the engraving desk, shaded under a screen of tissue paper. At the further end of the room stood a large cheval-glass, and in front of this, its back towards me, was a figure that excited my curiosity; so that remaining where I was, partly hidden behind a large easel, I watched it for awhile in silence. Above a heavily flounced blue skirt, which fell in creases on the floor and trailed a couple of yards or so behind, it wore a black low-cut sleeveless bodice, much too big for it, of the fashion early Victorian. A good deal of dark-brown hair, fastened up by hair-pins that stuck out in all directions like quills upon a porcupine, suggesting collapse with every movement, was ornamented by three enormous green feathers, one of which hung limply over the lady's left ear. Three times, while I watched, unnoticed, the lady propped it into a more befitting attitude, and three times, limp and intoxicated-looking, it fell back into its former foolish position. Her long, thin arms, displaying a pair of brilliantly red elbows, pointed to quite a dangerous degree, terminated in hands so very sunburnt as to convey the impression of a pair of remarkably well-fitting gloves. Her right hand grasped and waved with determination a large lace fan, her left clutched fiercely the front of her skirt. With a sweeping curtsey to herself in the glass, which would have been more effective could she have avoided tying her legs together with her skirt, a contretemps necessitating the use of both hands and a succession of jumps before she could disentangle herself, she remarked so soon as she had recovered her balance:

"So sorry I am late. My carriage was unfortunately delayed."

The excuse, I gathered, was accepted, for with a gracious smile and a vigorous bow, by help of which every hairpin made distinct further advance towards freedom, she turned, and with much dignity and head over the right shoulder took a short walk to the left. At the end of six short steps she stopped and began kicking. For what reason, I, at first, could not comprehend. It dawned upon me after awhile that her object was the adjustment of her train. Finding the manoeuvre too difficult of accomplishment by feet alone, she stooped, and, taking the stuff up in her hands, threw it behind her. Then, facing north, she retraced her steps to the glass, talking to herself, as she walked, in the high-pitched drawl, distinctive, as my stage knowledge told me, of aristocratic society.

"Oh, do you think so, really? Ah, yes; you say that. Certainly not! I shouldn't think of it." There followed what I am inclined to believe was intended for a laugh, musical but tantalising. If so, want of practice marred the effort. The performance failed to satisfy even herself. She tried again; it was still only a giggle.

Before the glass she paused, and with a haughty inclination of her head succeeded for the third time in displacing the intoxicated feather.

"Oh, bother the silly thing!" she said in a voice so natural as to be, by contrast with her previous tone, quite startling.

She fixed it again with difficulty, muttering something inarticulate. Then, her left hand resting on an imaginary coat-sleeve, her right holding her skirt sufficiently high to enable her to move, she commenced to majestically gyrate.

Whether, hampered as she was by excess of skirt, handicapped by the natural clumsiness of her age, catastrophe in any case would not sooner or later have overtaken her, I have my doubts. I have since learnt her own view to be that but for catching sight, in turning, of my face, staring at her through the bars of the easel, all would have gone well and gracefully. Avoiding controversy on this point, the facts to be recorded are, that, seeing me, she uttered a sudden exclamation of surprise, dropped her skirt, trod on her train, felt her hair coming down, tried to do two things at once, and sat upon the floor. I ran to her assistance. With flaming face and flashing eyes she sprang to her feet. There was a sound as of the rushing down of avalanches. The blue flounced skirt lay round her on the floor. She stood above its billowy folds, reminiscent of Venus rising from the waves, a gawky, angular Venus in a short serge frock, reaching a little below her knees, black stockings and a pair of prunella boots of a size suggesting she had yet some inches to grow before reaching her full height.

"I hope you haven't hurt yourself," I said.

The next moment I didn't care whether she had or whether she hadn't. She did not reply to my kindly meant enquiry. Instead, her hand swept through the air in the form of an ample semi-circle. It terminated on my ear. It was not a small hand; it was not a soft hand; it was not that sort of hand. The sound of the contact rang through the room like a pistol shot; I beard it with my other ear. I sprang at her, and catching her before she had recovered her equilibrium, kissed her. I did not kiss her because I wanted to. I kissed her because I could not box her ears back in return, which I should have preferred doing. I kissed her, hoping it would make her mad. It did. If a look could have killed me, such would have been the tragic ending of this story. It did not kill me; it did me good.

"You horrid boy!" she cried. "You horrid, horrid boy!"

There, I admit, she scored. I did not in the least object to her thinking me horrid, but at nineteen one does object to being mistaken for a boy.

"I am not a boy," I explained.

"Yes, you are," she retorted; "a beast of a boy!"

"If you do it again," I warned her, a sudden movement on her part hinting to me the possibility, "I'll kiss you again! I mean it."

"Leave the room!" she commanded, pointing with her angular arm towards the door.

I did not wish to remain. I was about to retire with as much dignity as circumstances permitted.

"Boy!" she added.

At that I turned. "Now I won't go!" I replied. "See if I do."

We stood glaring at each other.

"What right have you in here?" she demanded.

"I came to see Mr. Deleglise," I answered. "I suppose you are Miss Deleglise. It doesn't seem to me that you know how to treat a visitor."

"Who are you?" she asked.

"Mr. Horace Moncrieff," I replied. I was using at the period both my names indiscriminately, but for this occasion Horace Moncrieff I judged the more awe-inspiring.

She snorted. "I know. You're the house-maid. You sweep all the crumbs under the mats."

Now this was a subject about which at the time I was feeling somewhat sore. "Needs must when the Devil drives;" but as matters were, Dan and I could well have afforded domestic assistance. It rankled in my mind that to fit in with the foolish fad of old Deleglise, I the future Dickens, Thackeray and George Eliot, Kean, Macready and Phelps rolled into one, should be compelled to the performance of menial duties. On this morning of all others, my brilliant literary career just commenced, the anomaly of the thing appeared naturally more glaring.

Besides, how came she to know I swept the crumbs under the mat, that it was my method? Had she and Dan been discussing me, ridiculing me behind my back? What right had Dan to reveal the secrets of our menage to this chit of a school-girl? Had he done so? or had she been prying, poking her tilted nose into matters that did not concern her? Pity it was she had no mother to occasionally spank her, teach her proper behaviour.

"Where I sweep our crumbs is nothing to do with you," I replied with some spirit. "That I have to sweep them at all is the fault of your father. A sensible girl"

"How dare you speak against my father!" she interrupted me with blazing eyes.

"We will not discuss the question further," I answered, with sense and dignity.

"I think you had better not!" she retorted.

Turning her back on me, she commenced to gather up her hairpins, there must have been about a hundred of them. I assisted her to the extent of picking up about twenty, which I handed to her with a bow: it may have been a little stiff, but that was only to be expected. I wished to show her that her bad example had not affected my own manners.

"I am sorry my presence should have annoyed you," I said. "It was quite an accident. I entered the room thinking your father was here."

"When you saw he wasn't, you might have gone out again," she replied, "instead of hiding yourself behind a picture."

"I didn't hide myself," I explained. "The easel happened to be in the way."

"And you stopped there and watched me."

"I couldn't help it."

She looked round and our eyes met. They were frank, grey eyes. An expression of merriment shot into them. I laughed.

Then she laughed: it was a delightful laugh, the laugh one would have expected from her.

"You might at least have coughed," she suggested.

"It was so amusing," I pleaded.

"I suppose it was," she agreed, and held out her hand. "Did I hurt you?" she asked.

"Yes, you did," I answered, taking it.

"Well, it was enough to annoy me, wasn't it?" she suggested.

"Evidently," I agreed.

"I am going to a ball next week," she explained, "a grown-up ball, and I've got to wear a skirt. I wanted to see if I could manage a train."

"Well, to be candid, you can't," I assured her.

"It does seem difficult."

"Shall I show you?" I asked.

"What do you know about it?"

"Well, I see it done every night."

"Oh, yes; of course, you're on the stage. Yes, do."

We readjusted the torn skirt, accommodating it better to her figure by the help of hairpins. I showed her how to hold the train, and, I humming a tune, we commenced to waltz.

"I shouldn't count my steps," I suggested to her. "It takes your mind away from the music."

"I don't waltz well," she admitted meekly. "I know I don't do anything well, except play hockey."

"And try not to tread on your partner's feet. That's a very bad fault."

"I do try not to," she explained.

"It comes with practice," I assured her.

"I'll get Tom to give me half an hour every evening," she said. "He dances beautifully."

"Who's Tom?"

"Oh, father."

"Why do you call your father Tom? It doesn't sound respectful."

"Oh, he likes it; and it suits him so much better than father. Besides, he isn't like a real father. He does everything I want him to."

"Is that good for you?"

"No; it's very bad for me, everybody says so. When you come to think of it, of course it isn't the way to bring up a girl. I tell him, but he merely laughs, says it's the only way he knows. I do hope I turn out all right. Am I doing it better now?"

"A little. Don't be too anxious about it. Don't look at your feet."

"But if I don't they go all wrong. It was you who trod on mine that time."

"I know. I'm sorry. It's a little difficult not to."

"Am I holding my train all right?"

"Well, there's no need to grip it as if you were afraid it would run away. It will follow all right. Hold it gracefully."

"I wish I wasn't a girl."

"Oh, you'll get used to it." We concluded our dance.

"What do I do, say 'Thank you'?"

"Yes, prettily."

"What does he do?"

"Oh, he takes you back to your chaperon, or suggests refreshment, or you sit and talk."

"I hate talking. I never know what to say."

"Oh, that's his duty. He'll try and amuse you, then you must laugh. You have a nice laugh."

"But I never know when to laugh. If I laugh when I want to it always offends people. What do you do if somebody asks you to dance and you don't want to dance with them?"

"Oh, you say your programme is full."

"But if it isn't?"

"Well, you tell a lie."

"Couldn't I say I don't dance well, and that I'm sure they'd get on better with somebody else?"

"It would be the truth, but they might not believe it."

"I hope nobody asks me that I don't want."

"Well, he won't a second time, anyhow."

"You are rude."

"You are only a school-girl."

"I look a woman in my new frock, I really do."

"I should doubt it."

"You shall see me, then you'll be polite. It is because you are a boy you are rude. Men are much nicer."

"Oh, are they?"

"Yes. You will be, when you are a man."

The sound of voices rose suddenly in the hall.

"Tom!" cried Miss Deleglise; and collecting her skirt in both hands, bolted down the corkscrew staircase leading to the kitchen, leaving me standing in the centre of the studio.

The door opened and old Deleglise entered, accompanied by a small, slight man with red hair and beard and somewhat watery eyes.

Deleglise himself was a handsome old fellow, then a man of about fifty-five. His massive, mobile face, illuminated by bright, restless eyes, was crowned with a lion-like mane of iron-grey hair. Till a few years ago he had been a painter of considerable note. But in questions of art his temper was short. Pre-Raphaelism had gone out of fashion for the time being; the tendency of the new age was towards impressionism, and in disgust old Deleglise had broken his palette across his knee, and swore never to paint again. Artistic work of some sort being necessary to his temperament, he contented himself now with engraving. At the moment he was engaged upon the reproduction of Memlinc's Shrine of St. Ursula, with photographs of which he had just returned from Bruges.

At sight of me his face lighted with a smile, and he advanced with outstretched hand.

"Ah; my lad, so you have got over your shyness and come to visit the old bear in his den. Good boy. I like young faces."

He had a clear, musical voice, ever with the suggestion of a laugh behind it. He laid his hand upon my shoulder.

"Why, you are looking as if you had come into a fortune," he added, "and didn't know what a piece of bad luck that can be to a young fellow like yourself."

"How could it be bad luck?" I asked, laughing.

"Takes all the sauce out of life, young man," answered Deleglise. "What interest is there in running a race with the prize already in your possession, tell me that?"

"It is not that kind of fortune," I answered, "it is another. I have had my first story accepted. It is in print. Look."

I handed him the paper. He spread it out upon the engraving board before him.

"Ah, that's better," he said, "that's better. Charlie," he turned to the red-headed man, who had seated himself listlessly in the one easy-chair the room contained, "come here."

The red-headed man rose and wandered towards us. "Let me introduce you to Mr. Paul Kelver, our new fellow servant. Our lady has accepted him. He has just been elected; his first story is in print."

The red-haired man stretched out his long thin hand. "I have thirty years of fame," said the red-haired man, "could I say world-wide?"

He turned for confirmation to old Deleglise, who laughed. "I think you can."

"If I could give it you would you exchange with me, at this moment?"

"You would be a fool if you did," he went on. "One's first success, one's first victory! It is the lover's first kiss. Fortune grows old and wrinkled, frowns more often than she smiles. We become indifferent to her, quarrel with her, make it up again. But the joy of her first kiss after the long wooing! Burn it into your memory, my young friend, that it may live with you always!"

He strolled away. Old Deleglise took up the parable.

"Ah, yes; one's first success, Paul! Laugh, my boy, cry! Shut yourself up in your room, shout, dance! Throw your hat into the air and cry hurrah! Make the most of it, Paul. Hug it to your heart, think of it, dream of it. This is the finest hour of your life, my boy. There will never come another like it, never!"

He crossed the studio, and taking from its nail a small oil painting, brought it over and laid it on the board beside my paper. It was a fascinating little picture, painted with that exquisite minutiae and development of detail that a newer school was then ridiculing: as though Art had but one note to her voice. The dead figure of an old man lay upon a bed. A child had crept into the darkened room, and supporting itself by clutching tightly at the sheet, was gazing with solemn curiosity upon the white, still face.

"That was mine," said old Deleglise. "It was hung in the Academy thirty-six years ago, and bought for ten guineas by a dentist at Bury St. Edmunds. He went mad a few years later and died in a lunatic asylum. I had never lost sight of it, and the executors were quite agreeable to my having it back again for the same ten guineas. I used to go every morning to the Academy to look at it. I thought it the cleverest bit of work in the whole gallery, and I'm not at all sure that it wasn't. I saw myself a second Teniers, another Millet. Look how that light coming through the open door is treated; isn't it good? Somebody will pay a thousand guineas for it before I have been dead a dozen years, and it is worth it. But I wouldn't sell it myself now for five thousand. One's first success; it is worth all the rest of life!"

"All?" queried the red-haired man from his easy-chair. We looked round. The lady of the skirt had entered, now her own proper self: a young girl of about fifteen, angular, awkward-looking, but bringing into the room with her that atmosphere of life, of hope, that is the eternal message of youth. She was not beautiful, not then, plain one might almost have called her but for her frank, grey eyes, her mass of dark-brown hair now gathered into a long thick plait. A light came into old Deleglise's eyes.

"You are right, not all," he murmured to the red-haired man.

She came forward shyly. I found it difficult to recognise in her the flaming Fury that a few minutes before had sprung at me from the billows of her torn blue skirt. She shook hands with the red-haired man and kissed her father.

"My daughter," said old Deleglise, introducing me to her. "Mr. Paul Kelver, a literary gent."

"Mr. Kelver and I have met already," she explained. "He has been waiting for you here in the studio."

"And have you been entertaining him?" asked Deleglise. "Oh, yes, I entertained him," she replied. Her voice was singularly like her father's, with just the same suggestion of ever a laugh behind it.

"We entertained each other," I said.

"That's all right," said old Deleglise. "Stop and lunch with us. We will make ourselves a curry."

CHAPTER VI.

OF THE GLORY AND GOODNESS AND THE EVIL THAT GO TO THE MAKING OF LOVE.

During my time of struggle I had avoided all communication with old Hasluck. He was not a man to sympathise with feelings he did not understand. With boisterous good humour he would have insisted upon helping me. Why I preferred half starving with Lott and Co. to selling my labour for a fair wage to good-natured old Hasluck, merely because I knew him, I cannot explain. Though the profits may not have been so large, Lott and Co.'s dealings were not one whit more honest: I do not believe it was that which decided me. Nor do I think it was because he was Barbara's father. I never connected him, nor that good old soul, his vulgar, homely wife, in any way with Barbara. To me she was a being apart from all the world. Her true Parents! I should have sought them rather amid the sacred groves of vanished lands, within the sky-domed shrines of banished gods. There are instincts in us not easily analysed, not to be explained by reason. I have always preferred the finding, sometimes the losing of my way according to the map, to the surer and simpler method of vocal enquiry; working out a complicated journey, and running the risk of never arriving at my destination, by aid of a Continental Bradshaw, to putting myself into the hands of courteous officials maintained and paid to assist the perplexed traveller. Possibly a far-off progenitor of mine may have been some morose "rogue" savage with untribal inclinations, living in his cave apart, fashioning his own stone hammer, shaping his own flint arrow-heads, shunning the merry war-dance, preferring to caper by himself.

But now, having gained my own foothold, I could stretch out my hand without fear of the movement being mistaken for appeal. I wrote to old Hasluck; and almost by the next post received from him the friendliest of notes. He told me Barbara had just returned from abroad, took it upon himself to add that she also would be delighted to see me, and, as I knew he would, threw his doors open to me.

Of my boyish passion for Barbara never had I spoken to a living soul, nor do I think, excepting Barbara herself, had any ever guessed it. To my mother, though she was very fond of her, Barbara was only a girl, with charms but also with faults, concerning which my mother would speak freely; hurting me, as one unwittingly might hurt a neophyte by philosophical discussion of his newly embraced religion. Often, choosing by preference late evening or the night, I would wander round and round the huge red-brick house standing in its ancient garden on the top of Stamford Hill; descending again into the noisome streets as one returning to the world from praying at a shrine, purified, filled with peace, all noble endeavour, all unselfish aims seeming within my grasp.

During Barbara's four years' absence my adoration had grown and strengthened. Out of my memory of her my desire had evolved its ideal; a being of my imagination, but by reason of that, to me the more real, the more present. I looked forward to seeing her again, but with no impatience, revelling rather in the anticipation than eager for the realisation. As a creature of flesh and blood, the child I had played with, talked with, touched, she had faded further and further into the distance; as the vision of my dreams she stood out clearer day by day. I knew that when next I saw her there would be a gulf between us I had no wish to bridge. To worship her from afar was a sweeter thought to me than would have been the hope of a passionate embrace. To live with her, sit opposite to her while she ate and drank, see her, perhaps, with her hair in curl-papers, know possibly that she had a corn upon her foot, hear her speak maybe of a decayed tooth, or of a chilblain, would have been torture to me. Into such abyss of the commonplace there was no fear of my dragging her, and for this I was glad. In the future she would be yet more removed from me. She was older than I was; she must be now a woman. Instinctively I felt that in spite of years I was not yet a man. She would marry. The thought gave me no pain, my feeling for her was utterly devoid of appetite. No one but myself could close the temple I had built about her, none deny to me the right of entry there. No jealous priest could hide her from my eyes, her altar I had reared too high. Since I have come to know myself better, I perceive that she stood to me not as a living woman, but as a symbol; not a fellow human being to be walked with through life, helping and to be helped, but that impalpable religion of sex to which we raise up idols of poor human clay, alas, not always to our satisfaction, so that foolishly we fall into anger against them, forgetting they were but the work of our own hands; not the body, but the spirit of love.

I allowed a week to elapse after receiving old Hasluck's letter before presenting myself at Stamford Hill. It was late one afternoon in early summer. Hasluck had not returned from the City, Mrs. Hasluck was out visiting, Miss Hasluck was in the garden. I told the supercilious footman not to trouble, I would seek her there myself. I guessed where she would be; her favourite spot had always been a sunny corner, bright with flowers, surrounded by a thick yew hedge, cut, after the Dutch fashion, into quaint shapes of animals and birds. She was walking there, as I had expected, reading a book. And again, as I saw her, came back to me the feeling that had swept across me as a boy, when first outlined against the dusty books and papers of my father's office she had flashed upon my eyes: that all the fairy tales had suddenly come true, only now, instead of the Princess, she was the Queen. Taller she was, with a dignity that formerly had been the only charm she lacked. She did not hear my coming, my way being across the soft, short grass, and for a little while I stood there in the shadow of the yews, drinking in the beauty of her clear-cut profile, bent down towards her book, the curving lines of her long neck, the wonder of the exquisite white hand against the lilac of her dress.

I did not speak; rather would I have remained so watching; but turning at the end of the path, she saw me, and as she came towards me held out her hand. I knelt upon the path, and raised it to my lips. The action was spontaneous, till afterwards I was not aware of having done it. Her lips were smiling as I raised my eyes to them, the faintest suggestion of contempt mingling with amusement. Yet she seemed pleased, and her contempt, even if I were not mistaken, would not have wounded me.

"So you are still in love with me? I wondered if you would be."

"Did you know that I was in love with you?"

"I should have been blind if I had not."

"But I was only a boy."

"You were not the usual type of boy. You are not going to be the usual type of man."

"You do not mind my loving you?"

"I cannot help it, can I? Nor can you."

She seated herself on a stone bench facing a sun-dial, and leaning hack, her hands clasped behind her head, looked at me and laughed.

"I shall always love you," I answered, "but it is with a curious sort of love. I do not understand it myself."

"Tell me," she commanded, still with a smile about her lips, "describe it to me."

I was standing over against her, my arm resting upon the dial's stone column. The sun was sinking, casting long shadows on the velvety grass, illuminating with a golden light her upturned face.

"I would you were some great queen of olden days, and that I might be always near you, serving you, doing your bidding. Your love in return would spoil all; I shall never ask it, never desire it. That I might look upon you, touch now and then at rare intervals with my lips your hand, kiss in secret the glove you had let fall, the shoe you had flung off, know that you knew of my love, that I was yours to do with as you would, to live or die according to your wish. Or that you were priestess in some temple of forgotten gods, where I might steal at daybreak and at dusk to gaze upon your beauty; kneel with clasped hands, watching your sandalled feet coming and going about the altar steps; lie with pressed lips upon the stones your trailing robes had touched."

She laughed a light mocking laugh. "I should prefer to be the queen. The role of priestess would not suit me. Temples are so cold." A slight shiver passed through her. She made a movement with her hand, beckoning me to her feet. "That is how you shall love me, Paul," she said, "adoring me, worshipping me blindly. I will be your queen and treat you as it chooses me. All I think, all I do, I will tell you, and you shall tell me it is right. The queen can do no wrong."

She took my face between her hands, and bending over me, looked long and steadfastly into my eyes. "You understand, Paul, the queen can do no wrong, never, never." There had crept into her voice a note of vehemence, in her face was a look almost of appeal.

"My queen can do no wrong," I repeated. And she laughed and let her hands fall back upon her lap.

"Now you may sit beside me. So much honour, Paul, shall you have to-day, but it will have to last you long. And you may tell me all you have been doing, maybe it will amuse me; and afterwards you shall hear what I have done, and shall say that it was right and good of me."

I obeyed, sketching my story briefly, yet leaving nothing untold, not even the transit of the Lady 'Ortensia, ashamed of the episode though I was. At that she looked a little grave.

"You must do nothing again, Paul," she commanded, "to make me feel ashamed of you, or I shall dismiss you from my presence for ever. I must be proud of you, or you shall not serve me. In dishonouring yourself you are dishonouring me. I am angry with you, Paul. Do not let me be angry with you again.

And so that passed; and although my love for her, as I know well she wished and sought it should, failed to save me at all times from the apish voices whispering ever to the beast within us, I know the desire to be worthy of her, to honour her with all my being, helped my life as only love can. The glory of the morning fades, the magic veil is rent; we see all things with cold, clear eyes. My love was a woman. She lies dead. They have mocked her white sweet limbs with rags and tatters, but they cannot cheat love's eyes. God knows I loved her in all purity! Only with false love we love the false. Beneath the unclean clinging garments she sleeps fair.

My tale finished, "Now I will tell you mine," she said. "I am going to be married soon. I shall be a Countess, Paul, the Countess Huescar, I will teach you how to pronounce it, and I shall have a real castle in Spain. You need not look so frightened, Paul; we shall not live there. It is a half-ruined, gloomy place, among the mountains, and he loves it even less than I do. Paris and London will be my courts, so you will see me often. You shall know the great world, Paul, the world I mean to conquer, where I mean to rule."

"Is he very rich?" I asked.

"As poor," she laughed, "as poor as a Spanish nobleman. The money I shall have to provide, or, rather, poor dear Dad will. He gives me title, position. Of course I do not love him, handsome though he is. Don't look so solemn, Paul. We shall get on together well enough. Queens, Paul, do not make love matches, they contract alliances. I have done well, Paul; congratulate me. Do you hear, Paul? Say that I have acted rightly."

"Does he love you?" I asked.

"He tells me so," she answered, with a laugh. "How uncourtier-like you are, Paul! Do you suggest that any man could see me and not love me?"

She sprang to her feet. "I do not want his love," she cried; "it would bore me. Women hate love they cannot return. I don't mean love like yours, devout little Paul," she added, with a laugh. "That is sweet incense wafted round us that we like to scent with our noses in the air. Give me that, Paul; I want it, I ask for it. But the love of a hand, the love of a husband that one does not care for, it would be horrible!"

I felt myself growing older. For the moment my goddess became a child needing help.

"But have you thought" I commenced.

"Yes, yes," she interrupted me quickly, "I have thought and thought till I can think no more. There must be some sacrifice; it must be as little as need be, that is all. He does not love me; he is marrying me for my money, I know that, and I am glad of it. You do not know me, Paul. I must have rank, position. What am I? The daughter of rich old Hasluck, who began life as a butcher in the Mile End Road. As the Princess Huescar, society will forget, as Mrs." it seemed to me she checked herself abruptly "Jones or Brown it would remember, however rich I might be. I am vain, Paul, caring for power, ambition. I have my father's blood in me. All his nights and days he has spent in gaining wealth; he can do no more. We upstarts have our pride of race. He has done his share, I must do mine."

"But you need not be mere Mrs. anybody commonplace," I argued. "Why not wait? You will meet someone who can give you position and whom at the same time you can love. Would that not be better?"

"He will never come, the man I could love," she answered. "Because, my little Paul, he has come already. Hush, Paul, the queen can do no wrong."

"Who is he?" I asked. "May I not know?"

"Yes, Paul," she answered, "you shall know; I want you to know, then you shall tell me that I have acted rightly. Do you hear me, Paul? quite rightly, that you still respect me and honour me. He could not help me. As his wife, I should be less even than I am, a mere rich nobody, giving long dinner-parties to other rich nobodies, living amongst City men, retired trades-people; envied only by their fat, vulgarly dressed wives, courted by seedy Bohemians for the sake of my cook; with perhaps an opera singer or an impecunious nobleman or two out of Dad's City list for my show-guests. Is that the court, Paul, where you would have your queen reign?"

"Is he so commonplace a man," I answered, "the man you love? I cannot believe it."

"He is not commonplace," she answered. "It is I who am commonplace. The things I desire, they are beneath him; he will never trouble himself to secure them."

"Not even for love of you?"

"I would not have him do so even were he willing. He is great, with a greatness I cannot even understand. He is not the man for these times. In old days, I should have married him, knowing he would climb to greatness by sheer strength of manhood. But now men do not climb; they crawl to greatness. He could not do that. I have done right, Paul."

"What does be say?" I asked.

"Shall I tell you?" She laughed a little bitterly. "I can give you his exact words, 'You are half a woman and half a fool, so woman-like you will follow your folly. But let your folly see to it that your woman makes no fool of herself.'"

The words were what I could imagine his saying. I heard the strong ring of his voice through her mocking mimicry.

"Hal!" I cried. "It is he."

"So you never guessed even that, Paul. I thought at times it would be sweet to cry it out aloud, that it could have made no difference, that everyone who knew me must have read it in my eyes."

"But he never seemed to take much notice of you," I said.

She laughed. "You needn't be so unkind, Paul. What did I ever do for you much more than snub you? We boys and girls; there is not so much difference between us: we love our masters. Yet you must not think so poorly of me. I was only a child to him then, but we were locked up in Paris together during the entire siege. Have not you heard? He did take a little notice of me there, Paul, I assure you."

Would it have been better, I wonder, had she followed the woman and not the fool? It sounds an easy question to answer; but I am thinking of years later, one winter's night at Tiefenkasten in the Julier Pass. I was on my way from San Moritz to Chur. The sole passenger, I had just climbed, half frozen, from the sledge, and was thawing myself before the stove in the common room of the hotel when the waiter put a pencilled note into my hand:

"Come up and see me. I am a prisoner in this damned hole till the weather breaks. Hal."

I hardly recognised him at first. Only the poor ghost he seemed of the Hal I had known as a boy. His long privations endured during the Paris siege, added to the superhuman work he had there put upon himself, had commenced the ruin of even his magnificent physique, a ruin the wild, loose life he was now leading was soon to complete. It was a gloomy, vaulted room that once had been a chapel, lighted dimly by a cheap, evil-smelling lamp, heated to suffocation by one of those great green-tiled German ovens now only to be met with in rare out-of-the-way world corners. He was sitting propped up by pillows on the bed, placed close to one of the high windows, his deep eyes flaring like two gleaming caverns out of his drawn, haggard face.

"I saw you from the window," he explained. "It is the only excitement I get, twice a day when the sledges come in. I broke down coming across the Pass a fortnight ago, on my way from Davos. We were stuck in a drift for eighteen hours; it nearly finished my last lung. And I haven't even a book to read. By God! lad, I was glad to see your frosted face ten minutes ago in the light of the lantern."

He grasped me with his long bony hand. "Sit down, and let me hear my voice using again its mother tongue, you were always a good listener, for the last eight years I have hardly spoken it. Can you stand the room?

The windows ought to be open, but what does it matter? I may as well get accustomed to the heat before I die."

I drew my chair close to the bed, and for awhile, between his fits of coughing, we talked of things that were outside our thoughts, or, rather, Hal talked, continuously, boisterously, meeting my remonstrances with shouts of laughter, ending in wild struggles for breath, so that I deemed it better to let him work his mad mood out.

Then suddenly: "What is she doing?" he asked. "Do you ever see her?"

"She is playing in" I mentioned the name of a comic opera then running in Paris. "No; I have not seen her for some time."

He laid his white, wasted hand on mine. "What a pity you and I could not have rolled ourselves into one, Paul, you, the saint, and I, the satyr. Together we should have made her perfect lover."

There came back to me the memory of those long nights when I had lain awake listening to the angry voices of my father and mother soaking through the flimsy wall. It seemed my fate to stand thus helpless between those I loved, watching them hurting one another against their will.

"Tell me," I asked, "I loved her, knowing her: I was not blind. Whose fault was it? Yours or hers?"

He laughed. "Whose fault, Paul? God made us."

Thinking of her fair, sweet face, I hated him for his mocking laugh. But the next moment, looking into his deep eyes, seeing the pain that dwelt there, my pity was for him. A smile came to his ugly mouth.

"You have been on the stage, Paul; you must have heard the saying often: 'Ah, well, the curtain must come down, however badly things are going.' It is only a play, Paul. We do not choose our parts. I did not even know I was the villain, till I heard the booing of the gallery. I even thought I was the hero, full of noble sentiment, sacrificing myself for the happiness of the heroine. She would have married me in the beginning had I plagued her sufficiently."

I made to speak, but he interrupted me, continuing: "Ah, yes, it might have been better. That is easy to say, not knowing. So, too, it might have been worse, in all probability much the same. All roads lead to the end. You know I was always a fatalist, Paul. We tried both ways. She loved me well enough, but she loved the world also. I thought she loved it better, so I kissed her on her brow, mumbled a prayer for her happiness and made my exit to a choking sob. So ended the first act. Wasn't I the hero throughout that, Paul? I thought so; slapped myself upon the back, told myself what a fine fellow I had been. Then you know what followed. She was finer clay than she had fancied. Love is woman's kingdom, not the world. Even then I thought more of her than of myself. I could have borne my share of the burden had I not seen her fainting under hers, shamed, degraded. So we dared to think for ourselves, injuring nobody but ourselves, played the man and woman, lost the world for love. Wasn't it brave, Paul? Were we not hero and heroine? They had printed the playbill wrong, Paul, that was all. I was really the hero, but the printing devil had made a slip, so instead of applauding you booed. How could you know, any of you? It was not your fault."

"But that was not the end," I reminded him. "If the curtain had fallen then, I could have forgiven you."

He grinned. "That fatal last act. Even yours don't always come right, so the critics tell me."

The grin faded from his face. "We may never see each other again, Paul," he went on; "don't think too badly of me. I found I had made a second mistake, or thought I had. She was no happier with me after a time than she had been with him. If all our longings were one, life would be easy; but they are not. What is to be done but toss for it? And if it come down head we wish it had been tail, and if tail we think of what we have lost through its not coming down head. Love is no more the whole of a woman's life than it is of a man's. He did not apply for a divorce: that was smart of him. We were shunned, ignored. To some women it might not have mattered; but she had been used to being sought, courted, feted. She made no complaint, did worse: made desperate effort to appear cheerful, to pretend that our humdrum life was not boring her to death. I watched her growing more listless, more depressed; grew angry with her, angrier with myself. There was no bond between us except our passion; that was real enough, 'grand,' I believe, is the approved literary adjective. It is good enough for what nature intended it, a summer season in a cave. It makes but a poor marriage settlement in these more complicated days. We fell to mutual recriminations, vulgar scenes. Ah, most of us look better at a little distance from one another. The sordid, contemptible side of life became important to us. I was never rich; by contrast with all that she had known, miserably poor. The mere sight of the food our twelve-pound-a-year cook put upon the table would take away her appetite. Love does not change the palate, give you a taste for cheap claret when you have been accustomed to dry champagne. We have bodies to think of as well as souls; we are apt to forget that in moments of excitement.

"She fell ill, and it seemed to me that I had dragged her from the soil where she had grown only to watch her die. And then he came, precisely at the right moment. I cannot help admiring him. Most men take their revenge clumsily, hurting themselves; he was so neat, had been so patient. I am not even ashamed of having fallen into his trap; it was admirably baited. Maybe I had despised him for having seemed to submit meekly to the blow. What cared he for me and my opinion? It was she was all he cared for. He knew her better than I, knew that sooner or later she would tire, not of love but of the cottage; look back with longing eyes towards all that she had lost. Fool! Cuckold! What was it to him that the world would laugh at him, despise him? Love such as his made fools of men. Would I not give her back to him?

"By God! It was fine acting; half into the night we talked, I leaving him every now and again to creep to the top of the stairs and listen to her breathing. He asked me my advice, I being the hard-headed partner of cool judgment. What would be the best way of approaching her after I was gone? Where should he take her? How should they live till the nine days' talk had died away? And I sat opposite to him, how he must have longed to laugh in my silly face, advising him! We could not quite agree as to details of a possible yachting cruise, and I remember hunting up an atlas, and we pored over it, our heads close together. By God! I envy him that night!"

He sank back on his pillows and laughed and coughed, and laughed and coughed again, till I feared that wild, long, broken laugh would be his last. But it ceased at length, and for awhile, exhausted, he lay silent before continuing.

"Then came the question: how was I to go? She loved me still. He was sure of it, and, for the matter of that, so was I. So long as she thought that I loved her, she would never leave me. Only from her despair could fresh hope arise for her. Would I not make some sacrifice for her sake, persuade her that I had tired of her? Only by one means could she be convinced. My going off alone would not suffice; my reason for that she might suspect, she might follow. It would be for her sake. Again it was the hero that I played, the dear old chuckle-headed hero, Paul, that you ought to have cheered, not hooted. I loved her as much as I ever loved her in my life, that night I left her. I took my boots off in the passage and crept up in my stockinged feet. I told him I was merely going to change my coat and put a few things into a bag. He gripped my hand, and tears were standing in his eyes. It is odd that suppressed laughter and expressed grief should both display the same token, is it not? I stole into her room. I dared not kiss her for fear of waking her; but a stray lock of her hair, you remember how long it was, fell over the pillow, nearly reaching to the floor. I pressed my lips against it, where it trailed over the bedstead, till they bled. I have it still upon my lips, the mingling of the cold iron and the warm, soft silken hair. He told me, when I came down again, that I had been gone three-quarters of an hour. And we went out of the house together, he and I. That is the last time I ever saw her."

I leant across and put my arms around him; I suppose it was un-English; there are times when one forgets these points. "I did not know! I did not know," I cried.

He pressed me to him with his feeble arms. "What a cad you must have thought me, Paul," he said. "But you might have given me credit for better taste. I was always rather a gourmet than a gourmand where women were concerned."

"You have never seen him either again?" I asked.

"No," he answered; "I swore to kill him when I learnt the trick he had played me. He commenced the divorce proceedings against her the very morning after I had left her. Possibly, had I succeeded in finding him within the next six months, I should have done so. A few newspaper proprietors would have been the only people really benefited. Time is the cheapest Bravo; a little patience is all he charges. All roads lead to the end, Paul."

But I tell my tale badly, marring effects of sunlight with the memory of shadows. At the time all promised fair. He was a handsome, distinguished-looking man. Not every aristocrat, if without disrespect to one's betters a humble observer may say so, suggests his title; this man would have suggested his title, had he not possessed it. I suppose he must have been about fifty at the time; but most men of thirty would have been glad to exchange with him both figure and complexion. His behaviour to his fiancee was the essence of good taste, affectionate devotion, carried to the exact point beyond which, having regard to the disparity of their years, it would have appeared ridiculous. That he sincerely admired her, was fully content with her, there could be no doubt. I am even inclined to think he was fonder of her than, divining her feelings towards himself, he cared to show. Knowledge of the world must have told him that men of fifty find it easier to be the lovers of women young enough to be their daughters, than girls find it to desire the affection of men old enough to be their fathers; and he was not the man to allow impulse to lead him into absurdity.

From my own peculiar point of view he appeared the ideal prince consort. It was difficult for me to imagine my queen in love with any mere man. This was one beside whom she could live, losing in my eyes nothing of her dignity. My feelings for her he guessed at our first interview. Most men in his position would have been amused, and many would have shown it. For what reason I cannot say, but with a tact and courtesy that left me only complimented, he drew from me, before I had met him half-a-dozen times, more frank confession than a month previously I should have dreamt of my yielding to anything than my own pillow. He laid his hand upon my shoulder.

"I wonder if you know, my friend, how wise you are," he said. "We all of us at your age love an image of our own carving. Ah, if only we could be content to worship the white, changeless statute! But we are fools. We pray the gods to give her life, and under our hot kisses she becomes a woman. I also loved when I was your age, Paul. Your countrymen, they are so practical, they know only one kind of love. It is business-like, rich, how puts it your poet? 'rich in saving common sense.' But there are many kinds, you understand that, my friend. You are wise, do not confuse them. She was a child of the mountains. I used to walk three leagues to Mass each day to worship her. Had I been wise, had I so left it, the memory of her would have coloured all my life with glory. But I was a fool, my friend; I turned her into a woman. Ah!" he made a gesture of disgust, "such a fat, ugly woman, Paul, I turned her into. I had much difficulty in getting rid of her. We should never touch things in life that are beautiful; we have such clumsy hands, we spoil whatever we touch."

Hal did not return to England till the end of the year, by which time the Count and Countess Huescar, though I had her permission still to call her Barbara, I never availed myself of it; the "Countess" fitted my mood better, had taken up residence in the grand Paris house old Hasluck had bought for them.

It was the high-water mark of old Hasluck's career, and, if anything, he was a little disappointed that with the dowry he had promised her Barbara had not done even better for herself.

"Foreign Counts," he grumbled to me laughingly, one day, "well, I hope they're worth more in Society than they are in the City. A hundred guineas is their price there, and they're not worth that. Who was that American girl that married a Russian Prince only last week? A million dollars was all she gave for him, and she a wholesale boot- maker's daughter into the bargain! Our girls are not half as smart."

But that was before he had seen his future son-in-law. After, he was content enough, and up to the day of the wedding, childishly elated. Under the Count's tuition he studied with reverential awe the Huescar history. Princes, statesmen, warriors, glittered, golden apples, from the spreading branches of its genealogical tree. Why not again! its attenuated blue sap strengthened with the rich, red blood, brewed by toil and effort in the grim laboratories of the underworld. In imagination, old

Hasluck saw himself the grandfather of Chancellors, the great-grandfather of Kings.

"I have laid the foundation, you shall raise the edifice," so he told her one evening I was spending with them, caressing her golden hair with his blunt, fat fingers. "I am glad you were not a boy. A boy, in all probability, would have squandered the money, let the name sink back again into the gutter. And even had he been the other sort, he could only have been another business man, keeping where I had left him. You will call your first boy Hasluck, won't you? It must always be the first-born's name. It shall be famous in the world yet, and for something else than mere money.

I began to understand the influences that had gone towards the making, or marring, of Barbara's character. I had never guessed he had cared for anything beyond money and the making of money.

It was, of course, a wedding as ostentatious as possible. Old Hasluck knew how to advertise, and spared neither expense nor labour, with the result that it was the event of the season, at least according to the Society papers. Mrs. Hasluck was the type of woman to have escaped observation, even had the wedding been her own; that she was present at her daughter's, "becomingly dressed in grey veiling spotted white, with an encrustation of mousseline de soie," I learnt the next day from the Morning Post. Old Hasluck himself had to be fetched every time he was wanted. At the conclusion of the ceremony, seeking him, I found him sitting on the stairs leading to the crypt.

"Is it over?" he asked. He was mopping his face on a huge handkerchief, and had a small looking-glass in his hand.

"All over," I answered, "they are waiting for you to start."

"I always perspire so when I'm excited," he explained. "Keep me out of it as much as possible."

But the next time I saw him, which was two or three days later, the reaction had set in. He was sitting in his great library, surrounded by books he would no more have thought of disturbing than he would of strumming on the gorgeous grand piano inlaid with silver that ornamented his drawing-room. A change had passed over him. His swelling rotundity, suggestive generally of a bladder inflated to its extremest limits by excess of self-importance, appeared to be shrinking. I put the idea aside as mere fancy at the time, but it was fact; he became a mere bag of bones before he died. He was wearing an old pair of carpet slippers and smoking a short clay pipe.

"Well," I said, "everything went off all right."

"Everybody's gone off all right, so far," he grunted. He was crouching over the fire, though the weather was still warm, one hand spread out towards the blaze. "Now I've got to go off, that's the only thing they're waiting for. Then everything will be in order."

"I don't think they are wanting you to go off," I answered, with a laugh.

"You mean," he answered, "I'm the goose that lays the golden eggs. Ah, but you see, so many of the eggs break, and so many of them are bad."

"Some of them hatch all right," I replied. The simile was becoming somewhat confused: in conversation similes are apt to.

"If I were to die this week," he said, he paused, completing mental calculations, "I should be worth, roughly speaking, a couple of million. This time next year I may be owing a million."

I sat down opposite to him. "Why run risks?" I suggested. "Surely you have enough. Why not give it up, retire?"

He laughed. "Do you think I haven't said that to myself, lad, sworn I would a dozen times a year? I can't do it; I'm a gambler. It's the earliest thing I can recollect doing, gambling with brace buttons. There are men, Paul, now dying in the workhouse, men I once knew well; I think of them sometimes, and wish I didn't, who any time during half their life might have retired on twenty thousand a year. If I were to go to any one of them, and settle an annuity of a hundred a year upon him, the moment my back was turned he'd sell it out and totter up to Threadneedle Street with the proceeds. It's in our blood. I shall gamble on my death-bed, die with the tape in my hand."

He kicked the fire into a blaze. A roaring flame made the room light again.

"But that won't be just yet awhile," he laughed, "and before it does, I'll be the richest man in Europe. I keep my head cool, that's the great secret." Leaning over towards me, he sunk his voice to a whisper, "Drink, Paul, so many of them drink. They get worried; fifty things dancing round and round at the same time in their heads. Fifty questions to be answered in five minutes. Tick, tick, tick, taps the little devil at their elbow. This going down, that going up. Rumor of this, report of that. A fortune to be lost here, a fortune to be snatched there. Everything in a whirl! Tick, tick, tick, like nails into a coffin. God! for five minutes' peace to think. Shut the door, turn the key. Out comes the bottle. That's the end. All right so long as you keep away from that. Cool, quick brain, clear judgment, that's the secret."

"But is it worth it all?" I suggested. "Surely you have enough?"

"It means power, Paul." He slapped his trousers pocket, making the handful of gold and silver he always carried there jingle musically. "It is this that rules the world. My children shall be big pots, hobnob with kings and princes, slap them on the back and call them by their Christian names, be kings themselves, why not? It's happened before. My children, the children of old Noel Hasluck, son of a Whitechapel butcher! Here's my pedigree!" Again be slapped his tuneful pocket. "It's an older one than theirs! It's coming into its own at last! It's money, we men of money, that are the true kings now. It's our family that rules the world, the great money family; I mean to be its head."

The blaze died out, leaving the room almost in darkness, and for awhile we sat in silence.

"Quiet, isn't it?" said old Hasluck, raising his head.

The settling of the falling embers was the only sound about us.

"Guess we'll always be like this, now," continued old Hasluck. "Old woman goes to bed, you see, immediately after dinner. It used to be different when she was about. Somehow, the house and the lackeys and all the rest of it seemed to be a more natural sort of thing when she was the centre of it. It frightens the old woman now she's gone. She likes to get away from it. Poor old Susan! A little country inn with herself as landlady and me fussing about behind the bar; that was always her ambition, poor old girl!"

"You will he visiting them," I suggested, "and they will be coming to stop with you."

He shook his head. "They won't want me, and it isn't my game to hamper them. I never mix out of my class. I've always had sense enough for that."

I laughed, wishing to cheer him, though I knew he was right. "Surely your daughter belongs to your own class," I replied.

"Do you think so?" he asked, with a grin. "That's not a pretty compliment to her. She was my child when she used to cling round my neck, while I made the sausages, calling me her dear old pig. It didn't trouble her then that I dropped my aitches and had a greasy skin. I was a Whitechapel butcher, and she was a Whitechapel brat. I could have kept her if I'd liked, but I was set upon making a lady of her, and I did it. But I lost my child. Every time she came back from school I could see she despised me a little more. I'm not blaming her; how could she help it? I was making a lady of her, teaching her to do it; though there were moments when I almost hated her, felt tempted to snatch her back to me, drag her down again to my level, make her my child again, before it was too late. Oh, it wasn't all unselfishness; I could have done it. She would have remained my class then, would have married my class, and her children would have been my class. I didn't want that. Everything's got to be paid for. I got what I asked for; I'm not grumbling at the price. But it ain't cheap."

He rose and knocked the ashes from his pipe. "Ring the bell, Paul, will you?" be said. "Let's have some light and something to drink. Don't take any notice of me. I've got the hump to-night."

It was a minute or two before the lamp came. He put his arm upon my shoulder, leaning upon me somewhat heavily.

"I used to fancy sometimes, Paul," he said, "that you and she might have made a match of it. I should have been disappointed for some things. But you'd have been a bit nearer to me, you two. It never occurred to you, that, I suppose?"

CHAPTER VII.

HOW PAUL SET FORTH UPON A QUEST.

Of old Deleglise's Sunday suppers, which, costumed from head to foot in spotless linen, he cooked himself in his great kitchen, moving with flushed, earnest face about the gleaming stove, while behind him his guests waited, ranged round the massive oaken table glittering with cut glass and silver, among which fluttered the deft hands of Madeline, his ancient whitecapped Bonne, much has been already recorded, and by those possessed of greater knowledge. They who sat there talking in whispers until such time as old Deleglise turned towards them again, radiant with consciousness of success, the savoury triumph steaming between his hands, when, like the sudden swell of the Moonlight Sonata, the talk would rush once more into a roar, were men whose names were then, and some are still, more or less household words throughout the English-speaking world. Artists, musicians, actors, writers, scholars, droles, their wit and wisdom, their sayings and their doings must be tolerably familiar to readers of memoir and biography; and if to such their epigrams appear less brilliant, their jests less laughable than to us who heard them spoken, that is merely because fashion in humour and in understanding changes as in all else.

You, gentle reader of my book, I shall not trouble with second-hand record of that which you can read elsewhere. For me it will be but to write briefly of my own brief glimpse into that charmed circle. Concerning this story more are the afternoon At Homes held by Dan and myself upon the second floor of the old Georgian house in pleasant, quiet Queen Square. For cook and house-maid on these days it would be a busy morning. Failing other supervision, Dan and I agreed that to secure success on these important occasions each of us should criticise the work of the other. I passed judgment on Dan's cooking, he upon my house-work.

"Too much soda," I would declare, sampling the cake.

"You silly Juggins! It's meant to taste of soda, it's a soda cake."

"I know that. It isn't meant to taste of nothing but soda. There wants to be some cake about it also. This thing, so far as flavour is concerned, is nothing but a Seidlitz powder. You can't give people solidified Seidlitz powders for tea!"

Dan would fume, but I would remain firm. The soda cake would be laid aside, and something else attempted. His cookery was the one thing Dan was obstinate about. He would never admit that anything could possibly be wrong with it. His most ghastly failures he would devour himself later on with pretended enjoyment. I have known him finish a sponge cake, the centre of which had to be eaten with a teaspoon, declaring it was delicious; that eating a dry sponge cake was like eating dust; that a sponge cake ought to be a trifle syrupy towards the centre. Afterwards he would be strangely silent and drink brandy out of a wine-glass.

"Call these knives clean?" It would be Dan's turn.

"Yes, I do."

Dan would draw his finger across one, producing chiaro-oscuro.

"Not if you go fingering them. Why don't you leave them alone and go on with your own work?"

"You've just wiped them, that's all."

"Well, there isn't any knife-powder."

"Yes, there is."

"Besides, it ruins knives, over-cleaning them, takes all the edge off. We shall want them pretty sharp to cut those lemon buns of yours."

"Over-cleaning them! You don't take any pride in the place."

"Good Lord! Don't I work from morning to night?"

"You lazy young devil!"

"Makes one lazy, your cooking. How can a man work when he is suffering all day long from indigestion?"

But Dan would not be content until I had found the board and cleaned the knives to his complete satisfaction. Perhaps it was as well that in this way all things once a week were set in order. After lunch house-maid and cook would vanish, two carefully dressed gentlemen being left alone to receive their guests.

These would be gathered generally from among Dan's journalistic acquaintances and my companions of the theatre. Occasionally, Minikin and Jarman would be of the number, Mrs. Peedles even once or twice arriving breathless on our landing. Left to myself, I perhaps should not have invited them, deeming them hardly fitting company to mingle with our other visitors; but Dan, having once been introduced to them, overrode such objection.

"My dear Lord Chamberlain," Dan would reply, "an ounce of originality is worth a ton of convention. Little tin ladies and gentlemen all made to pattern! One can find them everywhere. Your friends would be an acquisition to any society."

"But are they quite good form?" I hinted.

"I'll tell you what we will do," replied Dan. "We'll forget that Mrs. Peedles keeps a lodging-house in Blackfriars. We will speak of her as our friend, 'that dear, quaint old creature, Lady P.' A title that is an oddity, whose costume always suggests the wardrobe of a provincial actress! My dear Paul, your society novelist would make a fortune out of such a character. The personages of her amusing anecdotes, instead of being third-rate theatrical folk, shall be Earl Blank and the Baroness de Dash. The editors of society journals shall pay me a shilling a line for them. Jarman, yes, Jarman shall be the son of a South American millionaire. Vulgar? Nonsense! you mean racy. Minikin, he looks much more like forty than twenty, he shall be an eminent scientist. His head will then appear the natural size; his glass eye, the result of a chemical experiment, a touch of distinction; his uncompromising rudeness, a lovable characteristic. We will make him buy a yard of red ribbon and wear it across his shirt-front, and address him as Herr Professor. It will explain slight errors of English grammar and all peculiarities of accent. They shall be our lions. You leave it to me. We will invite commonplace, middle-class folk to meet them."

And this, to my terror and alarm, Dan persisted in doing. Jarman entered into the spirit of the joke with gusto. So far as he was concerned, our guests, from the beginning to the end, were one and all, I am confident, deceived. The more he swaggered, the more he boasted, the more he talked about himself, and it was a failing he was prone to, the greater was his success. At the persistent endeavours of Dan's journalistic acquaintances to excite his cupidity by visions of new journals, to be started with a mere couple of thousand pounds and by the inherent merit of their ideas to command at once a circulation of hundreds of thousands, I could afford to laugh. But watching the tremendous efforts of my actress friends to fascinate him, luring him into corners, gazing at him with languishing eyes, trotting out all their little tricks for his exclusive benefit, quarrelling about him among themselves, my conscience would prick me, lest our jest should end in a contretemps. Fortunately, Jarman himself, was a gentleman of uncommon sense, or my fears might have been realised. I should have been sorry myself to have been asked to remain stone under the blandishments of girls young and old, of women handsome and once, no doubt, good looking, showered upon him during that winter. But Jarman, as I think I have explained, was no slave to female charms. He enjoyed his good time while it lasted, and eventually married the eldest daughter of a small blacking factory. She was a plain girl, but pleasant, and later brought to Jarman possession of the factory. When I meet him, he is now stout and rubicund, he gives me the idea of a man who has attained to his ideals.

With Minikin we had more trouble. People turned up possessed of scientific smattering. We had to explain that the Professor never talked shop. Others were owners of unexpected knowledge of German, which they insisted upon airing. We had to explain that the Herr Professor was in London to learn English, and had taken a vow during his residence neither to speak nor listen to his native tongue. It was remarked that his acquaintance with colloquial English slang, for a foreigner, was quite unusual. Occasionally he was too rude, even for a scientist, informing ladies, clamouring to know how he liked English women, that he didn't like them silly; telling one gentleman, a friend of Dan, a rather important man who once asked him, referring to his yard of ribbon, what he got it for, that he got it for fourpence. We had to explain him as a gentleman who had been soured by a love disappointment. The ladies forgave him; the gentlemen said it was a damned lucky thing for the girl. Altogether, Minikin took a good deal of explaining.

Lady Peedles, our guests decided among themselves, must be the widow of someone in the City who had been knighted in a crowd. They made fun of her behind her back, but to her face were most effusive. "My dear Lady Peedles" was the phrase most often heard in our rooms whenever she was present. At the theatre "my friend Lady Peedles" became a person much spoken of, generally in loud tones. My own social position I found decidedly improved by reason of her ladyship's evident liking for myself. It went abroad that I was her presumptive heir. I was courted as a gentleman of expectations.

The fishy-eyed young man became one of our regular guests. Dan won his heart by never laughing at him.

"I like talking to you," said the fishy-eyed young man one afternoon to Dan. "You don't go into fits of laughter when I remark that it has been a fine day; most people do. Of course, on the stage I don't mind. I know I am a funny little devil. I get my living by being a funny little devil. There is a photograph of me hanging in the theatre lobby. I saw a workman stop and look at it the other day as he passed; I was just behind him. He burst into a roar of laughter. 'Little! He makes me laugh to look at him!' he cluttered to himself. Well, that's all right; I want the man in the gallery to think me funny, but it annoys me when people laugh at me off the stage. If I am out to dinner anywhere and ask somebody to pass the mustard, I never get it; instead, they burst out laughing. I don't want people to laugh at me when I am having my dinner. I want my dinner. It makes me very angry sometimes."

"I know," agreed Dan, sympathetically. "The world never grasps the fact that man is a collection, not a single exhibit. I remember being at a house once where the chief guest happened to be a great Hebrew scholar. One tea time, a Miss Henman, passing the butter to someone in a hurry, let it slip out of her hand. 'Why is Miss Henman like a caterpillar?' asked our learned guest in a sepulchral voice. Nobody appeared to know. 'Because she makes the butter fly.' It never occurred to any one of us that the Doctor could possibly joke. There was dead silence for about a minute. Then our hostess, looking grave, remarked: 'Oh, do you really think so?'"

"If I were to enter a room full of people," said the fishy-eyed young man, "and tell them that my mother had been run over by an omnibus, they would think it the funniest story they had heard in years."

He was playing a principal part now in the opera, and it was he undoubtedly who was drawing the house. But he was not happy.

"I am not a comic actor, really," he explained. "I could play Romeo, so far as feeling is concerned, and play it damned well. There is a fine vein of poetry in me. But of course it's no good to me with this face of mine."

"But are you not sinning your mercies, you fellows?" Dan replied. "There is young Kelver here. At school it was always his trouble that he could give us a good time and make us laugh, which nobody else in the whole school could do. His ambition was to kick a ball as well as a hundred other fellows could kick it. He could tell us a good story now if he would only write what the Almighty intended him to write, instead of gloomy rigmaroles about suffering Princesses in Welsh caves. I don't say it's bad, but a hundred others could write the same sort of thing better."

"Can't you understand," answered the little man; "the poorest tragedian that ever lived never wished himself the best of low comedians. The court fool had an excellent salary, no doubt; and, likely enough, had got two-thirds of all the brain there was in the palace. But not a wooden-headed man-at-arms but looked down upon him. Every gallery boy who pays a shilling to laugh at me regards himself as my intellectual superior; while to a fourth-rate spouter of blank verse he looks up in admiration."

"Does it so very much matter," suggested Dan, "how the wooden-headed man-at-arms or the shilling gallery boy happens to regard you?"

"Yes, it does," retorted Goggles, "because we happen to agree with them. If I could earn five pounds a week as juvenile lead, I would never play a comic part again."

"There I cannot follow you," returned Dan. "I can understand the artist who would rather be the man of action, the poet who would rather be the statesman or the warrior; though personally my sympathies are precisely the other way, with Wolfe who thought it a more glorious work, the writing of a great poem, than the burning of so many cities and the killing of so many men. We all serve the community. It is difficult, looking at the matter from the inside, to say who serves it best. Some feed it, some clothe it. The churchman and the policeman between them look after its morals, keep it in order. The doctor mends it when it injures itself; the lawyer helps it to quarrel, the soldier teaches it to fight. We Bohemians amuse it, instruct it. We can argue that we are the most important. The others cater for its body, we for its mind. But their work is more showy than ours and attracts more attention; and to attract attention is the aim and object of most of us. But for Bohemians to worry among themselves which is the greatest, is utterly without reason. The story-teller, the musician, the artist, the clown, we are members of a sharing troupe; one, with the ambition of the fat boy in Pickwick, makes the people's flesh creep; another makes them hold their sides with laughter. The tragedian, soliloquising on his crimes, shows us how wicked we are; you, looking at a pair of lovers from under a scratch wig, show us how ridiculous we are. Both lessons are necessary: who shall say which is the superior teacher?"

"Ah, I am not a philosopher," replied the little man, with a sigh.

"Ah," returned Dan, with another, "and I am not a comic actor on my way to a salary of a hundred a week. We all of us want the other boy's cake."

The O'Kelly was another frequent visitor of ours. The attic in Belsize Square had been closed. In vain had the O'Kelly wafted incense, burned pastilles and sprinkled eau-de-Cologne. In vain had he talked of rats, hinted at drains.

"A wonderful woman," groaned the O'Kelly in tones of sorrowful admiration. "There's no deceiving her."

"But why submit?" was our natural argument. "Why not say you are going to smoke, and do it?"

"It's her theory, me boy," explained the O'Kelly, "that the home should be kept pure, a sort of a temple, ye know. She's convinced that in time it is bound to exercise an influence upon me. It's a beautiful idea, when ye come to think of it."

Meanwhile, in the rooms of half-a-dozen sinful men the O'Kelly kept his own particular pipe, together with his own particular smoking mixture; and one such pipe and one such tobacco jar stood always on our mantelpiece.

In the spring the forces of temptation raged round that feeble but most excellently intentioned citadel, the O'Kelly's conscience. The Signora had returned to England, was performing then at Ashley's Theatre. The O'Kelly would remain under long spells of silence, puffing vigorously at his pipe. Or would fortify himself with paeans in praise of Mrs. O'Kelly.

"If anything could ever make a model man of me", he spoke in the tones of one whose doubts are stronger than his hopes "it would he the example of that woman."

It was one Saturday afternoon. I had just returned from the matinee.

"I don't believe," continued the O'Kelly, "I don't really believe she has ever done one single thing she oughtn't to, or left undone one single thing she ought, in the whole course of her life."

"Maybe she has, and you don't know of it," I suggested, perceiving the idea might comfort him.

"I wish I could think so," returned the O'Kelly. "I don't mean anything really wrong," he corrected himself quickly, "but something just a little wrong. I feel, I really feel I should like her better if she had."

"Not that I mean I don't like her as it is, ye understand," corrected himself the O'Kelly a second time. "I respect that woman, I cannot tell ye, me boy, how much I respect her. Ye don't know her. There was one morning, about a month ago. That woman—she's down at six every morning, summer and winter; we have prayers at half-past. I was a trifle late meself: it was never me strong point, as ye know, early rising. Seven o'clock struck; she didn't appear, and I thought she had overslept herself. I won't say I didn't feel pleased for the moment; it was an unworthy sentiment, but I almost wished she had. I ran up to her room. The door was open, the bedclothes folded down as she always leaves them. She came in five minutes later. She had got up at four that morning to welcome a troupe of native missionaries from East Africa on their arrival at Waterloo Station. She's a saint, that woman; I am not worthy of her."

"I shouldn't dwell too much on that phase of the subject," I suggested.

"I can't help it, me boy," replied the O'Kelly. "I feel I am not."

"I don't for a moment say you are," I returned; "but I shouldn't harp upon the idea. I don't think it good for you."

"I never will be," he persisted gloomily, "never!"

Evidently he was started on a dangerous train of reflection. With the idea of luring him away from it, I led the conversation to the subject of champagne.

"Most people like it dry," admitted the O'Kelly. "Meself, I have always preferred it with just a suggestion of fruitiness."

"There was a champagne," I said, "you used to be rather fond of when we years ago."

"I think I know the one ye mean," said the O'Kelly. "It wasn't at all bad, considering the price."

"You don't happen to remember where you got it?" I asked.

"It was in Bridge Street," remembered the O'Kelly, "not so very far from the Circus."

"It is a pleasant evening," I remarked; "let us take a walk."

We found the place, half wine-shop, half office.

"Just the same," commented the O'Kelly as we pushed open the door and entered. "Not altered a bit."

As in all probability barely twelve months had elapsed since his last visit, the fact in itself was not surprising. Clearly the O'Kelly had been calculating time rather by sensation. I ordered a bottle; and we sat down. Myself, being prejudiced against the brand, I called for a glass of claret. The O'Kelly finished the bottle. I was glad to notice my ruse had been successful. The virtue of that wine had not departed from it. With every glass the O'Kelly became morally more elevated. He left the place, determined that he would be worthy of Mrs. O'Kelly. Walking down the Embankment, he asserted his determination of buying an alarm-clock that very evening. At the corner of Westminster Bridge he became suddenly absorbed in his own thoughts. Looking to discover the cause of his silence, I saw that his eyes were resting on a poster representing a charming lady standing on one leg upon a wire; below her, at some distance, appeared the peaks of mountains; the artist had even caught the likeness. I cursed the luck that had directed our footsteps, but the next moment, lacking experience, was inclined to be reassured.

"Me dear Paul," said the O'Kelly, he laid a fatherly hand upon my shoulder, "there are fair-faced, laughing women, sweet creatures, that ye want to put yer arm around and dance with." He shook his head disapprovingly. "There are the sainted women, who lead us up, Paul, up, always up."

A look, such as the young man with the banner might have borne with him to the fields of snow and ice, suffused the O'Kelly's handsome face. Without another word he crossed the road and entered an American store, where for six-and-elevenpence he purchased an alarm- clock the man assured us would awake an Egyptian mummy. With this in his hand he waved me a good-bye, and jumped upon a Hampstead 'bus, and alone I strolled on to the theatre.

Hal returned a little after Christmas and started himself in chambers in the City. It was the nearest he dared venture, so he said, to civilisation.

"I'd be no good in the West End," he explained. "For a season I might attract as an eccentricity, but your swells would never stand me for longer, no more would any respectable folk, anywhere: we don't get on together. I commenced at Richmond. It was a fashionable suburb then, and I thought I was going to do wonders. I had everything in my favour, except myself. I do know my work, nobody can deny that of me. My father spent every penny he had, poor gentleman, in buying me an old-established practice: fine house, carriage and pair, white-haired butler, everything correct, except myself. It was of no use. I can hold myself in for a month or two; then I break out, the old original savage that I am under my frock coat. I feel I must run amuck, stabbing, hacking at the prim, smiling Lies mincing round about me. I can fool a silly woman for half-a-dozen visits; bow and rub my hands, purr round her sympathetically. All the while I am longing to tell her the truth:

"'Go home. Wash your face; don't block up the pores of your skin with paint. Let out your corsets. You are thirty-three round the abdomen if you are an inch: how can you expect your digestion to do its work when you're squeezing it into twenty-one? Give up gadding about half your day and most of your night; you are old enough to have done with that sort of thing. Let the children come, and suckle them yourself. You'll be all the better for them. Don't loll in bed all the morning. Get up like a decent animal and do something for your living. Use your brain, what there is of it, and your body. At that price you can have health to-morrow, and at no other. I can do nothing for you.'

"And sooner or later I blurt it out." He laughed his great roar. "Lord! you should see the real face coming out of the simpering mask.

"Pompous old fools, strutting into me like turkey-cocks! By Jove, it was worth it! They would dribble out, looking half their proper size after I had done telling them what was the matter with them.

"'Do you want to know what you are really suffering from?' I would shout at them, when I could contain myself no longer. 'Gluttony, my dear sir; gluttony and drunkenness, and over-indulgence in other vices that shall be nameless. Live like a man; get a little self-respect from somewhere; give up being an ape. Treat your body properly and it will treat you properly. That's the only prescription that will do you any good.'"

He laughed again. "'Tell the truth, you shame the Devil.' But the Devil replies by starving you. It's a fairly effective retort. I am not the stuff successful family physicians are made of. In the City I may manage to rub along. One doesn't see so much of one's patients; they come and go. Clerks and warehousemen my practice will be among chiefly. The poor man does not so much mind being told the truth about himself; it is a blessing to which he is accustomed."

We spoke but once of Barbara. A photograph of her in her bride's dress stood upon my desk. Occasionally, first fitting the room for the ceremony, sweeping away all impurity even from under the mats, and dressing myself with care, I would centre it amid flowers, and kneeling, kiss her hand where it rested on the back of the top-heavy looking chair without which no photographic studio is complete.

One day he took it up, and looked at it long and hard.

"The forehead denotes intellectuality; the eyes tenderness and courage. The lower part of the face, on the other hand, suggests a good deal of animalism: the finely cut nostrils show egotism, another word for selfishness; the nose itself, vanity; the lips, sensuousness and love of luxury. I wonder what sort of woman she really is." He laid the photograph back upon the desk.

"I did not know you were so firm a believer in Lavater," I said.

"Only when he agrees with what I know," he answered. "Have I not described her rightly?"

"I do not care to discuss her in that vein," I replied, feeling the blood mounting to my cheeks.

"Too sacred a subject?" he laughed. "It is the one ingredient of manhood I lack, ideality, an unfortunate deficiency for me. I must probe, analyse, dissect, see the thing as it really is, know it for what it is."

"Well, she is the Countess Huescar now," I said. "For God's sake, leave her alone."

He turned to me with the snarl of a beast. "How do you know she is the Countess Huescar? Is it a special breed of woman made on purpose? How do you know she isn't my wife, brain and heart, flesh and blood, mine? If she was, do you think I should give her up because some fool has stuck his label on her?"

I felt the anger burning in my eyes. "Yours, his! She is no man's property. She is herself," I cried.

The wrinkles round his nose and mouth smoothed themselves out. "You need not be afraid," he sneered. "As you say, she is the Countess Huescar. Can you imagine her as Mrs. Doctor Washburn? I can't." He took her photograph in his hand again. "The lower part of the face is the true index to the character. It shows the animal, and it is the animal that rules. The soul, the intellect, it comes and goes; the animal remains always. Sensuousness, love of luxury, vanity, those are the strings to which she dances. To be a Countess is of more importance to her than to be a woman. She is his, not mine. Let him keep her."

"You do not know her," I answered; "you never have. You listen to what she says. She does not know herself."

He looked at me queerly. "What do you think her to be?" he asked me. "A true woman, not the shallow thing she seems?"

"A true woman," I persisted stoutly, "that you have not eyes enough to see."

"You little fool!" he muttered, with the same queer look, "you little fool. But let us hope you are wrong, Paul. Let us hope, for her sake, you are wrong."

It was at one of Deleglise's Sunday suppers that I first met Urban Vane. The position, nor even the character, I fear it must be confessed, of his guests was never enquired into by old Deleglise. A simple-minded, kindly old fellow himself, it was his fate to be occasionally surprised and grieved at the discovery that even the most entertaining of supper companions could fall short of the highest standard of conventional morality.

"Dear, dear me!" he would complain, pacing up and down his studio with puzzled visage. "The last man in the world of whom I should have expected to hear it. So original in all his ideas. Are you quite sure?"

"I am afraid there can he no doubt about it."

"I can't believe it! I really can't believe it! One of the most amusing men I ever met!"

I remember a well-known artist one evening telling us with much sense of humour how he had just completed the sale of an old Spanish cabinet to two distinct and separate purchasers.

"I sold it first," recounted the little gentleman with glee, "to old Jong, the dealer. He has been worrying me about it for the last three months, and on Saturday afternoon, hearing that I was clearing out and going abroad, he came round again. 'Well, I am not sure I am in a position to sell it,' I told him. 'Who'll know?' he asked. 'They are not in, are they?' 'Not yet,' I answered, 'but I expect they will be some time on Monday.' 'Tell your man to open the door to me at eight o'clock on Monday morning,' he replied, 'we'll have it away without any fuss. There needn't he any receipt. I'm lending you a hundred pounds, in cash.' I worked him up to a hundred and twenty, and he paid me. Upon my word, I should never have thought of it, if he hadn't put the idea into my head. But turning round at the door: 'You won't go and sell it to someone else,' he suggested, 'between now and Monday?' It serves him right for his damned impertinence. 'Send and take it away to-day if you are at all nervous,' I told him. He looked at the thing, it is about twelve feet high altogether. 'I would if I could get a cart,' he muttered. Then an idea struck him. 'Does the top come off?' 'See for yourself,' I answered; 'it's your cabinet, not mine.' I was feeling rather annoyed with him. He examined it. 'That's all right,' he said; 'merely a couple of screws. I'll take the top with me now on my cab.' He got a man in, and they took the upper cupboard away, leaving me the bottom. Two hours later old Sir George called to see me about his wife's portrait. The first thing he set eyes on was the remains of the cabinet: he had always admired it. 'Hallo,' he asked, 'are you breaking up the studio literally? What have you done with the other half?' 'I've sent it round to Jong's' He didn't give me time to finish. 'Save Jong's commission and sell it to me direct,' he said. 'We won't argue about the price and I'll pay you in cash.'

"Well, if Providence comes forward and insists on taking charge of a man, it is hardly good manners to flout her. Besides, his wife's portrait is worth twice as much as he is paying for it. He handed me over the money in notes. 'Things not going quite smoothly with you just at the moment?' he asked me. 'Oh, about the same as usual,' I told him. 'You won't be offended at my taking it away with me this evening?' he asked. 'Not in the least,' I answered; 'you'll get it on the top of a four-wheeled cab.' We called in a couple of men, and I helped them down with it, and confoundedly heavy it was. 'I shall send round to Jong's for the other half on Monday morning,' he said, speaking with his head through the cab window, 'and explain it to him.' 'Do,' I answered; 'he'll understand.'

"I'm sorry I'm going away so early in the morning," concluded the little gentleman. "I'd give back Jong ten per cent. of his money to see his face when he enters the studio."

Everybody laughed; but after the little gentleman was gone, the subject cropped up again.

"If I wake sufficiently early," remarked one, "I shall find an excuse to look in myself at eight o'clock. Jong's face will certainly be worth seeing."

"Rather rough both on him and Sir George," observed another.

"Oh, he hasn't really done anything of the kind," chimed in old Deleglise in his rich, sweet voice. "He made that all up. It's just his fun; he's full of humour."

"I am inclined to think that would be his idea of a joke," asserted the first speaker.

Old Deleglise would not hear of it; but a week or two later I noticed an addition to old Deleglise's studio furniture in the shape of a handsome old carved cabinet twelve feet high.

"He really had done it," explained old Deleglise, speaking in a whisper, though only he and I were present. "Of course, it was only his fun; but it might have been misunderstood. I thought it better to put the thing straight. I shall get the money back from him when he returns. A most amusing little man!"

Old Deleglise possessed a house in Gower Street which fell vacant. One of his guests, a writer of poetical drama, was a man who three months after he had earned a thousand pounds never had a penny with which to bless himself. They are dying out, these careless, good-natured, conscienceless Bohemians; but quarter of a century ago they still lingered in Alsatian London. Turned out of his lodgings by a Philistine landlord, his sole possession in the wide world, two acts of a drama, for which he had already been paid, the problem of his future, though it troubled him but little, became acute to his friends. Old Deleglise, treating the matter as a joke, pretending not to know who was the landlord, suggested he should apply to the agents for position as caretaker. Some furniture was found for him, and the empty house in Gower Street became his shelter. The immediate present thus provided for, kindly old Deleglise worried himself a good deal concerning what would become of his friend when the house was let. There appeared to be no need for worry. Weeks, months went by. Applications were received by the agents in fair number, view cards signed by the dozen; but prospective tenants were never seen again. One Sunday evening our poet, warmed by old Deleglise's Burgundy, forgetful whose recommendation had secured him the lowly but timely appointment, himself revealed the secret.

"Most convenient place I've got," so he told old Deleglise. "Whole house to myself. I wander about; it just suits me."

"I'm glad to hear that," murmured old Deleglise.

"Come and see me, and I'll cook you a chop," continued the other. "I've had the kitchen range brought up into the back drawing-room; saves going up and down stairs."

"The devil you have!" growled old Deleglise. "What do you think the owner of the house will say?"

"Haven't the least idea who the poor old duffer is myself. They've put me in as caretaker, an excellent arrangement: avoids all argument about rent."

"Afraid it will soon come to an end, that excellent arrangement;" remarked old Deleglise, drily.

"Why? Why should it?"

"A house in Gower Street oughtn't to remain vacant long."

"This one will."

"You might tell me," asked old Deleglise, with a grim smile; "how do you manage it? What happens when people come to look over the house, don't you let them in?"

"I tried that at first," explained the poet, "but they would go on knocking, and boys and policemen passing would stop and help them. It got to be a nuisance; so now I have them in, and get the thing over. I show them the room where the murder was committed. If it's a nervous-looking party, I let them off with a brief summary. If that doesn't do, I go into details and show them the blood-spots on the floor. It's an interesting story of the gruesome order. Come round one morning and I'll tell it to you. I'm rather proud of it. With the blinds down and a clock in the next room that ticks loudly, it goes well."

Yet this was a man who, were the merest acquaintance to call upon him and ask for his assistance, would at once take him by the arm and lead him upstairs. All notes and cheques that came into his hands he changed at once into gold. Into some attic half filled with lumber he would fling it by the handful; then, locking the door, leave it there. On their hands and knees he and his friends, when they wanted any, would grovel for it, poking into corners, hunting under boxes, groping among broken furniture, feeling between cracks and crevices. Nothing gave him greater delight than an expedition of this nature to what he termed his gold-field; it had for him, as he would explain, all the excitements of mining without the inconvenience and the distance. He never knew how much was there. For a certain period a pocketful could be picked up in five minutes. Then he would entertain a dozen men at one of the best restaurants in London, tip cabmen and waiters with half-sovereigns, shower half-crowns as he walked through the streets, lend or give to anybody for the asking. Later, half-an-hour's dusty search would be rewarded with a single coin. It made no difference to him; he would dine in Soho for eighteenpence, smoke shag, and run into debt.

The red-haired man, to whom Deleglise had introduced me on the day of my first meeting with the Lady of the train, was another of his most constant visitors. It flattered my vanity that the red-haired man, whose name was famous throughout Europe and America, should condescend to confide to me, as he did and at some length, the deepest secrets of his bosom. Awed, at all events at first, I would sit and listen while by the hour he would talk to me in corners, telling me of the women he had loved. They formed a somewhat large collection. Julias, Marias, Janets, even Janes, he had madly worshipped, deliriously adored so many it grew bewildering. With a far-away look in his eyes, pain trembling through each note of his musical, soft voice, he would with bitter jest, with passionate outburst, recount how he had sobbed beneath the stars for love of Isabel, bitten his own flesh in frenzied yearning for Lenore. He appeared from his own account, if in connection with a theme so poetical I may be allowed a commonplace expression, to have had no luck with any of them. Of the remainder, an appreciable percentage had been mere passing visions, seen at a distance in the dawn, at twilight, generally speaking, when the light must have been uncertain. Never again, though he had wandered in the neighbourhood for months, had he succeeded in meeting them. It would occur to me that enquiries among the neighbours, applications to the local police, might possibly have been efficacious; but to have broken in upon his exalted mood with such suggestions would have demanded more nerve than at the time I possessed. In consequence, my thoughts I kept to myself.

"My God, boy!" he would conclude, "may you never love as I loved that woman Miriam", or Henrietta, or Irene, as the case might be."

For my sympathetic attitude towards the red-haired man I received one evening commendation from old Deleglise.

"Good boy," said old Deleglise, laying his hand on my shoulder. We were standing in the passage. We had just shaken hands with the red-haired man, who, as usual, had been the last to leave. "None of the others will listen to him. He used to stop and confide it all to me after everybody else had gone. Sometimes I have dropped asleep, to wake an hour later and find him still talking. He gets it over early now. Good boy!"

Soon I learnt it was characteristic of the artist to be willing, nay, anxious, to confide his private affairs to anyone and everyone who would only listen. Another characteristic appeared to be determination not to listen to anybody else's. As attentive recipient of other people's troubles and emotions I was subjected to practically no competition whatever. One gentleman, a leading actor of that day, I remember, immediately took me aside on my being introduced to him, and consulted me as to his best course of procedure under the extremely painful conditions that had lately arisen between himself and his wife. We discussed the unfortunate position at some length, and I did my best to counsel fairly and impartially.

"I wish you would lunch with me at White's to-morrow," he said. "We can talk it over quietly. Say half-past one. By the bye, I didn't catch your name."

I spelt it to him: he wrote the appointment down on his shirt-cuff. I went to White's the next day and waited an hour, but he did not turn up. I met him three weeks later at a garden-party with his wife. But he appeared to have forgotten me.

Observing old Deleglise's guests, comparing them with their names, it surprised me the disconnection between the worker and the work. Writers of noble sentiment, of elevated ideality, I found contained in men of commonplace appearance, of gross appetites, of conventional ideas. It seemed doubtful whether they fully comprehended their own work; certainly it had no effect upon their own lives. On the other hand, an innocent, boyish young man, who lived the most correct of lives with a girlish-looking wife in an ivy-covered cottage near Barnes Common, I discovered to be the writer of decadent stories at which the Empress Theodora might have blushed. The men whose names were widest known were not the men who shone the brightest in Deleglise's kitchen; more often they appeared the dull dogs, listening enviously, or failing pathetically when they tried to compete with others who to the public were comparatively unknown. After a time I ceased to confound the artist with the man, thought no more of judging the one by the other than of evolving a tenant from the house to which circumstances or carelessness might have directed him. Clearly they were two creations originally independent of each other, settling down into a working partnership for purposes merely of mutual accommodation; the spirit evidently indifferent as to the particular body into which he crept, anxious only for a place to work in, easily contented.

Varied were these guests that gathered round old Deleglise's oak. Cabinet Ministers reported to be in Homburg; Russian Nihilists escaped from Siberia; Italian revolutionaries; high church dignitaries disguised in grey suitings; ex-errand boys, who had discovered that with six strokes of the pen they could set half London laughing at whom they would; raw laddies with the burr yet clinging to their tongues, but who we knew would one day have the people dancing to the music of their words. Neither wealth, nor birth, nor age, nor position counted. Was a man interesting, amusing; had he ideas and thoughts of his own? Then he was welcome. Men who had come, men who were coming, met there on equal footing. Among them, as years ago among my schoolmates, I found my place, somewhat to my dissatisfaction. I amused. Much rather would I have shocked them by the originality of my views, impressed them with the depth of my judgments. They declined to be startled, refused to be impressed; instead, they laughed. Nor from these men could I obtain sympathy in my disappointment.

"What do you mean, you villain!" roared Deleglise's caretaker at me one evening on entering the kitchen. "How dare you waste your time writing this sort of stuff?"

He had a copy of the paper containing my "Witch of Moel Sarbod" in his hand, then some months old. He screwed it up into a ball and flung it in my face. "I've only just read it. What did you get for it?"

"Nothing," I answered.

"Nothing!" he screamed. "You got off for nothing? You ought to have been whipped at the cart's tail!"

"Oh, come, it's not as bad as that," suggested old Deleglise.

"Not bad! There isn't a laugh in it from beginning to end."

"There wasn't intended to be," I interrupted.

"Why not, you swindler? What were you sent into the world to do? To make it laugh."

"I want to make it think," I told him.

"Make it think! Hasn't it got enough to think about? Aren't there ten thousand penny-a-liners, poets, tragedians, tub-thumpers, long-eared philosophers, boring it to death? Who are you to turn up your nose at your work and tell the Almighty His own business? You are here to make us laugh. Get on with your work, you confounded young idiot!"

Urban Vane was the only one among them who understood me, who agreed with me that I was fitted for higher things than merely to minister to the world's need of laughter. He alone it was who would listen with approval to my dreams of becoming a famous tragedian, a writer of soul-searching books, of passion-analysing plays. I never saw him laugh himself, certainly not at anything funny. "Humour!" he would explain in his languid drawl, "personally it doesn't amuse me." One felt its introduction into the scheme of life had been an error. He was a large, fleshy man, with a dreamy, caressing voice and strangely impassive face. Where he came from, who he was, nobody knew. Without ever passing a remark himself that was worth listening to, he, nevertheless, by some mysterious trick of manner I am unable to explain, soon established himself, even throughout that company, where as a rule men found their proper level, as a silent authority in all contests of wit or argument. Stories at which he listened, bored, fell flat. The bon mot at which some faint suggestion of a smile quivered round his clean-shaven lips was felt to be the crown of the discussion. I can only conclude his secret to have been his magnificent assumption of superiority, added to a sphinx-like impenetrability behind which he could always retire from any danger of exposure. Subjects about which he knew nothing, and I have come to the conclusion they were more numerous than was suspected, became in his presence topics outside the radius of cultivated consideration: one felt ashamed of having introduced them. His own subjects, they were few but exclusive, he had the knack of elevating into intellectual tests: one felt ashamed, reflecting how little one knew about them. Whether he really did possess a charm of manner, or whether the sense of his superiority with which he had imbued me it was that made any condescension he paid me a thing to grasp at, I am unable to say. Certain it is that when he suggested I should throw up chorus singing and accompany him into the provinces as manager of a theatrical company he was then engaging to run a wonderful drama that was going to revolutionise the English stage and educate the English public, I allowed myself not a moment for consideration, but accepted his proposal with grateful delight.

"Who is he?" asked Dan. Somehow he had never impressed Dan; but then Dan was a fellow to impress whom was slow work. As he himself confessed, he had no instinct for character. "I judge," he would explain, "purely by observation."

"What does that matter?" was my reply.

"What does he know about the business?"

"That's why he wants me."

"What do you know about it?"

"There's not much to know. I can find out."

"Take care you don't find out that there's more to know than you think. What is this wonderful play of his?"

"I haven't seen it yet; I don't think it's finished. It's something from the Spanish or the Russian, I'm not sure. I'm to put it into shape when he's done the translation. He wants me to put my name to it as the adaptor."

"Wonder he hasn't asked you to wear his clothes. Has he got any money?"

"Of course he has money. How can you run a theatrical company without money?"

"Have you seen the money?"

"He doesn't carry it about with him in a bag."

"I should have thought your ambition to be to act, not to manage. Managers are to be had cheap enough. Why should he want someone who knows nothing about it?"

"I'm going to act. I'm going to play a leading part."

"Great Scott!"

"He'll do the management really himself; I shall simply advise him. But he doesn't want his own name to appear.

"Why not?"

"His people might object."

"Who are his people?"

"How do I know? What a suspicious chap you are."

Dan shrugged his shoulders. "You are not an actor, you never will be; you are not a business man. You've made a start at writing, that's your proper work. Why not go on with it?"

"I can't get on with it. That one thing was accepted, and never paid for; everything else comes back regularly, just as before. Besides, I can go on writing wherever I am."

"You've got friends here to help you."

"They don't believe I can do anything but write nonsense."

"Well, clever nonsense is worth writing. It's better than stodgy sense: literature is blocked up with that. Why not follow their advice?"

"Because I don't believe they are right. I'm not a clown; I don't mean to be. Because a man has a sense of humour it doesn't follow he has nothing else. That is only one of my gifts, and by no means the highest. I have knowledge of human nature, poetry, dramatic instinct. I mean to prove it to you all. Vane's the only man that understands me."

Dan lit his pipe. "Have you made up your mind to go?"

"Of course I have. It's an opportunity that doesn't occur twice. 'There's a tide in the affairs—"

"Thanks," interrupted Dan; "I've heard it before. Well, if you've made up your mind, there's an end of the matter. Good luck to you! You are young, and it's easier to learn things then than later."

"You talk," I answered, "as if you were old enough to be my grandfather."

He smiled and laid both hands upon my shoulders. "So I am," he said, "quite old enough, little boy Paul. Don't be angry; you'll always be little Paul to me." He put his hands in his pockets and strolled to the window.

"What'll you do?" I enquired. "Will you keep on these rooms?"

"No," he replied. "I shall accept an offer that has been made to me to take the sub-editorship of a big Yorkshire paper. It is an important position and will give me experience."

"You'll never be happy mewed up in a provincial town," I told him. "I shall want a London address, and I can easily afford it. Let's keep them on together."

He shook his head. "It wouldn't be the same thing," he said.

So there came a morning when we said good-bye. Before Dan returned from the office I should be gone. They had been pleasant months that we had spent together in these pretty rooms. Though my life was calling to me full of hope, I felt the pain of leaving them. Two years is a long period in a young man's life, when the sap is running swiftly. My affections had already taken root there. The green leaves in summer, in winter the bare branches of the square, the sparrows that chirped about the window-sills, the quiet peace of the great house, Dan, kindly old Deleglise: around them my fibres clung, closer than I had known. The Lady of the train: she managed it now less clumsily. Her hands and feet had grown smaller, her elbows rounder. I found myself smiling as I thought of her, one always did smile when one thought of Norah, everybody did; of her tomboy ways, her ringing laugh, there were those who termed it noisy; her irrepressible frankness, there were times when it was inconvenient. Would she ever become lady-like, sedate, proper? One doubted it. I tried to picture her a wife, the mistress of a house. I found the smile deepening round my mouth. What a jolly wife she would make! I could see her bustling, full of importance; flying into tempers, lasting possibly for thirty seconds; then calling herself names, saving all argument by undertaking her own scolding, and doing it well. I followed her to motherhood. What a joke it would be! What would she do with them? She would just let them do what they liked with her. She and they would be a parcel of children together, she the most excited of them all. No; on second thoughts I could detect in her a strong vein of common sense. They would have to mind their p's and q's. I could see her romping with them, helping them to tear their clothes; but likewise I could see her flying after them, bringing back an armful struggling, bathing it, physicking it. Perhaps she would grow stout, grow grey; but she would still laugh more often than sigh, speak her mind, be quick, good-tempered Norah to the end. Her character precluded all hope of surprise. That, as I told myself, was its defect. About her were none of those glorious possibilities that make of some girls charming mysteries. A woman, said I to myself, should be a wondrous jewel, hiding unknown lights and shadows. You, my dear Norah, I spoke my thoughts aloud, as had become a habit with me: those who live much alone fall into this way, you are merely a crystal, not shallow, no, I should not call you shallow by any mans, but transparent.

What would he be, her lover? Some plain, matter-of-fact, business-like young fellow, a good player of cricket and football, fond of his dinner. What a very uninteresting affair the love-making would be! If she liked him, well, she would probably tell him so; if she didn't, he would know it in five minutes.

As for inducing her to change her mind, wooing her, cajoling her, I heard myself laughing at the idea.

There came a quick rap at the door. "Come in," I cried; and she entered.

"I came to say good-bye to you," she explained. "I'm just going out. What were you laughing at?"

"Oh, at an idea that occurred to me."

"A funny one?"

"Yes."

"Tell it me."

"Well, it was something in connection with yourself. It might offend you."

"It wouldn't trouble you much if it did, would it?"

"No, I don't suppose it would,"

"Then why not tell me?"

"I was thinking of your lover."

It did offend her; I thought it would. But she looked really interesting when she was cross. Her grey eyes would flash, and her whole body quiver. There was a charming spice of danger always about making her cross.

"I suppose you think I shall never have one."

"On the contrary, I think you will have a good many." I had not thought so before then. I formed the idea for the first time in that moment, while looking straight into her angry face. It was still a childish face.

The anger died out of it as it always did within the minute, and she laughed. "It would be fun, wouldn't it. I wonder what I should do with him? It makes you feel very serious being in love, doesn't it?"

"Very."

"Have you ever been in love?"

I hesitated for a moment. Then the delight of talking about it overcame my fear of being chaffed. Besides, when she felt it, nobody could be more delightfully sympathetic. I determined to adventure it.

"Yes," I answered, "ever since I was a boy. If you are going to be foolish," I added, for I saw the laugh before it came, "I shan't talk to you about it."

"I'm not, I won't, really," she pleaded, making her face serious again. "What is she like?"

I took from my breast pocket Barbara's photograph, and handed it to her in silence.

"Is she really as beautiful as that?" she asked, gazing at it evidently fascinated.

"More so," I assured her. "Her expression is the most beautiful part of her. Those are only her features."

She sighed. "I wish I was beautiful."

"You are at an awkward age," I told her. "It is impossible to say what you are going to be like."

"Mamma was a lovely woman, everybody says so; and Tom I call awfully handsome. Perhaps I'll be better when I'm filled out a bit more." A small Venetian mirror hung between the two windows; she glanced up into it. "It's my nose that irritates me," she said. She rubbed it viciously, as if she would rub it out.

"Some people admire snub noses," I explained to her.

"No, really?"

"Tennyson speaks of them as 'tip-tilted like the petals of a rose.'"

"How nice of him! Do you think he meant my sort?" She rubbed it again, but in a kinder fashion; then looked again at Barbara's photograph. "Who is she?"

"She was Miss Hasluck," I answered; "she is the Countess Huescar now. She was married last summer."

"Oh, yes, I remember; you told us about her. You were children together. But what's the good of your being in love with her if she's married?"

"It makes my whole life beautiful."

"Wanting somebody you can't have?"

"I don't want her."

"You said you were in love with her."

"So I am."

She handed me back the photograph, and I replaced it in my pocket.

"I don't understand that sort of love," she said. "If I loved anybody I should want to have them with me always.

"She is with me always," I answered, "in my thoughts." She looked at me with her clear grey eyes. I found myself blinking. Something seemed to be slipping from me, something I did not want to lose. I remember a similar sensation once at the moment of waking from a strange, delicious dream to find the sunlight pouring in upon me through an open window.

"That isn't being in love," she said. "That's being in love with the idea of being in love. That's the way I used to go to balls", she laughed, "in front of the glass. You caught me once, do you remember?"

"And was it not sweeter," I argued, "the imagination? You were the belle of the evening; you danced divinely every dance, were taken in to supper by the Lion. In reality you trod upon your partner's toes, bumped and were bumped, were left a wallflower more than half the time, had a headache the next day. Were not the dream balls the more delightful?"

"No, they weren't," she answered without the slightest hesitation. "One real dance, when at last it came, was worth the whole of them. Oh, I know, I've heard you talking, all of you, of the faces that you see in dreams and that are ever so much more beautiful than the faces that you see when you're awake; of the wonderful songs that nobody ever sings, the wonderful pictures that nobody ever paints, and all the rest of it. I don't believe a word of it. It's tommyrot!"

"I wish you wouldn't use slang."

"Well, you know what I mean. What is the proper word? Give it me."

"I suppose you mean cant," I suggested.

"No, I don't. Cant is something that you don't believe in yourself. It's tommyrot: there isn't any other word. When I'm in love it will be with something that is real."

I was feeling angry with her. "I know just what he will be like. He will be a good-natured, commonplace"

"Whatever he is," she interrupted, "he'll be alive, and he'll want me and I shall want him. Dreams are silly. I prefer being up." She clapped her hands. "That's it." Then, silent, she looked at me with an expression of new interest. "I've been wondering and wondering what it was: you are not really awake yet. You've never got up."

I laughed at her whimsical way of putting it; but at the back of my brain was a troubled idea that perhaps she was revealing to me the truth. And if so, what would "waking up," as she termed it, be like? A flash of memory recalled to me that summer evening upon Barking Bridge, when, as it had seemed to me, the little childish Paul had slipped away from me, leaving me lonely and bewildered to find another Self. Was my boyhood in like manner now falling from me? I found myself clinging to it with vague terror. Its thoughts, its feelings, dreams: they had grown sweet to me; must I lose them? This cold, unknown, new Self, waiting to receive me: I shrank away from it with fear.

"Do you know, I think you will be rather nice when you wake up."

Her words recalled me to myself. "Perhaps I never shall wake up," I said. "I don't want to wake up."

"Oh, but one can't go on dreaming all one's life," she laughed. "You'll wake up, and fall in love with somebody real." She came across to me, and taking the lapels of my coat in both her hands, gave me a vigorous shake. "I hope she'll be somebody nice. I am rather afraid."

"You seem to think me a fool!" I was still angry with her, without quite knowing why.

She shook me again. "You know I don't. But it isn't the nice people that take best care of themselves. Tom can't. I have to take care of him."

I laughed.

"I do, really. You should hear me scold him. I like taking care of people. Good-bye."

She held out her hand. It was white now and shapely, but one could not have called it small. Strong it felt and firm as it gripped mine.

CHAPTER VIII.

AND HOW CAME BACK AGAIN.

I left London, the drums beating in my heart, the flags waving in my brain. Somewhat more than a year later, one foggy wet December evening, I sneaked back to it defeated, ah, that is a small thing, capable of redress, disgraced. I returned to it as to a hiding-place where, lost in the crowd, I might waste my days unnoticed until such time as I could summon up sufficient resolution to put an end to my dead life. I had been ambitious, dwelling again amid the bitterness of the months that followed my return, I write in the past tense. I had been eager to make a name, a position for myself. But were I to claim no higher aim, I should be doing injustice to my blood, to the great-souled gentleman whose whole life had been an ode to honour, to her of simple faith who had known no other prayer to teach me than the childish cry, "God help me to be good!" I had wished to be a great man, but it was to have been a great good man. The world was to have admired me, but to have respected me also. I was to have been the knight without fear, but, rarer yet, without reproach, Galahad, not Launcelot. I had learnt myself to be a feeble, backboneless fighter, conquered by the first serious assault of evil, a creature of mean fears, slave to every crack of the devil's whip, a feeder with swine.

Urban Vane I had discovered to be a common swindler. His play he had stolen from the desk of a well-known dramatist whose acquaintance he had made in Deleglise's kitchen. The man had fallen ill, and Vane had been constant in his visits. Partly recovering, the man had gone abroad to Italy. Had he died there, as at the time was expected, the robbery might never have come to light. News reached us in a small northern town that he had taken a fresh lease of life and was on his way back to England. Then it was that Vane with calm indifference, smoking his cigar over a bottle of wine to which he had invited me, told me the bald truth, adorning it with some touches of wit. Had the recital come upon me sooner, I might have acted differently; but six months' companionship with Urban Vane, if it had not, by grace of the Lord, destroyed the roots of whatever flower of manhood might have been implanted in me, had most certainly withered its leaves.

The man was clever. That he was not clever enough to perceive from the beginning what he has learnt since: that honesty is the best policy, at least, for men with brains, remains somewhat of a mystery to me. Where once he made his hundreds among shady ways, he now, I suppose, makes his thousands in the broad daylight of legitimate enterprise. Chicanery in the blood, one might imagine, has to be worked out. Urban Vanes are to be found in all callings. They commence as scamps; years later, to one's astonishment, one finds them ornaments to their profession. Wild oats are of various quality, according to the soil from which they are preserved. We sow them in our various ways.

At first I stormed. Vane sat with an amused smile upon his lips and listened.

"Your language, my dear Kelver," he replied, my vocabulary exhausted, "might wound me were I able to accept you as an authority upon this vexed question of morals. With the rest of the world you preach one thing and practise another. I have noticed it so often. It is perhaps sad, but the preaching has ceased to interest me. You profess to be very indignant with me for making use of another man's ideas. It is done every day. You yourself were quite ready to take credit not due to you. For months we have been travelling with this play: 'Drama, in five acts, by Mr. Horace Moncrieff.' Not more than two hundred lines of it are your own, excellent lines, I admit, but they do not constitute the play."

This aspect of the affair had not occurred to me. "But you asked me to put my name to it," I stammered. "You said you did not want your own to appear, for private reasons. You made a point of it."

He waved away the smoke from his cigar. "The man you are posing as would never have put his name to work not his own. You never hesitated; on the contrary, you jumped at the chance of so easy an opening to your career as playwright. My need, as you imagined it, was your opportunity."

"But you said it was from the French," I argued; "you had merely translated it, I adapted it. I don't defend the custom, but it is the custom: the man who adapts a play calls himself the author. They all do it."

"I know," he answered. "It has always amused me. Our sick friend himself, whom I am sure we are both delighted to welcome back to life, has done it more than once, and made a very fair profit on the transaction. Indeed, from internal evidence, I am strongly of opinion that this present play is a case in point. Well, chickens come home to roost: I adapt from him. What is the difference?"

"Simply this," he continued, pouring himself out another glass of wine, "that whereas, owing to the anomalous state of the copyright laws, stealing from the foreign author is legal and commendable, against stealing from the living English author there is a certain prejudice."

"And the consequences, I am afraid, you will find somewhat unpleasant," I suggested.

He laughed: it was not a frivolity to which he was prone. "You mean, my dear Kelver that you will."

"Don't look so dumbfounded " he went on. "You cannot be so stupid as you are pretending to be. The original manuscript at the Lord Chamberlain's office is in your handwriting. You knew our friend as well as I did, and visited him. Why, the whole tour has been under your management. You have arranged everything most excellently; I have been quite surprised."

My anger came later. For the moment, the sudden light blinded me to everything but fear.

"But you told me," I cried, "it was only a matter of form, that you wanted to keep your name out of it because"

He was looking at me with an expression of genuine astonishment. My words began to appear humorous even to myself. I found it difficult to believe I had been the fool I was now seeing myself to have been.

"I am sorry," he said, "I am really sorry. I took you for a man of the world. I thought you merely did not wish to know anything."

Still, to my shame, fear was the thing uppermost in my heart. "You are not going to put it all on to me?" I pleaded.

He had risen. He laid his hand upon my shoulder. Instead of flinging it off, I was glad of its kindly pressure. He was the only man to whom I could look for help.

"Don't take it so seriously," he said. "He will merely think the manuscript has been lost. As likely as not, he will be unable to remember whether he wrote it or merely thought of writing it. No one in the company will say anything: it isn't their business. We must set to work. I had altered it a good deal before you saw it, and changed all the names of the characters. We will retain the third act: it is the only thing of real value in the play. The situation is not original; you have as much right to dish it up as he had. In a fortnight we will have the whole thing so different that if he saw it himself he would only imagine we had got hold of the idea and had forestalled him."

There were moments during the next few weeks when I listened to the voice of my good angel, when I saw clearly that even from the lowest point of view he was giving me sound advice. I would go to the man, tell him frankly the whole truth.

But Vane never left my elbow. Suspecting, I suppose, he gave me clearly to understand that if I did so, I must expect no mercy from him. My story, denounced by him as an outrageous lie, would be regarded as the funk-inspired subterfuge of a young rogue. At the best I should handicap myself with suspicion that would last me throughout my career. On the other hand, what harm had we done? Presented in some twenty or so small towns, where it would soon be forgotten, a play something like. Most plays were something like. Our friend would produce his version and reap a rich harvest; ours would disappear. If by any unlikely chance discussion should arise, the advertisement would he to his advantage. So soon as possible we would replace it by a new piece altogether. A young man of my genius could surely write something better than hotch-potch such as this; experience was all that I had lacked. As regarded one's own conscience, was not the world's honesty a mere question of convention? Had he been a young man, and had we diddled him out of his play for a ten-pound note, we should have been applauded as sharp men of business. The one commandment of the world was: Don't get found out. The whole trouble, left alone, would sink and fade. Later, we should tell it as a good joke and be laughed with.

So I fell from mine own esteem. Vane helping me, and he had brains, I set feverishly to work. I am glad to remember that every line I wrote was born in misery. I tried to persuade Vane to let me make a new play altogether, which I offered to give him for nothing. He expressed himself as grateful, but his frequently declared belief in my dramatic talent failed to induce his acceptance.

"Later on, my dear Kelver," was his reply. "For the present this is doing very well. Going on as we are, we shall soon improve it out of all recognition, while at the same time losing nothing that is essential. All your ideas are excellent."

By the end of about three weeks we had got together a concoction that, so far as dialogue and characters were concerned, might be said to be our own. There was good work in it, here and there. Under other conditions I might have been proud of much that I had written. As it was, I experienced only the terror of the thief dodging the constable: my cleverness might save me; it afforded me no further satisfaction. My humour, when I heard the people laughing at it, I remembered I had forged listening in vague fear to every creak upon the stairs, wondering in what form discovery might come upon me. There was one speech, addressed by the hero to the villain: "Yes, I admit it; I do love her. But there is that which I love better, my self-respect!" Stepping down to the footlights and slapping his chest (which according to stage convention would appear to be a sort of moral jewel-box bursting with assorted virtues), our juvenile lead—a gentleman who led a somewhat rabbit-like existence, perpetually diving down openings to avoid service of writs, at the instance of his wife, for alimony, would invariably bring down the house upon this sentiment. Every night, listening to the applause, I would shudder, recalling how I had written it with burning cheeks.

There was a character in the piece, a vicious old man, that from the beginning Vane had wanted me to play. I had disliked the part and had refused, choosing instead to act a high-souled countryman, in the portrayal of whose irreproachable emotions I had taken pleasure. Vane now renewed his arguments, and my power of resistance seeming to have departed from me, I accepted the exchange. Certainly the old gentleman's scenes went with more snap, but at a cost of further degradation to myself. Upon an older actor the effect might have been harmless, but the growing tree springs back less surely; I found myself taking pleasure in the coarse laughter that rewarded my suggestive leers, calling up all the evil in my nature to help me in the development of fresh "business." Vane was enthusiastic in his praises, generous with his assistance. Under his tuition I succeeded in making the part as unpleasant as we dared. I had genius, so Vane told me; I understood so much of human nature. One proof of the moral deterioration creeping over me was that I was beginning to like Vane.

Looking back at the man as I see him plainly now, a very ordinary scamp, his pretension not even amusing, I find it difficult to present him as he appeared to my boyish eyes. He was well educated and well read. He gave himself the airs of a superior being by freak of fate compelled to abide in a world of inferior creatures. To live among them in comfort it was necessary for him to outwardly conform to their conventions but to respect their reasoning would have been beneath him. To accept their laws as binding on one's own conscience was, using the common expression, to give oneself away, to confess oneself commonplace. Every decent instinct a man might own to was proof in Vane's eyes of his being "suburban," "bourgeois", everything that was unintellectual. It was the first time I had heard this sort of talk. Vane was one of the pioneers of the movement, which has since become somewhat tiresome. To laugh at it is easy to a man of the world; boys are impressed by it. From him I first heard the now familiar advocacy of pure Hedonism. Pan, enticed from his dark groves, was to sit upon Olympus.

My lower nature rose within me to proclaim the foolish chatterer as a prophet. So life was not as I had been taught, a painful struggle between good and evil. There was no such thing as evil; the senseless epithet was a libel upon Nature. Not through wearisome repression, but rather through joyous expression of the animal lay advancement.

Villains, workers in wrong for aesthetic pleasure of the art, are useful characters in fiction; in real life they do not exist. I am convinced the man believed most of the rubbish he talked. Since the time of which I write he has done some service to the world. I understand he is an excellent husband and father, a considerate master, a delightful host. He intended, I have no doubt, to improve me, to enlarge my understanding, to free me from soul-stifling bondage of convention. Not to credit him with this well-meaning intention would be to assume him something quite inhuman, to bestow upon him a dignity beyond his deserts. I find it easier to regard him merely as a fool.

Our leading lady was a handsome but coarse woman, somewhat over-developed. Starting life as a music-hall singer, she had married a small tradesman in the south of London. Some three or four years previous, her Juno-like charms had turned the head of a youthful novelist, a refined, sensitive man, of whom great things in literature had been expected, and, judging from his earlier work, not unreasonably. He had run away with her, and eventually married her; the scandal was still fresh. Already she had repented of her bargain. These women regard their infatuated lovers merely as steps in the social ladder, and he had failed to appreciably advance her. Under her demoralising spell his ambition had died in him. He no longer wrote, no longer took interest in anything beyond his own debasement. He was with us in the company, playing small parts, and playing them badly; he would have remained with us as bill-poster rather than have been sent away.

Vane planned to bring this woman and myself together. To her he pictured me a young gentleman of means, a coming author, who would soon be earning an income sufficient to keep her in every luxury. To me he hinted that she had fallen in love with me. I was never attracted to her by any feeling stronger than the admiration with which one views a handsome animal. It was my vanity upon which he worked. He envied me; any man would envy me; experience of life was what I needed to complete my genius. The great intellects of this earth must learn all lessons, even at the cost of suffering to themselves and others.

As years before I had laboured to acquire a liking for cigars and whiskey, deeming it an accomplishment necessary to a literary career, so painstakingly I now applied myself to the cultivation of a pretty taste in passion. According to the literature, fictional and historical, Vane was kind enough to supply me with, men of note were invariably sad dogs. That my temperament was not that of the sad dog, that I lacked instinct and inclination for the part, appeared to this young idiot of whom I am writing in the light of a defect. That her languishing glances irritated rather than maddened me, that the occasional covert pressure of her hot, thick hand left me cold, I felt a reproach to my manhood. I would fall in love with her. Surely my blood was red like other men's. Besides, was I not an artist, and was not profligacy the hall-mark of the artist?

But one grows tired of the confessional. Fate saved me from playing the part Vane had assigned me in this vulgar comedy, dragged me from my entanglement, flung me on my feet again. She was a little brusque in the process; but I do not feel inclined to blame the kind lady for that. The mud was creeping upward fast, and a quick hand must needs be rough.

Our dramatic friend produced his play sooner than we had expected. It crept out that something very like it had been seen in the Provinces. Argument followed, enquiries were set on foot. "It will blow over," said Vane. But it seemed to be blowing our way.

The salaries, as a rule, were paid by me on Friday night. Vane, in the course of the evening, would bring me the money for me to distribute after the performance. We were playing in the north of Ireland. I had not seen Vane all that day. So soon as I had changed my clothes I left my dressing-room to seek him. The box-office keeper, meeting me, put a note into my hand. It was short and to the point. Vane had pocketed the evening's takings, and had left by the seven-fifty train! He regretted causing inconvenience, but life was replete with small comedies; the wise man attached no seriousness to them. We should probably meet again and enjoy a laugh over our experiences.

Some rumour had got about. I looked up from the letter to find myself surrounded by suspicious faces. With dry lips I told them the truth. Only they happened not to regard it as the truth. Vane throughout had contrived cleverly to them I was the manager, the sole person responsible. My wearily spoken explanations were to them incomprehensible lies. The quarter of an hour might have been worse for me had I been sufficiently alive to understand or care what they were saying. A dull, listless apathy had come over me. I felt the scene only stupid, ridiculous, tiresome. There was some talk of giving me "a damned good hiding." I doubt whether I should have known till the next morning whether the suggestion had been carried out or not. I gathered that the true history of the play, the reason for the sudden alterations, had been known to them all along. They appeared to have reserved their virtuous indignation till this evening. As explanation of my apparent sleepiness, somebody, whether in kindness to me or not I cannot say, suggested I was drunk. Fortunately, it carried conviction. No further trains left the town that night; I was allowed to depart. A deputation promised to be round at my lodgings early in the morning.

Our leading lady had left the theatre immediately on the fall of the curtain; it was not necessary for her to wait, her husband acting as her business man. On reaching my rooms, I found her sitting by the fire. It reminded me that our agent in advance having fallen ill, her husband had, at her suggestion, been appointed in his place, and had left us on the Wednesday to make the necessary preparations in the next town on our list. I thought that perhaps she had come round for her money, and the idea amused me.

"Well?" she said, with her one smile. I had been doing my best for some months to regard it as soul-consuming, but without any real success.

"Well," I answered. It bored me, her being there. I wanted to be alone.

"You don't seem overjoyed to see me. What's the matter with you? What's happened?"

I laughed. "Vane's bolted and taken the week's money with him."

"The beast!" she said. "I knew he was that sort. Whatever made you take up with him? Will it make much difference to you?"

"It makes a difference all round," I replied. "There's no money to pay any of you. There's nothing to pay your fares back to London."

She had risen. "Here, let me understand this," she said. "Are you the rich mug Vane's been representing you to be, or only his accomplice?"

"The mug and the accomplice both," I answered, "without the rich. It's his tour. He put my name to it because he didn't want his own to appear, for family reasons. It's his play; he stole it"

She interrupted me with a whistle. "I thought it looked a bit fishy, all those alterations. But such funny things do happen in this profession! Stole it, did he?"

"The whole thing in manuscript. I put my name to it for the same reason, he didn't want his own to appear."

She dropped into her chair and laughed, a good-tempered laugh, loud and long. "Well, I'm damned!" she said. "The first man who has ever taken me in. I should never have signed if I had thought it was his show. I could see the sort he was with half an eye." She jumped up from the chair. "Here, let me get out of this," she said. "I just looked in to know what time to-morrow; I'd forgotten. You needn't say I came."

Her hand upon the door, laughter seized her again, so that for support she had to lean against the wall.

"Do you know why I really did come?" she said. "You'll guess when you come to think it over, so I may as well tell you. It's a bit of a joke. I came to say 'yes' to what you asked me last night. Have you forgotten?"

I stared at her. Last night! It seemed a long while ago, so very unimportant what I might have said.

She laughed again. "So help me! if you haven't. Well, you asked me to run away with you, that's all, to let our two souls unite. Damned lucky I took a day to think it over! Good-night."

"Good-night," I answered, without moving. I was gripping a chair to prevent myself from rushing at her, pushing her out of the room, and locking the door. I wanted to be alone.

I heard her turn the handle. "Got a pound or two to carry you over?" It was a woman's voice.

I put my hand into my pocket. "One pound seventeen," I answered, counting it. "It will pay my fare to London or buy me a dinner and a second-hand revolver. I haven't quite decided yet."

"Oh, you get back and pull yourself together," she said. "You're only a kid. Good-night."

I put a few things into a small bag and walked thirty miles that night into Belfast. Arrived in London, I took a lodging in Deptford, where I was least likely to come in contact with any face I had ever seen before. I maintained myself by giving singing lessons at sixpence the half-hour, evening lessons in French and German (the Lord forgive me!) to ambitious shop-boys at eighteen pence a week, making up tradesmen's books. A few articles of jewellery I had retained enabled me to tide over bad periods. For some four months I existed there, never going outside the neighbourhood. Occasionally, wandering listlessly about the streets, some object, some vista, would strike me by reason of its familiarity. Then I would turn and hasten back into my grave of dim, weltering streets.

Of thoughts, emotions, during these dead days I was unconscious. Somewhere in my brain they may have been stirring, contending; but myself I lived as in a long, dull dream. I ate, and drank, and woke, and slept, and walked and walked, and lounged by corners; staring by the hour together, seeing nothing.

It has suprised me since to find the scenes I must then have witnessed photographed so clearly on my mind. Tragedies, dramas, farces, played before me in that teeming underworld, the scenes present themselves to me distinct, complete; yet I have no recollection of ever having seen them.

I fell ill. It must have been some time in April, but I kept no count of days. Nobody came near me, nobody knew of me. I occupied a room at the top of a huge block of workmen's dwellings. A woman who kept a second-hand store had lent me for a shilling a week a few articles of furniture. Lying upon my chair-bedstead, I listened to the shrill sounds around me, that through the light and darkness never ceased. A pint of milk, left each morning on the stone landing, kept me alive. I would wait for the man's descending footsteps, then crawl to the door. I hoped I was going to die, regretting my returning strength, the desire for food that drove me out into the streets again.

One night, a week or two after my partial recovery, I had wandered on and on for hour after hour. The breaking dawn recalled me to myself. I was outside the palings of a park. In the faint shadowy light it looked strange and unfamiliar. I was too tired to walk further. I scrambled over the low wooden fencing, and reaching a seat, dropped down and fell asleep.

I was sitting in a sunny avenue; birds were singing joyously, bright flowers were all around me. Norah was beside me, her frank, sweet eyes were looking into mine; they were full of tenderness, mingled with wonder. It was a delightful dream: I felt myself smiling.

Suddenly I started to my feet. Norah's strong hand drew me down again.

I was in the broad walk, Regent's Park, where, I remembered, Norah often walked before breakfast. A park-keeper, the only other human creature within sight, was eyeing me suspiciously. I saw myself, without a looking-glass, unkempt, ragged. My intention was to run, but Norah was holding me by the arm. Savagely I tried to shake her off. I was weak from my recent illness, and, I suppose, half starved; it angered me to learn she was the stronger of the two. In spite of my efforts, she dragged me back.

Ashamed of my weakness, ashamed of everything about me, I burst into tears; and that of course made me still more ashamed. To add to my discomfort, I had no handkerchief. Holding me with one hand, it was quite sufficient, Norah produced her own, and wiped my eyes. The park-keeper, satisfied, I suppose, that at all events I was not dangerous, with a grin passed on.

"Where have you been, and what have you been doing?" asked Norah. She still retained her grip upon me, and in her grey eyes was quiet determination.

So, with my face turned away from her, I told her the whole miserable story, taking strange satisfaction in exaggerating, if anything, my own share of the disgrace. My recital ended, I sat staring down the long, shadow-freckled way, and for awhile there was no sound but the chirping of the sparrows.

Then behind me I beard a smothered laugh. It was impossible to imagine it could come from Norah. I turned quickly to see who had stolen upon us. It was Norah who was laughing; though to do her justice she was trying to suppress it, holding her handkerchief to her face. It was of no use, it would out; she abandoned the struggle, and gave way to it. It astonished the sparrows into silence; they stood in a row upon the low iron border and looked at one another.

"I am glad you think it funny," I said.

"But it is funny," she persisted. "Don't say you have lost your sense of humour, Paul; it was the one real thing you possessed. You were so cocky, you don't know how cocky you were! Everybody was a fool but Vane; nobody else but he appreciated you at your true worth. You and he between you were going to reform the stage, to educate the public, to put everything and everybody to rights. I am awfully sorry for all you've gone through; but now that it is over, can't you see yourself that it is funny?"

Faintly, dimly, this aspect of the case, for the very first time, began to present itself to me; but I should have preferred Norah to have been impressed by its tragedy.

"That is not all," I said. "I nearly ran away with another man's wife."

I was glad to notice that sobered her somewhat. "Nearly? Why not quite?" she asked more seriously.

"She thought I was some young idiot with money," I replied bitterly, pleased with the effect I had produced. "Vane had told her a pack of lies.

When she found out I was only a poor devil, ruined, disgraced, without a sixpence" I made a gesture expressive of eloquent contempt for female nature generally.

"I am sorry," said Norah; "I told you you would fall in love with something real."

Her words irritated me, unreasonably, I confess. "In love!" I replied; "good God, I was never in love with her!"

"Then why did you nearly run away with her?"

I was wishing now I had not mentioned the matter; it promised to be difficult of explanation. "I don't know," I replied irritably. "I thought she was in love with me. She was very beautiful, at least, other people seemed to think she was. Artists are not like ordinary men. You must live, understand life, before you can teach it to others. When a beautiful woman is in love with you, or pretends to be, you, you must say something. You can't stand like a fool and -"

Again her laughter interrupted me; this time she made no attempt to hide it. The sparrows chirped angrily, and flew off to continue their conversation somewhere where there would be less noise.

"You are the biggest baby, Paul," she said, so soon as she could speak, "I ever heard of." She seized me by the shoulders, and turned me round. "If you weren't looking so ill and miserable, I would shake you, Paul, till there wasn't a bit of breath left in your body."

"How much money do you owe?" she asked, "to the people in the company and anybody else, I mean roughly?"

"About a hundred and fifty pounds," I answered.

"Then if you rest day or night, Paul, till you have paid that hundred and fifty, every penny of it, I'll think you the meanest cad in London!"

Her grey eyes were flashing quite alarmingly. I felt almost afraid of her. She could be so vehement at times.

"But how can I?" I asked.

"Go straight home," she commanded, "and write something funny: an article, story, anything you like; only mind that it is funny. Post it to me to-morrow, at the latest. Dan is in London, editing a new weekly. I'll have it copied out and sent to him. I shan't say who it is from. I shall merely ask him to read it and reply, at once. If you've a grain of grit left in you, you'll write something that he will be glad to have and to pay for. Pawn that ring on your finger and get yourself a good breakfast", it was my mother's wedding-ring, the only piece of dispensable property I had not parted with, "she won't mind helping you. But nobody else is going to, except yourself."

She looked at her watch. "I must be off." She turned again. "There is something I was forgetting. B--" she mentioned the name of the dramatist whose play Vane had stolen "has been looking for you for the last three months. If you hadn't been an idiot you might have saved yourself a good deal of trouble. He is quite certain it was Vane stole the manuscript. He asked the nurse to bring it to him an hour after Vane had left the house, and it couldn't be found. Besides, the man's character is well known. And so is yours. I won't tell it you," she laughed; "anyhow, it isn't that of a knave."

She made a step towards me, then changed her mind. "No," she said, "I shan't shake hands with you till you have paid the last penny that you owe. Then I shall know that you are a man."

She did not look back. I watched her, till the sunlight, streaming in my eyes, raised a golden mist between us.

Then I went to my work.

CHAPTER IX.

THE PRINCESS OF THE GOLDEN LOCKS SENDS PAUL A RING.

It took me three years to win that handshake. For the first six months I remained in Deptford. There was excellent material to be found there for humorous articles, essays, stories; likewise for stories tragic and pathetic. But I owed a hundred and fifty pounds, a little over two hundred it reached to, I found, when I came to add up the actual figures. So I paid strict attention to business, left the tears to be garnered by others, better fitted maybe for the task; kept to my own patch, reaped and took to market only the laughter.

At the beginning I sent each manuscript to Norah; she had it copied out, debited me with the cost received payment, and sent me the balance. At first my earnings were small; but Norah was an excellent agent; rapidly they increased. Dan grew quite cross with her, wrote in pained surprise at her greed. The "matter" was fair, but in no way remarkable. Any friend of hers, of course, he was anxious to assist; but business was business. In justice to his proprietors, he could not and would not pay more than the market value. Miss Deleglise, replying curtly in the third person, found herself in perfect accord with Mr. Brian as to business being business. If Mr. Brian could not afford to pay her price for material so excellent, other editors with whom Miss Deleglise was equally well acquainted could and would. Answer by return would greatly oblige, pending which the manuscript then in her hands she retained. Mr. Brian, understanding he had found his match, grumbled but paid. Whether he had any suspicion who "Jack Homer" might be, he never confessed; but he would have played the game, pulled his end of the rope, in either case. Nor was he allowed to decide the question for himself. Competition was introduced into the argument. Of purpose a certain proportion of my work my agent sent elsewhere. "Jack Homer" grew to be a commodity in demand. For, seated at my rickety table, I laughed as I wrote, the fourth wall of the dismal room fading before my eyes revealing vistas beyond.

Still, it was slow work. Humour is not an industrious maid; declines to be bustled, will work only when she feels inclined, does not often feel inclined; gives herself a good many unnecessary airs; if worried, packs up and goes off, Heaven knows where! comes back when she thinks she will: a somewhat unreliable young person. To my literary labours I found it necessary to add journalism. I lacked Dan's magnificent assurance. Fate never befriends the nervous. Had I burst into the editorial sanctum, the editor most surely would have been out if in, would have been a man of short ways, would have seen to it that I went out quickly. But the idea was not to be thought of; Robert Macaire himself in my one coat would have been diffident, apologetic. I joined the ranks of the penny-a-liners, to be literally exact, three halfpence a liners. In company with half a dozen other shabby outsiders, some of them young men like myself seeking to climb; others, older men who had sunk, I attended inquests, police courts; flew after fire engines; rejoiced in street accidents; yearned for murders. Somewhat vulture-like we lived precariously upon the misfortunes of others. We made occasional half crowns by providing the public with scandal, occasional crowns by keeping our information to ourselves.

"I think, gentlemen," would explain our spokesman in a hoarse whisper, on returning to the table, "I think the corpse's brother-in-law is anxious that the affair, if possible, should be kept out of the papers."

The closeness and attention with which we would follow that particular case, the fulness and completeness of our notes, would be quite remarkable. Our spokesman would rise, drift carelessly away, to return five minutes later, wiping his mouth.

"Not a very interesting case, gentlemen, I don't think. Shall we say five shillings apiece?" Sometimes a sense of the dignity of our calling would induce us to stand out for ten.

And here also my sense of humour came to my aid; gave me perhaps an undue advantage over my competitors. Twelve good men and true had been asked to say how a Lascar sailor had met his death. It was perfectly clear how he had met his death. A plumber, working on the roof of a small two-storeyed house, had slipped and fallen on him. The plumber had escaped with a few bruises; the unfortunate sailor had been picked up dead. Some blame attached to the plumber. His mate, an excellent witness, told us the whole story.

"I was fixing a gas-pipe on the first floor," said the man. "The prisoner was on the roof."

"We won't call him 'the prisoner,'" interrupted the coroner, "at least, not yet. Refer to him, if you please, as the 'last witness.'"

"The last witness," corrected himself the man. "He shouts down the chimney to know if I was ready for him."

"'Ready and waiting,' I says.

"'Right,' he says; 'I'm coming in through the window.'

"'Wait a bit,' I says; 'I'll go down and move the ladder for you.

"'It's all right,' he says; 'I can reach it.'

"'No, you can't,' I says. 'It's the other side of the chimney.'

"'I can get round,' he says.

"Well, before I knew what had happened, I hears him go, smack! I rushes to the window and looks out: I see him on the pavement, sitting up like.

"'Hullo, Jim,' I says. 'Have you hurt yourself?'

"'I think I'm all right,' he says, 'as far as I can tell. But I wish you'd come down. This bloke I've fallen on looks a bit sick.'"

The others headed their flimsy "Sad Accident," a title truthful but not alluring. I altered mine to "Plumber in a Hurry, Fatal Result." Saying as little as possible about the unfortunate sailor, I called the attention of plumbers generally to the coroner's very just remarks upon the folly of undue haste; pointed out to them, as a body, the trouble that would arise if somehow they could not cure themselves of this tendency to rush through their work without a moment's loss of time.

It established for me a useful reputation. The sub-editor of one evening paper condescended so far as to come out in his shirt-sleeves and shake hands with me.

"That's the sort of thing we want," he told me; "a light touch, a bit of humour."

I snatched fun from fires (I sincerely trust the insurance premiums were not overdue); culled quaintness from street rows; extracted merriment from catastrophes the most painful, and prospered.

Though often within a stone's throw of the street, I unremittingly avoided the old house at Poplar. I was suffering inconvenience at this period by reason of finding myself two distinct individuals, contending with each other. My object was to encourage the new Paul, the sensible, practical, pushful Paul, whose career began to look promising; to drive away from interfering with me his strangely unlike twin, the old childish Paul of the sad, far-seeing eyes. Sometimes out of the cracked looking-glass his wistful, yearning face would plead to me; but I would sternly shake my head. I knew well his cunning. Had I let him have his way, he would have led me through the maze of streets he knew so well, past the broken railings (outside which be would have left my body standing), along the weedy pathway, through the cracked and dented door, up the creaking staircase to the dismal little chamber where we once, he and I together, had sat dreaming foolish dreams.

"Come," he would whisper; "it is so near. Let us push aside the chest of drawers very quietly, softly raise the broken sash, prop it open with the Latin dictionary, lean our elbows on the sill, listen to the voices of the weary city, voices calling to us from the darkness."

But I was too wary to be caught. "Later on," I would reply to him; "when I have made my way, when I am stronger to withstand your wheedling. Then I will go with you, if you are still in existence, my sentimental little friend. We will dream again the old impractical, foolish dreams, and laugh at them."

So he would fade away, and in his place would nod to me approvingly a businesslike-looking, wide-awake young fellow.

But to one sentimental temptation I succumbed. My position was by now assured; there was no longer any reason for my hiding myself. I determined to move westward. I had not intended to soar so high, but passing through Guildford Street one day, the creeper-covered corner house that my father had once thought of taking recalled itself to me. A card was in the fanlight. I knocked and made enquiries. A bed-sitting-room upon the third floor was vacant. I remembered it well the moment the loquacious landlady opened its door.

"This shall be your room, Paul," said my father. So clearly his voice sounded behind me that I turned, forgetting for the moment it was but a memory. "You will be quiet here, and we can shut out the bed and washstand with a screen."

So my father had his way. It was a pleasant, sunny little room, overlooking the gardens of the hospital. I followed my father's suggestion, shut out the bed and washstand with a screen. And sometimes of an evening it would amuse me to hear my father turn the handle of the door.

"How are you getting on, all right?"

"Famously."

Often there came back to me the words he had once used. "You must be the practical man, Paul, and get on. Myself, I have always been somewhat of a dreamer. I meant to do such great things in the world, and somehow I suppose I aimed too high. I wasn't practical."

"But ought not one to aim high?" I had asked.

My father had fidgeted in his chair. "It is very difficult to say. It is all so, so very un-understandable. You aim high and you don't hit anything, at least, it seems as if you didn't. Perhaps, after all, it is better to aim at something low, and, and hit it. Yet it seems a pity, one's ideals, all the best part of one, I don't know why it is. Perhaps we do not understand."

For some months I had been writing over my own name. One day a letter was forwarded to me by an editor to whose care it had been addressed. It was a short, formal note from the maternal Sellars, inviting me to the wedding of her daughter with a Mr. Reginald Clapper. I had almost forgotten the incident of the Lady 'Ortensia, but it was not unsatisfactory to learn that it had terminated pleasantly. Also, I judged from an invitation having been sent me, that the lady wished me to be witness of the fact that my desertion had not left her disconsolate. So much gratification I felt I owed her, and accordingly, purchasing a present as expensive as my means would permit, I made my way on the following Thursday, clad in frock coat and light grey trousers, to Kennington Church.

The ceremony was already in progress. Creeping on tiptoe up the aisle, I was about to slip into an empty pew, when a hand was laid upon my sleeve.

"We're all here," whispered the O'Kelly; "just room for ye."

Squeezing his hand as I passed, I sat down between the Signora and Mrs. Peedles. Both ladies were weeping; the Signora silently, one tear at a time clinging fondly to her pretty face as though loath to fall from it; Mrs. Peedles copiously, with explosive gurgles, as of water from a bottle.

"It is such a beautiful service," murmured the Signora, pressing my hand as I settled myself down. "I should so, so love to be married."

"Me darling," whispered the O'Kelly, seizing her other hand and kissing it covertly behind his open Prayer Book, "perhaps ye will be one day."

The Signora through her tears smiled at him, but with a sigh shook her head.

Mrs. Peedles, clad, so far as the dim November light enabled me to judge, in the costume of Queen Elizabeth, nothing regal; the sort of thing one might assume to have been Her Majesty's second best, say third best, frock, explained that weddings always reminded her how fleeting a thing was love.

"The poor dears!" she sobbed. "But there, there's no telling. Perhaps they'll be happy. I'm sure I hope they may be. He looks harmless."

Jarman, stretching out a hand to me from the other side of Mrs. Peedles, urged me to cheer up. "Don't wear your 'eart upon your sleeve," he advised. "Try and smile."

In the vestry I met old friends. The maternal Sellars, stouter than ever, had been accommodated with a chair, at least, I assumed so, she being in a sitting posture; the chair itself was not in evidence. She greeted me with more graciousness than I had expected, enquiring after my health with pointedness and an amount of tender solicitude that, until the explanation broke upon me, somewhat puzzled me.

Mr. Reginald Clapper was a small but energetic gentleman, much impressed, I was glad to notice, with a conviction of his own good fortune. He expressed the greatest delight at being introduced to me, shook me heartily by the hand, and hoped we should always be friends.

"Won't be my fault if we're not," he added. "Come and see us whenever you like." He repeated this three times. I gathered the general sentiment to be that he was acting, if anything, with excess of generosity.

Mrs. Reginald Clapper, as I was relieved to know she now was, received my salute to a subdued murmur of applause. She looked to my eyes handsomer than when I had last seen her, or maybe my taste was growing less exacting. She also trusted she might always regard me as a friend. I replied that it would be my hope to deserve the honour; whereupon she kissed me of her own accord, and embracing her mother, shed some tears, explaining the reason to be that everybody was so good to her.

Brother George, less lank than formerly, hampered by a pair of enormous white kid gloves, superintended my signing of the register, whispering to me sympathetically: "Better luck next time, old cock."

The fat young lady or, maybe, the lean young lady, grown stouter, I cannot say for certain, who feared I had forgotten her, a thing I assured her utterly impossible, was good enough to say that, in her opinion, I was worth all the others put together.

"And so I told her," added the fat young lady, or the lean one grown stouter, "a dozen times if I told her once. But there!"

I murmured my obligations.

Cousin Joseph, 'whom I found no difficulty in recognising by reason of his watery eyes, appeared not so chirpy as of yore.

"You take my tip," advised Cousin Joseph, drawing me aside, "and keep out of it."

"You speak from experience?" I suggested.

"I'm as fond of a joke," said the watery-eyed Joseph, "as any man. But when it comes to buckets of water"

A reminder from the maternal Sellars that breakfast had been ordered for eleven o'clock caused a general movement and arrested Joseph's revelations.

"See you again, perhaps," he murmured, and pushed past me.

What Mrs. Sellars, I suppose, would have alluded to as a cold col-la-shon had been arranged for at a restaurant near by. I walked there in company with Uncle and Aunt Gutton; not because I particularly desired their companionship, but because Uncle Gutton, seizing me by the arm, left me no alternative.

"Now then, young man," commenced Uncle Gutton kindly, but boisterously so soon as we were in the street, at some little distance behind the others, "if you want to pitch into me, you pitch away. I shan't mind, and maybe it'll do you good."

I informed him that nothing was further from my desire.

"Oh, all right," returned Uncle Gutton, seemingly disappointed. "If you're willing to forgive and forget, so am I. I never liked you, as I daresay you saw, and so I told Rosie. 'He may be cleverer than he looks,' I says, 'or be may be a bigger fool than I think him, though that's hardly likely. You take my advice and get a full-grown article, then you'll know what you're doing.'"

I told him I thought his advice had been admirable.

"I'm glad you think so," he returned, somewhat puzzled; "though if you wanted to call me names I shouldn't have blamed you. Anyhow, you've took it like a sensible chap. You've got over it, as I always told her you would. Young men out of story-books don't die of broken hearts, even if for a month or two they do feel like standing on their head in the water-butt."

"Why, I was in love myself three times," explained Uncle Gutton, "before I married the old woman."

Aunt Gutton sighed and said she was afraid gentlemen didn't feel these things as much as they ought to.

"They've got their living to earn," retorted Uncle Gutton.

I agreed with Uncle Gutton that life could not be wasted in vain regret.

"As for the rest," admitted Uncle Gutton, handsomely, "I was wrong. You've turned out better than I expected you would."

I thanked him for his improved opinion, and as we entered the restaurant we shook hands.

Minikin we found there waiting for us. He explained that having been able to obtain only limited leave of absence from business, he had concluded the time would be better employed at the restaurant than at the church. Others were there also with whom I was unacquainted, young sparks, admirers, I presume, of the Lady 'Ortensia in her professional capacity, fellow-clerks of Mr. Clapper, who was something in the City. Altogether we must have numbered a score.

Breakfast was laid in a large room on the first floor. The wedding presents stood displayed upon a side-table. My own, with my card attached, had not been seen by Mrs. Clapper till that moment. She and her mother lingered, examining it.

"Real silver!" I heard the maternal Sellars whisper, "Must have paid a ten pound note for it."

"I hope you'll find it useful," I said.

The maternal Sellars, drifting away, joined the others gathered together at the opposite end of the room.

"I suppose you think I set my cap at you merely because you were a gentleman," said the Lady 'Ortensia.

"Don't let's talk about it," I answered. "We were both foolish."

"I don't want you to think it was merely that," continued the Lady 'Ortensia. "I did like you. And I wouldn't have disgraced you, at least, I'd have tried not to. We women are quick to learn. You never gave me time."

"Believe me, things are much better as they are," I said.

"I suppose so," she answered. "I was a fool." She glanced round; we still had the corner to ourselves. "I told a rare pack of lies," she said; "I didn't seem able to help it; I was feeling sore all over. But I have always been ashamed of myself. I'll tell them the truth, if you like."

I thought I saw a way of making her mind easy. "My dear girl," I said, "you have taken the blame upon yourself, and let me go scot-free. It was generous of you."

"You mean that?" she asked.

"The truth," I answered, "would shift all the shame on to me. It was I who broke my word, acted shabbily from beginning to end."

"I hadn't looked at it in that light," she replied. "Very well, I'll hold my tongue."

My place at breakfast was to the left of the maternal Sellars, the Signora next to me, and the O'Kelly opposite. Uncle Gutton faced the bride and bridegroom. The disillusioned Joseph was hidden from me by flowers, so that his voice, raised from time to time, fell upon my ears, embellished with the mysterious significance of the unseen oracle.

For the first quarter of an hour or so the meal proceeded almost in silence. The maternal Sellars when not engaged in whispered argument with the perspiring waiter, was furtively occupied in working sums upon the table-cloth by aid of a blunt pencil. The Signora, strangely unlike her usual self, was not in talkative mood.

"It was so kind of them to invite me," said the Signora, speaking low. "But I feel I ought not to have come.

"Why not?" I asked

"I'm not fit to be here," murmured the Signora in a broken voice. "What right have I at wedding breakfasts? Of course, for dear Willie it is different. He has been married."

The O'Kelly, who never when the Signora was present seemed to care much for conversation in which she was unable to participate, took advantage of his neighbour's being somewhat deaf to lapse into abstraction. Jarman essayed a few witticisms of a general character, of which nobody took any notice. The professional admirers of the Lady 'Ortensia, seated together at a corner of the table, appeared to be enjoying a small joke among themselves. Occasionally, one or another of them would laugh nervously. But for the most part the only sounds to be heard were the clatter of the knives and forks, the energetic shuffling of the waiter, and a curious hissing noise as of escaping gas, caused by Uncle Gutton drinking champagne.

With the cutting, or, rather, the smashing into a hundred fragments, of the wedding cake, a work that taxed the united strength of bride and bridegroom to the utmost, the atmosphere lost something of its sombreness. The company, warmed by food, displaying indications of being nearly done, commenced to simmer. The maternal Sellars, putting away with her blunt pencil considerations of material nature, embraced the table with a smile.

"But it is a sad thing," sighed the maternal Sellars the next moment, with a shake of her huge head, "when your daughter marries, and goes away and leaves you."

"Damned sight sadder," commented Uncle Gutton, "when she don't go off, but hangs on at home year after year and expects you to keep her."

I credit Uncle Gutton with intending this as an aside for the exclusive benefit of the maternal Sellars; but his voice was not of the timbre that lends itself to secrecy. One of the bridesmaids, a plain, elderly girl, bending over her plate, flushed scarlet. I concluded her to be Miss Gutton.

"It doesn't seem to me," said Aunt Gutton from the other end of the table, "that gentlemen are as keen on marrying nowadays as they used to be."

"Got to know a bit about it, I expect," sounded the small, shrill voice of the unseen Joseph.

"To my thinking," exclaimed a hatchet-faced gentleman, "one of the evils crying most loudly for redress at the present moment is the utterly needless and monstrous expense of legal proceedings." He spoke rapidly and with warmth. "Take divorce. At present, what is it? The rich man's luxury."

Conversation appeared to be drifting in a direction unsuitable to the occasion; but Jarman was fortunately there to seize the helm.

"The plain fact of the matter is," said Jarman, "girls have gone up in value. Time was, so I've heard, when they used to be given away with a useful bit of household linen, maybe a chair or two. Nowadays, well, it's only chaps wallowing in wealth like Clapper there as can afford a really first-class article."

Mr. Clapper, not a gentleman in other respects of exceptional brilliancy, possessed one quality that popularity-seekers might have envied him: the ability to explode on the slightest provocation into a laugh instinct with all the characteristics of genuine delight.

"Give and take," observed the maternal Sellars, so soon as Mr. Clapper's roar had died away; "that's what you've got to do when you're married."

"Give a deal more than you bargained for and take what you don't want, that sums it up," came the bitter voice of the unseen.

"Oh, do be quiet, Joe," advised the stout young lady, from which I concluded she had once been the lean young lady. "You talk enough for a man."

"Can't I open my mouth?" demanded the indignant oracle.

"You look less foolish when you keep it shut," returned the stout young lady.

"We'll show them how to get on," observed the Lady 'Ortensia to her bridegroom, with a smile.

Mr. Clapper responded with a gurgle.

"When me and the old girl there fixed things up," said Uncle Gutton, "we didn't talk no nonsense, and we didn't start with no misunderstandings. 'I'm not a duke,' I says"

"Had she been mistaking you for one?" enquired Minikin.

Mr. Clapper commented, not tactfully, but with appreciative laugh. I feared for a moment lest Uncle Gutton's little eyes should leave his head.

"Not being a natural-born, one-eyed fool," replied Uncle Gutton, glaring at the unabashed Minikin, "she did not. 'I'm not a duke,' I says, and she had sense enough to know as I was talking sarcastic like. 'I'm not offering you a life of luxury and ease. I'm offering you myself, just what you see, and nothing more.'

"She took it?" asked Minikin, who was mopping up his gravy with his bread.

"She accepted me, sir," returned Uncle Gutton, in a voice that would have awed any one but Minikin. "Can you give me any good reason for her not doing so?"

"No need to get mad with me," explained Minikin. "I'm not blaming the poor woman. We all have our moments of despair."

The unfortunate Clapper again exploded. Uncle Gutton rose to his feet. The ready Jarman saved the situation.

"'Ear! 'ear!" cried Jarman, banging the table with the handles of two knives. "Silence for Uncle Gutton! 'E's going to propose a toast. 'Ear, 'ear!"

Mrs. Clapper, seconding his efforts, the whole table broke into applause.

"What, as a matter of fact, I did get up to say" began Uncle Gutton.

"Good old Uncle Gutton!" persisted the determined Jarman. "Bride and bridegroom, long life to 'em!"

Uncle Sutton, evidently pleased, allowed his indignation against Minikin to evaporate.

"Well," said Uncle Gutton, "if you think I'm the one to do it"

The response was unmistakable. In our enthusiasm we broke two glasses and upset a cruet; a small, thin lady was unfortunate enough to shed her chignon. Thus encouraged, Uncle Sutton launched himself upon his task. Personally, I should have been better pleased had Fate not interposed to assign to him the duty.

Starting with a somewhat uninstructive history of his own career, he suddenly, and for no reason at all obvious, branched off into fierce censure of the Adulteration Act. Reminded of the time by the maternal Sellars, he got in his first sensible remark by observing that with such questions, he took it, the present company was not particularly interested, and directed himself to the main argument. To his, Uncle Gutton's, foresight, wisdom and instinctive understanding of humanity, Mr. Clapper, it appeared, owed his present happiness. Uncle Gutton it was who had divined from the outset the sort of husband the fair Rosina would come eventually to desire, a plain, simple, hard-working, level-headed sort of chap, with no hity-tity nonsense about him: such an one, in short, as Mr. Clapper himself (at this Mr. Clapper expressed approval by a lengthy laugh) a gentleman who, so far as Uncle Gutton's knowledge went, had but one fault: a silly habit of laughing when there was nothing whatever to laugh at; of which, it was to be hoped, the cares and responsibilities of married life would cure him. (To the rest of the discourse Mr. Clapper listened with a gravity painfully maintained.) There had been moments, Uncle Gutton was compelled to admit, when the fair Rosina had shown inclination to make a fool of herself, to desire in place of honest worth mere painted baubles. He used the term in no offensive sense. Speaking for himself, what a man wanted beyond his weekly newspaper, he, Uncle Gutton, was unable to understand; but if there were fools in the world who wanted to read rubbish written by other fools, then the other fools would of course write it; Uncle Gutton did not blame them. He mentioned no names, but what he would say was: a plain man for a sensible girl, and no painted baubles.

The waiter here entering with a message from the cabman to the effect that if he was to catch the twelve-forty-five from Charing Cross, it was about full time he started, Uncle Gutton was compelled to bring his speech to a premature conclusion. The bride and bridegroom were hustled into their clothes. There followed much female embracing and male hand-shaking. The rice having been forgotten, the waiter was almost thrown downstairs, with directions to at once procure some. There appearing danger of his not returning in time, the resourceful Jarman suggested cold semolina pudding as a substitute. But the idea was discouraged by the bride. A slipper of remarkable antiquity, discovered on the floor and regarded as a gift from Providence, was flung from the window by brother George, with admirable aim, and alighted on the roof of the cab. The waiter, on his return, not being able to find it, seemed surprised.

I walked back as far as the Obelisk with the O'Kelly and the Signora, who were then living together in Lambeth. Till that morning I had not seen the O'Kelly since my departure from London, nearly two years before, so that we had much to tell each other. For the third time now had the O'Kelly proved his utter unworthiness to be the husband of the lady to whom he still referred as his "dear good wife."

"But, under the circumstances, would it not be better," I suggested, "for her to obtain a divorce? Then you and the Signora could marry and there would be an end to the whole trouble."

"From a strictly worldly point of view," replied the O'Kelly, "it certainly would be; but Mrs. O'Kelly", his voice took to itself unconsciously a tone of reverence, is not an ordinary woman. You can have no conception, my dear Kelver, of her goodness. I had a letter from her only two months ago, a few weeks after the, the last occurrence. Not one word of reproach, only that if I trespassed against her even unto seven times seven she would still consider it her duty to forgive me; that the 'home' would always be there for me to return to and repent."

A tear stood in the O'Kelly's eye. "A beautiful nature," he commented. "There are not many women like her."

"Not one in a million!" added the Signora, with enthusiasm.

"Well, to me it seems like pure obstinacy," I said.

The O'Kelly spoke quite angrily. "Don't ye say a word against her! I won't listen to it. Ye don't understand her. She never will despair of reforming me."

"You see, Mr. Kelver," explained the Signora, "the whole difficulty arises from my unfortunate profession. It is impossible for me to keep out of dear Willie's way. If I could earn my living by any other means, I would; but I can't. And when he sees my name upon the posters, it's all over with him."

"I do wish, Willie, dear," added the Signora in tones of gentle reproof, "that you were not quite so weak."

"Me dear," replied the O'Kelly, "ye don't know how attractive ye are or ye wouldn't blame me."

I laughed. "Why don't you be firm," I suggested to the Signora, "send him packing about his business?"

"I ought to," admitted the Signora. "I always mean to, until I see him. Then I don't seem able to say anything, not anything I ought to."

"Ye do say it," contradicted the O'Kelly. "Ye're an angel, only I won't listen to ye."

"I don't say it as if I meant it," persisted the Signora. "It's evident I don't."

"I still think it a pity," I said, "someone does not explain to Mrs. O'Kelly that a divorce would be the truer kindness."

"It is difficult to decide," argued the Signora. "If ever you should want to leave me"

"Me darling!" exclaimed the O'Kelly.

"But you may," insisted the Signora. "Something may happen to help you, to show you how wicked it all is. I shall be glad then to think that you will go back to her. Because she is a good woman, Willie, you know she is."

"She's a saint," agreed Willie.

At the Obelisk I shook hands with them, and alone pursued my way towards Fleet Street.

The next friend whose acquaintance I renewed was Dan. He occupied chambers in the Temple, and one evening a week or two after the 'Ortensia marriage, I called upon him. Nothing in his manner of greeting me suggested the necessity of explanation. Dan never demanded anything of his friends beyond their need of him. Shaking hands with me, he pushed me down into the easy-chair, and standing with his back to the fire, filled and lighted his pipe.

"I left you alone," he said. "You had to go through it, your slough of despond. It lies across every path, that leads to anywhere. Clear of it?"

"I think so," I replied, smiling.

"You are on the high road," he continued. "You have only to walk steadily. Sure you have left nothing behind you, in the slough?"

"Nothing worth bringing out of it," I said. "Why do you ask so seriously?"

He laid his hand upon my head, rumpling my hair, as in the old days.

"Don't leave him behind you," he said; "the little boy Paul, Paul the dreamer."

I laughed. "Oh, he! He was only in my way."

"Yes, here," answered Dan. "This is not his world. He is of no use to you here; won't help you to bread and cheese, no, nor kisses either. But keep him near you. Later, you will find, perhaps, that all along he has been the real Paul, the living, growing Paul; the other, the active, worldly, pushful Paul, only the stuff that dreams are made of, his fretful life a troubled night rounded by a sleep."

"I have been driving him away," I said. "He is so, so impracticable."

Dan shook his head gravely. "It is not his world," he repeated. "We must eat, drink, be husbands, fathers. He does not understand. Here he is the child. Take care of him."

We sat in silence for a little while, for longer, perhaps, than it seemed to us, Dan in the chair opposite to me, each of us occupied with his own thoughts.

"You have an excellent agent," said Dan; "retain her services as long as you can. She possesses the great advantage of having no conscience, as regards your affairs. Women never have where they"

He broke off to stir the fire.

"You like her?" I asked. The words sounded feeble. It is only the writer who fits the language to the emotion; the living man more often selects by contrast.

"She is my ideal woman," returned Dan; "true and strong and tender; clear as crystal, pure as dawn. Like her!"

He knocked the ashes from his pipe. "We do not marry our ideals," he went on. "We love with our hearts, not with our souls. The woman I shall marry", he sat gazing into the fire, a smile upon his face, "she will be some sweet, clinging, childish woman, David Copperfield's Dora. Only I am not Doady, who always seems to me to have been somewhat of a - He reminds me of you, Paul, a little. Dickens was right; her helplessness, as time went on, would have bored him more and more instead of appealing to him."

"And the women," I suggested, "do they marry their ideals?"

He laughed. "Ask them."

"The difference between men and women," he continued, "is very slight; we exaggerate it for purposes of art. What sort of man do you suppose he is, Norah's ideal? Can't you imagine him? But I can tell you the type of man she will marry, ay, and love with all her heart."

He looked at me from under his strong brows drawn down, a twinkle in his eye.

"A nice enough fellow, clever, perhaps, but someone, well, someone who will want looking after, taking care of, managing; someone who will appeal to the mother side of her, not her ideal man, but the man for whom nature intended her."

"Perhaps with her help," I said, "he may in time become her ideal."

"There's a long road before him," growled Dan.

It was Norah herself who broke to me the news of Barbara's elopment with Hal. I had seen neither of them since my return to London. Old Hasluck a month or so before I had met in the City one day by chance, and he had insisted on my lunching with him. I had found him greatly changed. His buoyant self-assurance had deserted him; in its place a fretful eagerness had become his motive force. At first he had talked boastingly: Had I seen the Post for last Monday, the Court Circular for the week before? Had I read that Barbara had danced with the Crown Prince, that the Count and Countess Huescar had been entertaining a Grand Duke? What [duplicated line of text] I think of that! and such like. Was not money master of the world? Ay, and the nobs should be made to acknowledge it!

But as he had gulped down glass after glass the brag had died away.

"No children," he had whispered to me across the table; "that's what I can't understand. Nearly four years and no children! What'll be the good of it all? Where do I come in? What do I get? Damn these rotten popinjays! What do they think we buy them for?"

It was in the studio on a Monday morning that Norah told me. It was the talk of the town for the next day, and the following eight. She had heard it the evening before at supper, and had written to me to come and see her.

"I thought you would rather hear it quietly," said Norah, "than learn it from a newspaper paragraph. Besides, I wanted to tell you this. She did wrong when she married, putting aside love for position. Now she has done right. She has put aside her shame with all the advantages she derived from it. She has proved herself a woman: I respect her."

Norah would not have said that to please me had she not really thought it. I could see it from that light; but it brought me no comfort. My goddess had a heart, passions, was a mere human creature like myself. From her cold throne she had stepped down to mingle with the world. So some youthful page of Arthur's court may have felt, learning the Great Queen was but a woman.

I never spoke with her again but once. That was an evening three years later in Brussels. Strolling idly after dinner the bright lights of a theatre invited me to enter. It was somewhat late; the second act had commenced. I slipped quietly into my seat, the only one vacant at the extreme end of the front row of the first range; then, looking down upon the stage, met her eyes. A little later an attendant whispered to me that Madame G-- would like to see me; so at the fall of the curtain I went round. Two men were in the dressing-room smoking, and on the table were some bottles of champagne. She was standing before her glass, a loose shawl about her shoulders.

"Excuse my shaking hands," she said. "This damned hole is like a furnace; I have to make up fresh after each act."

She held them up for my inspection with a laugh; they were smeared with grease.

"D'you know my husband?" she continued. "Baron G--; Mr. Paul Kelver."

The Baron rose. He was a red-faced, pot-bellied little man. "Delighted to meet Mr. Kelver," he said, speaking in excellent English. "Any friend of my wife's is always a friend of mine."

He held out his fat, perspiring hand. I was not in the mood to attach much importance to ceremony. I bowed and turned away, careless whether he was offended or not.

"I am glad I saw you," she continued. "Do you remember a girl called Barbara? You and she were rather chums, years ago.

"Yes," I answered, "I remember her."

"Well, she died, poor girl, three years ago." She was rubbing paint into her cheeks as she spoke. "She asked me if ever I saw you to give you this. I have been carrying it about with me ever since."

She took a ring from her finger. It was the one ring Barbara had worn as a girl, a chrysolite set plainly in a band of gold. I had noticed it upon her hand the first time I had seen her, sitting in my father's office framed by the dusty books and papers. She dropped it into my outstretched palm.

"Quite a pretty little romance," laughed the Baron.

"That's all," added the woman at the glass. "She said you would understand."

From under her painted lashes she flashed a glance at me. I hope never to see again that look upon a woman's face.

"Thank you," I said. "Yes, I understand. It was very kind of you. I shall always wear it."

Placing the ring upon my finger, I left the room.

CHAPTER X.

PAUL FINDS HIS WAY.

Slowly, surely, steadily I climbed, putting aside all dreams, paying strict attention to business. Often my other self, little Paul of the sad eyes, would seek to lure me from my work. But for my vehement determination never to rest for a moment till I had purchased back my honesty, my desire growing day by day, till it became almost a physical hunger, to feel again the pressure of Norah's strong white hand in mine, he might possibly have succeeded. Heaven only knows what then he might have made of me: politician, minor poet, more or less able editor, hampered by convictions, something most surely of but little service to myself. Now and again, with a week to spare, my humour making holiday, nothing to be done but await patiently its return, I would write stories for my own pleasure. They made no mark; but success in purposeful work is of slower growth. Had I persisted but there was money to be earned. And by the time my debts were paid, I had established a reputation.

"Madness!" argued practical friends. "You would be throwing away a certain fortune for, at the best, a doubtful competence. The one you know you can do, the other, it would be beginning your career all over again."

"You would find it almost impossible now," explained those who spoke, I knew, words of wisdom, of experience. "The world would never listen to you. Once a humourist always a humourist. As well might a comic actor insist upon playing Hamlet. It might be the best Hamlet ever seen upon the stage; the audience would only laugh, or stop away."

Drawn by our mutual need of sympathy, "Goggles" and I, seeking some quiet corner in the Club, would pour out our souls to each other. He would lay before me, at some length, his conception of Romeo, an excellent conception, I have no doubt, though I confess it failed to interest me. Somehow I could not picture him to myself as Romeo. But I listened with every sign of encouragement. It was the price I paid him for, in turn, listening to me while I unfolded to him my ideas how monumental literature, helpful to mankind, should be imagined and built up.

"Perhaps in a future existence," laughed Goggles, one evening, rising as the clock struck seven, "I shall be a great tragedian, and you a famous poet. Meanwhile, I suppose, as your friend Brian puts it, we are both sinning our mercies. After all, to live is the most important thing in life."

I had strolled with him so far as the cloak-room and was helping him to get into his coat.

"Take my advice", tapping me on the chest, he fixed his funny, fishy eyes upon me. Had I not known his intention to be serious, I should have laughed, his expression was so comical. "Marry some dear little woman (he was married himself to a placid lady of about twice his own weight); "one never understands life properly till the babies come to explain it to one."

I returned to my easy-chair before the fire. Wife, children, home! After all, was not that the true work of man, of the live man, not the dreamer? I saw them round me, giving to my life dignity, responsibility. The fair, sweet woman, helper, comrade, comforter, the little faces fashioned in our image, their questioning voices teaching us the answers to life's riddles. All other hopes, ambitions, dreams, what were they? Phantoms of the morning mist fading in the sunlight.

Hodgson came to me one evening. "I want you to write me a comic opera," he said. He had an open letter in his hand which he was reading. "The public seem to be getting tired of these eternal translations from the French. I want something English, something new and original."

"The English is easy enough," I replied; "but I shouldn't clamour for anything new and original if I were you."

"Why not?" he asked, looking up from his letter.

"You might get it," I answered. "Then you would be disappointed."

He laughed. "Well, you know what I mean, something we could refer to as 'new and original' on the programme. What do you say? It will be a big chance for you, and I'm willing to risk it. I'm sure you can do it. People are beginning to talk about you."

I had written a few farces, comediettas, and they had been successful. But the chief piece of the evening is a serious responsibility. A young man may be excused for hesitating. It can make, but also it can mar him. A comic opera above all other forms of art, if I may be forgiven for using the sacred word in connection with such a subject, demands experience.

I explained my fears. I did not explain that in my desk lay a four-act drama throbbing with humanity, with life, with which it had been my hope, growing each day fainter, to take the theatrical public by storm, to establish myself as a serious playwright.

"It's very simple," urged Hodgson. "Provide Atherton plenty of comic business; you ought to be able to do that all right. Give Gleeson something pretty in waltz time, and Duncan a part in which she can change her frock every quarter of an hour or so, and the thing is done."

"I'll tell you what," continued Hodgson, "I'll take the whole crowd down to Richmond on Sunday. We'll have a coach, and leave the theatre at half-past ten. It will be an opportunity for you to study them. You'll be able to have a talk with them and get to know just what they can do. Atherton has ideas in his head; he'll explain them to you. Then, next week, we'll draw up a contract and set to work."

It was too good an opportunity to let slip, though I knew that if successful I should find myself pinned down firmer than ever to my role of jester. But it is remunerative, the writing of comic opera.

A small crowd had gathered in the Strand to see us start.

"Nothing wrong, is there?" enquired the leading lady, in a tone of some anxiety, alighting a quarter of an hour late from her cab. "It isn't a fire, is it?"

"Merely assembled to see you," explained Mr. Hodgson, without raising his eyes from his letters.

"Oh, good gracious!" cried the leading lady, "do let us get away quickly."

"Box seat, my dear," returned Mr. Hodgson.

The leading lady, accepting the proffered assistance of myself and three other gentlemen, mounted the ladder with charming hesitation. Some delay in getting off was caused by our low comedian, who twice, making believe to miss his footing, slid down again into the arms of the stolid door-keeper. The crowd, composed for the most part of small boys approving the endeavour to amuse them, laughed and applauded. Our low comedian thus encouraged, made a third attempt upon his hands and knees, and, gaining the roof, sat down upon the tenor, who smiled somewhat mechanically.

The first dozen or so 'busses we passed our low comedian greeted by rising to his feet and bowing profoundly. afterwards falling back upon either the tenor or myself. Except by the tenor and myself his performance appeared to be much appreciated. Charing Cross passed, and nobody seeming to be interested in our progress, to the relief of the tenor and myself, he settled down.

"People sometimes ask me," said the low comedian, brushing the dust off his knees, "why I do this sort of thing off the stage. It amuses me."

"I was coming up to London the other day from Birmingham," he continued. "At Willesden, when the ticket collector opened the door, I sprang out of the carriage and ran off down the platform. Of course, he ran after me, shouting to all the others to stop me. I dodged them for about a minute. You wouldn't believe the excitement there was. Quite fifty people left their seats to see what it was all about. I explained to them when they caught me that I had been travelling second with a first-class ticket, which was the fact. People think I do it to attract attention. I do it for my own pleasure."

"It must be a troublesome way of amusing oneself," I suggested.

"Exactly what my wife says," he replied; "she can never understand the desire that comes over us all, I suppose, at times, to play the fool. As a rule, when she is with me I don't do it."

"She's not here today?" I asked, glancing round.

"She suffers so from headaches," he answered, "she hardly ever goes anywhere."

"I'm sorry." I spoke not out of mere politeness; I really did feel sorry.

During the drive to Richmond this irrepressible desire to amuse himself got the better of him more than once or twice. Through Kensington he attracted a certain amount of attention by balancing the horn upon his nose. At Kew he stopped the coach to request of a young ladies' boarding school change for sixpence. At the foot of Richmond Hill he caused a crowd to assemble while trying to persuade a deaf old gentleman in a Bath-chair to allow his man to race us up the hill for a shilling.

At these antics and such like our party laughed uproariously, with the exception of Hodgson, who had his correspondence to attend to, and an elegant young lady of some social standing who had lately emerged from the Divorce Court with a reputation worth to her in cash a hundred pounds a week.

Arriving at the hotel quarter of an hour or so before lunch time, we strolled into the garden. Our low comedian, observing an elderly gentleman of dignified appearance sipping a glass of Vermouth at a small table, stood for a moment rooted to the earth with astonishment, then, making a bee-line for the stranger, seized and shook him warmly by the hand. We exchanged admiring glances with one another.

"Charlie is in good form to-day," we told one another, and followed at his heels.

The elderly gentleman had risen; he looked puzzled. "And how's Aunt Martha?" asked him our low comedian. "Dear old Aunt Martha! Well, I am glad! You do look bonny! How is she?"

"I'm afraid" commenced the elderly gentleman. Our low comedian started back. Other visitors had gathered round.

"Don't tell me anything has happened to her! Not dead? Don't tell me that!"

He seized the bewildered gentleman by the shoulders and presented to him a face distorted by terror.

"I really have not the faintest notion what you are talking about," returned the gentleman, who seemed annoyed. "I don't know you."

"Not know me? Do you mean to tell me you've forgotten? Isn't your name Steggles?"

"No, it isn't," returned the stranger, somewhat shortly.

"My mistake," replied our low comedian. He tossed off at one gulp what remained of the stranger's Vermouth and walked away rapidly.

The elderly gentleman, not seeing the humour of the joke, one of our party to soothe him explained to him that it was Atherton, the Atherton, Charlie Atherton.

"Oh, is it," growled the elderly gentleman. "Then will you tell him from me that when I want his damned tomfoolery I'll come to the theatre and pay for it."

"What a disagreeable man," we said, as, following our low comedian, we made our way into the hotel.

During lunch he continued in excellent spirits; kissed the bald back of the waiter's head, pretending to mistake it for a face, called for hot mustard and water, made believe to steal the silver, and when the finger-bowls arrived, took off his coat and requested the ladies to look the other way.

After lunch he became suddenly serious, and slipping his arm through mine, led me by unfrequented paths.

"Now, about this new opera," he said; "we don't want any of the old stale business. Give us something new."

I suggested that to do so might be difficult.

"Not at all," he answered. "Now, my idea is this. I am a young fellow, and I'm in love with a girl."

I promised to make a note of it.

"Her father, apopletic old idiot, make him comic: 'Damme, sir! By gad!' all that sort of thing."

By persuading him that I understood what he meant, I rose in his estimation.

"He won't have anything to say to me, thinks I'm an ass. I'm a simple sort of fellow on the outside. But I'm not such a fool as I look."

"You don't think we are getting too much out of the groove?" I enquired.

His opinion was that the more so the better.

"Very well. Then, in the second act I disguise myself. I'll come on as an organ-grinder, sing a song in broken English, then as a policeman, or a young swell about town. Give me plenty of opportunity, that's the great thing, opportunity to be really funny, I mean. We don't want any of the old stale tricks."

I promised him my support.

"Put a little pathos in it," he added, "give me a scene where I can show them I've something else in me besides merely humour. We don't want to make them howl, but just to feel a little. Let's send them out of the theatre saying: 'Well, Charlie's often made me laugh, but I'm damned if I knew he could make me cry before!' See what I mean?"

I told him I thought I did.

The leading lady, meeting us on our return, requested, with pretty tone of authority, everybody else to go away and leave us. There were cries of 'Naughty!' The leading lady, laughing girlishly, took me by the hand and ran away with me.

"I want to talk to you," said the leading lady, as soon as we had reached a secluded seat overlooking the river, "about my part in the new opera. Now, can't you give me something original? Do."

Her pleading was so pretty, there was nothing for it but to pledge compliance.

"I am so tired of being the simple village maiden," said the leading lady; "what I want is a part with some opportunity in it, a coquettish part. I can flirt," assured me the leading lady, archly. "Try me."

I satisfied her of my perfect faith.

"You might," said the leading lady, "see your way to making the plot depend upon me. It always seems to me that the woman's part is never made enough of in comic opera. I am sure a comic opera built round a woman would be a really great success. Don't you agree with me, Mr. Kelver," pouted the leading lady, laying her pretty hand on mine. "We are much more interesting than the men now, aren't we?"

Personally, as I told her, I agreed with her.

The tenor, sipping tea with me on the balcony, beckoned me aside.

"About this new opera," said the tenor; "doesn't it seem to you the time has come to make more of the story, that the public might prefer a little more human interest and a little less clowning?"

I admitted that a good plot was essential.

"It seems to me," said the tenor, "that if you could write an opera round an interesting love story, you would score a success. Of course, let there be plenty of humour, but reduce it to its proper place. As a support, it is excellent; when it is made the entire structure, it is apt to be tiresome, at least, that is my view."

I replied with sincerity that there seemed to me much truth in what he said.

"Of course, so far as I am personally concerned," went on the tenor, "it is immaterial. I draw the same salary whether I'm on the stage five minutes or an hour. But when you have a man of my position in the cast, and give him next to nothing to do, well, the public are disappointed."

"Most naturally," I commented.

"The lover," whispered the tenor, noticing the careless approach towards us of the low comedian, "that's the character they are thinking about all the time, men and women both. It's human nature. Make your lover interesting, that's the secret."

Waiting for the horses to be put to, I became aware of the fact that I was standing some distance from the others in company with a tall, thin, somewhat oldish-looking man. He spoke in low, hurried tones, fearful evidently of being overheard and interrupted.

"You'll forgive me, Mr. Kelver," he said, "Trevor, Marmaduke Trevor. I play the Duke of Bayswater in the second act."

I was unable to recall him for the moment; there were quite a number of small parts in the second act. But glancing into his sensitive face, I shrank from wounding him.

"A capital performance," I lied. "It has always amused me.

He flushed with pleasure. "I made a great success some years ago," he said, "in America with a soda-water syphon, and it occurred to me that if you could, Mr. Kelver, in a natural sort of way, drop in a small part leading up to a little business with a soda-water syphon, it might help the piece."

I wrote him his soda-water scene, I am glad to remember, and insisted upon it, in spite of a good deal of opposition. Some of the critics found fault with the incident, as lacking in originality. But Marmaduke Trevor was quite right, it did help a little.

Our return journey was an exaggerated repetition of our morning drive. Our low comedian produced hideous noises from the horn, and entered into contests of running wit with 'bus drivers, a decided mistake from his point of view, the score generally remaining with the 'bus driver. At Hammersmith, seizing the opportunity of a block in the traffic, he assumed the role of Cheap Jack, and, standing up on the back seat, offered all our hats for sale at temptingly low prices.

"Got any ideas out of them?" asked Hodgson, when the time came for us to say good-night.

"I'm thinking, if you don't mind," I answered, "of going down into the country and writing the piece quietly, away from everybody."

"Perhaps you are right," agreed Hodgson. "Too many cooks - Be sure and have it ready for the autumn."

I wrote it with some pleasure to myself amid the Yorkshire Wolds, and was able to read it to the whole company assembled before the close of the season. My turning of the last page was followed by a dead silence. The leading lady was the first to speak. She asked if the clock upon the mantelpiece could be relied upon; because, if so, by leaving at once, she could just catch her train. Hodgson, consulting his watch, thought, if anything, it was a little fast. The leading lady said she hoped it was, and went. The only comforting words were spoken by the tenor. He recalled to our mind a successful comic opera produced some years before at the Philharmonic. He distinctly remembered that up to five minutes before the raising of the curtain everybody had regarded it as rubbish. He also had a train to catch. Marmaduke Trevor, with a covert shake of the hand, urged me not to despair. The low comedian, the last to go, told Hodgson he thought he might be able to do something with parts of it, if given a free hand. Hodgson and I left alone, looked at each other.

"It's no good," said Hodgson, "from a box-office point of view. Very clever."

"How do you know it is no good from a box-office point of view?" I ventured to enquire.

"I never made a mistake in my life," replied Hodgson.

"You have produced one or two failures," I reminded him.

"And shall again," he laughed. "The right thing isn't easy to get."

"Cheer up," he added kindly, "this is only your first attempt. We must try and knock it into shape at rehearsal."

Their notion of "knocking it into shape" was knocking it to pieces.

"I'll tell you what we'll do," would say the low comedian; "we'll cut that scene out altogether." Joyously he would draw his pencil through some four or five pages of my manuscript.

"But it is essential to the story," I would argue.

"Not at all."

"But it is. It is the scene in which Roderick escapes from prison and falls in love with the gipsy."

"My dear boy, half-a-dozen words will do all that. I meet Roderick at the ball. 'Hallo, what are you doing here?' 'Oh, I have escaped from prison.' 'Good business. And how's Miriam?' 'Well and happy, she is going to be my wife!' What more do you want?"

"I have been speaking to Mr. Hodgson," would observe the leading lady, "and he agrees with me, that if instead of falling in love with Peter, I fell in love with John"

"But John is in love with Arabella."

"Oh, we've cut out Arabella. I can sing all her songs.

The tenor would lead me into a corner. "I want you to write in a little scene for myself and Miss Duncan at the beginning of the first act. I'll talk to her about it. I think it will be rather pretty. I want her, the second time I see her, to have come out of her room on to a balcony, and to be standing there bathed in moonlight."

"But the first act takes place in the early morning."

"I've thought of that. We must alter it to the evening."

"But the opera opens with a hunting scene. People don't go hunting by moonlight."

"It will be a novelty. That's what's wanted for comic opera. The ordinary hunting scene! My dear boy, it has been done to death."

I stood this sort of thing for a week. "They are people of experience," I argued to myself; "they must know more about it than I do." By the end of the week I had arrived at the conclusion that anyhow they didn't. Added to which I lost my temper. It is a thing I should advise any lady or gentleman thinking of entering the ranks or dramatic authorship to lose as soon as possible. I took both manuscripts with me, and, entering Mr. Hodgson's private room, closed the door behind me. One parcel was the opera as I had originally written it, a neat, intelligible manuscript, whatever its other merits. The second, scored, interlined, altered, cut, interleaved, rewritten, reversed, turned inside out and topsy-turvy, one long, hopeless confusion from beginning to end, was the opera, as, everybody helping, we had "knocked it into shape."

"That's your opera," I said, pushing across to him the bulkier bundle. "If you can understand it, if you can make head or tail of it, if you care to produce it, it is yours, and you are welcome to it. This is mine!" I laid it on the table beside the other. "It may be good, it may be bad. If it is played at all it is played as it is written. Regard the contract as cancelled, and make up your mind."

He argued with force, and he argued with eloquence. He appealed to my self-interest, he appealed to my better nature. It occupied him forty minutes by the clock. Then he called me an obstinate young fool, flung the opera as "knocked into shape" into the waste-paper basket, which was the only proper place for it, and, striding into the middle of the company, gave curt directions that the damned opera was to be played as it was written, and be damned to it!

The company shrugged its shoulders, and for the next month kept them shrugged. For awhile Hodgson remained away from the rehearsals, then returning, developed by degrees a melancholy interest in the somewhat gloomy proceedings.

So far I had won, but my difficulty was to maintain the position. The low comedian, reciting his lines with meaningless monotony, would pause occasionally to ask of me politely, whether this or that passage was intended to be serious or funny.

"You think," the leading lady would enquire, more in sorrow than in anger, "that any girl would behave in this way, any real girl, I mean?"

"Perhaps the audience will understand it," would console himself hopefully the tenor. "Myself, I confess I don't."

With a sinking heart concealed beneath an aggressively disagreeable manner, I remained firm in my "pigheaded conceit," as it was regarded, Hodgson generously supporting me against his own judgment.

"It's bound to be a failure," he told me. "I am spending some twelve to fifteen hundred pounds to teach you a lesson. When you have learnt it we'll square accounts by your writing me an opera that will pay."

"And if it does succeed?" I suggested.

"My dear boy," replied Hodgson, "I never make mistakes."

From all which a dramatic author of more experience would have gathered cheerfulness and hope, knowing that the time to be depressed is when the manager and company unanimously and unhesitatingly predict a six months' run. But new to the business, I regarded my literary career as already at an end. Belief in oneself is merely the match with which one lights oneself. The oil is supplied by the belief in one of others; if that be not forthcoming, one goes out. Later on I might try to light myself again, but for the present I felt myself dark and dismal. My desire was to get away from my own smoke and smell. The final dress rehearsal over, I took my leave of all concerned. The next morning I would pack a knapsack and start upon a walking tour through Holland. The English papers would not reach me. No human being should know my address. In a month or so I would return, the piece would have disappeared, would be forgotten. With courage, I might be able to forget it myself.

"I shall run it for three weeks," said Hodgson, "then we'll withdraw it quietly, 'owing to previous arrangements'; or Duncan can suddenly fall ill, she's done it often enough to suit herself; she can do it this once to suit me. Don't be upset. There's nothing to be ashamed of in the piece; indeed, there is a good deal that will be praised. The idea is distinctly original. As a matter of fact, that's the fault with it," added Hodgson, "it's too original."

"You said you wanted it original," I reminded him.

He laughed. "Yes, but original for the stage, I meant, the old dolls in new frocks."

I thanked him for all his kindness, and went home and packed my knapsack.

For two months I wandered, avoiding beaten tracks, my only comrades a few books, belonging to no age, no country. My worries fell from me, the personal affairs of Paul Kelver ceasing to appear the be all and the end all of the universe. But for a chance meeting with Wellbourne, Deleglise's amateur caretaker of Gower Street fame, I should have delayed yet longer my return. It was in one of the dead cities of the Zuyder Zee. I was sitting under the lindens on the grass-grown quay, awaiting a slow, crawling boat that, four miles off, I watched a moving speck across the level pastures. I heard his footsteps in the empty market-place behind me, and turned my head. I did not rise, felt even no astonishment; anything might come to pass in that still land of dreams. He seated himself beside me with a nod, and for awhile we smoked in silence.

"All well with you?" I asked.

"I am afraid not," he answered; "the poor fellow is in great trouble."

"I'm not Wellbourne himself," he went on, in answer to my look; "I am only his spirit. Have you ever tested that belief the Hindoos hold: that a man may leave his body, wander at will for a certain period, remembering only to return ere the thread connecting him with flesh and blood be stretched to breaking point? It is quite correct. I often lock the door of my lodging, leave myself behind, wander a free Spirit."

He pulled from his pocket a handful of loose coins and looked at them. "The thread that connects us, I am sorrow to say, is wearing somewhat thin," he sighed; "I shall have to be getting back to him before long, concern myself again with his troubles, follies. It is somewhat vexing. Life is really beautiful, when one is dead."

"What was the trouble?" I enquired.

"Haven't you heard?" he replied. "Tom died five weeks ago, quite suddenly, of syncope. We had none of us any idea."

So Norah was alone in the world. I rose to my feet. The slowly moving speck had grown into a thin, dark streak; minute by minute it took shape and form.

"By the way, I have to congratulate you," said Wellbourne. "Your opera looked like being a big thing when I left London. You didn't sell outright, I hope?"

"No," I answered. "Hodgson never expressed any desire to buy."

"Lucky for you," said Wellbourne.

I reached London the next evening. Passing the theatre on my way to Queen's Square, it occurred to me to stop my cab for a few minutes and look in.

I met the low comedian on his way to his dressing-room. He shook me warmly by the hand.

"Well," he said, "we're pulling them in. I was right, you see, Give me plenty of opportunity.' That's what I told you, didn't I? Come and see the piece. I think you will agree with me that I have done you justice."

I thanked him.

"Not at all," he returned; "it's a pleasure to work, when you've got something good to work on."

I paid my respects to the leading lady.

"I am so grateful to you," said the leading lady. "It is so delightful to play a real live woman, for a change."

The tenor was quite fatherly.

"It is what I have been telling Hodgson for years," he said, "give them a simple human story."

Crossing the stage, I ran against Marmaduke Trevor.

"You will stay for my scene," he urged.

"Another night," I answered. "I have only just returned."

He sank his voice to a whisper. "I want to talk to you on business, when you have the time. I am thinking of taking a theatre myself, not just now, but later on. Of course, I don't want it to get about."

I assured him of my secrecy.

"If it comes off, I want you to write for me. You understand the public. We will talk it over."

He passed onward with stealthy tread.

I found Hodgson in the front of the house.

"Two stalls not sold and six seats in the upper circle," he informed me; "not bad for a Thursday night."

I expressed my gratification.

"I knew you could do it," said Hodgson, "I felt sure of it merely from seeing that comedietta of yours at the Queen's. I never make a mistake."

Correction under the circumstances would have been unkind. Promising to see him again in the morning, I left him with his customary good conceit of himself unimpaired, and went on to the Square. I rang twice, but there was no response. I was about to sound a third and final summons, when Norah joined me on the step. She had been out shopping and was laden with parcels.

"We must wait to shake hands," she laughed, as she opened the door. "I hope you have not been kept long. Poor Annette grows deafer every day."

"Have you nobody in the house with you but Annette?" I asked.

"No one. You know it was a whim of his. I used to get quite cross with him at times. But I should not like to go against his wishes now."

"Was there any reason for it?" I asked.

"No," she answered; "if there had been I could have argued him out of it." She paused at the door of the studio. "I'll just get rid of these," she said, "and then I will be with you."

A wood fire was burning on the open hearth, flashing alternate beams of light and shadow down the long bare room. The high oak stool stood in its usual place beside the engraving desk, upon which lay old Deleglise's last unfinished plate, emitting a dull red glow. I paced the creaking boards with halting steps, as through some ghostly gallery hung with dim portraits of the dead and living. In a little while Norah entered and came to me with outstretched hand.

"We will not light the lamp," she said, "the firelight is so pleasant."

"But I want to see you," I replied.

She had seated herself upon the broad stone kerb. With her hand she stirred the logs; they shot into a clear white flame. Thus, the light upon her face, she raised it gravely towards mine. It spoke to me with fuller voice. The clear grey eyes were frank and steadfast as ever, but shadow had passed into them, deepening them, illuminating them.

For a space we talked of our two selves, our trivial plans and doings.

"Tom left something to you," said Norah, rising, "not in his will, that was only a few lines. He told me to give it to you, with his love."

She brought it to me. It was the picture he had always treasured, his first success; a child looking on death; "The Riddle" he had named it.

We spoke of him, of his work, which since had come to be appraised at truer value, for it was out of fashion while he lived.

"Was he a disappointed man, do you think?" I asked.

"No," answered Norah. "I am sure not. He was too fond of his work."

"But he dreamt of becoming a second Millet. He confessed it to me once. And he died an engraver."

"But they were good engravings," smiled Norah.

"I remember a favourite saying of his," continued Norah, after a pause; "I do not know whether it was original or not. 'The stars guide us. They are not our goal.'"

"Ah, yes, we aim at the moon and hit the currant bush."

"It is necessary always to allow for deflection," laughed Norah.
"Apparently it takes a would-be poet to write a successful comic opera."

"Ah, you do not understand!" I cried. "It was not mere ambition; cap and bells or laurel wreath! that is small matter. I wanted to help. The world's cry of pain, I used to hear it as a boy. I hear it yet. I meant to help. They that are heavy laden. I hear their cry. They cry from dawn to dawn and none heed them: we pass upon the other side. Man and woman, child and beast. I hear their dumb cry in the night. The child's sob in the silence, the man's fierce curse of wrong. The dog beneath the vivisector's knife, the overdriven brute, the creature tortured for an hour that a gourmet may enjoy an instant's pleasure; they cried to me. The wrong and the sorrow and the pain, the long, low, endless moan God's ears are weary of; I hear it day and night. I thought to help."

I had risen. She took my face between her quiet, cool hands.

"What do we know? We see but a corner of the scheme. This fortress of laughter that a few of you have been set apart to guard, this rallying-point for all the forces of joy and gladness! how do you know it may not be the key to the whole battle! It is far removed from the grand charges and you think yourself forgotten. Trust your leader, be true to your post."

I looked into her sweet grey eyes.

"You always help me," I said.

"Do I?" she answered. "I am so glad."

She put her firm white hand in mine.

www.ingramcontent.com/pod-product-compliance
Lightning Source LLC
Chambersburg PA
CBHW060947030726
47503CB00003B/770